Charybdis

Charybdis

Published by Inkblot Books
Dayton Ohio
www.inkblotbooks.com
ISBN 1-932461-01-9

Cover image © 2003 Mark Carpenter
www.photogs.net/markc

Published in the United States of America

To Ian and Char, for information and inspiration

To Sandy and Tom, for always being there

And especially

To Mike and Curt
Who always believed the whirlpool would lift me up,
not suck me under

Charybdis

K.A. Thompson

February 1975

Chip

The hooker I was going to marry was dead. She plunged enough heroin into her body to wipe out half the county's addicts, and it was my fault. The official cause of death was listed as death by accidental overdose, but I knew the truth, and I'd spent the better part of a year living on the verge of an explosive temper tantrum because of it.

She died from a broken heart.

Being a first class son of a bitch is exhausting, and it took reaching my mental breaking point to be willing to admit the basic facts to myself. She knew what she was doing; her death was not an accident.

It took nearly a year, but I'd finally had enough of myself and the little dark cloud I wore like a crown.

My fingers fumbled over piano keys, plunking out sour notes that pinged off the walls of the empty restaurant. It sounded as empty and disjointed as I felt. I felt older than twenty two; at that age not everything should feel like such a sick, evasive pain. Some of it should go away.

I slammed my fist into the keys, and listened to the last

notes fade miserably. The damned broad was right—there was a huge black hole smack dab in the middle of my existence and I was going to walk right into it, eyes wide open, inching closer to it with every breath. Diving in head first would be easy if she'd leave me alone long enough to get a good running start.

Broad? Was that even a word then?

It didn't matter; it was the wrong way to describe her.

Kris Stevens was short; the top of her head barely reached my nose, and if I stood up straight when I hugged her, her head fit under my chin. She had sculpted brown hair, glittering brown eyes, and a confidence in dealing with me she didn't seem to have with anyone else. The woman was good at pushing me in the right direction and deep down I knew there wasn't much I would refuse her.

I used to think it was a shame she married my father. Life might have been less bitter if I had been able to pursue her first. The past year would have been different if I had, and the last six years might have been bearable.

With my head aching and knuckles throbbing from banging them into the piano keys, I got up and pushed my way past the tables and chairs. When had the restaurant become home? I hadn't even wanted it in the beginning. I was only nineteen years old, had no earthly idea how the place should be run, no clue what to do when it opened for business. They handed me the keys, told me to hire Ted, arranged tax breaks that I didn't understand and accountants to hide that fact, and that was it. I owned a restaurant.

Christ, nineteen years old. "This is your cover, Davis. Take care of it."

I had to admit, when I first stepped inside it was twice what I had expected or could have hoped for. The Charybdis dripped with the smell of success; light and shadows wove around each other, teasing and whispering of promised sex. There was a dance floor at the far end of the dining room; muted lighting made the tile floor look like marble, and the sound system gave off the impression of a live band playing just behind the curtain, where there was a small stage that served as storage space for the piano that was rarely used.

The bar was what had impressed me most; warm and dark, lined on one side by booths with thick comfortable benches and solid wood tables, and on the other side by the long, dark, bar itself, deep rich wood that always looked wet, with stools made for customer comfort, not designed to herd them in and out like cattle.

After three years, it felt closer to home than my apartment. If I never went back to that grim little studio again it wouldn't matter. I could easily live in the office. It was lonely, though, and I realized I didn't want to be alone anymore. All of it, including the office with the long, wide sofa and stone fireplace, was meant to be shared.

I started to reach for the phone. My fingers stopped just short of touching it. The last thing I wanted to hear was "I told you so."

But that wasn't Kris. She wanted me out of my shell; the year I had been hiding inside myself was too damned long. Life, as she put it often and pointedly, goes on whether you like it or not. You might as well learn to like it.

She didn't understand. How could she? I hadn't been square with her from day one.

Private hell is best suffered alone.

"Chip?"

Speak of the devil, though the devil never looked so good. "God, I thought I'd locked up."

"Nope." She leaned toward me, lips barely brushing a stubbled cheek. "Your front door is wide open and Ted is sweeping out the bar. I saw your clunker in the parking lot and thought I'd drop in and spy on you."

"A little out of your way, isn't it?" Of course it was. She was making sure I was alive and kicking.

And sober.

"I thought you might want to see a friendly face," she said. "Good day or bad?"

"I'm okay." My hand went to my chest; there was that weight again, the pressure that always seemed to slam into my chest, wrapping around me tightly. I leaned against the desk, closed my eyes and took a deep breath, knowing it would feel ragged going in and painfully hot coming out. When I opened my eyes, Kris was staring at me with enough love to melt a fudgesicle in the middle of December.

I didn't deserve that, not by a long shot.

The throbbing in my temples was joined by the twisting of a huge knot in my gut. Maybe I was losing the last marble I had pinging around in my skull, but it was time to come clean, allow her a glimpse of the reason I'd spent the last year hating the world and despising myself.

Explain about Brenda.

I met Brenda Webb when she was still in high school, a battered and bruised and terminally frightened soul. I never gave her much thought, other than wondering from time to time who had given her the latest welt or bruise, or why she stared down at her feet as she walked. Why she didn't smile or laugh or walk in a pack with fifteen other girls. She was not a part of my life and she was younger; I never had a reason to look twice or think beyond the moment.

Four years later that frightened mouse dropped onto a

stool at the bar, waved an impatient hand at me and snapped, "Don't worry, I'm not here to cruise your customers. I'm only here for a drink, so don't even start." She looked at me straight in the eye with a determination that dared me to tell her to leave, glaring as she reached for the ashtray.

I couldn't have cared less. I shrugged and told Ted to card her and not believe any date that aged her past eighteen years old, and walked out. Just another kid trying to play act at adulthood, hoping to walk out a little less sober than she had walked in. She mattered only as much as her final tab came to.

Ten minutes later I dropped onto the stool next to her and said flatly, "I know you."

She rolled her eyes. "You and every other horny guy on this side of the state line."

"You look different."

"As opposed to…?"

I leaned against the bar. "As opposed to the kid I remember from high school. Some girl who used to walk around holding her books to her chest so tight you'd think she was trying to keep her boobs from falling off."

She didn't give an inch. "Yeah, well maybe they were about to. So you went to Fairfield. Goody for you."

"I was there for awhile."

"One of those obnoxious jocks."

"I was never a jock."

"Just obnoxious." She lit another cigarette and took a deep draw from it, smoke curling at her fingertips. "So, you dropped out? What, gym class too difficult to handle?"

"Something like that."

"Don't get your jockeys in a wad," she snorted. "I remember you. Some freak junior who got his ass kicked out of school for shagging an English teacher. Word gets around."

"Shagging. What a nice way to put it."

"Well it wasn't some grand love affair was it?"

I had to smile. "No, not hardly."

So you boinked the English teacher, got caught, she gets suspended and you get thrown out of school… so then what?"

"I went to work."

"What a shame. I guess they won't be inviting you to all those lovely class reunions where you could sit around and brag about the A for effort you must have gotten."

"And you? What are you going to brag about at your class reunions?"

"Who says I'd be invited?"

"Why wouldn't you?"

"You're not the only one who didn't exactly leave in good graces," she said as she flicked the tip off her cigarette and stood up. "Some of us just got fed up with all the bullshit."

I watched as she blew through the door, my future stomping out in a cloud of anger and smoke.

A year and a few hundred packs of cigarettes later she was dead.

It was my fault.

I had to explain.

"Kris, I didn't love her. I think I cared, but I never loved her."

"Chip…"

"No, wait," I groped for the right words. "You don't understand. We had a hell of a lot of fun together, but I never fell in love with her. I felt the pressure to take the next step and to look more like the adult I was supposed to be and making the world think I was some sedate married man with a house and a white picket fence seemed to make sense."

She waited.

"Brenda was a junkie and she slept with anyone who could afford her price." My heart was pounding along with my head. "Somehow I thought it would work."

She stood there staring at me, mouth gaping. "Then why," she stammered, eyes flaming, "what the hell has been your problem? You lost a damned cover? You bastard!"

"You don't understand…"

"Understand what? You've been dragging all of us through hell all this time because you lost your goddamned *cover*?"

Okay, coming out I had known how wrong it sounded. But I thought Brenda knew. When I asked her to marry me, I was sure she knew how I felt. I only promised to try to help her straighten out and take control of her life. I certainly never told her that I loved her. I thought I had made that clear.

Really, Mr. Wonderful? What tipped you off?

Give me half a second and I can remember what she was wearing that last night, how her hair was cut, the perfume that teased my senses. Brenda Webb was only nineteen years old and she finally looked her age. Young and eager.

Kris dropped onto the sofa, refusing to look at me. Silently demanding an explanation.

"We were making wedding plans. She started talking about a wedding mass, white gown, the whole bit."

"You said no."

"I said it wasn't necessary." I said a lot of things, including pointing out that I didn't think she could make it through an entire ceremony unless she was stoned out of her mind. And then, ignoring the faint redness welling in her eyes, I told her that prostitutes don't wear white to their weddings. "After we stopped talking about the wedding itself she brought up the issue of kids. I blew up. I mean I really flew off the handle. In my heart I believe a baby needs two parents who love each other."

"Oh God, you said so."

Sighing, I nodded. "She loved me. She would have given up the men, and would have turned herself inside out to get off all the drugs, and I didn't have a clue. You know, I never would have been faithful. I'd have slept with any woman who gave me so much as a second glance. Hell, I *did*. The whole time we were together…"

The disappointed rage Kris stared at me with began to ebb. After a long time she said, "You don't know what would have happened. It might have been a decent marriage, but it probably would have been a disaster."

"I'll never know."

"You've spent the better part of a year beating yourself up because a hooker you didn't love in the first place tried to even the score by killing herself in your apartment." And killing everyone around me with my temper. "It's not grief, it's guilt."

Touché, Kris.

She stood and grabbed her purse. "Give it up, Chip. You didn't mean to hurt her and you certainly didn't kill her. I'm done feeling sorry for you."

I wasn't sure I wanted that. A perverse part of me cherished the attention she gave me out of pity.

Face it, I didn't have much else.

Kris

Ron closed the door, tossing his briefcase aside, and tugged at his tie. The lights were dim, *Earth, Wind, & Fire* barely audible from the other side of the room. I kept the volume down out of habit; he would hate it; rock music, in any shape or form, grated on his nerves.

"Let me guess." He took the wine glass out of my hand as he sat next to me. "You've been fending off Chip today."

"Just the usual."

"Why do you bother, Kris?" He sank back into the cushions, taking a sip of the cheap wine he'd paid top dollar for. Some connoisseur. "He's a big boy now. You don't need to watch over him the way you did when he lived with us."

"Ron, it is just so much bullshit." I pulled myself up and headed for the kitchen.

"What'd he do now?" He followed me to the kitchen and poured the wine into the sink. "You seem more than a little ticked at the boy."

He was never a boy, I thought absently, turning my attention to the water boiling on the stove. Fresh pasta; he'd better appreciate the effort.

"What"—his arms snaked around my waist and drew me back against him—"did he say this time?"

I leaned back and closed my eyes. It felt natural when he was like this, more concerned about me than about appearances. "I called your son a bastard. I said it before I realized it was coming out."

"He is one. What's the problem?"

"Ron!" I turned to look at him. Those were the same emerald green eyes I had stared into earlier, only twenty some odd years older and work weary, not guilt ridden. "It wasn't fair. I was angry but I had no right."

"Technically it's correct."

"Ron... okay, forget it. He's your son and if that's how you think of him, far be it for me to try to change your mind."

"Hey, come on..."

I broke away and went back to the living room, dropping back onto the sofa. Ron was too much like his son. Stubborn and unyielding. Infuriating. I loved them but there were times I wish they would both just go away for a long time.

It was just stress, sheer electric stress that never went away, tearing us into tiny pieces. It was relentless enough that Chip finding another cover for his life was probably the smart thing to do in spite of his poor selection.

Ron was my cover. A cover within a cover. Ron Gallery, supposed technical researcher, and Kris Stevens, whimsical bubbleheaded housewife.

I fought falling in love with him. The odds were stacked against us. We discussed one of us retiring when our contracts came up for renewal, when there was a graceful way to back out of this mess of a life. Get a normal job, live a normal existence.

Neither one of us was quite ready to give up the odd days of excitement, though I was close, some days paying attention to the dull ticking of a biological clock I was only recently aware of. All the excitement aside, it was becoming just a job, something I could get anywhere.

But there was Doug. The agency was my only tangible tie to him.

I never agreed that Chip should have been a part of it. He had been far too young to understand the danger and too reckless to accept the responsibility; now here he was trying to find his own cover. Just worried enough to find someone expendable.

Warm lips pressed against mine, lingering until I opened my eyes. "Dinner's ready," he whispered. "I love you."

Do you, really?

"Hmmm. I love you, too." I sat up, groggy. "I guess I

was more tired than I thought."

"My son, no doubt."

"I was thinking this afternoon," I said, letting him slip his arm around me. "This tailspin of his was started by a girl... maybe it's time for a girl to pull him out of it. He needs someone in his life right now."

"That's playing with fire and you know it. And it's not fair."

"What's not fair? He's a lonely man and he could use some company. Look, he's so far in the dumps it couldn't hurt to try."

He grimaced. "Maybe."

"Come on," I urged. "I know the perfect girl if you can get him to let his guard down long enough to consider it."

He knew I wouldn't give up, and it was true I knew Chip better than he did. So much for fatherhood; I doubt he expected any rewards.

"All right," he conceded. "Just don't expect a whole lot out of that kid."

Maybe you don't expect enough. You have no idea how terrific your son can be.

Chip

I groaned.

"A blind date?" I leaned back and waited for the inevitable. This had to be Kris's idea. "I'm not that hard up, Ron. I can find my own dates."

"Can you?" He flung his arms out, gesturing to the entire room. "Look at this, Chip. This office is your entire world. What kind of social life do you have?"

I followed his gesture. I was proud of the office, self-impressed by the only part of the restaurant I'd had a hand in.

It didn't matter if he was right and it had become a hiding place. I liked it there.

"Who is she?"

"Terry Stevens," he answered, pushing his black hair out of his eyes. "She's Kris's younger cousin."

Terrific. "Just how young?"

"Almost nineteen."

Another teenager. "I suppose," I sighed, telling myself that I would do it for Kris, I'd make the effort for her, "that it wouldn't hurt. I'll take her out but that's it. No promises."

"None expected." Ron leaned forward, resting his chin on clenched fists. "Listen, she's a really nice girl but she's been burned a little. She's not looking for any big romance. Just a friend."

"So naturally you thought of me."

"Actually, Kris thought of you first and then called Terry to see if she'd even be interested. Trust me, you'll like her."

"She anything like Kris?"

Ron shrugged.

"Hoookay. Give me the phone number."

What the hell. I had the feeling my goose was already cooked and ready for carving.

~

Chip

You want awkward? Walk into a woman's apartment without the slightest hint of what she's like, other than two or three odd hints gathered during a few hurried minutes on the phone. The only thing you've determined, up to the point when you ring the doorbell, is that the voice on the other end of the phone is intriguing. She could be a Royal Bitch In Training, but her voice is like soft music.

"Nice place." I wanted to bite the words back. What would she expect to hear? Your apartment is pretty much like all the others I've been in, except it smells a little better and you're obviously a better housekeeper than I am? My heart was pounding like the proverbial native drums and I wasn't sure I wanted to be there.

She didn't look anything like Kris. Terry Stevens had bright blue eyes, long blonde hair, and the top of her head didn't even reach my chin.

It took her about a minute to size me up; I was almost surprised that she didn't start ticking off the things wrong on her fingers. Dresses okay, nothing great. Hair a little too long, but not stringy. The beard could go. Basically, he's clean and makes a touch more than the minimal effort.

Well, I showered too, lady.

That fact didn't keep me from sweating. She stood next to me at the balcony door, the scent of her perfume clouding my senses. This petite blonde was not the kind of woman I was used to. Something about her was fresh and innocent, and deep down it made me nervous.

On the other hand, she seemed at ease with my being there. I babbled, she managed coherent conversation.

"You don't have to try so hard, Chip," she said with a smile. Beautiful smile.

"Try so hard to do what?" I was wondering what the hell she was doing to me. I had been there twenty minutes tops and was already beginning to feel the heat that crept through me when someone was getting under my skin. The feeling was as terrifying as it was good.

"Impressing me." Her smile deepened and traces of red crept into her cheeks. Those eyes nearly mesmerized me—witch's eyes I decided later—and as I looked down at her I barely heard what she was saying. "It doesn't take much."

I snapped back. "Take much to what?"

She laughed and patted me on the shoulder. "One hundred percent all American male."

"What? I lost something there. What doesn't take much?" She was staring through the glass door. I felt like an idiot.

"It doesn't take too much to impress me." She turned her head a touch and looked at me from the corner of her eye. "There's something about you I like. I'm not sure what it is yet."

"It can't be my natural charm."

"It must be your conversational talents," she teased.

There was a twinge of sorrow behind that smile. Was my being there picking open an old wound? "You've been through a lot. You can tell me if you want."

"Chip, I don't even know you."

I took a step towards her, my hand reaching to brush hair from her face. The movement felt natural, but when I touched her, I swear I felt a spark. "I have two good ears and I can keep my mouth shut."

"You have problems of your own."

I wondered how much Kris had told her. "That doesn't mean I can't listen. Maybe we can figure each other out."

She slid the balcony door open and sat in a red plastic chair. The night was cool and breezy—the town was nestled down in a valley less than a hundred miles from the coast and it was nearly always windy—and I could hear cars whizzing by on the parkway just a few hundred yards away. I dropped into the chair across from her, watching her eyes. For just a bare second I thought I saw a tear brimming there, but it was gone by the time she blinked.

"When Kris asked me to meet you I was really excited.

I honestly thought I was completely over everything and ready to move on."

"But you're not, and you want me to leave."

"No! That's not what I meant at all." Her nose crinkled as she thought; I wanted to reach out and touch the tip playfully. "I've only had one real relationship, and I thought it was the big one."

"So what happened?"

That light shrug of her shoulders was tantalizing. "Reality reared its ugly head, I guess. We were both way too young and he knew it. He decided we should wait or regret it later." She paused, sighing. "I'm not sure now that I loved him all that much, but back then I was positive I couldn't live my life without him. He was right, though, we were so young... It still hurt when he took off with someone else."

Son of a bitch. Somewhere in the world there existed as big a moron as I am.

"I'm sorry. No one deserves that."

But as long as there are men like me around, it'll happen.

"I'm okay now. But you've been through a lot, too."

"Wonderful, quiet, Kris," I muttered to myself. My heart had stopped beating so wildly, but the pressure that gripped at my chest was still there, pushing me further and further into the chair. "She didn't tell you enough to scare you away from me?"

"Evidently not. And I admit, my interest was piqued when she mentioned that you work together. She won't tell anyone what it is she does for a living." She studied my face, the hint of the smile that was tugging at the corners of my mouth. "What's the big secret?"

I shrugged. "So what is it that you do?"

"You're changing the subject."

"I am." I let the smile break. Time to quit brooding on what might have been and start examining what could be. "So? What occupies your day? School? Work? Both?"

"I'm just a plain old working stiff, counting the days until my first vacation."

"You're definitely not plain," I stammered. "I mean, you're not what I expected."

"Oh? Just what did you expect?"

Instructions for operation: open mouth and simultaneously insert both size 13 feet. "Not quite so much," I admitted. "Face it, when your stepmother sets you up, the last thing you expect is someone like you. Terry, you really are beautiful!"

Blushing suits her well.

"You figured I'd be quite large and zit-faced, didn't you? And if that had been the case this would be a very short evening and I would never see you again."

I didn't think it would be a good time to mention that I'd discovered before I could even drive that it was the plainer girls who tended to be a bit more grateful for the consideration, and were more inclined to put out. "Honestly, a girl doesn't have to be a knockout to get my attention."

She patted my arm. "Helps, though, doesn't it?"

I laughed, amazed that suddenly, in the flicker of that instant of contact, the pressure was gone.

Kris

Ron set his newspaper aside and checked his watch for the tenth time in an hour. He turned the TV on, staring at it blankly. Without thinking, he checked his watch again.

"We would have heard from Terry if he hadn't shown up," I told him. "He's there. They're probably having a good time."

He sighed heavily. "I know... It's just that Chip can forget about anything if it suits him." He turned the TV back off and reached for the newspaper again. "He didn't seem thrilled about this, Kris. He only agreed to see her because of you."

"Ron, he's there." I reached for the jacket I had tossed over the back of the sofa and slipped into it. "Come on. Go for a walk with me and quit thinking about your son. I swear, you weren't this worried the first time he crawled under a building with his hands full of explosive putty."

Terry

"It's after midnight," Chip said. "I really ought to go."

He seemed to hesitate, and I had half a mind to ask him to stay. He was nothing like the sad and dejected person Kris thought needed rescuing from himself; Chip was warm and comfortable, and easy to talk to. He was goofy and embarrassed for the first half hour, but at some point he relaxed enough to slip his arm behind me while we polished off a bottle of wine, watching the fire pop and crackle.

"Really, I have an important appointment in the morning."

"I have to work tomorrow, too. Six is going to come awfully early."

He nodded and stood, shuffling to the door. "I had a nice time, Terry. I'd like to call you again, if it's all right."

I followed him to the door. "Of course it is."

"Tomorrow? Or am I being too pushy?"

I laughed. "No, not pushy at all." I crept up on my toes and kissed his cheek. I was surprised, given the things Kris had told me, that this one little kiss was as far as he tried to get during the five hours we had been together.

"Good, then I'll see you..." He opened the door and

slipped out, calling goodnight as he walked down the hall-way.

I locked the door and leaned against it, imagining I could hear his footsteps fade into the night. He had made me laugh and he had listened to things I'd never tell another man. Not even, I realized, Matt.

Matt Rhuele was a teenage crush, a good first love. Chip… well, he might not have realized it at the time, but I was about to sink my sharp little fingernails into him, and hopefully make him like it.

Chip

Dan Martin's office always made me feel like I was twelve or thirteen years old, called into the principal's office for the inevitable sermon on my lack of self control and re-spect for others. It was bare, white walls that screamed with brightness, with just his battered desk and fake leather chair, a banged up metal file cabinet, and a hard wooden vinyl cov-ered chair for those who were forced to spend enough time there that sitting was required.

I wondered why he didn't spend a little money to hu-manize the place, make it less sterile and more welcome. If not for the fresh coat of paint—which I could still smell—it would be dingy.

"How's it going, Chip?"

I craned my neck to watch him come into the room. Dan was beginning to show his age, flecks of white peeking through the black at his temples. "I'm here. I suppose that counts for something."

His reply was a noncommitted grunt. "Your medical file keeps popping up on my desk. You've skipped at least a dozen appointments." He tossed the thick manila folder onto his desk and sat down. The warmth of his greeting was replaced with what I always thought of as Dan's Boss Face. He looked irritated and annoyed, like he was smelling something disgusting but trying to politely ignore it. "I want you to see Doug soon, so we can get back to work."

Doug Stone didn't care one way or the other if I showed up in the clinic for a checkup. He saw me at least three times a week in the gym and the doctor had never said a single word about how pressing it was to poke at me and peek into my nose and ears. "Dan, we get paid the same whether we work or not."

I could practically hear what he was thinking. *Smart assed kid.* "You have a contract. We haven't worked together as a team for over a year, and we'll have an assignment soon. *Soon.* I need you ready."

I shrugged. "Don't sweat it. I'm ready."

One flippant shrug too many. "You get your ass in to see Doug today. And shave off the damn beard and get your hair cut. You look like a bum."

"Yes, sir." I snapped a salute, deliberately mocking him. "Anything else, *sir*?"

Dan pointed his finger at me. "You owe us, Chip. You stick to the terms of your contract or I'll personally escort you to Leavenworth."

Before or after your ego explodes?

I leaned forward, whispering as if I were talking to a confidant. "I'll be a good little boy, Danny. I'll go see Dr. Doug and I'll be ready to go off and play with my little friends, okay?"

He bit off his retort. After a minute he shook his head and asked, "Okay, who is she?"

"Who's who?"

"Whoever it is that's turning you into a complete ass.

Has to be female."

I grinned.

"You haven't looked this happy in a very long time," he said.

At least a year.

I stood and pushed the chair out of my way. "I'll call Doug and make an appointment, and I won't miss this one, I swear. Anything else?"

"No," he grumbled. "Just be ready. I have a feeling whatever gets dropped into our lap will be a good one."

I liked Dan Martin, but there were too many times I thought he tried to play his boss card instead of just coming right out and asking. He was careful to avoid being the one to tick someone off; it had to be something official, it could never be as simple as the fact that he was royally pissed off. Someday, I thought, he'd play that card at the wrong time and it would be a fatal mistake.

That was just my opinion. Not everyone agreed.

Kris

I waited in the restaurant, glancing around nervously. I hated the feeling that I was sneaking around and despised how I would feel when I went home, but there were just those days when I had to get out and dive into a pool of privacy that my husband wasn't a part of. He wouldn't understand; he would boil over and stop listening, and probably accuse me of something that wasn't happening.

Not for lack of effort.

So why, I wondered, do I feel so guilty about meeting a friend for lunch? So he's male, but he is a friend.

I fidgeted, watching the door and watching the people around me. Doug was never late; usually I was early. Over eager? I suppose so. When he finally got there my nerves would calm and I'd feel less like a cheating little bitch and more like a person. I'd been like that from the moment we stepped outside the boundaries of our working relationship and decided to pursue a real friendship. How long had it been? I wasn't even sure.

One thing I did know was that I wanted to get past the idea of just being friends and to take it further; I gushed through that entire first lunch and came on to him with more effort than I'd ever put into my marriage. He ignored the obvious, and kept agreeing to see me. He never mentioned the overtures, and I knew he never would.

"Am I late?" He held his tie back to keep it from splashing into his water as he sat. "I got tied up at the clinic."

"No, you're not late." I bit back the warmth that pulsated through me. Doug's brooding dark eyes were a sharp contrast to his dirty blond hair, and the piercing way he looked at me always melted the frost I kept wrapped around myself. Every week it was a struggle to rebuild the coat of ice that shielded me from Ron's often unbearable advances. For all his good traits, my husband was an inadequate and infrequent lover, but I was minding that less and less.

"So where is it you're supposed to be this week?"

"At the mall," I laughed. "I'm taking a couple of harmless hours to window shop. One of these days I'll actually buy something to make it look good."

"You could"—he sipped at his water—"tell Ron you're having lunch with a friend."

"Doug, he would never understand. Any friend would have to be very female. Besides," I added, staring down at the table to make sure he wouldn't see any longing in my eyes, "he would be very hurt if I admitted I need to get away from him, even for a while."

"He needs to get back to work." He picked up the menu and looked at it, but I doubted he was reading it. "I saw Chip a little while ago and cleared him. We may be getting something tossed our way soon."

Dan blamed Chip for our inactivity, and the longer it went on the more vocal he was about that. I never thought that his depression was a valid reason for the rest of us to sit back on our collective asses, but it was true that except for the odds and ends fed to Ron and the routine medical work Doug managed at the clinic, not a thing had come our way. "Any rumors flying around about what it might be?"

"No telling. Dan's chomping at the bit, though." He put the menu down. "You should see Chip. He was pinging off the walls so much I had a hard time getting the exam done. It was like trying to do a checkup on a toddler."

I leaned forward, elbows on the table. Something to smile about, after all. "He went out with my cousin last night. I've been dying to find out how it went."

"Safe to say it went well." He leaned forward, too, his nose a few inches from mine. It would be so easy to lean in and steal a kiss. "What about you? Has it been a good week?"

"Yeah. Really good."

He sighed and pulled back. He knew I was lying; I couldn't reassure him. There were times he would press me for details, but for the most part he didn't want to be the one to reach out and rattle me. Even then, while Doug passed on our order to the waiter, he must have known I was grasping for control. It was like there was this line I had in my hands, with two ends I couldn't connect. Do I stay married for the sake of team continuity? Do I leave Ron and risk not being able to work with him? Do I jump in with both feet, grab the doctor by the hand and drag him to the nearest motel, contort myself trying to have the best of both worlds?

"Do you ever feel like a sneak?" I asked suddenly.

"No. Why should I?"

"I just mean… what do you tell your friends about your job?"

"I tell them the truth," he chuckled. "I'm a doctor."

"There are times I'd love to tell someone, just to see the reaction."

"No one would believe you," he said. "Look at you. You don't exactly fit anyone's idea of what a spy should look like."

"I'm not a spy," I defended, not at all serious. "I'm an operative. I use my charms to lure secrets out of ugly old men."

"Ever get laid by one?"

"Doug! I can't believe you just asked that!"

"Well?"

"Doug!"

He laughed and held up his hands defensively. "All right, you don't have to answer. Want to ask me?"

"You," I said, pointing an accusing finger at him, "probably take any and every opportunity to hop into the sack, whether it's on the job or not. You have a reputation, doctor. The stories do get out of the locker room."

We looked away from each other when the waiter brought the food. I glanced at him as his plate was put in front of him. I wished he had kept his mustache, but aside from that he was the same as he was every week. He made me laugh, and I wanted him.

Chip

"This," I sighed, sinking back against the edge of the couch, "is nice." I reached for Terry's hand and pulled her down next to me. "I was afraid you might not want to see me so soon."

"And I was beginning to think today that you weren't going to call at all." She placed the wine glass she was holding on the end table beside her. We were sitting on the floor, leaning against the sofa, our legs stretched out and feet touching. "By four o'clock I was sure I wouldn't hear from you."

"Didn't I say I would call? Or was I just thinking to myself that I couldn't wait to see you again?"

"Could have been a line." She was grinning.

"A line would have been 'let's do lunch.' I thought I was painfully obvious." I set my glass down and struggled to my feet. "I owe you a dinner out. Last night was great, but tonight I want to take you someplace nice."

She reached out for my hands and let me pull her to her feet. "All right. What do you have in mind?"

Oh, no, you don't really want to know that.

"Ever been to the Charybdis?"

"No," she laughed, "it's a little out of my league." She glanced down at her faded jeans. "Give me five minutes to change?"

She went into the bedroom and closed the door. I sat on the couch to wait, allowing myself the curiosity to really look around the apartment. It was fairly uncluttered; she had the sofa and two end tables, but other than 2 lamps she had no real furniture. Across the room there was a particle board bookcase crammed full of paperbacks. She was one up on me there; I hadn't cracked a book willingly since I was 10, and not at all after the day I stormed out of high school.

That could be a kick someday, the two of us curled up on a bed, her reading to me.

I had no idea what to do with the feelings that were

suddenly popping out at me from every direction. I was supposed to have control; I was supposed to know exactly what I wanted, how I was going to get it, and at what point I would walk away.

What other time I had not tried to get past the bedroom door on the first date? Ever?

"Better?"

She was standing in the doorway to her bedroom. The soft jeans, which I had been taken with anyway, had been replaced with a red dress, and her hair played loosely around her shoulders. My chest suddenly tightened and I sucked in a deep breath. "This is unjust."

"To whom?" She tried not to smile. "Me or you?"

"Me and every other red blooded man on the street." I could hear alarms going off in my head. Slow down with this one. The rules of the game obviously were not the same.

Once in the car, she reached out and ran a finger across my cheek. "You know, you look much better without the beard. You have such a nice smile. I'm glad you're not hiding it anymore."

I dug my fingers into the steering wheel. "I wish I could say it was my idea, but I only shaved it off under a direct threat from an extremely anal retentive boss."

"Just who is your boss?"

I glanced at her and smiled. "So you've never been to the Charybdis?"

"You're changing the subject again."

"Yes I am."

She sighed and gave up. "I've heard a lot about the Charybdis. I've been told they have a great dance floor and a killer bar."

"But," I pointed out, "you're only nineteen and can't go in the bar."

She turned in her seat. "It's not a problem. I pass for twenty one all the time."

"Trust me," I said, pulling the car into a vacant slot. I shut the engine off and looked at her, trying not to laugh. "I can't let you in the bar, I'm sorry."

"You can't *let* me in the bar?" She slammed the car door behind her. "Chip, you're not my mother. Hell, my mother would be in there doing shots with me!"

I leaned against the car, folding my arms on the roof and resting my chin on them. "No, but I could lose my liquor license." I nodded towards the front door. "Welcome to the Charybdis, Miss Stevens."

"This is yours?" *Surprise.*

I reached for her hand. "This is mine." As we walked to the door she began to drink in every detail; those blue eyes were dancing, hiding whatever doubt she probably had. The flurry of activity that erupted when we walked in told her I wasn't lying. "Well? Do you like?"

There were only a few tables open, lights dim except for the candles glowing in the center of each table. Music drifted from the far side of the dance floor where only a few couples clung to each other. "This is great," she murmured.

I led her by the hand to the dance floor. "Is this okay?"

She smiled and slipped into my arms, pulling herself close to me. We moved easily together, gliding from one side of the floor to the other, melting closer with every measure of the music. Her head fit perfectly under my chin, her fingers wove through mine as if they were molded together.

The thought crossed my mind that I hadn't even kissed this woman yet, but anyone watching us would think that we were joined at the soul.

June 1975

Chip

I sat at my desk staring at a calendar, ticking off the days since I had first laid eyes on the woman. I kissed her after the second date. It was one of those goodnight kisses that promised more than either of us were offering and left my head spinning and wanting much more. I kissed her before the third date and a dozen times during the fourth. I waited a month before I let my hands wander anywhere they shouldn't be, and it was another week before I realized her hands were often wandering, stopping just shy of anything that could have been mistaken as permission. But those kisses—I could have lived on those alone. I wanted the woman in the worst way and in the best way and every way in between, but those kisses could keep me going for the rest of my life.

It had been three months, two weeks, four days, and a few odd hours. It was the longest I had been happily celibate that I could remember. Hell, for that matter, it was the longest that I had been happy that I could remember.

This was something I wanted to make work, but I wasn't

sure that it was at all fair. She didn't know who I was or what I did. I didn't want her to become just my cover, the woman I hid behind so the world wouldn't notice what I was up to. Somewhere along the line, if I kept getting closer, she was bound to get hurt. I was reluctant to tell her how I was beginning to feel about her; as long as I never said those words, I never had to take them back.

Any shrink could have taken one look at me and said I was terrified of rejection. She had been in love before and stung by it; she might not be ready or willing to take that risk again. There was always that chance that she only wanted to be friends.

But close friends, I told myself, don't dance like that and you know it. The lady melts right into you and wants you as much as you want her. Maybe more.

Not possible. It just wasn't possible that she could want me more. I was just afraid of making the commitment.

The phone rang; I listened to it cut through the silence and waffled over answering. It could be Ron or Dan, or any one of another dozen people who could be telling me that I had an hour to get to work, two hours before I'd be leaving the country for some God forsaken hell hole in the middle of nowhere. I knew that call was coming soon; Dan was maniacally upbeat and practically drooling over the possibilities.

I didn't want to go anywhere.

I picked it up on the fifth ring, grumbling "Charybdis" before I had the receiver to my ear.

"Hey, handsome." Music to my ears. "Having a bad day?"

I chuckled. "No, I was just afraid you were someone I really didn't want to talk to. You know how irritating my many admirers can get, calling me all hours of the day and night."

"Ah, I'm sorry I bothered you then." She was laughing at me. "I can imagine all those women knocking on your door could be a little distracting."

"Yep. The men, too, you know."

"They're just jealous."

"Of course they are." I leaned back in my chair, staring up at the ceiling. "They all know that I have you so distracted they don't stand a chance."

"Just a little bit distracted," she allowed. "Would you like to come over and distract me some more?"

Foolish question. "Where would I be doing this distracting?" I asked, half hoping I could meet her at work, embarrass her in the law offices of Crusher and Colt with flowers and a kiss that would make her blush a bright, deep red and send the office gossip mill into overdrive.

"I'm at home." Too bad. "It's a beautiful day out there… I was hoping I could talk you into a walk down to the park. We could feed the ducks."

"That depends," I ventured. "Are we talking a walk for fitness, like you in sweats and me in grungy gym clothes, or are we talking just for fun, with you in shorts and me just ogling you?"

"You can ogle me in sweats," she laughed. "But I was thinking we'd go just for fun."

"And will that depraved little duck still be there?"

"I hope so!" She named the little feathered pervert 'Quackers' the first time we'd gone to the park pond together. He hopped off the back his most recent conquest and followed Terry closely, quacking as he waddled along behind her, and I was pretty sure he was asking over and over, "are you female, are you female?" All the bread crumbs and popcorn in the world couldn't convince him to turn around and go the other way. We lapped the pond and he kept pace, quacking at her the entire time.

"He's going to follow you home one of these days," I told her. "I don't think my feelings could take being displaced by a duck."

"Never."

"And do you promise to wear really short shorts and a tight t-shirt?"

"That depends... Do you promise to wear really tight shorts and a short t-shirt?"

"I will if you want me to," hoping she'd say yes.

I hung up to the sound of her laughter, wondering what, after all, she really wanted.

Quackers, as it turned out, was otherwise occupied when we finally made our way to the park. He never gave Terry a glance, too busy following one of the finer feathered females of the pond with his incessant chatter.

"I think I'm hurt," she laughed.

She was wearing shorts when I arrived at her apartment; careful, conservative shorts and a thick red t-shirt with 'Fairfield High' emblazoned across the front. Leftover gym class material that reminded me that I was, after all, in pursuit of a teenager. I wisely settled on something designed to not pique her curiosity, old gray sweatpants, but made sure the shirt was tight enough to carbonate at least one or two hormones.

We walked around the pond holding hands, and I felt like I was twelve again, having worked up the courage to wind my fingers through the seventh grade wonder woman's, swaggering proudly for the whole junior high to see and to notice that I was the one who she had picked for that week. I strutted around that pond like Quackers, hopefully with a bit more subtlety and self restraint.

After all, I was already fairly sure that Terry was female.

Across the pond there was a playground crawling with young children and their parents. It was usually loud, giggles and screams that cut through the air, something that a year before I would have hated. Then it would have been nothing but nerve wrangling noise emanating from out of control little brats. Terry and I stopped and planted ourselves under a tree, my arm wrapped around her, and watched them play. I noticed the smallest of the kids more often, and the noise was quickly becoming music. It was the sound of pure joy, tiny people just happy to be alive.

"I was never that small," I told her. "I think I was born 10 years old."

She settled against me. "I remember playing here when I was little. I also remember playing here when I was sixteen and cutting school."

"Shame on you."

"And you never cut school, I'm sure."

I watched as a duck ran from the edge of the grass and across the pond track, flapping its wings wildly as it headed for water. "How surprised would you be to hear that I dropped out when I was sixteen?"

"You did?" She lifted her head to look at me. "Why?"

"I had about a hundred reasons." None of which she wanted to hear.

"Okay. You want to leave it at that."

I nodded.

"That's all right. I had a blast in high school, it's hard for me to imagine wanting to leave."

I tugged at the sleeve of her shirt. "You went to Fairfield?"

"I'm a full fledged Falcon."

"If I had stayed I would have graduated the year after you got there, I think. Hell, we might even know some of the same people."

"Maybe… if I can get anyone to admit knowing you," she teased.

I pulled her back against me and kissed the top of her head. "I was well loved in high school, I'll have you know."

"I'll bet." I could hear the laughter in her voice. "But I don't want to hear about all your other women."

"Fair enough. What if I want to hear about all your social conquests?"

More laughter. "There were none. I dated but I was a good little girl."

Of that I had no doubt. Her hand was on my thigh and fingers were drawing absent minded little circles there, but I was sure she had no idea what she was doing to me. "When did you move out on your own?"

"Six months ago? Maybe seven. My dad retired and they bought a house up in Sacramento… I didn't want to go."

"I'm glad you didn't."

She turned and kissed my chin. "I think I'm glad now, too." With that, she pushed away from me and got to her feet. "Come on, let's start heading back before it gets cold."

Before it gets cold, I wondered, or before it warms up more than we'd like in public. Before she could step away I pulled her close enough for a lingering kiss, just enough to tease us both. Her hands went to my chest, and her arms were almost around my neck when I pulled back. "Anyone ever tell you you're a good kisser?"

"I suspected it."

No compliments on my performance. I reached for her hand and headed back over the dirt path around the pond, content enough that she was walking as close to me as she could without us tripping over each others feet.

When we reached the entry to her apartment building I stopped and gestured back to my car. "Are you going to let me take you out for dinner tonight? I brought a change of clothes just in case."

"I don't know, Chipper." She looked down at my sweatpants. "Those really are awfully sexy."

"I know... but I wouldn't want you to lose control."

"Sure you wouldn't." She frowned, but the lights in her eyes were dancing. "You go get your clothes and I'll go on and unlock the door. I promise, I'll try to control myself while you're changing."

Now I admit, while I was reaching into the trunk for my slacks and shirt, it occurred to me that her losing control wouldn't necessarily be a bad thing. But then like every other time that thought popped into my head I filed it under She's Not That Kind Of Girl, and resolved to respect that.

I expected her door to be open for me; I did not expect to hear her saying "Please, just go," as I reached for the door-knob.

Terry was on the far side of the living room, backed up against the glass balcony door. She looked frustrated, and when I walked in her eyes were pleading with me for help. The man standing near her was huge; I could only guess that he was at least 3 inches taller than me and outweighed me by a good fifty pounds. This guy, I thought in a flash, is a moose.

For just a brief moment my brain screamed, gut twisted, and I felt the stirring of a familiar rage. But Terry, seeing the change in my eyes, sighed and gestured to him.

"Chip, this is Matt. Matt"—she smiled at me—"this is Chip."

I didn't say a word. He glared at me, taking a territorial step towards Terry. She took a step back, still looking to me. I glared right back.

"This would be a lot less uncomfortable if someone else would say something," she pleaded.

"You were just leaving?" I offered.

"Wasn't planning on it."

"You might want to reconsider that."

Matt looked at her, a tight smile out of place on his lips. "We need to talk."

Terry was shaking her head, trying to move towards me, but every step she took he matched. I stayed rooted right where I was, watching how he moved, how his eyes changed from curious to angry, how each breath flared his nostrils. "She wants you to go," I said.

"She doesn't know what she wants."

"Matt," she seethed, "just go, please."

"We need to talk," he repeated. "I intend to do that. But not"—he gestured at me with his thumb—"with him here."

"I'm not going anywhere," I told him, as much for Terry's sake as his.

"You know what?" He stepped between us, poking a finger at my chest. "I'm in a lousy mood and I'm not here to take any crap from you. Just pick up your toys and go home, because she can't play anymore."

What the fuck? I swallowed as much of my building rage as I could, trying to ignore the familiar warning signs of hot flashes pulsating through my arms and legs. "Just what the hell it is that you want?"

"I came back for her," he nodded his head towards Terry, who was circling to move to a safe place behind me. "This is none of your business."

"It is now."

"Matt, I really don't want to talk," she insisted.

He ignored her. "This is *my* girlfriend," he boasted, looking right at me. "*My* fiancée. If anyone is leaving it'll be you."

"Your *what?*" She started towards him until I shot a warning look her way.

"I'm not going anywhere. If she wants to talk to you, fine, but I'm not budging."

"Like hell you aren't." He grabbed the front of my shirt, pulling me closer.

"You really don't want to do that."

His hand clenched the shirt tighter as he tried to leverage my feet off the floor. With my right hand I grabbed his wrist and turned it until it was locked and he couldn't move, and with my left hand I grabbed his curly black hair and forced his head back, sending him to his knees, bending over to get within an inch of his face. "I am not someone you want to fuck with," I warned.

He tried to jerk his head away, but the my grip wouldn't break. I used my thumb to put more pressure onto his hand, making the wrist lock even tighter and twice as excruciating. "We can play this game all night," I growled, "but you're still going to wind up being the one who leaves. Now do you want to go on your own, or can I show you the fast way out, over the balcony?"

"Dammit," he groaned, "I need to talk to her."

"For what?"

His voice was barely a whisper. "To get her back."

Terry put her hand on mine, trying to make me let go of his hair. "Chip, please…"

"You leaving?"

"All right," he groaned. "I'll leave."

I let his hair and wrist go, and watched him crumple to the floor. He sat there for a few seconds, and then slowly, embarrassed, got up. I didn't miss the anger burning in his eyes, though he barely glanced up, and he didn't look at Terry at all as he stormed out.

When the door clicked shut, I closed my eyes and ran my fingers through my own hair. I didn't want to look at Terry and see the fear that had to be there. I didn't want to have to explain the kind of pain I had just inflicted on her former boyfriend. I only wanted to blink and have it back to the moment before I stepped through the door, when my temper was under control and I felt relatively sane.

Her arms were around me before I opened my eyes, and she was trembling, but I wasn't sure if it was anger or fear.

"I'm sorry," I whispered against her hair. "Are you okay?"

Her face was buried against my chest. I could feel her nod.

"I could have handled that better… I should have handled that better."

"I'm glad you were here," she said, voice muffled against my shirt. "He'll be back, Chip. Matt doesn't give up easily once he has a wild hair up his butt."

"Would he hurt you?"

She shrugged. "I don't think so… but that wasn't the same Matt I dated."

"But you do think he'll come back."

"I know he will, Chip. He's the kind of person that keeps

trying until something else distracts him."

I sucked in a deep breath and pulled back. If I wanted to test the waters of our relationship, it seemed as good a time as any. "Then let's not be here when he does," I said. "Go away with me for a few days. My stepfather has a house on the coast that we can use."

"Run away from big bad Matthew?"

"It's not running away." I reached out to touch her face, to brush away the lone tear that had managed to work its way over her eyelashes. "It's being inaccessible. Besides, if I see him again and I think for a second he might hurt you, I'll kill him."

"I'm sorry," she sighed, laying her head against my shoulder. "I'm sorry I got you into this."

I wrapped my arms around her a little tighter. "I'm not."

She pulled back and looked into my eyes, seeing that look she had missed before, realizing suddenly that I was serious: I would kill him if I thought he would hurt her.

"We can go play in the sand and soak up the sun," I told her. "Just for a few days. Take the time to calm down..."

"I'll go," she told me, her hand settling on my chest, "but not because of him. If we go, it's because of us."

"Fair enough."

So she definitely felt something for me. Now it was a question of how much I should tell her, and if I should even let it get that far.

Kris

I am, Ron often told me, the Goddess of Thou Shall Not Sit On Thy Ass. He grumbled it as he pushed the vacuum cleaner across the floor. As far as he was concerned, housework was definitely woman's work, and he only did it on occasion to appease the angry goddess, hoping that she'd be grateful later.

I half watched as I ran a brush through my hair. I could see his reflection in the mirror; he flipped the switch on the vacuum and left it in the corner, turning to look at me. His eyes roamed the entire length of my body. I knew the nightgown was just sheer enough for him to see through. I'd bought it just before we married, knowing then that it would drive him wild. Putting it on was a mistake in judgment; the last thing I wanted was to put up with him pawing at me.

Suddenly self conscious I put the brush down and reached for a robe. There was pain in his eyes then, as if he knew I'd seen him watching and couldn't stand it.

He walked away and I stared at myself in the mirror, hating what I was doing to him, knowing that I couldn't help it. He had no clue, and I couldn't tell him.

Chip

Buck naked, I pulled the closet open to stare into the full length mirror hanging on the inside of the door. I knew my body was decent; I spent enough hours in the gym working out to get it that way. I watched what I ate, I bled sweat through hours spent pushing weights around, and I jogged; the end result was worth the effort. My waist was flat and hard, legs well built, chest broad enough to satisfy my ego— but I knew it wasn't just ego; I worked damned hard for it. I had decided in my teens that the time it would take to build the muscle would be worth it in the long run. I used my body for bait, and until then, I hadn't been ashamed of it.

The scars that crossed my chest made me cringe. The one long line that ran practically from nipple to nipple stood out the most, a thick white ridge that hadn't faded with time.

It would be the one Terry would notice first, and I wasn't sure that I was ready to answer the inevitable questions.

I reached for a shirt along with cutoff shorts. I didn't have the answers to give her.

She was waiting for me on the front porch of the beach house, leaning against the old wooden rails, looking down the beach where a little boy was digging in the sand, his mother sunning herself beside him. The sound of seagulls popped like firecrackers, dulled only by the sound of lapping waves.

"You look thoughtful," I said when she didn't turn at the sound of the door closing. "Something wrong?"

She turned and smiled, stretching her arms above her head. "Just daydreaming a little."

My stomach did a quick flip flop. She shouldn't do that.

We spread a blanket out on the beach and settled on it, feeling the heat from the sand creep through it. She whipped off her shirt and began slathering sun tan lotion on, offering me the bottle. I shook my head no, trying not to stare.

She knew what she was doing to me then, I was sure of it.

"So tell me, what do you daydream about when you're out here?" she asked, rubbing the lotion onto her legs.

I drew my knees up to my chest and rested my arms on them, staring out at the ocean to keep from being distracted by the sight of her hands rubbing her legs. I didn't want to tell her that during the frequent trips there with my mother and brother I dreamed mostly of having a normal family, to feel like a ordinary person for once. Instead I told her, "Just the average stuff, I suppose. Hero to the world, preteen fantasies... kid stuff."

"Has it been long since the last time you were here?" She shoved the bottle aside and laid back, turning on her side toward me.

"Long time," I mumbled. "I came out here alone a lot after my mother died, but it got to where I was staying longer and longer and kept finding reasons to not go home. So I quit coming." I sighed and stretched out beside her. "What about you? What kind of fantasies did you have as a kid?"

"I'm too chicken to have fantasies," she laughed.

"Come on, " I prodded. "Spill it. I won't laugh."

"You won't laugh because I won't tell you."

"You were a little pervert, weren't you?"

"Pot, meet kettle." She poked at my side with a sharp finger, but was smiling. "I buried myself in cheesy romance novels. I didn't have to fantasize."

That would explain the bookcase crammed with paperbacks.

"And what about now?" I asked.

"I'm not telling you anything, Chip! How did we get from daydreams to fantasy anyway?"

"I'm just curious."

"You're just nosy." She was trying to sound angry, but it wasn't working. "I still cave in to an occasional cheap, trashy romance novel... Keeps me from getting frustrated."

"About...?"

"Stop it," she laughed. Then she cocked her head and ventured, "so... what keeps you from getting frustrated?"

Did she want to know?

"What makes you think I'm not frustrated now?"

She blushed, deep and wild, and turned away from me. I'd flustered the woman, and it made me laugh.

"Didn't you have any boyfriends along the way to keep that frustration in check?"

"I had boyfriends," she allowed.

"But...?"

"God, you *are* a nosy little shit!"

I nodded proudly. "I've never read a cheap romance novel, but unless it was loaded with porn, I don't see what it would do for anyone's frustration."

"I was a very young teen when I started reading those," she laughed. "We're talking along the lines of things like some two dimensional little tart spouting off 'love me, love me, love me' being enough to thrill me to the point of curling my toes." She was laughing hard now, burying her face in her hands. "Oh, God, I don't believe I'm telling you this."

"If it makes you feel any better, I was stealing Playboy magazines from the Seven-Eleven when I was twelve."

"Didn't that just frustrate you even more?"

"It was educational," I reasoned.

"I'll bet."

"Embarrassed?"

She peeked at me from the corner of her eye. "Maybe a little. But I think that's exactly what you want."

I wasn't about to tell her exactly what I wanted. I just raised an eyebrow and smiled, leaving it at that. I could have reached out and grabbed her right there, to hell with the kid playing down the beach, to hell with anything, but she still didn't know enough to make it fair. This wasn't like the line of women who had been in and out of my life, women who didn't matter and weren't going to be around long enough for me to give a rat's ass what they thought or cared about. She didn't deserve to be shoved into that long line of faceless memories.

The time just wasn't right to even imply a commitment. Not until I knew she was safe.

Kris

"Where is he?"

Ron settled back into the chair, vinyl squealing, and everyone's eyes were on him. "I don't know," he replied evenly, staring straight at Dan. "I don't know that he's gone anywhere at all."

Dan's hands were gripping the edge of the desk so tightly his fingers turned white. Every word that had tumbled from him from the moment he came into the office dripped with venom. He didn't bother to pretend he was trying to control his anger. "He damn well knew we were on call," he said through clenched teeth.

Of course Chip knew. He just didn't care.

I stood behind Ron, leaning with my hands on the back of his chair. "Maybe you just missed him, Dan. When did you call?"

Doug had been standing quietly, leaning against the far wall, eyes darting back and forth between Ron and Dan and myself. Silently soaking in every detail, making mental notes about the condition of this once tight team. "We looked everywhere, Kris," he said. "I've been to his apartment, his girlfriend's apartment... he didn't show up at the gym last night, either. I've looked everywhere he normally would be."

"That still doesn't mean he's missing," I said.

Doug shrugged. He knew Chip better than anyone and probably did know where he was, but he'd never say so, not in front of Dan, who was so close to exploding his face was turning red. He was clenching and grinding his teeth so hard I could see his jaw move in and out. Doug noticed, too, barely shaking his head in wonder.

"We just go without him," Ron offered.

"No!" Dan shot out of his chair, pointing an accusing

finger at Ron. "I'll be damned if I'll let that little bastard screw us out of a choice assignment again!"

"Nothing is so good that it can't be delayed a day or two."

I wondered if Ron really believed that. Had he been in Dan's shoes, staring at the first real piece of work he'd been trusted with in a year, would he be so willing to brave the world with someone important missing? You don't leave your muscle behind, not when you can avoid it.

"You find that kid," Dan insisted.

"What happens if we don't find him?" I asked. "Can we go without him? Any chance of that at all?"

"No!" Dan pounded his fist into the desk. "If he's not here by tonight we lose the assignment, and if we lose it I swear I will chew him up into so many pieces you'll be able to stuff him into a little plastic baggie."

"He is," Ron pointed out, calmly and quietly, "only twenty two years old and would be much better off away from all of this." He stood up, planting his hands flat on Dan's desk, leaning forward to face him. A challenge dripping with testosterone. "All *you* can see is your precious career going down the toilet. Chip's life can go on without it. He *needs* to go on without it. Take the assignment, find someone to re-place him, and let's just go."

Dan flushed with anger. "You find that bastard son of yours, Gallery, or I swear I'll take you down with him."

Chip

From where I sat on the porch, in the dark, I could watch Terry through the big bay window. If not for the hardly-there bright pink bikini, she'd be the picture of domesticity. I cooked dinner—cheap steaks tossed onto a too-hot grill and lumpy

mashed potatoes—and she cleaned up. I offered to help, rea-
soning that even I was capable of washing a dish or two; after
all, I had been living on my own for a while and didn't always eat at the restaurant. I had been known to use real dishes
once I a while. Even utensils. She pushed me out of the kitchen
with the order to just find someplace to sit down, relax, go
watch the stars or the waves or something.

I preferred to watch her.

Terry was as boyishly slim as she could get and still be
completely feminine. When she reached high over her head
to slide plates into the cupboard I noticed some real defini-
tion in her stomach, and leg muscles that stood almost taunt
against her skin. She was in shape but not freakishly so, not
like the muscle bound steroid goddesses of the gym.

This was the longest time I'd ever taken to just watch a
woman move and appreciate her just for being her, though
not without my own prurient thoughts.

Watching her move back and forth through the house
was like dancing with her, those fluid movements that made
my heart pound and head spin. When I thought about the first
time we danced together at the restaurant, I could feel the
electricity between us. I almost kissed her a dozen times,
fought the urge to tilt her face up to mine and just melt lips
together with the whole world looking on.

And when I did finally kiss her, standing at her door that
night, every inch of her was screaming surrender. Arms looped
possessively around my neck, body pressed as close to mine
as she possibly could; those lips were warm and wet and promised something more than I was willing to take.

She tossed a dishtowel aside and walked over to the other
side of the living room, bending low to turn the stereo on.
She fiddled with the knobs until she found a station that came

in clearly, soft music that rode on the air out to the porch. I could have stayed right where I was, on a hard rickety lawn chair under clear night sky with a full moon, stayed outside where it was safe, but I found myself getting up and heading for the door.

Lord, give me strength...

She turned when she heard me come in and she smiled, holding her arms out to me, inviting me to dance. I slipped my arms around her and pulled her close, wondering what in the world I was going to do.

"You look worried," she said. "Something wrong?"

Astute observation, woman. What do I do with a teenage witch who deserves a whole lot better than anything I can give her? I shook my head and said, "No... I was just thinking."

"Don't hurt yourself, now."

"Very funny."

I wanted to pull her close and just hold her, but she had other ideas. She tilted her head to the side, eyes twinkling, and just looked up at me. I knew what she wanted to hear; I wanted to say it, but dammit, I was afraid. It was binding, a verbal commitment, once said I couldn't take it back, not without tearing her heart out.

But then, I could be breaking her heart if I kept it to myself.

If anyone had told me, when I was nineteen and hopping from one warm bed to the next, that in just a few short years I'd be standing in the middle of my stepfather's beach house with the woman of every man's dreams wrapped in my arms and that I'd be terrified right down to my toenails, I'd have laughed and called them a liar. I wasn't afraid of women. I used women. I let women use me.

So what do I do, say something and take the chance that it would break her heart someday, or keep quiet and break it right there on the spot?

I bent my head towards hers, lips brushing together lightly. "I love you," I whispered. "I love you very much."

She started to say something, but I closed my mouth over hers. It was out there, and I didn't want to hear "but we barely know each other." I did entertain the thought, when I felt her tongue on my teeth, that what I was most afraid of was not hearing it back. Who's heart might get broken, and did I even have a heart still?

My mind was screaming at me to stop, loud clanging alarms going off in every corner of my brain, but my fingers slipped curiously under the bikini top, tracing feather soft lines on her skin. I kissed her chin, her ear, sliding my lips down to her neck. She let out a small little gasp and pulled herself closer to me.

"This doesn't have to happen now," I whispered. "Not if you don't want it."

Without a word she took my hand and headed for my bedroom. We were hardly through the door before she leaned hard against me, pressing kisses into my neck and on my ear. Her hands worked to pull the shirt over my head, quick fingers unzipping my shorts, her lips barely leaving my skin. I pulled the string that held her top together and felt it brush against my leg as it fell to the floor. With lips fused to mine, she pulled me down onto the bed, hands running over my shoulders, over my chest.

I pulled back long enough to ease off the rest of her swim suit, and trailed kisses from her hip to her neck, lingering here and there, tasting the salt on her skin, licking away drops of sweat.

Her eyes were closed and she was trembling, though her hands were moving gently over my skin.

The light bulb went off in my brain. "You're a virgin," I whispered, almost a question, not expecting an answer.

She opened her eyes, pupils wide and dark, breath coming in quick little gasps. "God, don't you stop now, Chip."

"Are you sure?"

She answered with a kiss, as soft and gentle as it was demanding. I let my hands and lips roam her body, touching her softly, listening for every moan and every sigh. When I was sure the trembling wasn't fear but fire, I gently pushed her onto her back. Her hands were holding my face, and with kisses trailing over her lips and chin, I thrust once hard, until I was completely inside her, afraid to hear her cry out.

Her fingers feathered across my neck to my chest and she began to move with me, breath hot and wet against my neck. I felt her shudder just slightly, and let myself go, knowing I couldn't expect anything more for her, not this time.

I buried my face against her neck, afraid to look into her eyes and see pain and disappointment.

"I'm sorry," she whispered after a long time. "I should have told you."

I lifted my weight to my elbows and pulled away gently, curling onto my side so I could hold her close. "God, don't apologize," I murmured against her hair. "I never even asked. I just assumed..." I touched her cheek, urging her to look at me. "You are so wonderful." My finger traced over her lips, and then I kissed her. "Why me?"

"Chip..." A soft kiss on my chest. "I've never wanted to be with anyone else."

"I've never been anyone's first..." I stopped, wanting to bite off my tongue.

She laughed softly. "It's okay. I was pretty certain all along that you're not little Mr. Innocence. I just hope you're not angry."

"Angry?" I sat up and looked down at her, hair all wild and splayed out over a pillow. "Terry, no. Christ, how could I be mad about this? I love you so much."

She reached for my hand. "I love you, too."

Blue eyes just boring into mine. They were still dark and wild, and fixated on mine. I smiled and leaned over to kiss her. "You can look, you know."

"What?"

"You won't go blind if you peek," I teased. "Here"—I laid back and closed my eyes—"I'll lay perfectly still and I won't watch you, and you can peek all you want."

"Open your eyes," she laughed.

"Nope, not until I know you've had a good look."

"I peeked plenty, Chip."

I could feel her hair tickling my face, and her breath on my lips. "You kept your eyes closed almost the whole time," I told her. "Either that or you were looking right at my face."

"I'm sly."

"Not that sly."

The bed moved as she slid closer to me, lying on her side. She was quiet for a minute, then leaned over and kissed the nipple closest to her. "You don't want me to peek," she laughed.

"I don't?"

Her hand was on my stomach, fingers playing over the lines between muscle. "You want me to touch."

I opened one eye. "I wouldn't mind," I allowed.

"And I didn't touch enough, did I?" She was smiling, not all that serious.

"You did just fine," I assured.

"But I could do better." Not a question. "I admit, I was afraid to. Am afraid to."

Both eyes open. "It's okay."

Her fingers picked at hair, tugging very gently. "You have completely different body parts, mister. I might break something."

"I'm willing to risk it."

"I'm not even sure... oh, close your eyes again, I'm about to make a confession and I don't want you staring at me."

"Okay." I chuckled and closed them. "And how long has it been since your last confession?"

"Well I've never told anyone *this*."

I sucked in a sharp breath as her hand slipped lower.

"This isn't just my first time, Chipper... It's like my first first time. I mean... God, this is embarrassing."

"I won't laugh."

"I know you won't." She traced invisible lines along the length of me, watching, I was sure, the reaction she was getting. "I'm not one for just grabbing body parts. On anyone."

"I didn't think you were."

"I mean..." She sucked in a deep breath.

I opened an eye. She was staring down at my chest, not even paying attention to what she was doing to me. "You mean," I finished for her, closing my eye again, "not even yourself?"

"Not even," she admitted after a while.

"Why?"

"I think," she whispered with that hint of laugher, "that I was always afraid my fingers would fall off."

I opened my eyes and lifted my head to kiss her. "They won't."

"Oh, sure, you of the I-steal-Playboy confidence."

"That was when I was twelve and didn't have much control of all my body parts." I rolled to my side and pushed her to her back. "Watch…" I slid my hand up her thigh and touched her carefully, slowly. "I swear, my fingers will not fall off."

"Oh, God…"

"And neither," I murmured against her stomach, trailing kisses past her navel, "will my tongue."

Sharp fingernails grabbed at my hair. "Chip…"

I waited until I knew she was just at the point of arching off the bed, breathing ragged and hands tugging at my ears, before I joined her, both of us thrashing wildly on the sheets together, so caught up in the moment that it when it was over I could only breath out, "damn…."

Kris

Saturday morning Ron stood on a jetty overlooking the beach, trying hard to look inconspicuous as he searched out his son's car next to the house. He wore a white t-shirt and baggy shorts, his hairy legs too white to belong to someone who spent any real time there. He was watching through binoculars, wanting to keep distance between us and the house, hoping we wouldn't be seen.

He had known where Chip would be. From the moment Dan grouched that Chip was nowhere to be found, Ron had known right where his son was. "He's here," he grunted. "At least his car is."

He hopped off the rocks, handing me the binoculars.

"Dan better be happy. I don't like spying on my own kid."

"Chip knows the rules. Someone should always be able to get a hold of him."

"They want to be alone, Kris."

"Still..."

"Come on. He didn't tell anyone where he'd be for the very reason that he doesn't want any of us to come knocking on his door. I can't just barge in there and drag him away."

He was right. "There are crazy about each other, aren't they?"

"Exactly." He took a deep breath and set his hands on his hips, staring at me exactly the way he did when I said something that surprised or stumped him. "Remember how awkward it was the first time we went away together? How embarrassing it was to have to give Dan our entire agenda, right down to the times we expected to be out of the hotel room? I don't want to do that to Chip." He looked back over the jetty and sighed. "I want him to finally have a real life."

"So what do we do?"

"We go back without him."

I shook my head. "You heard Dan. Chip's finished if we don't show up with him in tow."

Ron nodded sadly and started for the car, parked a mile up the beach. "I'll take the heat," he finally said. "I won't lie to Dan, we know where he is and that he's safe, but I'll be damned if I'm going to be the one to puncture another hole in Chip's heart. If we drag him out of there now he'd hate us forever." He stopped and looked at me. "Kris, we don't even know what he's told her. What would it do to her?"

"You'd do this much for him?" I asked. His pain was seeping out so thickly I could feel it.

"I couldn't do jack shit for him when he was growing up, but I can do this."

"Dan will hang you from the rafters by your gonads, Ron."

"I love my son. What else can I do?" He started walking again, his head hung low. "Why in the hell did I allow him to get mixed up in this in the first place?"

"Chip never gave you a whole lot of choice," I reminded him.

"I know," he sighed. "And now he's going to pay for it. I should have seen it coming."

Chip

It was early when I woke, Terry's leg thrown across my thighs, her arm across my stomach and face buried into the pillow next to my head. I don't think I moved all night, just laid there on my back with her curled around me; I knew she was tired and I didn't want to so much as twitch and wake her.

Somewhere at the foot of the bed there was a tangled sheet, but I couldn't reach it with my toes and couldn't make a grab for it without moving her over. I stared up at the ceiling and absorbed the warmth she radiated, willing myself to feel every point of contact between us.

God, what have I done to her?

Telling her I loved her was one thing, taking advantage of that was another.

I couldn't even be honest enough with myself to admit that I'd gotten exactly what I wanted, one night with the woman who—increasing every minute—meant more to me than the world itself. It wasn't fair, not by a long shot. I had all the details and she only had hints.

Carefully, hoping to not wake her, I shifted to my side. If I was going to scare her off later, I wanted to spend the morning watching her sleep, drinking in every detail, from the way she crinkled her nose as she slept to the way her hair spilled across the pillows. Any other time I'd be doing whatever I could to wake the woman, have one last good roll in the hay before I got up to leave, and I wouldn't even promise to call.

So what happened to me, at what point did I become human?

She drew in a deep even breath, stretching against me. As I leaned over to plant a kiss on her bare shoulder she whispered, "Well good morning to you, too," a hint of laughter tumbling out sleepily.

"I was watching you," I admitted. "You look incredible."

"I am incredible."

God, she's just a teenager.

Light was streaming through the cracks in the curtains now, dust motes dancing in the slivers of light that beamed across the bed. Off in the distance a coast guard cutter sounded it's horn, a deep lazy sound that was almost mournful. Terry was snuggling up against me, her arms sliding around mine, trying to draw me close.

"I need food first," I groaned.

While I plugged the coffee pot in she hunted through cupboards for cups, standing on her toes to peek past glasses made from jelly jars and bowls made from old pink melmar. She found them in the back, holding them up triumphantly as she brought them to the table. I sat down across from her, dropping spoons and packets of sugar onto the table.

"We have to talk," I told her, not wanting to look up and see that look of 'oh, no, he got what he wanted and it's over.'
"You may hate me."

"Not a chance, mister. I love you."

"I know." I reached for her hand, staring down at the lines that crossed her palm, running a finger over them. "You know there's a lot I haven't told you about myself."

"Yes, I know. It's frustrating."

Will she even believe me? With that thought came the reaffirmed idea that once she did know, she might not want to stay, and that it would be easier for her to back away. She had to have that option, as much as I hated it, and I had to be the one to give it to her. "I have to give you the chance to walk away from me and not look back. I should have told you before things went this far. I swear, I never wanted to hurt you."

She pulled her hand back. "Okay, now you're scaring me."

"I know." I looked up from the table and into her eyes. There was pure bewilderment, fear and unasked questions beaming back at me. When this conversation was over, would she think last night had been a colossal mistake? That look was breaking my heart, just the idea that I could lose her in the next 30 seconds, but it wasn't my choice to make. "I work for the government, Terry. I'm a field agent for the U.S. Defense Agency."

I waited, giving her time to absorb.

"And?"

"I'm not a spy... not in the typical sense anyway. I go after things, equipment the U.S. wants, weapons, sometimes people. Mostly recovery of information and intelligence. Sometimes it can be dangerous... My contract runs for over a year still but even then I'll have a hard time breaking away from it."

"Ron? And Kris?"

I nodded. "I'll understand if when we get home you don't want to see me again. I can't ask you to live like that, always wondering where I am and what I'm doing."

She got up from the table and went over to the bay window, staring out at the beach and the waves; the clouds were getting thicker and dark. "How often do you do it? I mean, when and what do you really do?"

"I haven't done anything for over a year. Before that... three or four major cases a year. Sometimes a few odd short ones. When I do work—it could be just about anything, anywhere. I can't give you concrete details."

She leaned against the wall by the window, arms crossed at her chest, eyebrows knotted in confusion. I waited while she sorted through the bits and pieces pinging around in her brain.

"Have you ever killed anyone?" she asked without looking at me.

I closed my eyes for a moment; I couldn't give her half-truths and expect her to be able to see what she may or may not be getting in to. In one long slow breath I said, "Yes."

"Do you enjoy it? Your job?"

"Not anymore." I didn't add that I used to thrive on it, the more danger pulsating around me the better. I pushed away from the table and went over to her, standing behind her with my arms around her waist. "I would walk away from it right now if I could. I don't know what the next assignment is, I only know that it will be soon."

"Have you ever come close to being killed?"

"No."

"Will they ever let you go?"

"I don't know."

"I suspected," she said thickly, "that you were into something heavy right from the beginning. You steered away from the subject so many times it had to be serious. This is not going to knock me off balance." She turned in my arms and hugged me, hard. "I love you, no matter what."

I sighed hard and stared out the window, more afraid than I'd ever been in my life.

Kris

"What," Ron asked in response to Dan's explosion, "did you expect me to do? Bust the door down and drag them out of bed? Aside from scaring the hell out of Terry—who is a civilian in case you've forgotten—I can't tell him what to do anymore."

"You never could," Dan spat. He paced the office as if it were a cage. "We have a job to do!" He turned on his heel to face Ron. "We had a job to do."

Ron shrugged. "So there will be another. Chip made a small mistake. We're all entitled."

"Small?" Dan drew in a sharp breath. "This is my career, dammit. You go back and get him, Ron. I want that son of a bitch back here yesterday!"

Ron just sat there and stared. Dan's face turned a little more red with each word that spewed out of his mouth. The veins in his neck stood out in rapt attention, and his eyes were bloodshot.

"I don't care how you do it," he growled. "Just do it."

"I have no intention of driving back down there. If you want him that badly, then call him, or go after him yourself. I won't risk losing him."

"Do, it, dammit!"

"Like hell. And what's the point anyway? You said yourself we don't have this job now." He was keeping his cool for once. "He's just a young kid who wants to spend a lost weekend with his girlfriend. Can't you understand that?"

Dan slumped into the chair behind his desk and nodded,

the fire burned out as quickly as it had erupted. "Of course I understand. But understand this: before the whole fiasco with that dead fiancee of his, Chip was blazing a trail through this department so fast we could have all grabbed his tail and gone along for the ride. The agency considered him the backbone of this team. He just lost the chance to really shine."

"What was the assignment?"

"He had the chance," Dan groaned, "to steal—and help Kris fly—one of the newest MiG fighters. Fresh off the block, probably not even painted yet. They gave it to someone else."

"So?" Ron shot out of his chair. "So they both get to live instead. Goddamn, taking my wife and my kid in one blow?"

"This was his chance to move up to his own team, Ron."

"I don't give a bucket of shit if it meant a promotion into the assistant SG slot. I want him out of this whole mess, Dan."

Dan nodded slowly. "I'm sure that's a done deal. The Secretary General wants to handle this himself. Chip's not only done, he's probably on his way to Leavenworth."

Chip

Halfway home I understood what it was I wanted. The realization jolted me so powerfully I swerved in the road, tires squealing. Terry was dozing in the seat beside me, her lips curled up in a half smile.

The woman is saving you from yourself, so what are you going to do about it?

I glanced over at her, resisting the urge to reach over and touch her. Instead, I dug my fingers into the wheel and kept steering for home.

How much was she willing to risk?

Doug

I swirled my drink, watching the ice cubes spin around in the glass. I was already beginning to feel drunk; ordering it had been a mistake. On my best days I didn't hold liquor well. One or two good drinks could damn near put me under the table. Halfway through my first drink I realized I could barely fix my eyes on anything for more than a second; everything seemed to just slip and fade off to one side.

I took a long, slow sip, enjoying the feeling as it burned down my throat. Kris was late, probably trying to think of an excuse to get away from her husband.

She'd better come soon, I thought, or she'll have to scrape me off the floor.

Most of the time it made no sense to me, meeting her every week without fail, fifty two times a year, a minimum annual debit of one hundred and four hours out of my life. She was painfully obvious how far she wanted to take this so-called friendship. There wasn't a week that went by that she didn't at least hint that she wanted to leave the drinks and the food behind and find some warm place to crawl into bed. Every week I pretended not to hear, or to not take her seriously. As much as I was tempted, I had the feeling that deep down she did still love her husband.

This would be a really great time to break the whole thing off, I thought. Put half a bottle of wine down her and then tell her this is it, no more. Then get up and walk away without looking back. Once she'd had enough to drink it would be easy.

I looked up, staring across the room. She was there, scanning tables for me. The familiar stab shot through me and I knew I'd be back the next week, and the week after that.

Chip

My first intentions were to drop Terry's bag by her bedroom door, spend a few minutes saying goodnight, and then to head home; not to the Charybdis, but to my own cramped studio apartment. I was bone weary by that point, my eyes burning with fatigue, and my head was beginning to swim.

I put the bag by her bedroom door and then dropped onto the sofa, groaning, "I am so tired. I feel like I haven't slept in a month."

She sat next to me, our shoulders touching, her hand on my thigh. "The purpose of this weekend wasn't to rest, it was to forget, which I did. For now, anyway."

Back to reality and all the baggage we were bringing into this relationship. "Don't worry about him. He was just nuts because he realized he'd made a huge mistake by leaving you. Besides, if he bothers you again, I'll break his face open."

"You will not!"

I would, but didn't say so. "I'd better go," I said, leaning over for a kiss. "I'll never get any sleep if I don't."

She kissed me, but it was quick. "Don't go."

"Darlin'," I moaned, half grumbling, "I can barely move and certain parts of me are screaming."

"How's that?"

"Ya done rubbed me raw."

She laughed and reached for my hand. "I promise, I'll let you sleep. Just don't leave me alone tonight."

I bet she's afraid of sounds in the night, too, cringes at the wind whistling down the chimney.

"You're worried he'll pop out of the corner when you least expect it?"

She nodded, biting her bottom lip. "Something like that."

"All right…" I grabbed another kiss. "I'll stay." I expected to see a flicker of relief there in her eyes, but what I saw reminded me more of victory. She'd won.

It wasn't that I minded, I just wasn't used to being the one who was manipulated.

"Don't worry," she set her head on my shoulder, "this is as far as I expect to get tonight."

I was genuinely surprised. "Really now."

"Amazed?"

"I think I'm insulted. You must be tired of me already, because I was sure you were insatiable."

"Oh I am," she teased, "but you're afraid it will fall off."

"Another night with you and it will." I stole another quick kiss. "Have we created a monster this weekend? The volcano hath erupted, and there's no plugging it back up."

"I said," she growled playfully, "that I would let you sleep. I think I can keep my hands off you for one night. Beyond that, there are no guarantees." She stood up, reaching for my hand. "Come on, you can't sleep on my couch. I want you in my bed."

"Wanton woman that you are." I followed her into the bedroom. It was as soft as I'd expected it to be, very bright and feminine. The collection of stuffed animals strewn all over the room would have struck me as odd if I hadn't realized she was holding on to one last vestige of her childhood. She could play house and be the grown up, but the bedroom was a part of an old home she could never go back to.

I sat on the edge of the bed, kicking my shoes off. "You know, there is one really big thing we never bothered with this weekend that we should have."

"What's that?" She was standing in front of the dresser mirror, slowly pulling a brush through her long hair.

Our eyes met in the mirror. "I don't mean this to sound as crass as it probably does... but I'm not ready to be a father. I honestly didn't think we'd be sleeping together this weekend or I would have taken care of it before we left. Once we got started... I just never thought about it. I'm hoping it's not too late."

"Well if it is, I'll stick a candle in the window and tell everyone I'm waiting for three wise men to come strolling in from the east. You'll be off the hook."

"Fat chance. If your wise men showed up they'd all tell you the same thing. Blow the candle out, because no one is buying it. And I would not be off the hook, not by a long shot. I'm not that big of a coward."

She set the brush down and came over to me. "I'm not pregnant, so don't worry about it." She pushed me back onto the mattress. "You're just trying to spoil my mood."

"But it's not going to work, is it? Should I give it up so easy?"

"Somehow I think I'm the one who should be saying that." She stretched out next to me, kicking her own shoes off. "Tsk, now is it so bad?"

"It's not so bad at all," I said quietly, fingers working to unhook her bra. "I definitely enjoy making love with you."

"I enjoy Oreo cookies and chocolate milk," she snickered. "Was that a compliment or not?"

"Was a compliment, woman."

"Well you're not so bad yourself, mister."

"I try hard."

"I noticed."

"I don't want you to wonder if this is as good as it gets. When I'm with you it feels like all the pieces are falling into place, and it all seems perfect... maybe it's a little early to pursue the subject."

"The subject of what?"

The thought that someday she just might want another lover shot through my brain like an arrow on fire. That was possible, wasn't it? Someone is your first for a reason, the implication that there's going to be a second. She might love me, but that didn't mean she wanted my body and only my body for the rest of her life. She wasn't even expecting the question, her eyes clouded with confusion over my sudden change in mood. I was serious, she was bewildered.

"Marriage," I said. "I can't imagine what my life would be now without you and I don't want to. I want you to be my wife."

Those blue eyes grew wide with surprise. She looked stunned for just a minute, and then laughed. "You mean one minute you're worried you might have knocked me up and the next you want to get married? Does this go hand in hand?"

Ouch.

"No. I love you, woman. I would die for you…" I stopped, suddenly thinking that I understood. "That's it, isn't it? You're afraid that's exactly what will happen."

"Chip," she sighed, "I told you that I loved you no matter what, but that doesn't mean I'm not scared."

"I know." That's it, I opened myself up to it and she's going to turn me down. "All right, I'm sorry. But I had to ask."

"Hey…" She touched my chin, turning my face towards hers. "I don't just want your body tonight, I want it every night." Tears brimmed at her lashes, but she blinked and they were gone. "We must have a good fifty or sixty years left in us."

"But will you marry me?"

"Chip, " she laughed. "I'm saying yes."

"Seriously?" The breath I had been half holding came out in one steady stream. "If I give you fifty or sixty years it will fall off."

She pulled away from me, removing off her bra and she stood. "I'm going to try," she promised.

"Oh God," I moaned, drawing myself up so that I was sitting at the head of the bed, legs stretched out. I watched as she slowly stripped, my head beginning to pound with my heartbeat. "You promised."

She crossed in front of the bed, knowing I was watching every movement. Carefully, she reached down to me, pulling at my belt with one finger. "I know," she whispered. "I lied."

~

Chip

Anyone driving by the building that housed the west coast headquarters of the United States Defense Agency—a name that didn't address its purpose and opened itself to ridicule among the intelligence community—would be hard pressed to figure out what it was and why it was smack dab in the middle of nowhere. It was an ugly 5 story beige square plopped incongruously in the heart of agriculture, a blink of an eye off the Interstate, and so sorely out of place that people naturally slowed down to look and wonder whose brilliant idea it was to build in the middle of a pasture.

The few people who did take the nearest exit and backtrack to actually go inside were greeted by a myriad of small offices on the first floor; a receptionist welcomed them to IntelliTech, asked which division they were looking for and to whom would they like to speak, and invariably sent them on their way with the impression that the odd beige building was nothing more than the repository for a company of technical researchers, the nerdy kids they had picked on in school now grown up and putting those freakish brains to work for the betterment of the world.

It would have taken a detailed map and a willing guide to actually find anything resembling technical research in the building. There were huge room-sized computers in the basement, along with the men who kept them running and programmed, and a fair sized medical clinic on the fifth floor, but that was as close as it got to technology.

The offices that mattered were on the second through fourth floors, easily accessible from the inside, much more difficult to get to from the outside. It was the standard construction policy for every agency building world wide: put what doesn't matter much on the floors where access is more likely from someone repelling from the roof or trying to drive a tank through the front door, and bury the rest.

Dan's office was tucked safely in the middle of the third floor, just three doors down from the office of the enigmatic Secretary General. I stepped out of the elevator and headed down the hall, my shoes squeaking on newly waxed tile, and steeled myself for the sharp contrast between the relative warmth of the decorated hall and the sterile emptiness of Dan's little cell.

Ron had already prepared me to face the wrath of Hurricane Danny; I knew going in that his temper had reached the point of volcanic eruptions and he was taking all the little things and building them up until they were monumental.

"He wants you to think you're headed for a federal prison," Ron told me. "By now he may have even come up with a credible reason to threaten you with it."

I was guilty of lack of foresight, but I couldn't believe

my decision to wander off without permission was reason enough to string me up by the short hairs. "So he's waiting there for me with handcuffs?"

"Sure," Ron snorted. "I think the worst you have to worry about is having the SG drape you over his knee for a good spanking."

Ron was sure that Dan was reacting to something else, something he wasn't sharing. His temper could be nothing more than out of control fear. He certainly babbled on, and wasn't making sense.

Given the warning, I was prepared for an angry and out of control Dan. I was even prepared for a nonsensical Dan. I wasn't prepared for the highs and lows he could throw at me in a five minute time span.

"Sorry won't cut it this time," he grunted when I entered his office. He was rocking in his chair, springs squealing. "In a few minutes you'll be going through Barstow's door"—he pointed in the general direction of the Secretary General's office—"and I don't honestly know if you'll be coming back here."

"Hello to you, too."

"Close the damn door."

I pushed it closed with my foot and then dropped into the chair in front of his desk. "I went away for the weekend, Dan. It's not that big a deal."

"It *is* a big deal!" He jumped out of his seat and nearly shot across the desk. "This isn't the Army, Chip, this is worse. You fucked up. You won't get the benefit of a court martial or anything resembling a fair hearing. You don't even get to plead for mercy. Alex Barstow doesn't have to say two words to you—I'm sure he's already made up his mind."

"And he's decided that because I missed one lousy case

that I should stand in front of a firing squad with a rose clenched between my teeth and an American flag waving in one hand?"

Cold gray eyes glared at me.

"They sent someone else to get the plane, Dan. It was one case. Losing it is not the end of the world."

Dan threw his hands in the air and turned away. Head hanging, he gripped the edge of his desk, and it was as if all the life sucked out of him with a single breath. The man deflated right there in front of me. "Barstow is a military type zealot, Chip" he said. "When I first signed on, he was so inflexible with the rules that you didn't dare sneeze unless it was an approved and documented activity." He sighed hard and turned around. "I was on a team that missed out on a waste-case, something anyone with three brain cells and half a clue could have done. We didn't make it because one of the men was sleeping off a bender in a hotel room and we couldn't find him. He could have shown up drunk and it would have been all right…"

"But? They stuck a grenade up his ass and tossed him off the Golden Gate Bridge because no one knew where he was?"

"Might as well have. Barstow decided to make an example out of him. The last time I saw him he was nothing but a mass of bloody bruises and was being shipped out to God knows where in the back of an ambulance."

I ran my fingers through my hair, trying not to laugh. "So the SG is going to try to beat the snot out of me for all this?"

"I doubt he'll lay a hand on you."

"Not personally, anyway."

He didn't respond, didn't nod or shake his head, just stared.

I got out of the chair, reaching for the door. "I won't play any games, with him, Dan. It's a crock of shit and you know it."

"Don't try to force his hand," Dan warned. "You *are* expendable."

I slammed the door behind me. Of course I was expendable. So was Dan, and I wondered if that wasn't who he was most concerned about. The agency didn't really need any of us.

Alex Barstow's office was like entering a whole other world; I stepped off hard tile onto blood red carpet that was so thick I could feel my feet sink into it. His windows had long flowing drapes pulled apart and tied off to the sides with thick black cords that practically disappeared into the dark red drapes. His walls were covered with old paintings in heavy dark wood frames, and his desk, which spanned nearly half of the back wall, dug into the carpet.

He sat behind the desk and watched as I closed the door behind me, fingers drumming, waiting.

"Sir," I said as evenly as I could. I didn't offer my name or my hand, and I didn't sit in either of the black leather chairs that faced him. I stopped just behind them and waited.

He arched an eyebrow, then nodded. "Sit down," he finally said. "We can dispense the introductions, you know who I am."

"Of course."

I felt like I did when I was in sixth grade, sitting there in the principal's office, wondering just how bad the punishment for throwing an eraser at the music teacher could possibly be. I fidgeted then; now I casually crossed one leg over the other and waited, hoping I looked as collected as I wanted him to think I was.

"You," he said flatly, "made a mistake."

"Possibly."

"Your team leader spent the better part of two days looking for you. We had to deploy another team to do your job. The loss in operating time may very well result in a negative outcome."

An alarm went off in my head. They knew where I was; Ron found me on the first day. Dan knew that—so why didn't the Secretary General know that? "If I held my team back," I said, "then I apologize. If we lose the plane, I accept the responsibility."

He picked up a folder from his desk. "You're a good field agent," he said. "You've been sent out twenty seven times in the six years you've been with us."

"Yes."

"And twenty seven times you've been instrumental in the success of your team."

Where was he going, I wondered. I felt like I was about to be tripped up, or that he was looking for something he could use to crucify me with. "At best," I said, "I've been secondary to the team's success."

The folder fell back to the desk. "Your first case. What was it?"

I had to think carefully. The first time I did anything officially I was a little over sixteen years old, after bullying my way into the agency by following Ron and Kris halfway around the world in hopes of finding something better than summer school and fending off my stepfather. "China," I finally remembered. "The objective was to destroy intelligence information. Some of the key components were embedded into the building itself... we did the job and left."

"According to your records, you scaled three quarters of

the way up an eight story building, crawled through at least a quarter mile of air conditioning ducts to set up explosives, and came out the same way. No one else on your team was able to get into the building."

No one else was as skinny as I was when I was sixteen. I didn't belly my way through those air ducts because I was dripping with courage. I did it because I was the only one who fit.

"And your last assignment." He opened the folder, flipping through pages until he found what he was looking for. "Do you know what Dan Martin said about you, officially?"

I shook my head.

"'He frequently displayed courage beyond the call of duty, including risk to his own life on several occasions. Instrumental in the rescue of our medical operative. Was also solely responsible for the recovery of a female operative, preventing a potentially fatal attack. He sustained multiple injuries; however, he did not withdraw himself from the case. His actions resulted in the safe return of the entire team. Recommend retention.'" He closed the file and pushed it away.

"There's more to that story," I said. "My team may have come out of it unscathed but…"

"I'm aware of the entire story," he said, cutting me off. "Your team was handed an assignment and you were unavailable. It made you look unreliable and irresponsible."

"Mr. Barstow, I'm fully aware of what I did."

"And are you aware of the repercussions?"

I was aware of what Dan thought would happen to me. There was nothing hanging from the ceiling in Alex Barstow's office that could be used to hang me by, no medieval torture devices. "I'm aware the outcome could be unpleasant."

"I understand you've had a tough year."

"Not entirely."

"I'm giving you an excuse," he said bluntly. "I've interviewed other team members. I've been told about the events of this last year, and I was aware that you had been on a medical out for most of that time. However, Dr. Stone tells me there was nothing to keep you from completing this assignment."

"Nothing official, no."

"I'd like to fire you, but I can't. You still have a contract and haven't done anything that would merit dissolving it. I could assign you to spend the rest of your time with us in the basement as a file clerk, or I could suspend you without pay until further notice."

He shrugged, as if it didn't matter one way or the other to him. I could spend the next year cleaning the bathrooms with my toothbrush and a Q-tip.

"I want you to turn your weapon and identification card to your team leader. During your suspension you'll accumulate no pension benefits and you lose your medical coverage."

I stood, slowly exhaling. "Yes, sir."

The Secretary General extended his hand. "Goodbye, Mr. Davis. Have a nice day."

~

Chip

Ron leaned against the bar, drink in hand. He was crowded on all sides by half drunken people pushing to find open seats and available ashtrays; his eyes were red, blinking frequently against the smoke that hung in layers in the air. He waited while I served a customer, taking liberal sips of his drink.

"Sounds like you did well, son," he said, trying to talk above the noise. "You played your cards right on this one."

I swept crumbs off the counter and then topped off his drink. "Someone must have gone to bat for me, Ron. Dan was sure Barstow was going to have me drawn and quartered... I think the guy wanted me to squirm for a few minutes, but that was it. Hell, I was afraid to squirm."

He laughed and finished his drink in one long draw. "That's my boy. Cold as ice."

"Not this time." I took his glass and set it behind the bar, expecting him to protest. "I didn't want to blink wrong, breath wrong, or sniff wrong. What I wanted to do was get down on my knees and beg, just in case Dan was closer to being right than he was wrong."

"I am really sorry, Chip," he said, reaching for the pretzel bowl. "If I'd just knocked on the damn door and brought you home it would be a non-issue."

I waved him off. "Forget it. I think this is one I'd rather have avoided anyway."

Ron cupped his chin in his hands and pursed his lips thoughtfully. "Could've been the big one for you. If you'd brought that plane home and in one piece you could have had anything you wanted."

Not to mention that there was a time when I would have given my right arm and a shot at my soul for the chance to steal that plane. "Too risky." I tossed ice cubes into a glass and poured Ron a soft drink. "The better bet for me is to just stay home right now, and with any luck, I can ride it out until they just cancel my contract."

"You're one damn lucky sumbitch." He lifted the glass in a toast. "I only wish I'd been the one to save your butt."

"Who did?"

"Kris," he said. "And Doug. They went in early this morning to plead your case. She says Doug laid it on thick about our last assignment and everything you went through after Brenda... he insinuated he was going to have you medically boarded out of the agency. They would have had to pension you for life."

"Then I owe him. Come on," I said, gesturing towards the door. "My office is a hell of a lot quieter."

"How did Dan take it?" Ron asked as he closed the office door behind him. He settled back onto the couch that set against the wall opposite the desk; it was wide enough for two people to snuggle on it comfortably, though it had never been used for the purposes I intended when I bought it. All that time with Brenda and I'd never let her set one foot inside the office.

"I dunno about him," I grunted as I dropped next to him. "Dan tried to get me to wet my pants a little with some odd story about a friend of his that Barstow supposedly beat to a pulp over a missed case."

"I know the story. It's true... but it's not as if the SG dished out any punishment himself. This yo-yo got so shit-faced he didn't know if his ass was in the air or what, and let a briefcase full of sensitive documents vanish into thin air. Dan's team tried to cover it up and make it look like he'd just drunk himself into a lost weekend... didn't work. They all got caught. The guy tried to fight his way out of the building, and security fought back."

Dan had been with the agency longer than I had been alive; any screwups along the way would explain why he was still doing legwork and not sitting behind a desk all the time, enjoying the comfort of sending other, younger people out for all the gruntwork.

"Dan lit up like a Christmas tree when I walked back into his office," I said. "He didn't even seem to mind when I turned in my gun."

"He got rid of his little troublemaker," Ron laughed. "Have you told Terry any of this?"

"Not yet. I didn't want to tell her over the phone."

He was twirling his drink, little droplets of water spinning off the glass onto the floor. "How much does she know, son?"

"Just enough." I grinned and elbowed him in the side. "I asked her to marry me."

"No kidding?" He set the drink aside. "Well, did she give you an answer?"

"She said she would."

Ron leaned back and smiled. "I feel like that girl has pulled you right out of the grasp of hell," he said, slapping my knee. "Damn, I wish your mother was here to see you now. She would love Terry. She's perfect for you."

My mother would have loved Terry, I'm sure, but I knew that had she lived, there would be no Terry in my life simply because there never would have been a Kris. Ron would still be living his life hoping she'd leave my stepfather to be with him. He never would have looked twice at Kris.

"Why didn't she marry you, Ron?" I asked.

"Because Grant meant stability," he sighed. "I meant confusion and fear. I think she believed we'd drift apart after she married him and we could all live happy little white picket fence lives."

"And Grant knew?"

He nodded. "At some point he realized it wasn't over... You have to understand, he *did* love your mom. He was determined to stick by those vows and your mother thought of the whole mess as a holy sacrament—I could never talk her into getting an annulment. Too Catholic to leave, not enough to stop from cheating." He closed his eyes, a long, sad blink. "Believe it or not Grant cared enough to make sure I was never shut out of your life... he really did love you. It wasn't until your brother came along that you started fighting with him so much. The gap just got so big..."

"He tried to kill me, Ron" I reminded him. "That's not love. I still have the scars to show for it."

"I know he hates himself for that," he said, and got up from the couch. "I loved your mom right up to the end, Chip. I still do."

"I know."

I rested my head on the back of the sofa, shutting my eyes, listening to the click of the door as it closed. I suddenly felt very tired, and very lonely. I hadn't given my mother much thought in a long time; I could barely remember what she looked like. When she died I was filled up with so much rage and hate, mostly because I was left there with Grant, that I shoved her into a neat little corner somewhere in my mind and only thought about her when I had to, or when she crept out of that dusty hiding place to poke at my conscience.

My hand went to my chest, feeling for the long scar that tore from nipple to nipple. This was something my mother never would have forgiven. She would have killed Grant with her bare hands.

August 1975

Kris

Chip and Terry's wedding couldn't have been held on a more miserable day. I woke up to the sound of rain battering the windows and wind whipping leaves off the trees. It was cold and the dark clouds seemed to envelope everything, hiding the hills that dotted along the city, swallowing whole the soul of the day.

Inside the chapel it was warm but not very bright. Rain swirled on the stained glass windows, bright pinpoints of light reflecting from the candles burning in nearly every nook and corner of the church. The air was heavy with the scent of cinnamon and hot wax, yet it was comforting against the chill we had come in from. Ron closed his eyes and inhaled a slow deep breath, saying that it smelled like home.

The groom stood on the altar and watched as his bride came down the aisle on her father's arm, his eyes beaming with more love than I had seen in anyone for as long as I could remember. The pain that had been reflected in those eyes for so long was no where to be seen; he took her hand and smiled so warmly that he didn't even seem to be the same person.

They had chosen to forgo a wedding mass, something I was sure earned Chip no points with Terry's mother and very few with his stepfather, who sat very quietly—and alone—in the back pew. Sheila couldn't have known that Chip hadn't set foot inside a Catholic church since his mother died, and Grant, while he surely knew, wouldn't like it but he also wouldn't hold it against the man Chip had become.

He shared Chip's faltered faith on more levels than one; Ron told me once that Grant Davis had been a deeply religious man when they first met, his faith ground down by anger and the pain of betrayal.

They spoke their vows to each other with quiet astonishment; Chip seemed certain that it was just a dream and if he took his eyes off Terry for just a moment, she'd be gone when he looked back. Terry held his hand as if she were holding his heart, very gently, but with a certainty I nearly envied.

I hadn't felt that sure when I married Ron. Terry looked at Chip and knew without a doubt that she was the only person in his world and would be forever. I kept glancing at Doug, who stood next to Chip, uncomfortable in his tuxedo, wondering if he remembered the ceremony, and if he had seen then the doubts I must have had. He saw none in Chip. None in Terry.

They decided against a reception; the plans for the wedding had been throw together quickly and neither one of them had the patience to wait for anything other than Chip's own restaurant to be available for a celebration. That could wait, they said. Give us a week for our honeymoon and we'll party all you want.

Their first kiss as husband and wife was both passionate and restrained, ten seconds of pure joy that had half their guests in tears, those who knew Chip's personal demons and how gracefully Terry had embraced him.

Chip and Terry made their way down the aisle quickly, pausing only when he realized his stepfather was there. Grant stood, holding out an envelope, staring uncertainly at Chip, who took it without a word and escaped through the chapel door with his hand grasped tightly by his new wife.

Grant watched them leave from the chapel stairs, standing in the rain as the car pulled away. Ron left me just inside the door so he that he could take a few minutes alone with Grant, and I, as much as I hated myself for it, made sure I was where I could hear them both.

I wanted to know what was in the envelope.

"I'm glad you came," Rod told him. "What was it you gave him?"

Grant turned; he didn't seem at all surprised to find Ron there with him. I expected to see tempers flare and anger drip off them like the rain, but instead I saw two old friends who couldn't find a way past the sadness of their former lives. "It was just a letter," Grant replied. "Pat wrote it the day David was born. She asked me to make sure Chip got it on his wedding day, if she wasn't able to give it to him herself."

Ron looked down the road where he could see Chip's tail lights fade into the rain. "Some day he'll heal," he said.

"I'd give my soul for that... it won't ever happen."

Ron nodded, almost thoughtfully. "At least you've had the chance to know him as a son, Grant. I've never really had that. And you have David."

A child whose very existence tore at Ron's heart. David was proof positive that the woman he loved didn't live the chaste marriage he had assumed.

"You never had more children." More of a question than a statement.

"Me? No. You should be grateful Pat got what she wanted out of life, Grant. All she ever wanted to be was a mother. That's a choice my wife will never have."

"You have a son."

"He's my flesh and blood, but he's not her son."

"But he *is* yours."

"And yet he never took my name. I didn't bring him into this world. I wasn't there to pick him up when he fell, when he said his first word, or the first time he got his heart broken. I wasn't there."

Grant turned his face to the sky, letting the rain wash over him. "I love that boy, Ron. As much as if he were my own son."

"I know," Ron said, turning to come back into the chapel. I leaned against the back pew, feeling as if my soul was about to bleed through my skin and pool on the carpet.

Why did I never know?

Why did he never tell me I had no choice?

Terry

Chip's hands are strong and have these little calluses on his palms, right where his fingers begin, battle scars from his almost daily war with free weights. His knuckles are usually red from pounding on a heavy bag in the gym, and even the heel of his palm has skin thickened from the years of driving it into the canvas of the bag.

How, I wondered out loud, could someone with hands that rough be so gentle with them?

"It's a gift," he laughed.

We decided to spend our honeymoon back at the beach house where we knew we would be alone and not distracted by friends or family, or even other strangers who would be in any tourist spot we could think of. I wanted a few days of nothing but the two of us; we could always find time later to see the Grand Canyon, or be greeted with a lei in Hawaii.

From the time he had told me he loved me, right there in the beach house living room, until our wedding day, it had only been three weeks. He woke up the morning after we got back, dragged me from sleep with a long, slow kiss that left me wanting so much more, and announced that until I had a ring on my finger, we would both be sleeping alone.

He bounded out of the bed before I could grab him and change his mind, and he stuck to his decision. He did nothing more than kiss me for the next three weeks. I grumbled a lot, and pouted a few times, but I wasn't half as annoyed as I wanted him to think. We waited just long enough to be able to honestly tell my parents that no, we weren't marrying because we had to, but because we couldn't stand the idea of living apart. We made arrangements to hold a small ceremony in a nondenominational church, risking the ire of my staunchly Catholic mother, and ran at full speed toward starting a future together.

I knew my mother was sitting at the kitchen table at home, muttering to herself—and to my father if he would sit still to listen—that as sure as the sun would shine again, she'd be a grandmother long before she should be. My father would probably think that a good thing, or at least something he would have to accept and be glad about.

I made a mental note to send my mother flowers in nine months with the message "Well, we told you so!"

The rain had let up by the time we got there, the air sticky and smelling like fish. Chip unloaded the car while I took off my wedding gown and hung it carefully in the closet; I was suddenly struck with the idea that I didn't have a clue what to do. Put clothes on and go help him, or just throw the covers back and wait for him in bed?

When I heard him opening cupboard doors, I sighed and slipped into a robe. He was putting up groceries. It was his wedding night, he had a woman waiting in his bedroom, and he was putting up groceries.

"I wanted you to see how domesticated I can be," he chuckled.

"I can train you for domestic duties later."

He shoved a bag full of dry food into the pantry. "And did you, hmmm, *want* something?"

"Well not anymore!"

He was laughing as I stomped off in a pretentious huff into the living room. I waited by the bay window, watching as the waves lapped up onto the beach, frothy little bubbles forming on the sand with each one. The rain began again, drop by drop at first, then sure and steady. After only a minute I felt his arms slide around my waist from behind, and his breath on my ear.

"Ah, now, Mrs. Davis," he whispered with a brogue, "I would be wanting you in the worst way, don't y'know?"

I laughed and turned my face to his. "Where did that come from?"

"A gift from my mother, who was a fine Irish lass with a musical lilt to her tongue." His arms went around me tighter and he placed a warm kiss on my neck. "'Tis a fine gift to have, something from your mother, something a man would only do in front of the woman he loves."

"I married an Irishman."

"That you did." He tugged on the belt of my robe. "And this Irishman loves you, woman. He wants you right here in front of God and all the angels."

We made love there in the living room, in front of the bay window to the sound of the waves and rain dancing on the glass. If God was watching, I'm pretty sure he approved.

Chip

At some point during the night we wandered from the living room floor into the bedroom. Terry fell asleep, curled in my arms. I watched her for the longest time in the dim light; her mouth was turned up in a slight smile and her breath was warm and wet, streaming across my chest. She stirred when I kissed her forehead, pulling her body closer to mine.

"Chip?" Her voice was barely a whisper.

"It's late," I whispered, nuzzling my face to her head; her hair smelled like strawberries. "You should sleep."

"So," she protested, "should you. Why are you still awake?"

"Because I wanted to watch you, and make sure you didn't get away."

"Oh, sure," she snickered. "I do this every other week, I marry some poor misunderstood sucker and then leave him the next morning."

"That's what I read on the mens' room wall."

She poked my ribs. "You're awful."

"I hope not," I said, dropping kisses on her nose and chin. "I'd never want to disappoint you."

She lifted her head onto the pillow to fit her body more intimately with mine. "I'm just a rank amateur, mister. If anyone's going to disappoint, it'll be me."

"Not a chance."

"Should I have warned you the first time? I didn't want to scare you off."

"You have no idea what it means to me to know I was

first. And last." I paused when she kissed me. "Does it bother you that I wasn't…?"

More soft kisses. "No. What you did before you met me is none of my business."

"Do you want to know?"

"Not tonight," she murmured. "The only thing I want to hear tonight is that you love me, and that you're willing to teach me what I need to know to make you happy."

"I'm happy now," I told her. "I can't imagine anything better."

Terry

Chip's face was less than an inch from mine, his green eyes glittering in the half light, with a sleepy look that seemed more satisfied than tired. When I shivered he pulled the blankets up around us, then rubbed my back with his hand.

"Explain to me," I said, kissing his lips, "why when we make love you always call out to God."

He didn't miss a beat. "Because it's so much like dying, I figure I have to hedge my bet."

Kris

"You're going to do what?" Dan asked, dumbfounded.

I swallowed nervously, not wanting to look up from the floor. "You heard me, Dan. It's the only way to preserve my sanity."

"But you haven't told him yet."

I looked up at him and shook my head. "Should I? He's been lying to me for the last five years. I don't feel like I owe him a damn thing."

"After five years you at least owe him an explanation. You can't just leave him and not tell him why."

I listened to the click of my heels echo in the hall. The corridor felt long and empty this time of the day, early morning before all but a few people would show up for work. "I wanted to let you know before all hell breaks loose. I know how badly this will affect the team."

"Chip took care of that. It's not a problem." He stopped and turned to me, taking my hands in his. "Five years is a lot to throw away... I'd hate to think you were jumping the gun."

"I'm honestly torn, Dan. A part of me loves him but I can't get past this *thing* and I know I can't live with him anymore."

"You said he lied," he pressed. "It is too personal for me to ask?"

I gently pulled my hands away. There was no way I could tell him all the things that had been thundering through my head in the short time since the wedding. There was all that anger and hurt, and something else that I couldn't quite put my finger on. But he had omitted something essential from day one, and it was killing me. "It's not what he lied about," I said, walking again. "It's what he never told me."

"I won't ask if it hurts too much."

It hurts...

"The long and short of it... He can't have children," I said. "All this time I never realized, and I had to find out by spying on him at Chip's wedding. How sad is that for a factoid of my life?"

He squinted at me warily. "Do you really need a baby to make you happy?"

"Dan, I feel like he reached into my chest and just ripped my heart out. If I had know then, I wouldn't have married him."

"Having kids in this business is usually a mistake..."

"I never intended to stay this long! And I should have known all along, I should have had the choice!" I let the tears that had been threatening all morning spill. "I feel like I'm too goddamn old now, and he took those years from me."

Dan reached out to hold me. "Maybe you should give it some time, at least long enough to make a decision when you're not this angry. Give him a chance to defend himself."

I pulled back and wiped the tears off my cheeks. "Is this coming from you as my boss or as my friend?"

"I'm not your boss anymore. If anything came out of that fiasco with Chip, it was showing me I'm just plain tired now. I'm thinking about retiring."

"Are you serious?"

He nodded. "I am. Kris, please, don't walk away from Ron just yet. Give yourself time to absorb the blow first. It may not be the end of the world after some time."

"What if I were to tell you I might want someone else?"

"It wouldn't matter. Don't throw your marriage away without giving it a chance. You could regret it in the long run."

I tried to look into his eyes, but he looked away.

"Trust me," he said.

"All right," I conceded. "I'll give it a chance. Just one."

He nodded slowly; he wasn't smiling and his eyes were distinctively cold. For a moment, I thought he really didn't believe I should try.

Chip

Blood dripped in steadily flowing ripples from my wrists, some of it falling to the ground, some of it running in thin lines down the length of my arms, little red beads that popped up off my skin like drops of sweat. I could feel my arms being stretched out, my shoulders straining with the effort to keep the pain from turning into white hot agony. I tried to lift my head but couldn't, and the air was slowly being sucked from my lungs. I could feel pain in my side, and knew if I opened my eyes and looked down my feet would be a mass of blood and bruises.

It was a mistake, I should be somewhere else. With someone else. My ears buzzed with the sounds of hundreds of people murmuring and chanting. It pounded in my head, throbbing wildly against the inside of my skull. I tried to open my mouth to scream but I couldn't draw a breath deep enough. I was being sucked into darkness, I wanted to scream for someone to help.

"Chip!"

I woke with a start, sweat dripping from my face. My hair was wet and plastered to my forehead. I picked up Terry's hand from my chest and placed a kiss into her palm.

"That must have been one hell of a dream," she whispered. "Are you all right?"

"Just a nightmare."

"You were shouting." She pulled the blankets around us tighter, and with a kiss eased back onto the pillows. A soft, cool morning breeze was pouring in through the window, making the hair on my head turn cold. Her hand slid across my chest, fingers tracing the line that ran almost all the way across it, slightly raised and rough against the smoothness of her own skin. "How did this happen?"

I hugged her tight for a moment, then sighed and relaxed. "It was just a fight."

She pulled herself out of my embrace and lifted herself up onto an elbow. "Just a fight?" she repeated. "Chip, who did this to you?"

"It was a long time ago, Terry. It doesn't matter anymore."

"I can't imagine someone wanting to hurt you like this. You won't tell me?"

"It's not a huge secret… most of these scars have been here since I was fourteen."

"My God," she grimaced, falling back onto the pillows. "You were just a kid."

"Hardly." I could still taste the fear, the wild feeling that I was about to die. If I closed my eyes I could see the glint of the knife as it slashed at me, and the fingers gripping the handle. "I had a fight with my stepfather," I said after a while. "I don't even remember why."

She touched the scar again and cringed. "How could he do this?" she wondered out loud. "Chip, how could he do this?"

"He took a knife," I said, "and he cut me open. It doesn't matter anymore."

She rested her head against my shoulder. I was sure she could feel how hard my heart was pounding; she knew how much it still mattered to me, how deep those scars really were, and how much she hated Grant Davis.

December 1975

He grieved as he watched the months creep by. The woman had distanced herself from him so far that he was ready to give up; her moods were dark and stormy, and the tension that filled the room when they were together was unbearable. He had hoped that patience was the key, that he would be able to wait her out, and everything would be all right.

But it was not all right.

Her anger was as unyielding as it was passionate. She refused to speak unless she had to; nights had become long and painfully dark. She stayed on her side of the bed, her back always facing him.

He would admit only to himself that he was crushed and confused. She had pulled away so far that he knew there was no room left for any more strain or the relationship would snap. There was no place for compromise; the marriage was on her terms or not at all.

What frustrated him most was the silence. She had never said what sparked her anger. One day she simply stopped talking. Sometimes he would catch her staring, her eyes filled with a hurricane of rage, but she would never say why.

The times he found himself reaching for the door were more frequent, thinking it would be so easy to walk through it and never look back. But he didn't need the pain, he was already filled with more desperation than he felt he could handle. It was a familiar pain, the ache of loss and hope denied he had felt before.

He wondered if she even knew what she was doing to him. He stopped trying to hide the torment he felt, he stopped pressing for answers, and kept to himself. There was the work that had to be done. He just couldn't remember anything he had said or done that would push her that far away.

More nights than he cared to admit he found himself home alone, or out alone, and he tried to drown out the pain. He drank often now, not even tasting the liquor that burned white hot down his throat. It helped to go home numb, to collapse in a stupor. The hangovers were easier to handle than the pain.

The work would have to make up for it all, someday it would be his redemption. It couldn't be his downfall, he knew, because he was already in hell, and nothing else he did would matter.

Chip

Terry reached over my shoulder and slapped at the alarm clock until it stopped ringing. I forced an eye open and peered at her. "What time is it?" I groaned.

She still had her hand on the clock, probably contemplating throwing it across the room. "Five thirty. Get up, Chip, you've only got an hour before you have to meet Dan."

I moaned and buried my face into the pillow, stubbornly closing my eyes. "I'll call him. It's too damned early."

"Get up," she ordered, tossing the blankets off, well out of my easy reach. The snap of sudden cold was enough to send me bolting from the bed and reaching for the robe I'd left in a heap on the floor before crawling into bed. Terry followed me, going into the bathroom to turn on the shower. I stumbled in behind her, pulling her into a lazy embrace.

"You're mean, woman. It would have take me maybe ten minutes to get there."

"But it's going to take you the other forty minutes to shower, shave, and pull your clothes on. It's your own fault for agreeing to a meeting this early."

"Hmmm." I slipped out of the robe and into the shower, pulling her with me. "Relax," I chuckled. "I won't bite unless you ask me to."

She slid her arms around my neck and brushed wet lips against mine. "I'm not objecting. You just don't have the time right now."

"Humor me."

"I'd like to." She lathered soap into her hands, rubbing it onto my chest. "Did Dan give you any idea what he wanted to see you about?"

"Nope." I squinted, water spraying off her shoulders and into my face. "I got the feeling it wasn't something I was supposed to ask him on the phone."

She motioned for me to turn so that she could lather soap across my back. I stuck my head under the spray, hands leaning on the slippery tile, enjoying the feeling of her hands sliding across my skin. After a quiet moment her arms went around me. "They want you back, don't they?" she asked.

I turned back around and pulled her close. "I don't know."

"Can you refuse if they do?"

"No, not really." I rinsed and then slapped the water off

and reached for a towel, wrapping it around her neck and shoulders. "Don't sit here all morning stewing," I said. "Even if they do want me for something, that doesn't automatically mean it's a bad thing."

She went back into the bedroom, sitting at the edge of the bed as she dried her hair. "What could possibly be good about it?"

"Well..." I tossed my towel aside and reached for underwear and jeans, "There was some talk of making me clean the latrines on the second through fifth floors with a toothbrush."

"Chip..."

"I'm only half kidding."

"You're making me rethink letting you out that door," she sighed.

I was tucking my shirt into my jeans, and stopped. "It's not too late. Given a choice between crawling back into bed with you or going out there and to see the Grinch, it's a no brainer."

"Zip your pants up, wonder boy."

I leaned over the bed and kissed her, letting my fingers trail from her jaw down her neck, very softly moving until my hand stopped just at her navel. She was still wet from the shower and starting to shiver. "Now are you sure about that?"

"Go to work, Chip." She threw the pillow and me and laughed. "You're impossible."

It was no surprise to find that the diner Dan chose to meet at was one of the oldest, cheapest, and least clean places in town. Ambiance obviously wasn't his foremost concern when deciding where to take us for breakfast. Doug and I arrived first, wiping the table off with napkins before we sat in the booth. Coffee, we agreed. Anything more than coffee would risk finding out exactly how much intestinal fortitude we both had.

"Any idea what he wants?" I asked, sipping at the coffee. I grabbed more sugar, stirring enough in to leave a thick scum at the bottom of the cup.

"No idea." His eyes were heavy, dark circles beneath them. "He sounded pretty down when he called last night."

"When in the last two or three years has he not sounded down? Hell, look at this place. It's one step away from a used roach motel."

As good as Dan was at his job—and I suspected at one time he had been among the best—one of his personal quirks was that he was tight with a buck, even when it came directly out of an expense account.

"What about you? How's married life treating you?"

"You should try it sometime," I laughed. "It'll do wonders for your disposition."

"I haven't even had a decent date in over a year."

"Maybe you should actually ask someone out." I lifted an eyebrow, only half jesting. "When was the last time you really put yourself out there?"

"About a year ago."

"Try over a year and a half, Doc. You're about two Our Fathers and a Hail Mary away from becoming a monk."

"I bet a monk would get more action."

"You'd look lousy in the robe."

He pretended to consider it. "I have the legs for it. And it could be very freeing. All that fresh air swirling around my—"

I'm sure he would have coughed up an entire list of monk-robed possibilities and innuendo about women and knowing them in the biblical sense, but Dan slid into the booth next to him, his briefcase banging on the table. He looked beyond tired, his hair streaked with gray, and the stiffness I used to kid him about—geez, Dan, you're walking with a broomstick up your ass—had given way to a pronounced slouch. He looked like a completely whipped Ricky Ricardo, a thin little man with age and stress wrapped around him tighter than the skin on his bongo drums. "Gentlemen," he said, "thank you for coming."

"What's up, Dan?" Doug asked, watching Dan pop open the briefcase and pull out two long thin envelopes. "Christmas cards? Cash?"

He handed one to each of us. "Your contracts. The team is being dissolved."

Doug snapped to attention. "What?"

"The team," Dan repeated grimly, "is being dissolved."

I tore open the envelope and pulled out the papers that were inside. There was Dan's signature, and stamped across the bottom in bright red letters were the words *terminated with reserve*. "Just what does this mean?"

"It means you're free to go. The option on your contract has been dropped. Potentially you could be recalled, but it's not likely. They want you gone. But you," he said to Doug, "you'll be offered another position. I doubt you'll get field work this time, most likely you'll get your chance to just be a doctor again."

"What if I decline?" Doug asked.

Dan drew a deep breath. "Well, you can begin your outprocessing. That would take about thirty days."

I shoved the papers aside. "This is too easy. What strings are attached? They're just going to let us walk away?"

"Apparently."

"And the restaurant? Do I lose that as well?"

"There was a board of director's meeting last night addressing that specific issue, Chip," he said dryly, shaking his head as if in wonder. "The final decision boiled down to the fact that no one else can even spell Charybdis, so the papers to resume possession can't be filed..."

"Very funny, Dan." I clapped him on the shoulder. "But it's nice to see you still have a sense of humor."

Doug was folding his contract, slipping it into his jacket pocket. "Whose idea was this? I know we had a lousy year, but we don't warrant this."

"Maybe *you* haven't," I offered.

"It was my decision," Dan said. "I decided to cut the team off last week. We're not stable enough as a unit to function efficiently any longer."

"I don't get it," I said. "The group can do fine without me."

"It's not you, Chip."

"Then who?"

He leaned back heavily and sighed. "Kris and Ron. There's no possible way they can work together anymore." He paused, considering. "She's half a step away from leaving him."

Doug shot up in his seat. "What?"

"I don't understand, Dan," I said. "What makes you think she's going to leave him?"

"She told me as much, Chip. She brought it up three or four months ago but I don't think anything has changed. I can't hold this team together when half of it can't stand each other."

Or when part of it is doing slow backstrokes through a pool of depression.

How long had it been since I'd spent any time at all with either one of them? Terry saw Kris all the time but never hinted at problems between them. The last time I saw Ron was shortly after our wedding; he was looking for wood tools to finish carving designs into the hand held crossbow he was building. He was proud of it, boasting that the everything from the design to the final coat of wood stain was his, and that he was sure it would actually work. "God, I didn't know. Where the hell have I been?"

"Probably in bed," Doug snorted.

"Which is where I would rather be than face either one of them right now," Dan said sadly. "You two, I knew you'd be at least grown up about this. Ron will shit bricks and Kris..." He shook his head. "I'm no good with women who cry."

I held my hand out. "Give me their contracts," I told him. "I've made Kris cry enough times that I'm almost immune."

"I should do my own dirty work, but thanks."

"I'm not kidding. I don't know a damn thing about my own father's marriage imploding... this will give me a way to worm my way into it without being nosy outright."

He reached back into his briefcase for two more envelopes. "Thank you. You can act on my authority. Ron will be offered another contract."

"And Kris?"

"No. The option wasn't offered and I didn't press for it."

"You're firing her!" Doug accused. "Just what the hell is she supposed to do now? Bus tables for Chip?"

Dan raised his eyebrows and looked at Doug. "What's it to you, Doctor?"

"Kris will be fine," I interrupted. "She can take care of herself." I studied Doug's face, too, the surprise and the rage. He didn't care that our team was now a memory and he wasn't upset about potentially losing his own job. It was Kris, and I found that more than a little interesting. "Dan, what do I offer her if she rejects the terms? What if she wants an option?"

"There are no more options for her, Chip. She'll get eighteen months severance, plus any accrued benefits. The same goes for you, Doug, if you pass on this."

Doug nodded.

"But Chip," he said, "I'm sorry. They're not offering you anything beyond releasing you from any immediate obligations."

"I get to keep the restaurant. That's good enough."

"I've known a lot of friendships the drew the line at this point," he said quietly.

It wouldn't be fair to tell Dan then that I felt nothing but relief and wanted more than anything to bolt from the crappy little diner and find my wife to tell her the good news. He wanted something, for one of us to reach out and tell him it would be all right, we'd all stay friends and live happy little lives together until we were all old and gray and had shriveled up prunes for bodies. He wanted to hear that.

Later, I'd wish I had told him.

The first person I called when I got to my office was Terry; she answered on the second ring and I asked her, giving her no time to press for details on my meeting with Dan, to meet me for a late lunch. If she was as elated as I hoped she'd be, I wanted to see her face when I told her, not hear her squeal over the telephone.

It took several more phone calls to find Ron. I left message after message in his office, even venturing to think he might brave the gym. I sat there racking my brain, trying to figure out where else he could be when he called back, wanting to know why half the building's occupants were running up to him to tell him to call his son. He was worried and I did nothing to reassure him, only asked him to stop by for a drink.

I had an entire bottle of Seagram's waiting and used it liberally to loosen him up before handing him his contract.

"So, we're being fired?"

I poured pretzels from a bag into a bowl and set them on the bar in front of Ron. "No," I said, popping one in my mouth, "I'm being fired. You they want to keep for some odd reason. It certainly can't be cause of your charm."

He drained his glass in one long draw, and then pushed it towards me. "Refuel me, son. I want to get stewed."

I laughed and poured him another. "You're still gainfully employed," I reminded him. "Some of us have to get day jobs."

"Sure, son, you look real worried."

"Well hell, everyone else who's getting canned gets eighteen months pay. I sure as hell wouldn't have minded that."

Ron's eyebrows peaked at that. "You need money?"

"No, we're doing fine and I get to keep the restaurant. I just need something to grouch about."

"I can grouch enough for the both of us."

I picked up the bottle and poured myself a drink and refreshed his. "What's up, Ron?" I asked, serious now. "You're sucking this stuff down like water."

"Very astute." He set the glass down. "This just makes life a little easier to deal with."

"For today, okay. But I don't want to be there when they're standing over your death bed watching your liver turn you different shades of yellow."

"I should live that long…"

"Come on."

"I'm sorry. Life really has been hell lately."

"Anything I can help with?"

"Crack my wife's head open and find out what's going on in there?" he asked, face pinched. "She hasn't said more than two or three words at a time to me for the past four months. When she looks at me, she's got this hate in her eyes… Jesus, I don't even know what I did. I've said every damn thing I can possibly think of. I've begged and I've pleaded with her and she won't say a goddamned word!"

I slipped out from behind the bar and sat on the stool next to him. "Not another woman involved?"

"No!"

I help up a hand. "Take it easy, I'm just asking." Doug's angry face came to mind, and the idea that there might be another man was spinning through my head.

"She's just slipping away from me, Chip. She's slamming the door"—he held up a fist and knocked on an imaginary door—"and no matter how loud I bang she won't let me in."

"You want me to talk to her? There's a good chance she'll listen to me."

He stared straight ahead. He had nothing left to lose and he knew it; all the pride in the world couldn't save him from needing to know what was going wrong, even if he had to use his son to find out. "Sure," he said, sliding off the stool. He patted me on the shoulder as he went past. "Sure."

"What was that all about?" Terry asked, passing him on his way out the door. "Is he all right?"

I watched him go through the door, waited until it clicked

shut. "I don't know yet." I set down my glass and held my arms out to her.

"How did it go with Dan?" she asked, hugging me.

"It went well." I took her hand and led her into the office. "He fired me."

"And that's good?"

"It means I don't have to worry about a call at three in the morning telling me I'm headed for Timbuktu. I lost all our medical benefits, though." I thought for a moment and shrugged. "What the hell... Dan dissolved the entire team."

"He fired all of you?"

"No. Doug has options and so does Ron. They'll just be reassigned to other duties."

"Kris?"

"No. They dropped her. And I'm the lucky stiff that gets to break the news to her."

"Chip, that's not fair. That's not your job."

"It's okay, I volunteered." I sat on the top of my desk, heels banging against the bottom edge. "I'd rather it came from me, and I really need to talk to her. Something big is brewing between her and Ron."

"Sure you want to get involved?"

"Don't want to, but I owe Kris. She's pulled me out of deep holes more than once. Hell," I added, "look at you and me. She pulled that off, didn't she? And she'll be here soon anyway."

"You don't think she'll be upset?"

"Not at me, no."

She stood in front of me, hands on my thighs, worry flooding her eyes. "I obviously don't know the whole story. Can I do anything?"

"Just stay with me while I talk to her. Something has

gone sour and I promised Ron... I have to talk to her."

She leaned in and planted a kiss on my forehead. "I'll stay," she promised. "Maybe I can help somehow."

"I am so drained." I put my arms around her waist and pulled her closer, burying my face against her shoulder. "This is going to be one long assed day."

"So have someone else lock up tonight," she said. "Come home early. I could make it worth your while."

Or me make it worth your while, I chuckled to myself, noting how quickly her heart beat against my chest and the steadily increasing warmth of her skin. I pressed my lips to her neck, right where I could feel her pulse. Much too easy to arouse, I was thinking, though not really sure if the thought was intended for her or myself. Her virgin curiosity had grown into full blown wantonness, and with just a little effort I could have had her surrendering right there on the sofa just a few feet away. I could suffer through a few false protests and indignation.

"Break it up, you two!" Kris smiled brightly as she waltzed through the door. She looked great, I surmised quickly, looking up from Terry's neck. Much better than I expected. "Well, strangers," she added, "how has life been treating you?"

Reluctantly, I pulled away from Terry. "Just super," I answered, body aching. Impeccable timing on her part. "But you'd better sit down."

"Ooh," she sat next to Terry on the sofa. "This sounds serious."

"It is." I pulled the envelope from the inside pocket of my sports coat and handed it to her. "First off, we've been fired."

"What?"

"You and I... They're returning our contracts and terminating our services. The team is being put out to pasture with all the other old, unwanted goats."

She took the envelope and looked inside. "This isn't so bad, Chip. It could have waited."

"But I couldn't have." I looked wondered what demons she had lurking inside. "I talked to Ron just a few minutes ago. He's in awful shape."

"He can find another job. We all can."

"Kris…" I sucked in a deep breath. Where to start and what to say? "He's in a hell of a lot of pain right now. The man is dying inside because he thinks he's going to lose you."

She closed her eyes and bit her bottom lip. When she finally opened them, she could barely meet my gaze. I could almost see the wheels spinning at break neck speed as she finally reached her decision. "He is."

My mind reeled. "But why?" I managed. "What has he done that's so awful?"

The turmoil that passed over her face was almost frightening. In less than a minute I saw anger and hurt and fear cloud her eyes, and worry knotted on her brow. She buried her face in her hands, and then ran her fingers through her hair, grappling for the right words. "It's so damned complicated," she finally whispered.

I waited.

"It's a whole lot of little things and one really big one… but Chip, he's your father, I can't pull you into the middle of this."

"I'm already there."

She shook her head uncertainly. "How did you know? Is Ron sniffing around trying to find out if I'm confiding in anyone?"

"Dan," I told her.

Pure fury erupted in those brown eyes. "That son of a bitch!"

"I know, it wasn't his to tell... but he did and it's out here in the open, and you're hurting as much as Ron—only he doesn't know what the problem is."

"I just can't live with him anymore, Chip" she cried. "Do you know what I found out at your wedding? What he was telling your stepfather but never bothered to tell *me*? Son of a bitch, I was standing there behind him listening to him tell Grant of all people that he can never have children again. Grant! He never told *me*!"

I squinted at her. "You're leaving Ron because he's sterile? Excuse me, Kris, but that's pretty lame."

"You don't understand," she groaned. "He has a son, he has you. Your mother gave him the one big thing I never will."

"But Ron doesn't even know what the problem is," I pointed out.

"Wait a minute," Terry interrupted. She had been so quiet and I had been so fixated on Kris I nearly forgot she was there. "This has nothing to do with having a baby, does it? Not directly anyway."

Kris knotted her eyebrows.

"It's Pat, isn't it? You're not angry with Ron because he can't father a baby, you're angry about Chip's mother."

Kris sank back into the sofa cushions, looking very much like a lost little girl who only wants someone who will hold her and tell her she's safe. "I am so tired of living with a ghost. I'm just a poor substitute. Ron will never love anyone as much as he loves her."

"Then you have to let him go," I insisted. "Stop torturing the man and tell him. You've got to end it one way or the other."

"I've tried," she cried. "I can't find the right way to tell him."

I slipped off the desk and knelt in front of her, slipping my fingers between hers, holding her hands with what I hoped was reassurance. "Tell him exactly what you told me. You've got to talk to him before he dives off into the deep end. He doesn't have a clue and that's not fair... give the man a chance."

She pulled her hands away and left, slamming the door. I looked at Terry helplessly, afraid to move, not trusting my own reflexes, just hoping that Kris would trust me again.

Kris

When I reached the apartment I felt totally alone and without a friend in the world. I knew Chip was right; I should have leveled with Ron from the beginning, those first days when I became aware that I was not as happy as I pretended to be. The anger I felt was so deep and took so long to bubble to the surface that when I realized a rift was forming between us I found it almost impossible to face. I wasn't sure I wanted to.

I don't know how long I sat there—it could have been five minutes or it could have been an hour—before Ron walked in. He could tell I had been crying, and when he lowered himself onto the sofa next to me I wasn't sure I could stop.

He was gentle, brushing the wetness from my cheeks with his thumb, asking very softly, "What's wrong?"

"Ron..." My voice caught in my throat and I almost succumbed to a fresh onslaught of tears. I shivered when he put his arms around me and drew me close, goosebumps popping up on my skin, little boils of agony that I could not control.

"Kris, you have to tell me what's wrong," he said. "I can't live like this anymore. I can't sit here and watch you eat me alive with your eyes and I can't handle this sadness. What did I do?"

"I can't do this right now," I sputtered. I pulled away and went over to the window, leaning against the sill. I stared out at nothing, just gazed blankly into my own fog. He followed me there, slipping his arms around me.

"I have to know." He was still quiet, measuring everything he said. "You have so many things going on inside of you, and I don't have the foggiest notion what they are." I turned in his embrace and hugged him back, not quite ready to let go. "I need you," he murmured, "and I'm losing you."

I held my breath. His heart was pounding hard and fast, beating against me wildly. How hard would he take it, knowing I was going to leave, that I didn't feel like I had any choice? Finally I told him, "I know I'm hurting you. I just don't know what else to do."

"Tell me."

I pulled away from him. I forced myself to meet his gaze, torn by the cruelty of the months of silence I had forced on him. It was justifiable, wasn't it? Silence in payment for the years of omission, the accrued interest of a fact that could have changed my life had I known. I looked into those green eyes and with slow, careful words, began the process of breaking his heart.

Everything poured out of me in one long rush of half thought out words and accusations.

He nearly jumped back, stunned, his face pinched with confusion. "Wait, we never discussed having children, Kris. Not once."

"What was I supposed to think?" I demanded. "I've never

seen you reach for a condom and I know damn well I've been bothered with the pill!"

"So you just assumed." The shock gave way to anger and his jaw set, face hard. He crossed over to the fireplace and leaned against the mantel. "You've been treating me like shit for as long as I can remember. You sit there and stare at me, you won't do more than grunt at me! All because I can't father a goddamned baby? What the fuck!"

"Stop it! I've never been given a choice in this. You have Chip!"

"Bullshit!" He slapped at the wood of the mantel, spinning to face me. "I fathered a baby twenty three years ago on a wild, freak chance, Kris. I was never his father, and he's never been mine. I didn't raise him. I didn't get to help him grow up. Jesus!" His hands went to his hair, digging sharp fingers into his head. He sniffed hard and when he looked at me again it was not the man I knew, those were someone else's eyes. "Chip is just my flesh and blood. I was *never* his father. All he ever had was his mother."

"And you were there, waiting for her to leave her husband."

"What's that got to do with anything now? The woman dropped dead from a heart attack nine years ago!"

"Ron, she gave birth to your child and it still eats at you that she stayed married to Grant. You hate her for that."

"I love her for that!"

And there it was. Nothing past tense about his feelings. I pointed an accusing finger at him. "There has not been one day that she hasn't crept into your head and insinuated herself into the most intimate moments of your life. You're going to love her until the day you die."

He stared at me blankly. "What do you want me to do?

Flip a switch and turn it off? Kris," he said, biting back the anger. "I love you. More than you'll ever realize. Do you think for one minute that if something happened to you I'd just stop? That's not the way it works. It would never happen. I will love *you* until the day that I die, and even beyond that."

Pain was stabbing at my temples. I took a deep breath and rubbed at them, willing my head to clear. "You will never, not ever, love me the way you love her."

"Of course not." He stepped closer to me, forcing me to look at him. "You're two totally different people."

"She's always been there, Ron. She's like this phantom hanging over our bed, it just doesn't go away."

"No, that's not true." He was breathing hard, full of fear, eyes moist and turning red.

"I can feel her between us, Ron. It doesn't matter what we're doing. She's there when we're watching TV together, she's there when we're making love."

"No…"

"This hurts so much because it's true, you know that." I wanted to hug him, to hold him for just a few minutes, but instead I reached for his hands. He was trembling, he knew what was coming and he had no way to stop it. Whispering, I said, "I'm not in love with you anymore, Ron. I'm sorry. I am so sorry."

He blinked, letting tears spill over. "I will always love you," he murmured again. "Always."

Terry

I flung the curtains back and carefully lifted the bedroom window. The room was hot, so hot that all I could do was toss and turn, tangling the sheets at my feet. Chip lay there soundly, sleeping as he always did, on his back, arms folded over his stomach. I rarely found him on his side at night, unless he fell asleep holding me.

I half sat on the widow sill, letting the cool air pour in to cut through the heat, moonlight and starlight spilling across the bed. I watched him sleep for the longest time, the slow rise and fall of his chest, the way his hair fell across his forehead. I couldn't imagine ever falling out of love with him, or keeping secrets strong enough to break us apart. My cousin was at home drowning in her vows, and I was with Chip silently thanking God for mine.

I only half believed the innuendo of his temper and the stories I was being told about his youth. He was far too gentle a person to be filled with that much rage, but the scars across his chest, those told a story much different than what I wanted to believe. I tried to picture the wild fear he must have felt, sheer horror of a knifed slashed out, and passionate hatred for the man wielding the blade. And Chip had admitted that he had killed before. It just didn't fit. It wasn't him.

The sheepish man in the office earlier, that was him. He was playful and passionate, a not terribly subtle seducer with warm hands and deft lips and a knack for saying the right thing. He backed away from fights. That was one thing about him that did irritate me; he refused to fight. He ran away from mere hints of trouble between us, preferring to back away from a potential argument with boyish charm or sex.

I couldn't imagine wanting to live without him.

I went back to bed and stretched out next to him. He stirred but didn't wake. I pushed his arms from his stomach, very gently rubbing his chest. When he didn't move, only sighed in his sleep, I caught my finger in the waistband of his underwear, wondering what I could possibly do to him before he woke up.

~

*"I'm going to lose them both," he thought wildly, sitting
alone in the dark with a half empty bottle of tequila dangling
from his fingers. "I've signed away my son's respect and I've
pushed my wife out of my life. Goddamn, I'll lose them both.
I am such an amazing fuck up, I'm going to lose them both.
When his mother died I thought I had felt the worst of it all.
How wrong could I have been? That was nothing. God, that
was nothing. This is despair."*

January 1976

Chip

Coward that I am, with the pressure building from both sides of the Gallery War, I packed bags for Terry and myself, threw them in the back seat of my tired old Mustang, kidnapped her from work, and headed for the coast. In less than a week we went from being glad when one of them would just pop in to say hello to dreading the possibility.

I felt like I was a kid again, sneaking off to the beach to avoid my stepfather's confusing dark mood swings. His house away from home was safe, it was quiet and always available for prolonged periods of intense navel contemplation and extended bouts of inebriated meditation.

With Terry there I didn't feel pressed to drink myself into a stupor. I just spread myself on a blanket on the sand and soaked up the sun and cool California winter air. I was half asleep when she dashed out of the cold water and flung herself beside me, spraying me with icy droplets. I jumped; she laughed.

"You're too easy, Irish," she laughed.

"For—?" I lifted my sunglasses and peered down the

beach. "There be kidlets here, woman, don't you be getting any ideas about the nasty things you want to do to me."

"I always have ideas." She bent over and kissed me. "But I'll be good while we're outside in front of God and the neighbors."

"It's overrated, you know," I said.

"What is?"

"Sex on the beach. You get sand in places where sand doesn't belong."

She swatted at me playfully. "I don't want to know."

"You sure? We could always sneak out here after dark."

"You're turning red," she said, ignoring me. "Flip over before you're too burnt to hug me later."

I rolled onto my stomach and laid my head on crossed arms. "My real wife would rub suntan lotion onto my back."

"Oh, really?" She laughed. I heard the bottle flip open and felt the cold of the lotion as she dribbled it on my back, then warms hands begin to slide across my skin. "My real husband still hasn't told me why we're really here."

"You just married a lazy bum, that's all."

"I'll squirt this whole bottle down your shorts, mister. Now tell me why we I took off work for a week."

She had a finger under the waistband of my shorts and I had no doubt she'd follow through. "I didn't want to be there when the bomb went off," I said. "Kris filed for divorce."

She stopped rubbing. "I don't understand. Kris never mentioned anything being wrong before last week. She never hinted at it."

"I didn't see it coming, either."

"Ron never told you how miserable he was?"

"No... We talked a lot about work, about hobbies... Christ, he asked about us and it never occurred to me to ask about them. It's hard to believe it's over"

"It could have been over before it really began, Chip."

"What's that supposed to mean?"

"Well, it's true, isn't it? Kris has always felt like a distance second to your mother. That's not where she wanted to be." She looked at me curiously, studying my face. "Ron loves her," she added, "but she's just not the great love of his life."

"I know," I sighed, "and I'm sorry."

"Why? It's not your fault."

"Maybe. Maybe not."

"Chip, this isn't your fault."

"I'm a constant reminder to both of them, Terry. Ron looks at me and sees what he wanted to have with my mother but could never quite get a grasp on. Kris looks at me and sees what she can never have with Ron, something he gave someone else but not her. I'm a walking reminder—danger here. Do not trespass."

"That's not true, Chip. Kris loves you. I don't think any of this will change that."

"I know." Her hands were rubbing again, slowly. "She's been my friend since the day we met. I'm honestly closer to her than I am to him."

"Then you know she wouldn't blame you for how badly their marriage went. It's not your fault for being alive."

"Still… I pushed myself into their lives when I shouldn't have. Me being there had to have made it that much more difficult."

She didn't understand and I didn't expect her to. I walked into their brand new marriage and became a fixture in their home and in their jobs. Kris never had a choice and Ron was so terrified that he'd lose the last thing he had of my mother than he wouldn't push me away.

I was a human billboard, one that advertised in neon overtones that there was someone else standing between them. How they ignored it for so long, I don't know, but if I had stayed away, they might have had a chance.

Doug

I pushed the food around on my plate, not really caring about eating. Kris was as relaxed as I had ever seen here, eyes dancing brightly and warmth bubbling over. She was finally comfortable, and the last thing I wanted to do was hurt her.

"Are you sure this is what you want to do?" I asked.

She looked up, surprised. "Doug, I wouldn't do it if I weren't. I don't want to live with him anymore. Things haven't been right for a long time and you of all people know it."

I pressed my lips tightly together. What I wanted to do was to take her away right then, turn my back on everything else, and hide us both away. What I had to do, though, was pressing down on me so hard I wasn't sure I could get the breath to say the words. "Kris," I set my fork down, "this is going to have to be the last time we see each other for a while."

"What?"

"Look, if you're really going to divorce Ron you can't give him any ammunition against you. If he's angry enough he can try and twist this into adultery."

"So? Let him."

"Think about it," I urged. "You just lost your job and it might be a long time until you get your severance pay. You may need his financial support, even if it's just until you get back on your feet. You can probably go into court and prove mental cruelty, but if the judge thinks you're screwing around with me, you'll wind up with nothing."

"I won't need anything from him."

"Maybe not, but I won't be the one who messes it up for you."

"Doug…"

I shook my head. "No, Kris. I care about you. Until your divorce is final we'd better not see each other."

"I have no choice?"

That look in her eyes was tearing at me. Yet another man making decisions for her. I took a deep breath and said firmly, "No. But I promise, when it's over I'll still be here."

Her eyes filled with tears. "Doug, you'd better leave now because I think I'm going to cry and I don't want you to see me like this."

I got up from the table, dropping enough money next to my plate to cover the bill. Walking out that door, I felt angry at myself and angry at Ron for just existing, and prayed that when it was finally over, she'd still want me there.

Chip

Terry admitted, standing under a hot shower at three in the morning, that I was right. Sex on the beach was overrated and resulted in sand being in places where she didn't want it to be.

"It was cold," she grumbled, "it was sticky and wet," more grumbling, "and my butt cheeks might grate like sandpaper for a week."

I resisted exercising the right to say I Told You So.

"But"—warm, soapy fingers touched the tip of my nose—"you were wonderful."

Well, yeah, but I wasn't the one with my butt digging into the sand, either.

It was midmorning before either of us woke; we talked

long into what was left of the night, cuddled up under heavy blankets, talking about everything and nothing, avoiding anything that might bring us back to the reason we were there. Somewhere around four I learned that my teenage witch had wanted to be the first female President when she was seven years old—because, if she were leader of the Free World, then no one could force her into bed before 9 p.m.—and had aspirations of acting when she was thirteen.

"Every school play from eighth grade on," she told me. "As long as I didn't have to sing, I was there. I didn't care how small the part was, I just wanted to be in it."

She gave that dream up when she thought she wanted to become someone's wife, realizing now it was just another way to playact.

She woke first, jerking her trapped hair out from under my cheek. I stirred and slowly opened my eyes, not wanting to wake up. I had no clue what time it was but I was sure I'd only been asleep for about five minutes.

"Morning," she whispered, dropping a kiss on my nose before she crawled out of bed.

I grunted a reply but smiled anyway. I was drowsy but not so far gone that I missed the fact that the woman was strutting around the bedroom without a stitch on and she wasn't reaching for a robe. I rolled onto my side and watched her, a little voice in my head telling me to look closer. Pay attention.

Well of course I was looking close. I was married, not dead.

She swayed clumsily and braced herself against the wall. The little voice shouted *get your ass out of that bed*!

"I stood up too fast," she said when I jumped up.

"That's not all that's happening pretty damned fast. Is

there something you've been meaning to tell me?"

She looked up at me, blue eyes shining. "And what am I supposed to tell you?"

I reached for the closet door, yanking it open with one hand and pulling her toward it with the other. I stood behind her, pressing my body against hers, standing there sideways while looking into the mirror. "This," I said, running fingers over the edges of her breasts, "and this," I slid my hands down to her belly.

"Oh great," she moaned, leaning her head back against my shoulder. "I'm getting fat and you think it's funny."

I placed a soft kiss behind her ear. She really didn't know, did she? "Think," I half whispered. "When was your last period?"

"What?" She was watching me in the mirror, eyebrows knotted together.

"Are you pregnant?"

Her gaze followed mine in the mirror to the hand I had on her stomach. Eyes widening suddenly, the thought had never occurred to her. She had simply lost track along the way.

"I know you had one right before we got married," I said, filling in the silence, "and maybe three weeks after. It's been almost four months, hasn't it?"

Her hand covered mine. "How can you tell?"

"I know your body," I said. "You're not getting fat, not unless it's baby fat."

She pulled away from me and sat at the edge of the bed. "Chip," almost a whisper, "I'm sorry."

"What?" I sat next to her, gently rubbing her back. "Why are you sorry?"

"You said you weren't ready for this. The night you proposed, you were worried because we hadn't used any protection and you didn't think you were ready to become a father."

I pulled the hair away from her face so I could see her eyes. "That was only because everything was still so new for us," I said. "And I honestly don't believe in having babies without a commitment... not to mention how unfair it would have been to you with my job."

"What about now?" She looked pale and scared; it reminded me of being fifteen again, getting caught making out in the back seat of a car in the girl's driveway. What Will Daddy Do?

"Well... we won't know until we get home and you can see Doug or someone if you even are pregnant. But I hope so."

She looked up at me hopefully.

"Terry, I love babies."

Her arms shot around me. "God, I love you."

"I love you, too." I bent over and kissed her belly. "And I love you, too."

"You could be talking to a vacuum," she snickered.

"You have about 400 billion eggs in there, woman. Surely one of 'em at some point will be our son or daughter."

"What do you want, Chip? A boy or a girl?"

"I want," I said, leaning back onto the bed, "whatever God gives us. Do you have a preference?"

"That depends," she paused, crinkling her nose when she laughed. "I hope we have a boy. A son just like his father."

"Then I'll pray for a daughter."

"Why?"

"You never knew me as a kid, Terry. I was the Davis's bastard son and I tried to live up to it. If you're stubborn enough to want a son like me, keep in mind you're in for one hell of a time and a whole lot of heartache."

"Come on, you weren't that bad."

I slid off the bed and reached for my jeans. What could I tell her without giving her glaring examples that would only scare her? Let her worry that her twelve year old son might disappear for days on end and come home reeking of cheap wine, not giving a damn if anyone was going nuts looking for him? Or that her fifteen year old son might hotwire the car and crash it into a tree out by the lake? How would she feel hearing that her seventeen year old son just might convince a girl to give him a blow job while he was speeding down the Interstate at 90 miles an hour, laughing at the idea he could lose control of the car and kill them both?

"I was that bad," I finally said, slipping into a shirt and heading for the kitchen.

Less than a minute later she was out there with me, grabbing the orange juice container before I could take a swig from it. She pulled glasses from the cupboard and filled them, quietly going through the motions of making breakfast.

"How much do you know about Brenda?" I asked, cutting through the silence.

She set a carton of eggs on the counter, looking at me with a mixture of confusion and irritation. "I know that you were engaged to her. That you say you didn't love her... And that she's gone."

"Did you know she was a prostitute?"

Disbelief. "What?"

"And that she was an addict?"

"Chip..."

"And that I only asked her to marry me so that I would have what I thought was a plausible cover, someone to hide behind in case there was ever any suspicion about what kind of life I was leading? Someone expendable."

She didn't know what to say.

I sat at the kitchen table, my hands cupped around a glass of juice I didn't want, my eyes glued to the glass because I couldn't force myself to look at my wife. "Terry, I was not a nice person... I've never been a nice person, not until you came into my life."

Silence. She was waiting for me to finish.

"You are completely different from anything I've ever had. Right from that first time I saw you... there was no pressure there. You didn't have any wild expectations. I didn't feel like I had to perform to prove what kind of man I was. You're the first person I didn't want to use and then throw away." I finally looked up at her. "I've always been afraid of the responsibility, Terry. And I didn't want to hurt you."

"I know," she whispered.

"You fell in love with me, not the danger in my life, not my family's money... I didn't want you to ever think I was after something cheap." I pushed away from the table and went over to her, reaching for her hands. "I think I knew from that first minute we laid eyes on each other that this was hopeless. I couldn't let go of you if my life depended on it but I can't put you through hell to be with me either. Or to raise my kids."

"You won't."

"Terry... I gave my mother nothing but hell right up until the day she died. I hurt her at every turn. I love you too much to ask you to put up with that."

Her arms went around me. "It will never be like that," she murmured. "Our baby will never be hurt the way your parents hurt you." A cool hand went to my chest, tracing the scar there. "I promise."

"I want to be a good father…"

"You will be."

"With the examples I've had?"

She took my face between her hands and pulled me towards hers, kissing me slowly. "You learned from them, Chip. You learned what not to do, and I swear, if you ever spiral out of control, I'll yank you back so fast your head will spin."

Doug

Even before I could shut the door and get across the office to my desk, Terry was pinging out of her chair. I tried not to smile and give anything away but she was so excited I couldn't help it. "Congratulations," I told her. "Someone shot the rabbit and put it out of its misery."

She squealed and shot to her feet, throwing her arms around my neck.

"You're not happy, are you?"

"OhmygawdImgoingtohaveababy!"

"I'm sorry, I had hoped this would be good news."

And please don't squeal again.

I retreated behind the desk where she couldn't break my neck if the impulse for another ballistic hug struck. "Have you been feeling all right lately?"

"I've felt fine, no morning sickness… no symptoms at all."

I laughed. "Well…"

"I've been busy! I lost track!"

"Okay."

"You stop teasing me," she demanded with a laugh. "Your job is to tell me what to do next."

"Pelvic exam."

That wasn't what she was expecting. She flushed red

and looked away.

"You've had one before?"

More red.

"No premarital exam, no pap smear, nothing, ever?"

She shook her head. Still blushing and looking like she wanted to slide under the tile.

"Well, it's definitely the next step. Complete exam, we'll do the pap smear, and then see if we can pinpoint about how far along you are."

"Okay."

"I don't have to be your doctor, Terry. I'll understand if I make you uncomfortable."

"You don't…"

I didn't believe her. "And I'll understand if you think Chip will feel awkward. I take care of pregnant field agents and I've even delivered a few dozen babies, but I can find you someone else."

She smiled a bit sheepishly. "No, it's all right. It wouldn't matter *who* was doing the exam… I'm going to be uncomfortable and completely mortified no matter what."

"Good."

"But what about the doctor?" she asked. "Will *he* be uncomfortable?"

I smiled and motioned her out the door towards an exam room. "The doctor is a professional," I reminded her. "He won't admit it if he is."

Terry

The restaurant had become familiar enough to me it was almost like a second home. I could walk through the dining room and spot regular customers, and I could usually tell what the special was on smell alone; I found it frustrating that I still couldn't worm my way into the bar. I tried, now and then, to slip in and sit at the far end of the bar when it was crowded, but Ted always spotted me and would bodily escort me to Chip's office. I don't care if you're the bosses wife, he always grumbled, but you don't sit at my bar until it's legal.

He would bring soft drinks to the office for me, even a virgin daiquiri now and then, but I wasn't allowed to desecrate his beloved bar.

I loved to sit in the office, to stretch out on that monstrous sofa and stare into the fireplace. At first it had struck me as odd that the office was as luxurious as it was, knowing how simple everything else in Chip's life had been. His apartment was a one room hole in the wall with a mattress on the floor and a small transistor radio in the corner. He drove an old beater that looked like it had shed its own paint in embarrassment. When I got to know him better I realized the office was his lifeline, the closest thing to home he'd had since he was a boy. It was concrete in his chaotic life, and comfortable because nothing else was.

He was sitting at his desk when I got there, staring deeply into a stack of paperwork. His hair fell forward, shaggy and badly in need of being cut. I watched him from the doorway for a long time, not wanting to break his concentration.

I just couldn't picture him as an out of control teenager, wild and full of fire. The boy he described and the man I shared my bed with were worlds apart. The man who held me at night and whispered such sweet things couldn't be the same boy who had torn so angrily through life

"Hey, mister," I said finally. "Got a few minutes?"

He looked up from his desk and smiled. "Anytime," he said, reaching for me. I sat on his lap, planting a firm kiss on his lips.

"Hi, Daddy," I whispered.

"You mean it? We really are pregnant?" He held me tight for a moment. "Wow," he exhaled sharply. "A baby."

"Doug thinks I'm about three months along."

"Wow."

"Feeling a little monosyllabic?"

"Yes…" He was grinning, though, holding me tightly on his lap and rocking the chair back and forth. "We're gonna have a munchkin."

"I'll have the munchkin, you have the coronary."

"Doug is sure?"

"Positive."

"Oh my God…"

"Happy New Year!" I laughed. "It's too bad we didn't know before Christmas. This would have been one heck of a present for my parents."

"Oh sure, and your mother would have grabbed the nearest calendar and starting counting. If you have this baby early, she's going to come after me with claws bared."

"She'll only be unhappy for about 30 seconds," I assured him.

"And your dad?"

"My dad will pick me up, start to twirl me around the room, and then put me down as fast as he can because he'll be afraid of hurting the baby. Then he'll punch you in the arm and call you an old dog, and offer you a beer, or three or four. After that… If I know my dad he'll try very hard to not cry."

"I know the feeling," he whispered.

"I knew it. Deep down you're just an old marshmallow."

"I am now. Have I told you lately how much I love you?"

"Every day, but I don't get tired of hearing it."

"We have to celebrate," he decided suddenly. "I'll take

you anywhere, do anything you want tonight."

"How about," I said, leaning my forehead against his, "we stay at home tonight, order pizza in, cuddle up on the couch, and just tell each other how wonderful we are. And how perfect our baby is going to be."

"She's already perfect. She has you for her mother."

"You're getting the idea already." I kissed him again, slowly and softly. "I need to go tell Kris before she hears it from Doug."

He nodded. "Tell her gently, I don't know how she'll feel about it."

"She'll take it just fine," I assured him. "Probably better than if she were still with Ron."

"How do you figure that?"

"Because," one more kiss and then I got up, "if she stayed with him, she'd be a grandmother, and she doesn't want to be that old."

"Are you serious? You're pregnant?" Kris laughed and reached for me. When we pulled apart, her eyes automatically darted to my stomach. "You two don't believe in wasting any time, do you?"

"We didn't plan this… It's a total surprise."

"But you are happy about it, right?" she asked almost frantically. "Chip will be such a good daddy, and you"—she pointed at me—"you're going to be a natural."

I had my doubts. I grew up an only child, my cousins were all older than I was, and friends didn't parade their brand new siblings out in front of me; I'd only held a baby once or twice in my entire life and had never so much as thought about changing a diaper.

"Trust me, you'll catch on in nothing flat. I can't wait to see what your kid will look like."

"Chip, I hope."

"Chip is gorgeous," she agreed, "but you're not lacking in the looks department either, kid."

I plopped down on the hard motel room bed, staring up at the ceiling. "Can I ask you something extremely personal?"

"Sure."

I pointed up. "Just who is it besides yourself you expect to be looking at in that mirror?"

"God," she groaned, laughing along with me, turning red. "This is what you get when you check into a motel where half the rooms are pay-by-the-hour."

"Uh huh."

"Look, I swear, you would have a much better time in this room than I do. All that does is remind me I'm alone."

I stared up at myself. "I wonder whose bright idea that was. It had to be a man."

Kris looked up, too. "Oh?"

"Think about it. I don't think I'd want to be here staring up at some guy's ass, not unless it was one hell of an ass."

"What about Chip? You can bring him here and do a thorough study of all his gluteal curves."

"Kris!"

"Well? The room is yours if you want it. You'd just have to tell me if the mirror is worth it."

"Why not just get some guy up here and see for yourself?"

She sighed and stared back up at the mirror. "I tried," she confessed. "He doesn't want to see me until my divorce is final."

"Are you serious? There's someone else?"

"No, not yet. But there could be soon if Ron doesn't contest the divorce."

I sat up on the bed and turned to face her. "Is that why you left him? You're in love with someone else?"

"I'm in lust with someone else," she corrected. "I'm divorcing Ron for a lot of reasons."

"Do you really want a baby that much?"

She shook her head. "No, I don't think I want one at all anymore, but having that option taken away from me was just the final straw. He's got this place inside I just can't get to and he's fiercely protective of it."

"You can't live with that."

"Could you? How would you feel if Chip was only half there emotionally? No matter what you did or said or how hard you tried to be the perfect wife he kept you at arms' length…"

"God, Kris, I'm sorry."

"It's all right now. I just want to untangle myself from him and get on with things."

"What about this other guy?" I asked. "The guy you're so madly in lust with. Could it get serious?"

"Oh hell, I don't know," she sighed. "You'd think after so many years I could read Doug like a book but I don't have a clue where it is he wants to go."

"Doug?" I clasped my hand over my mouth, stifling a laugh. "You have the hots for Doug Stone?"

Kris closed her eyes and moaned. "Yes, Doctor Douggie. I've spent the last year and a half trying to push him into the sack and he won't budge."

"Really? He won't sleep with you?"

"Not as long as I'm married, he won't. I know he cares about me, Terry, but he's even refusing to see me until a judge says my marriage is over."

"Why?"

"He's afraid Ron will find out and twist it to get his way

in the divorce. Doug and I used to meet for lunch—and I mean just lunch—every week and he won't even do that now."

"Any idea how long the divorce will take?"

"My lawyer says four or five months as long as Ron doesn't put up a fight." She laughed grimly. "He said it should be easy since there's no children involved. Maybe I should fight for custody of Chip."

"Not a chance! I get custody of Chip, you get liberal visitation."

"I hope he doesn't feel torn in all this," she said, sitting up. "Losing him as a friend is not something I want to have happen just because I can't live with his father."

"You won't lose him. He just wants to stay as neutral as possible, I think."

"You really are lucky, Terry. He loves you so much he gushes. He's a totally different person, you've tamed him so much."

I still couldn't see him all that wild and I said so.

"He was like a caged animal sometimes," she said. "It was like he was always one step away from self destruction."

"I can't picture Chip being mean."

"No, he wasn't a mean person. He had a hard edge that wasn't always controlled."

I knew he had a temper; I'd see it flare when he encountered Matt. I'd never seen that edge, though.

"You know, I was damn near raped a couple years ago. I let a situation get out of control and found myself overpowered by this giant of a man... I didn't even have my weapon on me. Chip popped out of nowhere. Terry, I watched him take on this guy with his bare hands. They fought like animals until Chip caught back of his head and started to pummel him face first into a wall. He just pounded his head there, over and over like a basketball, and when he finally stopped there wasn't much left of this guy's face. He had a terrifying look on his face, and right about the time I thought I'd have to find someone to peel him off this guy he snapped back to reality and rushed over to help me. It was like there wasn't this man lying there in a pool of blood with his brain running down the stucco. You'd have thought I'd just twisted an ankle and he was helping me get up."

"What about the other guy?" I asked, stomach churning.

"Dead. And probably better off that way."

I took a long slow breath. "What else has he done, Kris?"

"I've already said too much, I can tell. You don't want to know."

"He's so gentle with me..."

"He wants to be gentle with you, Terry. That boy I worked with is not your Chip. That boy would have never been happy with one woman, expecting a baby no less."

My hand went to my stomach. "He really is happy."

"Don't push to know too much, Terry," she advised. "Just let him be the way he is now and be grateful."

April 1976

Doug

The thing that disturbed me most was the way she kept creeping into my head, lurking there in the corner of every idea and hiding behind every notion. The trouble was that I wasn't sure I wanted her out of there. I missed those lunch meetings. Until I called it off I didn't realize how important that connection to her had been and how much it stroked my ego to know that she wanted me.

I hadn't realized that all along I wanted her just as much.

Sitting there in the dark, it was easy to reach for the phone and dial the numbers I had been tempted to for months. I didn't have to close my eyes to summon up the courage; the darkness engulfed my senses to the point that I felt detached. The sound of the phone ringing in my ear seemed a world away.

The line crackled, and her voice was there. "Hello?"

"It's Doug," I said, my own voice echoing in my ears. "I need to see you tonight… it's important."

"Where are you?"

I felt tired, drained. "At home."

"Doug, are you all right?"

I nodded to myself. "I'm fine. I just need for you to come over as soon as you can. The door's unlocked... you can just come on in."

"I'll be right there."

I hung up, feeling like I was moving in slow motion. This could be a very big mistake, I told myself. I could be setting myself up for one hell of a downfall.

I waited, staring out the window at the night sky. It was clear and crisp, stars twinkling brightly. Right then it seemed like I could reach out and grab one, wrap my fingers around it gently and bring it back.

What could I say to her? We had known each other almost my entire adult life and worked together for five years. And the lunches. Over a year of our lives, hours stolen away from other people, time that no one else knew about. Had it been fair for me to walk away when she probably needed me the most? I fought that idea, replaying the scene in my head over and over. I knew I had hurt her, but I sometimes wondered who was the more wounded.

The slow turn of the doorknob, the muffled click of the door as it swung open and then closed. I still didn't know what to say to her, keenly aware she expected something urgent.

"Doug? Why is it so dark in here?"

"Please, don't turn the lights on."

I heard her toss her purse aside, and a coat. Footsteps coming towards me.

"Are you all right? You sounded upset on the phone."

I could see her now, less than an arms' length away. What to say to her? I knew what I wanted to do, certainly, if I could just move. She was looking at me with so much concern and I couldn't say a thing. It didn't matter what I was thinking, the words were stuck somewhere between my brain and my mouth.

"Doug?"

I took a deep breath and reached for her. I kissed her softly at first, very carefully tasting the sweetness of her lips. When the surprise gave way she slid her arms around my neck and returned the kiss with enough passion to take my breath away. All the apprehension that had gripped at me, the certainty that it was too late and she would reject any of my overtures slipped away. The only thing left was the fire inside and the fuel she was feeding it with each touch.

"You tell me now," I breathed, "if this is wrong and I'll never say another word about it. But if you want me as much as I want you, I need to know."

She answered with a kiss, flaming lips that seared into mine. Her hands worked feverishly, pushing the shirt from my shoulders, and I knew that at the very least, this night was ours.

"I don't want to know," she said later, "if you called me because you felt sorry for me or because you were horny and couldn't find anyone else. I'm just glad you called."

"I missed you." She pulled herself up against me, laying her head on my shoulder. It felt natural, like she'd been there all along. "I called you because I couldn't stop thinking about you."

She laughed softly. "So you just thought you'd call and give me a tumble."

"Come on... I didn't plan this. I didn't even know what to say to you once you got here."

"I think you said it all."

"I don't think that I've said enough." She stiffened next to me, waiting. "I never should have walked away in the first place, Kris. I haven't wanted anyone else in my life from that first time we decided to ditch Ron and Chip go out alone. Any time I'd even come close to asking someone else out I felt like I was cheating on you."

She pulled away, propping herself up on the pillows next to me. "I'm not sure I want to hear this, Doug."

"Why not?"

"I've been married... all I wanted from you was sex."

I swallowed hard. "What about now?"

"I'm not ready to just jump into another relationship, Doug. I'm not even completely out of the last one."

"Then this is it?" I looked away, fighting to compose myself. "You got what you wanted and that's it? You're a decent fuck, doctor, but goodbye?"

"No." She touched my cheek, gently urging me to look at her. "It's not just sex anymore. I just don't want any strings attached."

"So you want me, but you intend to play the field also, so to speak?"

"No... you don't understand. I can't handle a string of one night stands. I just don't want to feel obligated for anyone's happiness but my own."

"I'm not asking you to marry me, Kris."

"Good, because technically I'm not available."

For those few hours, I had forgotten. "I don't want anyone else in my life," I told her. "I won't ask you to do anything you're not ready for, but it's only fair to tell you that I want you. I can wait."

She kissed my cheek. "I could agree to a mutually exclusive, non-binding, no strings attached, very intimate friendship."

I thought for a moment, trying to interpret. "You mean," I said when I finally understood, "that you want to date me and have sex?"

"In a nutshell, yes."

"But you don't want a relationship."

"Not in the sense that either one of us should expect marriage proposals or wedding rings."

"Just good sex?"

"No, I expect great sex. But I also expect the sex to be mutually exclusive."

"I won't sleep around if you won't."

"Don't judge me on the track record of my marriage," she said. "I may have been willing to cheat on my husband and I could have cared less if he was sleeping around, but I don't think I could take that right now. Have all the female friends you want, just keep your pants on."

"Is anyone else allowed to know about this." I asked, thinking of Ron, "or are we still sneaking around?"

"Terry already knows about this incredible lust I have for you. She'll take one look at me and know."

I slid in the bed and pressed kisses into her neck and shoulders. "If Terry knows then Chip will soon. Will it matter to you if Ron knows?" I stopped and glanced up at her. "I don't know how badly you feel deep down about him, but I don't think the man deserves to have his heart shredded."

She pulled my head back to her neck, urging me not to stop. "I won't live my life tip-toeing around his feelings," she sighed, a small moan escaping. "It's time I started worrying about my own."

"And just what are you feeling?" I murmured against her neck, lips sliding on her flesh.

She started to answer, but with her fingers digging into my back, all I heard was "Oh, God."

~

"Come on—lift," Chip urged. "You just don't have your heart in it today."

I grimaced, settling the weight bar back into the cradle. Sweat was running off me and every muscle was screaming in outraged protest. "I'm just tired. I doubt I got more than a couple hours sleep last night."

He motioned me off the bench and took my place, slipping his hands around the bar and pushing, bringing the weight down to his chest. "Try sleeping with a pregnant woman," he grunted between presses. "She's either getting up every ten minutes to go to the bathroom or pressing that gut up against me and the baby kicks…"

"That doesn't sound too bad, but I think I'll take my sleepless nights over yours." I helped him ease the weights back into the cradle. "I'm not sure I could handle a pregnant woman right now."

"Just who is it you are handling?" he laughed, sitting up.

I handed him a set of dumbbells and watched him curl the weights forward. "What makes you think I'm handling anyone?"

"Just a wild guess," he grunted, trying not to fight the weight up. "You don't look terribly unhappy."

"Didn't say I was."

He switched the weight from one hand to the other, drawing slow ragged breaths. "You're sleeping with someone," he said like it was a matter of fact.

"And how do you figure that, oh wise one?"

"Well, I'm not stupid and I'm not blind." He set the dumbbell at his feet. "Remember the day Dan gave us back our contracts?"

I nodded.

"You got all hot and bothered when Dan said Kris was leaving Ron. And you were spitting fire because she was let go." He picked up a towel, wiping sweat from his face. "So? Did you finally get her to put out?"

"Christ, Chip!"

"Well?"

"Terry told you, didn't she? Kris said she knew that something might happen between us."

"No," he laughed, "Terry never said a thing, but you sure as hell just did. Man, I haven't seen that look on your face in a long, long time. Could only be attributed to extremely satisfied primal urges."

"You wouldn't believe it if I told you." I reached for my own towel. "I'm not even sure I believe it and I was there."

"Well come on, Doctor." He followed me from the weight room to the locker room. "That woman was nine out of ten of my major teenage fantasies. Spill the details."

Laughing, I peeled off my sweat soaked shirt. "That's a little personal don't you think?"

He considered it for a minute, stripping off his own sweaty clothes and wrapping a towel around his waist. "The way I see it," he said, "personal is subjective. You see my wife naked about every other week these days. If that's not personal…"

"That's different. That's professional."

"But it's my only good argument. Humor me." He headed for the shower room and I followed. "Don't get me wrong, I think it's great. Get it while you can. But I want details."

I stepped in front of a shower head and turned it on, letting the water beat into my face. "I almost made a real mess of it," I confessed. "I wasted a lot of time I could have spent with her."

"Qué?"

"We've been friends for a long time, Chip. This could have happened over a year ago if I wasn't so fucking stupid."

"Are you the reason behind her divorce?"

"No." I soaped and rinsed, then slapped the shower off hard. "Until last night it was totally innocent. I wasn't about to get involved with a married woman, much less someone whose husband I worked with. She just…"

"She wouldn't?"

"No, *I* wouldn't." I started drying off, anything to avoid his gaze. "She made it clear a year ago that an affair would be welcome." I wrapped the towel around my waist and went back to the lockers. I sat down on the bench, back pressing into the cold metal lockers. When he came back in I said, "The day she came to tell me she was leaving Ron I told her we shouldn't see each other at all, not until it was final. I walked away. Can you believe that? I left her sitting in your damn restaurant, crying."

"But it worked out okay, didn't it?"

"I was going nuts… so I called her last night and asked her to come over. When she walked in I couldn't thing of a damned thing to say to her. I was afraid she'd blow me off for being such a prick."

"So what'd you say?"

"Nothing. I just let the hormones take over."

"Are you frigging serious? She walked into your apartment and you laid her without saying a word?" He stepped into his jeans, zipping them. "You're priceless, Doug. That took guts."

I shrugged. "We talked later." I rolled the wet towel into a ball and tossed it into the basket across the room. "But she pulled a slightly weird one on me."

"Kris? Kinky?"

"Get your mind out of the gutter. It's not what she did, it's what she said." I stopped to think, trying to remember her exact words. "She says she doesn't want a relationship. She wants what she calls a mutually exclusive, non-binding, intimate friendship."

"She wants to go steady."

"Very funny."

"Think about it." He bent over to tie his shoes. "What she wants is sole screwing rights."

"God, you're crude."

"But I am right... right?"

I waved him off. He was right and knew it.

"Take what you can get, Doug. What she's offering doesn't sound half bad."

"What if I want more?"

"Give her some time. Sounds like you've been offered everything short of a trip down the aisle. She just doesn't want to admit that."

"I know... Christ, I'll be glad when their divorce is final. I've spent a year of my life listening to the crap that he..."

He put up a hand, stopping me. "Whoa. Doug, I'm glad you two have each other and I'm all for it. For your sake I hope someday she marries you if that's what you want... but Ron *is* my father."

"I'm sorry, I wasn't thinking."

"It's okay." He finished dressing and then sat on the bench, thumbs hooked through belt loops. "I'm curious why

Ron never figured it out if you two were seeing each other for so long. Innocent or not, it would have mattered to him."

"The man does fancy himself as some kind of super spy," I supposed. "Maybe he didn't see it because he didn't want to." I pulled on my shoes. "Did he renew his contract?"

Chip sighed hard. "Signed back on to go solo."

"What, no team at all? He's a Maverick?"

"He's getting into some nasty stuff, Doug" Chip said. "Maverick Renegade Class Two. He'll be dead within a year."

I watched him shuffle out of the locker room, suddenly very grateful I'd connected with Kris. As angry as she was with the man, she would need a cushion if something went wrong. Ron would be lucky to stay alive six months, let alone a year.

The thought kept spinning around in my head—holy shit. Ron is an assassin.

Kris

Terry picked aimlessly at her food, grumbling that anything she ate would feel like a lead ball in her stomach. Just sitting there was an exercise in discomfort. She swore that the baby was a sadist, one hand swinging from her ribs and the other gripped tightly around her bladder. Chip, she reported, was a fountain of patience but she was tired of having to find each and every restroom every time she dared to venture out. They celebrated her birthday with a candlelight dinner in Chip's office; being there meant avoiding the search for a public facility. Work was impossible; she barely fit in the space between her desk and the wall and couldn't concentrate with all the commotion rolling inside. Chip agreed—far too happily in her opinion—that it was time to leave her job.

I tried not to smile. Chip barely tolerated her working in the first place. His enlightened feminist beliefs clashed loudly with his caveman mentality.

I sat at the table across from her, slowly stirring my drink with a straw. I was a french fry away from bubbling all over the booth, and she knew I was holding something back, biting it back every time it threatened to spill out.

"We've been sitting here for half an hour," she said, taking a small bite, "and you've hardly said two words. If you don't tell me now I swear I'm going to jump up on this table and start singing."

"Please don't. I'm just in a good mood, I suppose."

She watched the smile break on my face and matched it with her own. "It's Doug, isn't it?" she asked. "You finally nailed him!"

"He nailed me," I laughed. "Clear out of the blue I get this frantic phone call saying he *has* to see me. He sounded so upset that I got over there so fast I'm surprised I didn't get a least a dozen speeding tickets... I hadn't been there two minutes and he was all over me."

She rubbed her belly, trying to quiet the kicking baby inside. "Whatever happened to waiting for your divorce to be final?"

"Who know? Who cares?"

"I'm guessing you don't!" She sighed hard and struggled to get out from behind the booth. "I'll be back in a minute, Kris. I swear, this kid..."

I watched as she waddled across the room. It amazed me that someone Terry's size could handle so well the strain of getting that big. At first, even though I never would have admitted it, I was a touch jealous. There was a small, whiny voice in the back of my head that kept whimpering that it just wasn't fair. No one should be that happy when my own life is falling apart. But watching her grow, I couldn't help but get caught up in the excitement. Chip and Terry's absolute joy was infectious.

"Hey, lady, have you seen my beautiful wife?"

Chip dropped into the seat next to me and then kissed me on the cheek. He looked ragged and tired, dark circles under his eyes. "I'll give you a wild guess where she is."

"I can hear the flush from here." He picked up Terry's drink and took a sip. "So how's your life treating you these days?"

"My life's terrific. You look like hell."

He ran his fingers through his hair, nodding in agreement. "I would kill for one uninterrupted night's sleep," he groaned. "I can't even imagine how Terry feels."

"Huge, restless, uneasy... how do you think you'd feel if you were seven months pregnant?"

He pretended to consider it. "I think it could make me a very rich man."

I rolled my eyes at him. "Your husband is a moron," I told Terry as she sat down.

She met Chip's gaze as he leaned across the table to kiss her. "I've suspected as much sometimes," she snickered. To him she asked, "How'd the workout go?"

"Mine was great, but Doug..." He shook his head. "The poor guy was so weak he could hardly get a weight off and he could barely keep his eyes open. And he's got these horrible scratches running all the way across his back. Someone really raked him."

Terry stared at me, mouth gaping. "Kris!"

Chip nearly doubled over laughing. I know he could feel my eyes burning huge, gaping holes into his head. "I'm sorry," he finally said. "I couldn't resist."

"Can you explain why the whole world knows?" I demanded.

"Nobody knows," Terry said. "He's just being an ass."

"Honestly," Chip said, "I didn't mean to embarrass you, but you don't expect Doug to keep quiet about the single most important night of his life, do you?"

This was not what I wanted to hear. "You think it meant that much?"

Chip nodded, poking at his wife's food. "Is this a serious relationship, or am I being too nosy?"

"You're being too nosy." I watched him pop a french fry into his mouth and added, "We're just good friends, Chip."

"That might win you an award for the understatement of the year."

"Look"—I was begging to feel testy—"I don't expect you to understand or to approve, but I need Doug in a way I don't think you can appreciate."

"Try me. I can appreciate just about anything if I've been given a good explanation."

"Let it go," Terry pleaded quietly. "It's none of your business."

"Fine, I'll shut up." He slid out of the booth. "Just for the record, Kris, I do understand, but in the long run my approval means absolutely nothing. Sleep with whomever you want. Like Terry said, it's none of my goddamn business."

We both watched him storm off.

"Kris, I'm sorry," Terry said. "I don't know what got into him."

"Don't be so quick to apologize. He's tired. And that little outburst was more my fault than his."

"Don't make excuses for him," she sighed. "He could

learn to keep his nose out of other peoples' lives."

I wasn't so sure. I'd never thought twice about butting into his before. "Do you mind if I go talk to him for a few minutes?" I asked. "I don't want any hard feelings over something this stupid."

She waved me off. "No, go ahead. I'll try to sneak in the bar and see how long it takes Ted to throw me out."

I knocked on his door before pushing it open. He was sitting on the couch, long legs stretched out in front of him. His eyes had that far away look that told me he hadn't heard me knock and probably wasn't anywhere in this dimension.

"Okay," I said, dropping onto the couch next to him. "I'm sorry."

He glanced at me, not even moving his head. "Sorry for what? My wife is right. It's none of my business."

"But I think it is."

"All right," he grumbled, turning his head to look at me, "I'll bite."

"I'm divorcing your father, Chip... the marriage was over a long time before I got the courage to walk out, but I know that has to hurt you. And Doug... he's been there every time I needed a shoulder to cry on. But he's not the reason I left Ron."

"I didn't say he was." He shifted uncomfortably, sitting upright and turning to me. "Kris, I think it's terrific, I really do. You and Doug are friends and I don't see a thing wrong with that, but you've got to realize that Doug wants more from you than you probably want from him."

"I'm not ready for that, Chip."

"But Doug is," he stressed gently, adding, "Look, I'm not saying marry the guy the minute the ink is dry on your divorce decree, but you have to keep it in your head that

Doug's feelings are running pretty deep."

I smiled and kissed his cheek before getting up from the sofa. When I got to the door, I stopped at the sound of his voice.

"Don't do to Doug what I did to Brenda," he cautioned. "Don't ever make him think there's a chance for anything more than you're willing to give."

Chip

Sitting there on the office couch, half asleep, I wondered how Ron was doing.

I didn't feel as though I was betraying the man by supporting Kris; something inside told me that I should, that my father's feelings should come first, but it was very easy to squash that thought when it popped up. I didn't remember Ron doing me any special favors; besides, Kris did look radiant. Walking away from her marriage was probably a turning point, and who better than Doug to be there for her? He was more level headed than any of us; the only person I knew more secure was Ted.

I tried to doze there, wishing my brain would just drop to a lower gear for five minutes, long enough to quit thinking and fall asleep. I was almost there, feeling like I was a sigh away from dropping off, when soft, warm lips landed on mine, pulling me away from bleary semi-consciousness.

"Hi, stranger," Terry whispered as my eyes slowly opened. "I was beginning to think you were lost in there."

"You hate me, don't you?" I moaned. "You can't stand to see me sleeping."

She grinned and tousled my hair as she struggled to sit next to me. "If I can't sleep…"

"This little guy giving you a hard time?" I set my hand

on her stomach, rubbing slowly and gently. I could feel the baby move, slowly, a gentle fluttering that always amazed me.

"This is one of those days I'm having fifth and sixth thoughts about this," she said. "I'm tired of being tired. I even walk funny now."

I slid my arms around her the best I could. "I know you're tired. I promise, it'll be worth it in the end."

"I know." She sighed and pushed against my arm, trying to sit up straight. "I have to be in Doug's office in about half an hour. What are my chances of getting you to take me?"

"Do I have to watch?" I stood and held out my hands to help her get up.

"No... but it's not as bad as you think."

"Oh sure," I groaned. "He just straps your legs up and probes places I'd rather not think about. I prefer to not watch my best friend do that to my wife. I'll wait in his office."

"What will you do when I go into labor, Chip?" she asked as we left the restaurant. "Doug is going to be right down there pulling the baby out."

I opened the car door for her, helping her in. "I'll deal with that when the time comes." I closed her door and went to the other side, easing behind the wheel.

"It really bothers you, doesn't it? You can't stand the idea of him seeing me bare ass naked."

I shook my head and turned the ignition key. "He's a doctor, Terry. He sees naked people all the time."

I pulled the car from the parking lot, trying to ignore my wife's laughter.

"Your sole job now is to follow this list. You will be provided as much information possible on each individual—

known work habits, friends, family, hobbies, possible loca-
tions—and you will take this list and eliminate each one by
one. Any method you use is purely discretionary. If you have
any questions about the terms of your contract or if you have
any misgivings about the current nature of your work, say so
now. You won't get another chance."

He reached forward and plucked the stiff black plastic
card from the older man's hand. He slipped it into his breast
pocket, not bothering to take a second look. The time for that
was later, when he was alone, wondering at what point he
had become the single most stupid person on the planet.

Doug

"Well, pops," I said as I came into the office, "your wife
is doing just fine. She should be ready to go in a few minutes." I slung my lab coat over the back of the chair and sat,
eyes on Chip.

"What about the baby?" He tossed aside the magazine
he had been thumbing through.

"The baby is good. Nice strong heart beat and kicks like a
mule." I leaned back in the chair, fingers drumming on the desk.
"I have to talk to you, though. It's personal and I don't want to
embarrass you. Well, I do, but it wouldn't be professional."

"Shoot. You endured a pretty good ribbing from me, I suppose I can take it."

"The baby is already getting big," I said. "It's also sitting
kind of low. We really want to avoid anything that could possibly put Terry into early labor."

He waited for the shoe to drop.

I stopped drumming my fingers. "No sex until after the
baby is born. Any stimulation could start contractions."

"No sex at all?"

He looked like a six year old being denied dessert. What, no cookies, not even a crumb? "No intercourse, that could rupture the membranes. No oral sex either. If you blew air into her it could cause an embolism and could kill both her and the baby. And that goes both ways, Chip. Any activity that arouses her could potentially induce labor."

He considered it briefly. "Doug," he said slowly, "breathing arouses Terry."

"Then quit breathing."

He laughed nervously. "I'm pretty sure I can handle it, but have you told her?"

"I thought," I told him half seriously, "that she was going to gouge my eyes out."

Chip

Lying in bed that night, she fumed. "It's not fair! Two months! You can't touch me for two months!"

"I can hold you," I offered, not wanting to mention the weeks after birth when she'd probably put it dead last on her list of Things I Find Appealing.

"Oh, great. That'll do wonders for my libido."

I sighed in exasperation. Another sleepless night while she ranted and raved and got it out of her system. "Come on. It's not so terrible."

"Not for you!" she spat. "You can start dating the bar of soap in the shower."

"I won't," I promised. "I don't need to."

"Sure."

I felt her slide out of bed and heard the soft padding of her feet on the floor. "It really won't be that bad," I called after her. "As uncomfortable as you're getting, I doubt you'd want to anyway."

"Dream on," she snapped.

"Dammit, Terry," I said, jumping out of bed, "would you rather have sex now or a healthy baby later?" I met her at the bathroom door, light streaming in from the window softly outlining her. "Why is this making you so angry?"

"I don't know," she sobbed, falling into a hug.

I could feel her tears against my chest, and felt utterly helpless. I didn't know what to say and doubted she knew what she wanted to hear. "Just think," I whispered, still holding her tight, "in just two months the baby will be here and you won't feel so miserable all the time."

"I'll still be fat."

"You'll still be beautiful." I led her back to bed, drawing her tight to me when we crawled back under the sheet. We were quiet for the longest time, silence peppered with her sniffles. "You know what," I said when I was sure she was done crying, "we still have a ton of things we need to get for this munchkin. Maybe tomorrow we could go out and get the crib and anything else you think a kid needs."

"You hate shopping even for your own clothes," she pointed out.

"Well... you could go with Kris if you'd rather not put up with me. I don't know anything about baby stuff."

She chuckled. "Neither do I. Unless you think it'll be pure torture, I'd rather you and I went together. It's your baby, too."

Yes, and I have the checkbook and a couple credit cards, I told myself. But to her I just said, "It'll be fun. I'll buy you gross things for lunch, too. So go to sleep so you'll have the energy to manage me on a shopping binge."

Anything to keep her from blowing up again.

It was going to be a very long two months.

June 1976

Chip

"I'm going to hurt you, Chip," Terry moaned angrily. "As soon as this is over, I swear to God, I'm going to do damage."

I tried to smile and grasped her hand, wincing as she squeezed back hard. Sweat was dripping from her face, her hair wet and matted at her forehead, and the venom in her eyes would have terrified me any other time. Every time a contraction gripped at her she hated me with the passion of a drama queen.

As the contraction faded she relaxed her grip on my bruised hand and pushed it away. "You are never, ever, touching me again."

I took a soft cloth from the bedside stand and patted away the sweat from her face. "Just say the word and Doug will get someone in here to give you something for the pain."

"Well why the hell didn't you remind me of that an hour ago!" she snapped. "I'm dying here... do something!"

"All right." I kissed her softly on the forehead.

"Do that again and I'll rip your lips off!"

"It's okay. Just try to relax."

"You relax, goddammit!" A weave of pain washed over her face and her hand shot out to mine. "Get Doug," she hissed. "Now!"

I jumped out the of the chair and scurried toward the door. She had been angry and full of fire from the moment her water broke, hours earlier, in my office. She was embarrassed and didn't want to walk through the restaurant in wet clothes; I literally had to pick her up and carry her out to the car. She was in misery from the start; the first contraction hit and she nearly doubled over from the pain.

Doug checked her and then eased the sheet back over her legs. "It's not quite time yet, Terry," he said, probably fearing the look in her eyes. "I'd give it another couple of hours."

"Nobody warned me," she growled, sucking in deep breaths, "that it was going to hurt so much."

"Yes, I did," Doug assured her. "We talked about that at least three weeks ago. You just wouldn't listen. Now, do you want something for it?"

"Now, dammit!"

I glanced nervously from Terry to Doug and back again. "What are you going to give her?"

"Personally, nothing. I'll have the anesthesiologist come up and numb her from the waist down so she won't feel a thing and she won't try to push too soon."

Great, I thought wearily. Maybe he can numb her lips while he's at it.

Doug

"Chip may survive all this," I told Kris when I joined her in the waiting room.

"What about Terry?" She reached up and turned off the old black and white TV. "How's she doing?"

"She's fine, even if she doesn't think so." I eased back, trying to stretch my legs out. Whoever had planned the waiting room had never intended for it to be used. The chairs were hard and the lighting so poor I knew I'd have a raging headache if I stayed long. "Listening to her now, if Chip even thinks about thinking about breathing near her again in this lifetime, he's toast."

She laughed. "Will it be much longer?"

"Could be." I stretched my arms over my head. Dozing would be easy if the chairs weren't like concrete. "A couple hours at the very least."

"You look beat."

I nodded, stifling a yawn. "Not as beat as Terry," I managed. "She finally asked for something for pain, so her mood should do a one-eighty soon." The yawn, which I tried to hold back, broke through. "I shouldn't be so tired."

"My fault." She reached over and rubbed her hand across my cheek. "Can I buy you dinner when this is all over?"

"Might be breakfast," I yawned. "I'd rather you just came home with me. We could pick something up on the way there, and you can pull me off the table when I fall asleep with my face in the Frosted Flakes."

"All right," she chuckled.

I struggled to my feet, fighting the weariness that was seeping into my bones. "Remind me," I mumbled, "to never again play obstetrician."

He watched his objective walk, oblivious and confident, across the carefully manicured lawn, bend over to pick the newspaper up off the sidewalk, and then turn to go back in-

side. He held his breath and squeezed the trigger, waiting just long enough to watch as his target pitched face forward onto the grass.

Chip

"Push now, Terry."

I helped her rise up off the table, holding her, watching the strain on her face as she bore down. Her eyes snapped shut, breath caught up in the tremendous effort.

"Okay," Doug said. "Relax."

In the mirror on the wall behind Doug, I could see the baby's head starting to show. Terry collapsed back onto the table, my hands at her shoulders, rubbing gently.

Doug looked up, peering over his green surgical mask. "Just one or two more good ones should do it. Are you ready?"

She grunted her reply.

"Okay, then... now."

She pushed again, hard, her face bright red and contorted with effort.

"One more time."

Again, she bore down. The blood in my own head was pounding; hers had to have been surging.

I looked up in time to see Doug grasping the baby's shoulders, suctioning out its nose, wiping at its eyes.

"Well what do you know," he beamed. "You've got yourselves a boy."

I let out the breath I hadn't realized I was holding, my hands grappling to hold Terry. "A boy," I said, mostly to myself. "We have a son."

Her eyes followed the nurse holding her baby, watching as she hurried to place drops in his eyes and to clean him off. Just a minute later she gently laid the baby across Terry's chest, making sure we could see our new son's face.

"Look at him, Chip," she marveled. She reached out to touch him, her fingers feather soft against his brand new, tender skin. Big blue eyes stared back at her, a look of astonishment and irritation that screamed "who the hell are you?"

"Has he got a name yet?" Doug asked.

"Nicholas," I whispered. "Nicholas Christopher." My finger barely brushed against the baby's cheek, and in that moment I knew I was as close to heaven as I would ever get.

July 1976

Chip

Ron missed his own divorce hearing, leaving his lawyer to stumble through repeated apologies and to agree, reluctantly, with the judge that if his client couldn't be bothered to appear then he surely wouldn't mind the support judgment he was about to issue. Kris didn't care, she only wanted to get it over with. When she walked out of the court room she had her divorce and a promise for generous monthly support.

No one knew where Ron was and no one had heard from him in weeks, so when he strolled into my office as if he didn't have a care in the world, I was more than a little irritated.

"Well," he said as he breezed through the door, "I hear you're a daddy now. Congratulations."

What in the hell could he want? "Yeah, thanks," I grunted. "I'm not even going to ask where the hell you've been."

"Good, because I wouldn't tell you anyway."

I tossed my pencil down and pushed papers aside. "Been working hard?"

"Very." He shrugged it off, and for the first time in my

life that I could recall, pulled out a cigarette and lit it. "It's a living, Chip, that's all," he explained, inhaling deeply.

"You couldn't pay me enough, Ron. Some of us can't be bought."

Smoke curled from his lips. "And some of us have our price."

I stared at him, trying to figure out where his head was at. There was something about his attitude, something I couldn't put my finger on. He just sat there, puffing away, his eyes roaming the room. "What'd you come back for? Somehow I doubt it's got a whole lot to do with this sudden urge to be a grandfather."

He blew smoke out the side of his mouth, away from me. "I needed to see Kris," he said. "But... it doesn't seem like she has any room for me in her life now."

"No reason she should."

He flipped the butt of his cigarette into the fireplace, his eyes following it and lingering there for a moment. "I showed up at her place around ten last night, figured I'd surprise her. Hell, the surprise was on me."

"She wouldn't talk to you?"

"Oh, she talked to me, all right. No problem there. We sat in the living room like a couple of polite strangers, and she started catching me up on things going on around here... I didn't expect Doug to come stumbling out of her bedroom damn near naked." He stared back to the dying embers of his cigarette. "When did she start seeing him?"

"Couple months ago," I guessed. "Why?"

Ron slowly rose from his chair. He paced the room wearily, hands jammed into pockets and eyes half closed. After a while he asked, "Did she leave me for him, Chip?"

"It's none of my business, Ron. You'd have to ask her."

"Dammit, Chip. You know, just tell me!"

"No," I replied after a long time. I didn't know if he had the right to know or even the right to ask, but he was suddenly standing there in a pool of pain and I didn't want to be the one to shove him under. "Doug had nothing to do with it. It must have been four or five months after you two split before they got together." As an afterthought I added, "They both say it's not serious. They're just friends."

"Bullshit." He dropped back into the chair. "It's really over," he said, as if he just then understood. "I really thought that if I gave her some time and some space that we could manage to work it out. I thought she still loved me."

I tried to empathize with the man, but couldn't do it. Maybe if he'd had the guts to stay and face Kris when she was most angry, but Ron found a way to cut and run.

He shifted uncomfortably, aware that I was staring and not saying anything. "How's Terry?" he asked. "And the baby?"

"They're both fine." I was starting to feel uneasy, wishing he would just get up and go. I could sense the danger he had shrouded himself in—it was familiar and cold—and I wanted no part of it. I didn't want to know what he had been doing and didn't want even a chance that the subject would come up.

"Kris says he's a beautiful kid. I wish I could see him."

"You will," I said, only half believing it. "Right now he and Terry are getting to know each other and it wouldn't be a good time. She hardly lets anyone near him."

"Not even you? He's your son, too."

I was surprised that he'd think for even a minute she would keep me away from my own son. "Look," I said testily, "Nicky is only a few weeks old. She lugged him around for nine months, she can damn well have this time with him. And where the hell do you get off coming in here with attitude dripping all over the place? No one has heard from you in months… hell, you didn't even know we were going to have a baby! None of us owes you anything, Ron."

He stared me straight in the eye. "No," he agreed, "but I owe myself. I'm not cutting myself off again, son. I can't live that way."

"You chose to. You're the one who decided to sign on the dotted line again. There's no way you can expect the rest of us to wait around for the ax to fall. We won't do it."

"It's a job, son, nothing more."

I clenched my teeth, trying not to over react. "In my book, Ron, you're a murderer. Nothing more."

~

Nicky's insistent cries of hunger lulled me from a deep sleep, reaching through a cloud of dreams to pull me—almost willingly—awake. I flung an arm across the bed, knowing Terry wouldn't be there, and then crawled from the bed, grumbling; I'd promised to be the one to get up with him to give her a chance to sleep through the night. She had probably bolted out of bed at the first whimper.

I headed for the living room where she cuddled with him on the sofa, gently urging him to take the bottle. I lingered at the doorway, watching her, transfixed by the bond that was already there and how naturally Terry reacted to him. It was a connection with him she beat me to by nine months, something that would have bothered me if it didn't fascinate me so much.

The first night he was home I was completely baffled by his nonstop crying and clueless how to stop it. While Terry, still exhausted and sore, tried to sleep, I paced his bedroom and the living room with him, his tiny head resting on my shoulder, patting and rubbing him softly on the back. He had been fed and he was dry, and he would not stop crying. He was only three days old and I was already a failure as a father.

She woke after a while and called for me to bring him into bed with us, laying him across her chest, where he settled almost immediately and drifted off. Her heart beat, she explained. He missed it.

I wondered how long it would take him to trust my heart as easily.

"'Morning, love," I whispered, carefully sitting next to her on the sofa. My eyes settled on Nicky, sucking eagerly on the bottle Terry held for him, his eyes closed tight against the effort. He had Terry's blue eyes and patchy blonde hair that for the most part reminded me of Einstein on a bad hair day.

"How long will we be graced with your presence?" she asked sleepily.

I reached over, brushing my fingers against Nicky's soft cheek. "As long as it takes," I murmured. "He looks like he's already asleep."

She smiled lazily. "Almost," she said. "If I put him down now he'll start crying again. I'll just let him nurse it for a while... You go on back to bed, Chip. You look like hell."

"Oh, you're wonderful for my ego, woman," I grunted, but went back to bed anyway, shuffling slowly through the dim living room. I slipped wearily between the sheets, feigning sleep, hoping that if I pretended I would fall there quickly. A few minutes later, though, and the bed sagged with Terry's weight.

I reached out for her. "It was supposed to be my turn," I whispered, placing a kiss behind her ear. "You were supposed to sleep."

"We're both awake now." She pushed me onto my back, hair falling all around my face. "At least I hope you're fully awake."

"I am now…"

Her lips melted into mine, slow deliberate kisses that reached right down to my toes.

When I was finally able to catch my breath a good half hour later I whispered, "Motherhood has been very good to you… Do you have any idea how hard it's been for me to lie here and not be able to touch you?"

"I wouldn't have stopped you."

I laughed, nuzzling my head next to hers. "No, I'll bet you wouldn't have."

"I've missed this," she whispered into my ear.

"It was worth the wait."

She pulled closer to me, an arm flung over my waist. I waited until I heard the soft, steady rhythm of her breathing before I was sure she was no longer awake, then eased myself out of her half embrace. I crawled out of bed and went to the window, looking out at the street below. The early morning was hot and black, humidity pressing down like a steamy blanket. There was no moon or stars lighting the sky, but the darkness took on a dull gray edge near the fuzzy light of the street lamps that dotted the parkway.

The day ahead was going to be hot and miserable, and I knew there was no hope of rain for at least another month or two, not unless we were graced with some freakish storm.

I opened the window as quietly as I could, hoping there would be some breeze to cut through the heat and then stood there practically willing the wind to whip up. Any other time and I'd be stomping through the apartment, closing doors and windows and swearing under my breath about wanting just one day without that damned wind ripping through the valley, but standing there soaked in sweat, I would have welcomed it.

Terry turned in the bed and sighed, one foot kicking away the sheet. I could barely see her outline in the dark, but I could hear the change in her breathing, and knew I'd woken her up when I opened the window.

"Go back to sleep," I whispered.

"I can't. There's a naked man standing by my window and I'm afraid he's about to jump and get away from me."

"He's hot."

"Well, I *know* that," she snickered. "Why aren't you in bed?"

"I think I'm up for good. Go back to sleep, I'll get Nicky when he wakes up."

She patted the mattress. "Come back to bed, Irish. Even if it's just long enough for me to fall asleep again."

"You just want my body," I accused, sliding back into the bed next to her. "I'm all sticky and sweaty, though…"

"So am I. Think how the baby must feel."

"I'll turn a fan on in his room," I promised. "This heat is just going to get worse. Can a little guy like that get through it without duct taping ice cubes to his body?"

"I think he'll be okay, Chip," she laughed.

"I'll go buy a couple of air conditioners tomorrow. He's too little, he'll sweat off half his body weight and disappear."

"For that kind of money you could hire someone to stand over his crib and fan him with palm fronds all day."

"I just might do that, too."

She rolled over and kissed me. "He'll be fine."

"And I'll be buying air conditioners for both bedrooms."

"You worry too much."

"That's my job. I hunt and gather and worry."

"You're very good at it, too." Then, after a few moments quiet and a heavy sigh, "Can we afford that?"

"We can," I assured her.

"It sounds expensive."

"Now who's worrying?"

"That's *my* job. I cook and clean and worry. And in between cooking and cleaning, I worry. I feed Nicky, and I worry. I change a diaper, or give him a bath, and I worry..."

"And why do you worry so much?"

"It's biological. I'm a mother."

"Well..." I lifted myself up on an elbow to look at her. "You're a very good mother and you don't need to worry so much. We have enough money to indulge an occasional whim, and no one could take better care of that baby than you do."

Her hand went to my chest, tugging at the lone hair I had managed to grow. "Can I tell you something that might sound really stupid?"

"It depends. Is this something I'll find so funny I can't help but laugh and then wind up getting pushed out of bed onto the floor?"

"Maybe." She sighed deeply, her fingers letting go of the hair. Her hand stayed on my chest, warm and wet and not moving. "I'm scared, Chip. I mean I am really scared. I don't know anything about little boys much less raising one, and I just know I'll screw him up somehow."

"That's not stupid."

"It's not rational, either!" She sniffed, trying not to cry.

"Would it make you feel any better if you knew I was just as scared? That little boy is an awesome responsibility. I don't know anything about babies other than that they cry and poop a lot... we'll figure it out."

"And screw him up along the way…"

"Not a chance."

"We're the blind leading the blind, Chip!"

"But we have your parents to help us through anything we can't figure out on our own," I pointed out, "and we have my three wonderful parents as the prime examples of what not to do. And we love him, Terry. We can fuck up along the way and he'll still be fine."

She sniffed again and snuggled up against me, ignoring the heat and the sweat. "Have I told you lately how much I love you?"

"I think you've mentioned it once or twice."

"Remind me to mention it more often."

"Yes, ma'am." I kissed her on the forehead, hugging her tight. "Now go back to sleep. I'll go get a fan for Nicky and I'll get him when he wakes."

I started to get up, but she wouldn't let go.

"Ter?"

"I'm not done with you, yet, mister," she grumbled lightly. "I want things from you."

"Such as?" I started to say when her lips covered mine.

"Lots of things," she murmured, rolling onto her back and pulling me with her. "All the things you haven't been able to do for the last three and a half months."

"All those things right now?"

"Well…" Her hands were on my cheeks, pulling my face down to hers. "Just a few things for now. The rest later."

"And your order of preference?"

She pretended to think about it. "Start with my lips and work your way down," she laughed. "Let's see if your tongue really will fall off."

~

As far as I knew, my stepfather had never asked for help from anyone. He was this formidable presence, indomitable and forbidding. He had money and the power that went with it, and if something came up, his wallet was usually the solution. In the short line of people that he would lower himself to turn to, I suspected I was dead last, so when the phone cut through the quiet morning, I was not prepared to hear his voice.

"Jeremy?" No one, not even my wife on our wedding day, called me by my given name. I hated it, and Grant was the only person who made a habit out of using it. "I need your help," he pleaded. "I need to talk to you if you can spare the time."

Past his voice I could hear the sound of traffic. He was probably standing at the 7-11 down the street, staring up at the apartment building, waiting for permission before he dared to even think of walking up that flight of stairs and knocking on our door. While I waited I watched Nicky sleeping in his play pen just a few feet away, thumb rooted firmly in his mouth. He could barely lift his head and couldn't roll over to save his life, but that boy could find his thumb in the darkest of night.

"Who was on the phone?"

Terry stumbled out of the bedroom half asleep and disheveled, her hair flying in all directions. "My stepfather," I said, sounding surprised even to myself. "He's coming over."

"Here? What the hell for?"

"Don't know. But he did sound worried or scared. I'm not sure which."

"Why should you care? It's not like he's ever done anything for you."

"There was something about his voice... It won't kill

me to let him in and listen to what he has to say."

Terry turned back for the bedroom, mumbling to herself. She didn't think much of the man in the first place, but she wasn't about to let him see her half dressed.

Grant looked old. He hadn't hit sixty, but his hair was flecked with gray and his face was etched with lines of worry and loneliness; he was not the imposing opponent I remembered from just a few short years before.

"I need your help," he repeated, sitting in the chair near the fireplace. "I can't find your brother and no one has seen him for at least a week."

It surprised me that he was even looking. "I haven't seen David since you shipped him off to that damned boarding school. It's been at least three years."

There was a sadness that permeated Grant's normally reserved composure and he nearly winced at the hint he'd abandoned his only son. "He's had some trouble lately," he said. "He's either afraid to come home, or he can't."

I tried to picture my younger brother running scared. The last time I had seen Dave he was terrified and trying hard to fit his little boy fears into the nearly grown body he'd discovered thrust on him practically overnight. He was awkward and uncomfortable in his adolescence, and painfully shy; just 14 years old and a day away from being sent to a private school halfway across the state, too scared to protest the unjustness of the decision and too hurt at being told to go that he didn't know how to ask to stay.

"The headmaster thinks," Grant went on, "that David was selling narcotics in the dormitories. They wanted to expel him but had no concrete proof... Jeremy, David's grades were never better, and he was a top notch athlete. I refuse to believe..." He choked back the rest, swallowing hard.

Stress was definitely taking its toll on Grant. He sat there fighting to believe that the worst was a lie, he needed to believe the best in his son. "Did the headmaster say he thought Dave was using drugs or just selling them?"

"Selling…"

"All right. So Dave knew he was about to be expelled, hopefully on false charges. Just what is it you want from me?"

For the first time, Grant's eyes brightened. "I know you know people who could help, Jeremy. I'm begging you, please help me find him. He's only seventeen."

A year older than I was when I tore out of Grant's house for the last time. I glanced down at Nicky, who was still sleeping and sucking away at his thumb as if life itself depended on it. I would do anything, even bow down to my worst enemy, to save my son. Grant was doing just that, begging the one person who had every reason to tell him no.

If he had asked me just a short year before, I would have thrown him out of the apartment and told him to go to hell.

Nicky changed everything.

"I don't know what I can do yet, but I may be able to call in a few favors," I told him. "Someone can probably track him down in a day or two."

Pure relief flooded his face. "Jeremy…"

"I'll try to find him," I interrupted, "but that doesn't mean I'll make him come home. If he's safe and out of trouble, I'll leave him alone or help him find someplace to live, whatever he needs. But I won't force him to come home."

"That's all I want. I just want to know he's safe."

His eyes shifted to the baby; I could almost feel his restraint, the urge to reach out and touch one of those chubby cheeks. I bent over the playpen and lifted the baby carefully, placing him in Grant's arms. "His name is Nicholas," I said. "Nicky."

Grant stared with fascination at Nick's tiny face, and those lips that were sucking away hard, even in slumber. "He's beautiful. When was he born?"

Unaware that we'd even had a child, I realized. Another thing he had in common with Ron. "Six weeks ago."

A slow smile crept onto Grant's face. "God, don't let him grow up too fast," he said, sounding almost like a prayer. He handed Nicky back to me carefully, practiced, knowing how to admire the baby yet not wake him. "He looks so much like you."

I settled him back into the playpen, gently rubbing his back when he stirred. Grant had walked to the door, waiting for me to finish.

"Please," he said, "let me know."

"It might take a day or two."

The door slowly closed, the quiet click of the latch catching. I had never seen Grant frightened, like a man who knew already he'd lost everything.

When I knocked on Dan Martin's office door I expected the same depressingly bare and glaringly white walls as always. Those things never change. But Dan himself, that was a surprise. The worry lines that had been practically tattooed on his forehead were gone, and he was surprisingly upbeat.

"I'm sorry, but I can't do anything," Dan said. "I'm afraid I won't be here to help you on this one. I'm leaving."

"Seriously?" That was not what I expected to hear. I pulled the old wood chair up to his desk and sat down. "Is this your choice, Dan?"

"My choice. After the team melt down I realized my heart just wasn't in it anymore. No, wait, that's not even true. I realized I damn well hated it and had been hating it for a couple of years. Barstow offered me the mayor's position with a new group, but…"

"You turned it down?"

He nodded. "They've had me for thirty years, Chip, that's long enough. I'm buying a condo up at Tahoe and the biggest damn boat I can afford, and I'm going to spend the next thirty years fishing and looking for her."

I bit. "Her?"

"You know. *Her.* The one I've been too busy to notice. The older clone of the one you married. I'm not too old to jump into the game."

"Maybe too ugly," I laughed.

"Hey, you managed to find someone," he shot back, an old sparkle in his voice. "Which reminds me, I haven't even seen that new son of yours. Doug tells me he's incredible."

"He is, Dan. You wouldn't believe the difference that kid has made already."

"Now is it the baby that's made the difference, or the wife? I can tell there's a difference, Chip. You don't look like you want to crawl out of your own skin anymore."

"It wasn't that bad."

"Like hell. You wanted to die. Literally."

"Maybe for a little while, after Brenda…"

He cut me off. "Long before her. Don't you realize, that's what made you valuable to us right from the beginning? You *wanted* to die, and a dead man has no fear of walking into a bad situation."

"I was sixteen," I reminded him.

"I didn't know that at the time," he said. "All I saw was someone who was fearless and could think straight when everything was exploding around us. Someone who had the balls to bullshit his way in without caring what it was he was getting into. I knew you were Ron's son, but that was about it."

I leaned back in the chair and crossed my legs. "No clue I was just a kid?"

"Ron never said a word, not until it was too late."

"Yeah well… I don't think he's ever wanted to be up for Father of the Year."

"He might be able to help you find your kid brother," Dan pointed out.

That thought had already crossed my mind, but finding Ron to enlist his help would be as difficult as finding Dave without it. "What about Doug? Can he get into the system and find out if Dave might have been arrested somewhere between school and home?"

"I don't see why not."

"I've never seen my stepfather like this, Dan. If it were anyone but Dave…"

"Kids run away all the time, Chip. You find some girl he's interested in, and I bet you find him."

"You think Grant is over reacting?"

"It's his son. He's entitled to over react."

"All right. I'll go wander upstairs and see if Doug is around." I got of the chair and shook Dan's hand. "Stop by the restaurant once in a while, we have an excellent senior citizen's discount."

I left his office listening to him laugh.

It was nice to see him in a good mood after all this time.

Dave, Doug pointed out, is a seventeen year old upper class white boy wearing a ridiculous looking school uniform. How many places could a kid like that hide? His friends are probably all rich white boys who could be convinced to spill his whereabouts with the right threat.

He agreed with Dan: find the girl and you probably find the boy.

Doug insisted, however, that I stay out of it. "Don't give them even half a reason to suck you back into this, Chip," he said. "If anyone sees you in here playing around, the implication would be that you're back. You're not."

"I just want to see if he's been busted for anything, Doug. It would take two minutes."

"And if you didn't find that, you'd want two more minutes to run checks on every single John Doe in California, another two minutes to look for warrants on anyone who resembles your brother, then you'd want to talk to the FBI liaison… Just let me do it."

"Then what do I do?"

"You go home and sit on your overstuffed sofa and watch your son drool."

"That'll kill ten minutes."

He rolled his eyes. "Just go do something. I'll call you in a couple hours."

I left and wandered towards Sears, bought the two air conditioners, and went home to install them. Three hours later and twenty degrees cooler, I plopped down on the sofa, lying on my side, and proceeded to do what the doctor had ordered; I watched my son lay on a blanket on the floor, his little arms and legs jerking all over the place, drool and formula trickling out the corners of his mouth.

When the phone rang it jolted me upright, heart racing from the rush of adrenaline. I snatched up the receiver before it could ring a second time and scare Nicky.

"You've got to get down to Dan's office," Doug said.

"What is it?"

"Just get here like ten minutes ago."

The phone clicked dead and I put the receiver down, wondering what was so important he couldn't even offer a hint over the phone. I doubted it was Dave; if it were I wouldn't be headed to Dan's office. Doug would have been at my door, dragging me off to wherever my brother was.

"I have to leave for a little while," I told Terry. "I don't know what's up, but Doug wants to see me." I kissed her before I left, and called out as I was shutting the door behind me, "Don't wait up."

I could hear voices in Dan's office halfway down the hall. I recognized Doug's voice and Kris's as well, but the sound of two others were unfamiliar. I walked through the door and stopped dead in my tracks.

"Holy shit."

"Don't touch anything," Doug warned. He gestured to two men who were rifling through Dan's desk and trash can. "They're looking for a note."

Dan was hanging from the ceiling by his neck, his head twisted to one side and pure terror etched onto his face. His blood red eyes bulged from their sockets, scratch marks covered his neck and his fingers were marred with rope burns. The room smelled faintly of urine, and from the doorway I noticed his socks were wet.

It took me a few minutes to stop gawking and start looking. The old wood chair I had been in just hours earlier was tipped onto its side under his feet, and the rope around his neck was thick and corded. I kept looking from the chair to Dan and back again, making mental measurements.

"There's no note," I finally said.

Everyone in the room stopped what they were doing to look at me. I took a few tentative steps towards Dan's body, digging in my pockets for a handkerchief. I wrapped it around my hand and carefully set the chair upright, directly under his feet.

There was at least three inches clearance.

"Shit," Dough muttered.

"There's not a snowball's chance that he did this to himself," I said to no one in particular.

Doug and Kris both stared at the chair, unwilling to look up at Dan.

I looked at one of the men who had been going through the desk. "Cut him down."

Three days later I was in the passenger seat of Doug's convertible, speeding towards San Francisco and, I hoped, my brother. Doug had found mention of someone fitting Dave's description, right down to the slate gray slacks and navy blue blazer of his school uniform, on a routine check through police blotters, and within half an hour we were on our way.

He carried the blotter printout in his coat pocket, showing it to the desk sergeant on duty, who led us down a long dark hallway, through swinging doors, into one of the coldest rooms I had ever been in. It reminded me of Dan's office, bare and uninspired, but with walls covered by giant stainless steel file drawers.

The sergeant slowly pulled open a drawer on the far wall and pulled the sheet off of the face of the blond teenager inside.

I looked down at the face of the brother I hadn't seen in three years, the boy who had grown into a man when I wasn't looking.

The boy who wasn't coming home.

~

My soul was pricked by nightmares for several weeks. I remained as passive as I could through both funerals and ignored my own birthday, holding tight the emotions I was afraid would erupt into a tantrum, but at night, there was no escaping the recurring hell of my dreams.

Damn you, Chip, you used me, goddammit, you used me. The slamming of a door, the bang that echoed in my head for days after finding her dead in my own apartment, the floor in my dreams littered with spent syringes. *You used me, you used me, you used me...*

You should be careful, Chip, all things considering. This girl is special.

Yes, oh masterful father. I'll be careful. I'm always careful. Why the hell do you care anyway, you're never here. You've never been here. Where the hell were you when I was bleeding from my chest so hard I thought my life was over? Where the hell were you when my son was born?

I've known a lot of friendships that draw the line here.

Get away, get home, go tell the wife that you're free, but don't ever tell someone that it's okay, one ending doesn't have to lead to another. Walk away and be happy, don't bother telling him you've no intention of losing a friend. Go ahead, go on. Go on.

I'm begging you, please help me find him. He's only seventeen. His grades were never better, he was a top notch athlete.

Well, you're too late to notice that, old man. He was a good kid and he was alone and he went looking for something to fill that emptiness and he found it with a spoon and a syringe. I didn't find him fast enough, I didn't look for him personally, I didn't find him, I didn't find him, I didn't find him...

My arms are stretched out so tight that my neck feels like it will break off from my shoulders and my chest feels wrapped so tight that I can't draw in more than half a breath. Where were you? Where are you? I didn't find him, I didn't look, I didn't find him, I didn't find him, I didn't find him...

I woke with a start, hair matted to my head with sweat. I looked to be sure my wife was asleep, then slipped out of bed and quietly made my way across the dark living room to my son's room. He slept soundly and didn't wake as I lifted him from his crib. I held my son close, feeling that quick little heart beat speeding in his chest. I stood there in the dark, my son cuddled against me, and let myself cry for the first time that I could remember.

March 1977

Chip

"How long has he been there?" I asked Ted, nodding towards the end of the bar. It was just three o'clock, and the bar was vacant save the one customer.

"About half an hour," Ted replied. "I went ahead and served him because he's one of your friends, Chip, but he got drunk fast and doesn't want to quit. He's drinking just to get drunk so I'm cutting him off."

"I'll take care of it," I said, my gazed fixed on Doug, who was sitting on the last stool at the bar, staring blankly ahead, his mind anywhere but there. He didn't look quite drunk to me, not yet, more like someone so lost in thought that it would take an explosion big enough to register on the Richter scale to bring him back. "Would you mind getting some coffee? We might be able to sober him up a little. I'll make sure he gets home."

"Home may be the last place he wants to go." Ted turned to reach for the coffee pot, one eye still on Doug. "A guy like that getting stewed so early in the day usually has a reason and most of the time it has to do with home."

"I don't doubt you." I didn't remember seeing Doug pull down more than a drink and a half before, and that little bit was always enough to plaster him to the floor. It was usually the other way around; Doug was always the one to peel me up and make sure I landed home in one piece.

"Bar's closed," I said, sliding on the barstool next to him. "Ted thinks you're past your limit."

"I'm still conscious, aren't I?" Doug muttered, still staring straight ahead.

"Looks like it."

"Then I haven't reached my limit."

I reached over and took his glass, sliding it down the bar out of his reach. "You have here. Ted won't serve you any more. He doesn't like the way you're slugging it down and I tend to agree with him."

He sighed hard and closed his eyes. "Fine. I'll just sit here until I'm sober and then start all over again."

Ted set the coffee mugs in front of us, slowly filling each one. "I called the kitchen," he said to me. "Someone will be out with a couple sandwiches in a few minutes. Just don't let him eat so fast that he barfs on my clean floor."

"Thanks, Ted." I pushed the coffee towards Doug. "You heard the man, Doug. Eat, drink, and be merry, but don't puke on the linoleum."

Doug allowed himself a tight smile, sipping at the hot coffee. It wasn't what he wanted, but even through the cloud of liquor he knew me well enough to know he wouldn't make it two steps out the door. There was no point of even thinking about going somewhere else. "I'm not that drunk," he mumbled.

"Good. Then a few cups of this and a decent lunch and you should be just fine."

"Yeah, sure. Just fine." He set his cup down and finally turned to me. "I shouldn't have brought this here. I should have realized your booze nazi bartender wouldn't let me drink till I found oblivion."

"Not Ted." There was a panic in Doug's eyes, an edge of fear that was totally out of character. "I think you're wrong, though, it was probably a smart idea to bring whatever lured you to the bottle here." I glanced up at the waiter who brought the food. "Eat. You'll feel better."

Doug took a small bite, and swallowed carefully, waiting to see if his stomach would heave back at him. His stomach growled loud enough that I could hear it, making me wonder when the last time was that he'd thought to eat. "How's Nicky?" he asked between bites.

"Nicky? Nicky's great. Pulls himself up on the furniture, crawls like lightning."

"Kris says he's talking some, too."

"A few words. Mostly 'oh shit.'"

"We all know who he got that from."

"What's bugging you, Doug?" I finally asked. "I don't believe you came in here this early just to toss a few down."

"I came," he said evenly, "to ask about Nicky."

"Bullshit. You see him all the time and if you were that bent on knowing how he was you'd be at the zoo with Kris and Terry, holding your nose at the stink and complaining about it. You sure as hell wouldn't be here molding your ass into a barstool and getting blind drunk."

He pushed the food around and finally pushed away the plate. "Probably not," he agreed after some thought. He picked at a damp cocktail napkin, staring down at his hands. "Kris is pregnant."

"Are you fucking serious?"

He nodded.

"Well hell, getting drunk celebrating I could understand, but you look like crap."

Doug spun on his seat. "Oh, it's terrific all right. Kris doesn't want the commitment, remember? The best I can ever hope for is just really good friends who see each other naked once in a while. She'll never marry me, Chip... what I get is a seat on the sidelines while she calls all the goddamned shots!"

"Whoa, take it easy. A baby can change a lot of things. What did she say when she told you?"

His head was in his hands. "She hasn't told me. Her doctor called me on a consult today. The guy has no idea that I'm the baby's father."

I should have been surprised, but I wasn't. "You're going to have to talk to her, Doug. She's got to know that you know."

"Does she?" He looked up, shaking his head. "Maybe she doesn't want me to know. Maybe she won't even go through with it."

"I thought she wanted a baby."

"Past tense. Wanted, not wants. She's just happy being Nicky's indulgent aunt or cousin or whatever. The urge to have one was just another one of her flaky spur of the moment whims."

"Talk to her," I urged.

"I have begged her a hundred times to marry me," he moaned. "This won't change her mind. She's determined to be so fucking independent that even if she does have the baby she'll want to do it on her own."

"Or maybe not."

"I don't know what the hell Ron did to her, but it sure as

hell has made her gun shy when it comes to making a commitment."

I couldn't argue with him. "If you handle it right, she still might marry you, you know."

"How?"

"Tell her you already know about the baby. Tell her you're happy about it and you want this kid more than anything... but you respect her right to do it without a wedding ring as long as she doesn't cut you out of the kid's life. Just don't let her scare you away and don't let her pull away. She'll warm to the idea once she knows you're not going anywhere."

"You're assuming that she's even going to have this baby. I know Kris, she might not."

I poured him another cup of coffee. "Talk fast," I told him, "and don't stop talking until it's too late for her to do anything about it."

Terry

My cousin's idea of a relaxing day out was to drive an hour to San Francisco, or go in the opposite direction to Sacramento, and spend the day walking around the zoo. Kris was a zoo addict; she declared Nicky old enough to appreciate the sights and smells of all the animals, and piled us into her car for a trip to William Landt Park in Sacramento.

Nicky was impressed enough to sleep through most of it; I was just grateful for a nice spring day and the chance to get out of the house and more than an hour of adult conversation.

Kris was preoccupied with her own thoughts and talked about as much as Nicky did. She paused and lingered more than she normally would, barely glanced up from the ground and avoided looking at me altogether. I assumed it was a fight with Doug and didn't want to pry, as curious as I was.

It wasn't until we were in the dark, cool quiet of the reptile house that I realized how deep her thoughts were running. Kris was snaring at a rattlesnake, watching it slither slowly across the bottom of the tank, her forehead pressed against the glass.

"I'm pregnant," she blurted out.

I pulled the stroller up alongside her, leaning against the rail that was supposed to separate the curious from the potentially dangerous. "You don't seem terribly excited about the prospect."

"I'm not." She lifted her head and turned, slowly moving to the next exhibit. "If this had happened two years ago I would have been thrilled. But not now."

I reached out and touched her arm. "What's wrong with now, Kris? Having a baby with Ron would have been a mistake, but with Doug? It could be the greatest thing to ever happen to you."

"It could also be the worst." She stepped outside, blinking hard against the sudden bright light. "I'm thirty six years old now, Terry. Do you know how much could go wrong?"

"Come on. You're not too old."

"I'm on the wrong side of the hill for this."

"Isn't it worth the chance?"

She shook her head, frowning. "I couldn't take it if something went wrong."

I stopped walking, leaning heavily against Nick's stroller. "You mean you wouldn't accept anything less than a perfect child? You can't have a baby and not have the responsibility."

"That's what I mean!" She spun on her heel defiantly. "It takes someone very special to go through that and survive. I'm not having a baby I can't give one hundred per cent to. I'm not trying to be selfish, I just know my limitations."

"In the words of my overly wise father, el toro poop." I pulled the strolled to a nearby bench and sat, digging into the diaper bag for a bottle. Nicky watched every movement, and his hands shot out, trying to grab it before I could get the top off. "Have you told Doug yet?" I asked, pulling him onto my lap.

"I haven't decided whether or not I should."

I stared at her, incredulous. "You've got to be kidding! He has every right to know. It's his baby, too." I handed the bottle to Nicky and then suddenly wondered. "Isn't it?"

"Yes, of course it is. But there's no reason to tell him if I decide to not have it."

"God, I don't believe you," I swore. "Doug doesn't deserve this. How do you think he'll feel if he ever finds out? He'll never trust you again. Is that what you want?"

"No. Losing him is the last thing I want."

"How do you think you'll feel if you have an abortion and then realize you *do* want a child with him?"

"Terry, it…"

"No. Look at Nicky, Kris. He was never an 'it.'"

"I didn't mean..."

"You can't go back and change it," I said, not letting her finish. "Look at this little boy. How can you not want Doug's child?"

She reached out and brushed her fingers against his chubby cheek. Nicky grinned, dropping the bottle from his mouth, a bright four toothed smile that had to melt her heart. "You and Chip make beautiful babies, that's for sure."

"And you'll never know if you and Doug do unless you give yours a chance." I handed Nick over to her, knowing he'd be just as content on her lap. "I can't imagine my life without him now. There's not a thing in this world I would trade the little time we've had together for. I *live* for him, Kris."

She held him close, his warm little body squirming to get loose. "I remember when you were his age. Your mom would let me sit and hold you for hours, and you'd sit still for it, too. We'd curl up on the couch and I'd read to you or sing songs... God, I was only about fifteen and thought I knew everything."

"And now?"

"Now I don't even know what I want from day to day."

"Then how can you make up your mind about something this big by yourself? Kris, you have to tell Doug. Even if you decide you don't want the baby, at least he can help you. He'd know all the risks."

"Once I tell him he'll stop thinking like a doctor and start thinking like a potential father. Doug is so hot to get married he'd do anything. A baby would just give him more ammunition to work with."

"So? Doug loves you. I'm surprised you're not married already."

"I'm not ready for that much commitment, Terry."

"Bull. The commitment is already there. Neither of you sees anyone else, you probably spend most nights together... If the situation was reversed and Doug didn't want marriage, we'd be sitting here bitching about what a selfish pig he is, out for nothing more than steady sex."

She almost smiled. "Once I marry Doug the choice is made. I can't back out." She settled Nick back into his stroller. "If I ever remarry it's going to be for the rest of my life. I refuse to make the same mistake again."

"You love Doug, don't you?"

She nodded.

"Then it's not a mistake. Even if it ended down the line, it still wouldn't be a mistake. Look at your marriage to Ron."

"I'd rather not."

"Kris, it wasn't a mistake. If not for you and Ron, I never would have found Chip, and look how good we are for each other. I can't believe you're afraid to take the chance to be happy."

"I'm already happy."

"All right." I got up and started to push Nick along. Kris followed, taking long steps to catch up. "If you're so happy," I asked her, "then why does it look like you're fighting to not cry?"

"Why is this so important to you, Terry? You have your baby and your husband. Why the hell does it matter to you whether or not I have this kid?"

"Because I think you'd wind up hating yourself if you had an abortion. It's not a morality thing, Kris, I just think you'd despise yourself."

"But the choice is mine."

"Don't leave Doug out of it."

"No." She stopped walking and forced me to turn to her. "When it all comes down to it, the choice *is* mine. It's my body, not his. And I'll be the one with a live human being to take care of when it's all over."

"Don't fluff your ego too much," I warned. "Did it ever occur to you that Doug could raise this baby just as easily? Nine months out of your life and you make him a happy man forever."

"What... just turn my baby over to him and walk away?"

"Why not? You don't want it and you'll lose him if you get rid of it. So why not have it and then turn your back on both of them?"

"Terry, stop it. I haven't decided anything."

"Talk to him," I urged. "Do it or you'll hate yourself for the rest of your life."

He drove the same route he had been following for six weeks. He moved the car along slowly, eyes constantly darting to the beige and gray buildings that loomed ahead. He felt like he should be pleased with himself, satisfied with the dedicated care he took in his work and the ease with which he accomplished it. The truth was, he hated it and hated himself for doing it. It had been a long time since he had tried to convince himself that it was just a living. He stopped trying to justify it, and only did it because he had to, because if he didn't his son would pay the price.

He couldn't even remember the last time he had seen his son; he'd never seen his grandson. Most nights he tried to form a mental image of what the boy looked like and what he would be doing, but it was heartbreaking. He stopped thinking of going home; nobody would be comfortable with him around. There was no sense tormenting them.

Slowly, he eased his car into the parking lot. It was a battered blue Chevy that had long since had a really good day. It was inconspicuous, though, a car no one would remember, which was what he wanted.

The climb to the top of the stairs was longer than it had ever seemed before, the well worn briefcase in his hand increasingly heavy with each forward step. This was planned, every last detail. He knew when his mark would leave the building across the street, linger at the news stand, and when he would turn to face the window before crossing the street to the parking lot. He did it every day without fail.

He pried the window open, the fresh air snapping back

at him. The briefcase squealed miserably as he opened it, but he paid no attention to the sound, knowing it would be lost in the regular din of the building.

Silence was his foremost consideration. He needed to be quiet, but not so quiet that he would stand out. His chosen weapons were always quiet enough to be overlooked in the everyday music of life.

He perched there, waiting, his eyes glued to the door across the street. When his mark came out, right on schedule, he took aim. First the news stand, to chat for a moment and to buy a paper. Everything else moved in slow motion; he gently squeezed the trigger as his mark moved in to line and turned to face the window. He exhaled slowly, watching the chaos that unfolded before him. Slowly, he pulled the crossbow apart and placed it in the briefcase and stepped back from the window.

He watched from the bowels of the room for a moment longer to be certain he hadn't been seen, and then joined the throng of people rushing to see what had happened. He only stopped for a moment to throw the briefcase in his car and ran, along with fifty other people, to gawk at the dead man with an arrow through his head.

Doug

The hangover I'd hoped to avoid came crashing down on me four hours after Chip shoved me into a taxi and sent me in the general direction of the medical offices I shared in a downtown office complex with two other agency physicians. It was a rotation that worked, there were always two of us there, no matter where in the world the third might be. I sat at the desk in my private office with the intentions of reviewing the file of every patient I had seen during the week, anything to get my mind off myself.

My head throbbed from the afternoon binge and my stomach churned with the protests of hunger and fear. I could still taste vodka and coffee and the grease of the salami sandwich Chip had urged me to eat.

I grabbed the first file and opened it, staring blankly, seeing the page but not reading the words, trying to quiet the small voice in my head that would not go away.

It could be, that voice whispered, that it's not meant to be. Just a passing phase in our lives, two lonely souls who needed each other but were never meant for each other. She may have carried my baby but that didn't also mean that there wasn't someone else out there waiting for her, the great love of her life who nursed the pains of longing, wondering where she was.

It didn't matter how right it felt, not if it was something never destined to happen.

Did I love her enough to let her go? The thought pricked at my conscience; could I gracefully walk away if I had to?

Could I live with her without the baby?

She trusted me enough to let me tell her often that I wanted to marry her, knowing I wouldn't press hard enough to send her running into the night. I wasn't sure if she trusted me enough to share the fact of our child.

Talk fast and don't stop talking…

When she walked into the office, her face flushed with the first hints of springtime sunlight, it was everything I could do to not blurt out the facts as I knew them, and the solution as I wanted it to be. She greeted me with a kiss and settled into a chair in front of the desk, purse perched on her lap like so many of my patients did when they waited to hear the news, good or bad.

"You look tired," I said, noting her eyes, sad eyes.

"A little. Terry and I spent the afternoon wandering around the zoo with Nicky today and the traffic coming home was awful... I think Nicky had a good time, though."

"Nicky's a terrific kid," I ventured.

"He is. I hope Chip and Terry have a couple more like him."

But what about you? I stood up, walking around to the other side of the desk, and reached for her hands. "I should stay and finish going over these files." I looked down at her, finding those brown eyes a confusing mixture of warmth and invitation, but just beyond that, fear. "I would much rather take you out to dinner."

"Doug, you eat out so much I'm surprised you have a stomach left."

"Blame my mother," I said, taking her hand and guiding her out through the waiting room. "She never taught me to cook. Come on, it'll do us some good. Where to?"

"My place."

"Yours?"

"I'll cook for you tonight. If you watch, you might even learn something."

You must not be ready to toss me out on my ass if you're willing to cook for me.

Going home wasn't what I had in mind. I wanted to get her to a public place, somewhere we could talk but she couldn't make a public scene. Once I let her know, even hinted, that I knew there was a baby she could fly into a rage or break down into sobs so hard she wouldn't be able to stop. In public she would keep enough composure that I could handle her; I wasn't as confident about in private.

We rode in silence to her apartment, static cutting through

the car radio. I stayed one step behind her through the parking lot and up the stairs, allowing only fear to keep me from grabbing her at various points along the way to hold her and tell her everything would be all right.

"So," she said, walking into the kitchen, "what are we hungry for tonight?"

I shrugged, peering over her shoulder into the refrigerator. "It would be a hell of a lot easier if we just called for a pizza."

"Well that's a nice home cooked meal."

"It's been a bitch of a day, Kris," I said, pushing the refrigerator closed. "All I want to do is kick back and relax with you, and if you're in here cooking it'll just heat up the entire apartment..."

She relented to the bite of anger in my voice. "Okay, that's fine... call it in while I go change clothes."

I watched her leave the kitchen and then reached for the phone. My gut was twisted in knots but I wasn't sure if it was from all the drinking I'd done earlier or from the fight I expected. I called in the order and then went back into the living room, tossing my suit coat over the back of her sofa. I stood there, staring at the bedroom door. She was in there half dressed, and it would be so easy to just walk in and convince her to commit in the heat of passion.

I wanted that commitment on fair ground, though, and I wanted to hear from her own lips about the baby slowly growing inside her.

She came out of the bedroom wearing a baggy t-shirt and virtually nothing else, a Monopoly game box in hand. "Something to pass the time while we wait for the pizza," she said.

You're thinking about a stupid kids game when you have a bombshell to drop on me?

I sat on the floor in front of the fireplace, crossing my legs uncomfortably, my eyes following her every move as she turned on a light and came back. *You have half an hour or I'll tell you what you might not want me to know...*

She sat across from me and reached over to yank at my tie. "Take off that awful dress shirt. You look more uncomfortable than I've ever seen you."

"Anything else you want removed while I'm at it?"

"Anything else is up to you."

I took off the shirt and tossed it onto the sofa. "You could be looking for trouble if I start taking things off."

"Don't worry," she said as she handed me the dice. "If I see anything I haven't seen before, I'll shoot it."

"Thanks a lot."

We fell silent as we played, my mind miles away from the game.

"Doug," she said when I finally looked away, "is something wrong?"

"I don't know. I get the feeling I should be asking you that."

She set the dice down and stared at the game board for a long time. "Okay, you're right, there is something and I don't think you're going to like it one bit."

"I love you, you know."

She threw her arms around my neck and hugged me hard. "I know you do, Doug. You didn't have to say it for me to know."

"Whatever it is can't be that bad."

She pulled back far enough to look into my eyes. The game board was scattered, little green houses and dice all over the carpet. "Yes, it can be... You might hate me"—she broke off, voice cracking.

"Let me tell you something," I said, pulling her with me from the floor to the couch. "I will *never* hate you. What I am is terrified of losing you. I'll do anything—and I mean anything—to keep that from happening."

"I'm not so sure." Tears were threatening to spill over and she swallowed hard against the lump in her throat. "I found out his morning that I'm pregnant."

I let my breath out slowly, marveling that she had managed to say it. "You're not happy about it."

She bit her lip, forcing herself to speak. "I haven't decided yet if I want to go through with it. I don't know if it's a good idea."

I pulled her close, afraid that if I let go she would bolt from the apartment. "Why?"

"I'm getting too old… my chances of getting through it unscathed get smaller every day." She broke away from the embrace, startled to see the tears misting in my eyes. "I wasn't even sure I was going to tell you."

"I know how you feel about marrying me." When she started to respond, I placed a finger over her lips. "I won't pressure you, not even now, but I'm begging you to really think it through. I *do* want this child."

"But at my age…"

"Your age isn't that big a factor. And if you're honestly worried about carrying a baby with birth defects, there are tests."

"Time is running out, Doug. I have to decide soon."

I refused to let her look away from me. "When I was in medical school," I said, heart beating so hard it felt like it was in my throat, "I had to sit in on an abortion. The mother had bone cancer, it was basically her or the baby… They cut her open so they could look for other signs of cancer—Jesus

Christ. The surgeon pulled out this three month old fetus still in the amniotic sac and held it up by tweezers so we could see it. Kris, the baby was still alive, kicking and sucking its thumb, and we had to watch it *die*."

Tears were streaming down her face and she tried to look away, but I turned her face back to me. "We already know that a baby starts forming habits in the womb. That baby inside you is very much alive, and you have to know that if you get rid of it, it *will* feel pain. I won't stop you because I can't, but you have to know I am against the idea with every fiber in my soul."

"Stop it!" she finally managed. "Don't do this to me, Doug. This is hard enough without you laying a guilt trip on me. This is *my* body, dammit! I don't know that I can push it so hard for the next seven months. I don't know if I have what it takes to be a mother."

"You don't have to go through any of it alone."

She collapsed against me, her hands desperately holding on to my t-shirt. "What if I decide to not have this baby. How will we be then?"

"I told you, I'll still be here. And whether you marry me or not I plan on spending the rest of my life with you. Just swear to me you won't rush into anything without thinking about it long and hard."

"All right," she agreed after a while. "And I won't keep you out of it."

I pulled away from her to answer the door. My head felt fuzzy and I was exhausted, barely able to keep my brain one step ahead of my mouth. My mind was screaming at me to fight for my son or my daughter, but the simple truth was that as much as I wanted to be a father to this baby, I wanted her more.

When I paid for the pizza and closed the door she was coming out of the kitchen with two coke bottles in hand. Her eyes were red with tears and she was trembling.

"The kids got good timing," I said after a while, trying to force some of the pizza down. "Don't know if that's good or bad." I tossed a half eaten slice back into the box, aware that Kris was only picking at hers.

"It's raining," she whispered, getting up to take the box into the kitchen.

I got up and walked over to the balcony door. The rain swirled in puddles on the concrete and I stared into them, feeling empty and hopeless.

"It's getting late," I said when she returned.

"You don't have a curfew." She took my hand and leaned into me, staring out at the rain with me. "Stay the night."

"I don't think I can."

"I don't want anything from you tonight, Doug. Just for you to stay."

Terrified of being together and terrified of being alone. "I suppose," I sighed, "that I need the company, too." I turned and kissed the tip of her nose. "I still want to marry you, Kris. I don't expect you to say yes, but I mean it."

The corners of her mouth turned up in a sad smile. "I promise, I'll think about it."

Chip could be right; talk fast enough and talk long enough, and she just might change her mind.

Chip

"You guys have a good day?" I asked Terry while I pulled my wet jacket off. She was sitting on the floor in front of the sofa with Nicky, stacking bright red and blue wood blocks for him to knock over.

"I did. Your little munchkin here," she chucked him under the chin, "took all the fresh air as a cue to snooze the afternoon away. The only time he woke up was to stuff his face."

"That's my boy," I laughed. I kicked off my shoes—I hated dress shoes—and sat on the floor across from them, holding out my arms to my son. "Come on, Nicky. Give Daddy a hug."

Nicky looked at me and smiled but didn't move.

"He's got a mind of his own. Kind of like someone else in this family who can be a little bullheaded."

"You're not that bad."

"Funny." She leaned over and kissed me full on the mouth, lips lingering there for a moment. "How was your day today?"

"It was different. Doug showed up right after the lunch rush and rooted himself to the bar with every intention of still being there at closing time. Ted had me practically giving him coffee through an IV."

"Are you serious? Doug's not a drinker."

"He was today."

Terry stacked the blocks again for Nicky, his eyes dancing with delight. With a single swipe of his hand he sent them flying.

"Shit!"

"No, no, Nicky," I tried not to smile. "No shit."

He grinned at me. "No shit."

"That's great," Terry moaned. "What else will you teach him tonight?"

"Sorry, wasn't thinking…"

"You and my cousin," she said absently.

I scooped Nicky onto my lap and planted a kiss on top

of his head. "Kris told you?"

She looked up from the blocks. "How could you know, Chip? She was with me all day."

"Why do you think Doug was guzzling down half my vodka supply?" Nick wiggled away, crawling back to Terry and his blocks. "He talked to her doctor this morning."

"Oh, my God. She's considering not even telling him. I don't think she wants to have this baby."

We both looked at Nicky. "That's too bad. Kris would be a wonderful mother. She'll have to tell him, though. She would never be able to look him in the eye again if she didn't."

"She's terrified, Chip. I don't think she knows what she really wants and I'm afraid she'll do something she'll regret." She handed Nicky a block, pointing to the stack. He set it on top and giggled before knocking it over. "I even suggested she have the baby and give it to Doug, then walk away if she couldn't face being a family."

Nicky took a blue block and shoved it in his mouth, drool running down his chin.

"Could you do that?" she asked. "If I couldn't be here for whatever reason, could you raise Nicky on your own?"

"Darlin' I don't even want to think about that..."

"But if it was a choice between life without him, knowing I hadn't wanted him, or life with him and me walking away, could you do it?"

"You'd never walk away, Ter."

"But if I did. If something happened and I couldn't be his mother, if I just wasn't here."

Nicky took the block from his mouth and crawled over to me, setting it on my leg, warm spit seeping through my slacks. "If I were Doug," I sighed, "and you were Kris... Yes, I'd take the baby and raise him alone if I had to. But you'd be welcome back in our lives when you finally found that place inside that would let you come home."

Nick pulled himself up using my arm to balance, sticking the wet block into my mouth.

"If you can see that," Terry cried, "and I can see that, why can't Kris?"

"She will," I mumbled around the block. Nick grabbed it and threw it towards the stack, his fingers gripping my shirt tightly. He leaned towards my face, and with his mouth wide open, planted a kiss on my cheek that included baby teeth marks. "I bet Mommy wants a kiss too, tiger," I told him, kissing him back.

Terry held her arms open, and he dropped to his hands and knees and crawled to her.

"Mommy mommy," he squealed.

"Kris will marry him," I said, certain of it. "She just needs time to get used to the idea. As soon as she realizes Doug won't bolt, she'll relax enough to let it happen."

"She knows he won't leave. I think that's what scares her."

Nicky curled up in her lap and stuck his thumb in his mouth, eyes getting heavy. "Bedtime?" I asked.

"Past."

I stood and reached for him. "Did you eat for Mommy tonight?"

"Like a pig," she answered for him.

"And did we take a bath?"

"We did. He just needs to be changed."

"Well, Daddy will change diapers and clothes if Mommy will get a water bottle."

I put Nicky in his crib, pulling off his clothes and diaper. "So, little man," I said to him, reaching for a diaper, "didn't you want to see all the lions and tigers and monkeys today? Your Aunt Kris *will* quiz you on them later. For the rest of your life she's going to take you to the zoo so you better start paying attention."

He just grinned, kicking his legs when I pulled a shirt over his head. "What do we have here?" I ran my thumb over a red mark under his arm. "Your Uncle David had one of these right here, too. I used to tell him it was a hickey from all those girls who chased him around on the playground. Is that what you've got? Did some little eight month old wonder woman lay one on you?"

"Chip, you're horrible."

"You're interrupting some important man-talk, woman," I said. "He was about to tell me about this hot chick he's seeing."

"Well Casanova here will be wanting his bottle." She held the bottle over the rail of the crib and he snatched it from her, stuffing the nipple into his mouth.

"Shouldn't he be learning to sleep without that?" I asked.

"He's not ready, yet, Chip. Don't rush him. It's only water."

I turned out the light by the bed and reached out for her. We stood there in the half light, watching Nicky drift off, his quick little breaths interrupted only by the loud sucking on his bottle.

"Have you ever considered having another one?" she whispered.

I moaned to myself. There was no considering here. She had already decided, and only needed my cooperation.

Doug

Religion and faith in a higher being was never my strongest suit; I wasn't raised to be particularly pious and hadn't seen much while growing up to convince me that there was anyone or anything out there with the power to point and exert influence on the good and bad in the world. I fell somewhere between agnostic and atheist, my belief suspended enough to not blame God for the occasional agonies in my life, but neither did I give any credit that might be due.

I spent the night lying in Kris's bed, listening to the rain ping off the windows, alternately staring at the ceiling and watching her sleep. She slept on her side, curled around a pillow with her knees drawn up towards her stomach. Her breathing was soft and slow, but even in sleep her face was drawn with worry.

There had to be a way to convince her that she could have everything and that it was something to embrace, not fear.

I slid my hand under the pillow and rested it on her belly. It would be weeks before I would be able to feel any movement but just knowing that the baby was there and still safe, gave me the feeling that I was connecting, and in that moment I believed in God with a power and certainty that seared right through my soul.

You have to give her a sign, I prayed silently. *Let her see what it is she needs. Just don't let this baby die.*

Chip

I shot straight up, instantly awake, when a blood curdling scream sliced through the morning and yanked me from sound asleep to completely alert in less than a second. My heart thundered wildly in my chest and a rush of adrenaline propelled me from the bed in one swift movement, my head pounding hard when she screamed again.

I raced from the bedroom, sprinting across the living

room, hurdling over the toys we'd left scattered on the floor, to my son's bedroom. Terry stood there, ashen and shaken, her eyes wild with fear and face contorted in pain.

"Chip, Nicky's not here," she cried. "He's gone."

I looked at the empty crib. "Can he climb out yet? Maybe he's somewhere in the apartment."

"No, no he isn't," she insisted. "He's gone."

There was no way, I realized, looking at my son's empty bed, that he could have gotten out of it without creating enough noise to wake both us and the people downstairs. He would have fallen and started screaming, or pulled the whole thing over on its side. I looked over at the window across the room; the air conditioner was still barricaded and locked into place. The bathroom door was shut, and the eye hook I'd put on it to keep Nick out was still clasped.

"Don't touch anything," I told her. "Just back out into the living room and don't touch anything."

She stood there, staring numbly at the crib.

"Terry!" I snapped. "Get out!"

She nodded and slowly backed out through the door. I made a quick survey of the room; the stack of diapers on the night stand was gone, along with the assortment of toys Terry kept stored under the crib. Clothes hung sloppily over an open drawer. Nicky's water bottle, abandoned after he fell asleep, was at the foot of the crib, but the pacifier he slept with yet rarely put in his mouth was gone.

I left the room, careful not to touch even the door, biting back the raw terror that was beginning to boil. Calm, I told myself. Stay calm and think, find the right switch to flip so that you can keep your wife from falling apart and so that you can figure this out.

Terry was rooted in place just a few feet into the living

room, staring numbly at his bedroom, her breathing just a measure away from gasps. I reminded her again not to touch anything, and slipped into the kitchen and picked up the phone, dialing blind. "I need help fast," I said when Kris answered. "I have to call in a few favors and I need them within the next two minutes. Doug will need to make all the contacts for me."

I explained what I wanted, and when I hung up the phone I was shaking so hard I could barely get the receiver back onto the cradle.

"I called Kris," I told Terry after I was able to regain enough composure to go back to the living room. "She and Doug will help, we can find Nicky."

She blinked hard, trying to absorb what I was saying, but all she knew was that her son was not there. "The police…"

"The police don't have the same resources, Terry. I swear to you, we can find him long before they could even finish a report. He'll be okay, I promise."

"Don't…"

I tried to put my arms around her, but she tore away. She couldn't cry, there was too much terror swirling around us both for any tears to come. "How can they help, Chip? Who would do this?"

"I don't know who would do this," I said helplessly, wanting to hold her. "Doug will bring field agents from investigations … they'll look around Nick's room for prints and hair or anything else that might help. Someone else will canvas the building, find anyone who might have seen something…"

"How could I not hear him, Chip?" she asked wildly. "I never heard him cry. I never heard anything." She was gasping now, rocking on her feet and shouting. "Chip, why didn't we hear anything?!"

"I don't know."

I got my arms around her before she fell to the ground, panic gripping at her in huge sobs, and held her tight while she rocked on the floor and cried harder than I had ever seen someone cry in my life.

Kris

When we walked into their apartment they were both were sitting on the floor, holding on tight and trying hard to not completely fall apart. Terry didn't look up at the men who shot through the living room, directed to Nick's bedroom by Doug. She was clinging to Chip like a life preserver, and it took considerable urging to get her to move from the floor to the sofa, where she tumbled from Chip's arms into mine.

"Terry," I said gently, "look at me. You have to look at me."

Reluctantly, she nodded and looked up.

"I have to warn you, those men are going to tear Nick's room to pieces, and they won't take the time to put anything back. When you go back in there every drawer will be empty and on the floor, they'll take his sheets, and there will be powder coating every surface they can find. It's going be a huge mess... can you handle that?"

She nodded numbly.

"Before they leave," I went on, "we'll need hair samples from you and from Chip, and we'll also need your fingerprints. Do you understand?"

Another slow nod.

"Has anyone besides you and Chip been in Nick's room in the last couple of weeks?"

"No," she replied thickly. "Just you, I think, maybe Doug."

"You need to think hard. Have you gotten any strange letters or phone calls lately? Anything that seemed out of the ordinary at the time? Someone offering to help you carry groceries up from the car, maybe? Someone asking for help looking for a lost kid or pet when you had Nick with you?"

"No."

Chip was leaning against the back of the couch, watching as his son's room was ripped apart, looking more confident that he should have—looking more like the Chip I knew from years past. He was soaking in every detail, making mental notes that would burn into his memory. "I can't think of anything, either," he said. "No threats, no warnings... nothing."

I turned toward him. "What about your stepfather, Chip? Would he try something like this to hurt you? Payback for losing Dave?"

"Grant? Kris, the man is a bastard, not a lunatic."

He turned his attention back to the chaos in Nicky's room. His crib mattress had been stripped and the sheet placed in a plastic bag; dusting powder floated through the air; even a baby bottle was wrapped in plastic.

Doug came out of Nick's room and looked at Chip. "You'd better get dressed. I assume you want to go to the lab with us."

"How much longer?"

"Ten, maybe fifteen minutes." He watched Chip go into the other bedroom, and then motioned for me to walk across the room with him.

I glanced at Terry, who was staring blankly at the floor, and then followed him. "What is it?"

He pulled me into the bedroom. "They found some blood on one of the crib's side rails," he whispered. "It's not much but it should be enough to get a type on it."

"You think it's Nicky's?"

"I doubt it. I looks more like someone reached down at the corner of the crib and scraped themselves on the rail. The thing is, the blood is fresh, so this didn't happen very long ago."

I went over to the crib and looked down at the rail. The was a very small jagged edge at the tip, flecked with red. "Any tissue?"

"On the top side of the tip," one of the men said quietly, understanding we didn't want Terry to hear.

"Anything else?" I asked.

"No, ma'am. There are tons of fingerprints but most of them are smudged and appear to be from the baby."

I watched as they finished bagging Nicky's things. "Any ideas on motivation?"

Both of the men working shook their heads. Doug shrugged and said, "Could be anything, even random. Nicky's a good looking, personable little kid and he has no fear of strangers. We could be looking at black market, or some whacked out woman who wants her own baby... a personal gain kidnapping."

"Ransom? Chip's stepfather isn't exactly down in the middle class, you know."

"But Chip is. If he has any money stashed away he doesn't show it. He drives a ten year old car and lives in a small apartment on one of the busiest streets in town. I'd put ransom at the bottom of my list."

He steered me from the room, glancing warily at Terry. "I think it would be better if you stayed here with her. I don't want her alone, and on the off chance this *is* for ransom, I want you to field every phone call that comes into this house. Don't let her talk to anyone. We don't need crazed grandparents down here"—he watched Terry slowly get up off the couch and move towards the front door—"and we need her to stay put."

"What is it, Terry?" I asked, afraid she was about to run out the door.

She pointed to a rattle on the floor, wedged up against the wall. "Nicky hasn't played with that in over a month. It was in the night stand, Kris. I remember seeing it there yesterday."

Doug took a small plastic bag and gently pushed the rattle into it. "Good eyes," he muttered, more to himself than to her. "We still need a clear set of your prints, Terry."

As she wiped the ink off her hands, she sniffed back more tears. "Kris, you have to stay with me," she pleaded. "I can't be here by myself."

"I'm not going anywhere."

She tried to manage a grateful smile, but she couldn't. Her head hung wearily from her shoulders, the full shock beginning to set in. "They have to find my baby," she cried. "They have to find him."

I rushed to hold my cousin, feeling awkward and useless. "They're the best of the best," I told her gently, "and Chip is one better than that. He'll find Nicky, Terry, I know he will." I pulled back a little, finding it hard to let go. Terry's eyes were red and puffy, tears streaming down her cheeks. "Trust me. Chip will find him. He's never, I swear *never*, failed to finish the job once he's started."

And knowing him on the job, I realized, I didn't want to be there to clean up after him when he did finish it.

Chip

I barely recognized Alex Barstow out of his standard black suit and matching tie. The man that came through the double doors wearing gray sweatpants and a sweatshirt with the sleeves cut off was completely different from the man I once thought I might have to beg mercy from. Even his sneakers, tattered white Converse high tops, didn't seem to fit.

"Chip," he said casually, stretching out in the chair next to mine, "they called me about your boy. I came right over to see if there's anything I can do."

We were sitting outside the lab door, where Doug was supervising the print and blood tests. "Just let me abuse your lab for a while longer," I said. I felt distinctly uneasy sitting next to Barstow; he belonged behind the dark wood desk, surrounded by everything blood red.

"Anything. You have run of the place."

I muttered my thanks.

"All things considered, I think we owe you this much."

Owed me what, I wondered, but didn't care enough to ask. He stood up and held out his hand. "I'll be in my office if there's anything I can personally do. Don't hesitate."

He wandered off, leaving me to stew there alone. Doug wouldn't let me past the door to the lab, afraid I was too emotionally involved to not interfere. So I sat there and waited, seconds stretching into minutes that seemed to stretch into eternity. I could not fathom, on any level, why someone would invade our home and steal our child.

Two hours later Doug stepped out of the lab and sat next to me. "We may have something," he said. "The blood on the crib was O positive, but Terry and Nick are both A positive."

"So am I."

"They also recovered several hairs from the sheets and carpet. Most are blonde or brown—Terry's or Nick's or yours—but they did find a few strands of black hair."

"Prints?"

"One really good one on the rattle Terry found. It's being run through DMV and the FBI."

"So if this person doesn't drive in California or doesn't have a record, we may be shit out of luck."

Doug shook his head and looked away. "I'm going to say something you're not going to like, but you have to consider it under the circumstances. No one has seen Ron in a long time, I checked his records and the blood type matches... if the prints don't pan out I'd suggest we have someone go after him first."

"Are you crazy?" I couldn't believe he was even suggesting this. "Look, Doug, you might not like the man but you have to be out of your fucking mind to think he would do this! No one in my family did this, not Grant, and especially not Ron!"

He waited for the tirade to end. "Ron kills people for a living," he reminded me. "From what I hear, he's gotten very good at it. Don't try to tell me he doesn't have it in him."

"What motive?" I demanded. "Ron has absolutely no goddamned reason to kidnap his own grandson."

"Take it easy... I'm only saying it's something to consider if the print doesn't pan out."

I settled back, my head against the wall. I hadn't heard from Ron since Nicky was just six weeks old; the man had never seen his grandson and there was no telling what was running through his mind. My gut refused to consider it, but my brain was spinning in all directions.

"All right," I said, feeling exhausted. "Can we run a check and see if there's a log of any threats made against me after I was suspended? Someone I might have offended on duty who would use my son to get back at me?"

"Already checked," he said. "There's no record of anyone

either in or outside the agency threatening you or filing complaints. I checked for anything on Kris and myself, too. I don't think it's agency related."

"A disgruntled employee then? Maybe I fired someone..."

The lab door jerked open, and the tech that stepped outside was both flustered and excited. "We've got an ID. DMV records coughed up a nice one."

"Spill it," Doug ordered. I braced myself, expecting the worst.

"Your perp is Alvin Matthew Rhuele, last known address is right here in town."

My head started to spin. "Alvin"—I muttered, trying to place the face with the name. My fists clenched and every muscle in my body tightened with rage, and the name finally tumbled out like a curse. "Matt Rhuele."

"You know him?"

"Vaguely." I shot out of the chair. "I want an info sheet on everything known about this son of a bitch. I want to know who his family is, who his friends are, who he hangs out with, who he sleeps with..."

"Slow down, Chip," Doug cautioned. "You're not going after him yourself."

"Like hell I'm not."

"You are *way* too close to this. Give me two minutes to make a phone call, you know the SG will authorize a team to go after him."

"Not a fucking chance," I hissed. "This one is mine. I promised Terry."

"You don't have the authority to take him into custody."

"Custody? Hell Doug, when I'm done with this bastard there won't be anything left of him to take anywhere."

"Hold on." He grabbed at my arm when I started to walk

away. "You go after him like this and you'll get Nicky hurt."

I continued on down the corridor, leaving him to catch up. "I do everything by the book," I told him. "Always have."

"Your book or theirs?"

"The one that matters."

He stopped me before I could barge into the Secretary General's office. "You walk in there," he said, "and you're committing yourself all over again."

"My boy is missing," I reminded him. "I'll do whatever I have to in order to get him back."

"Not this."

"Fucking Christ, Doug, let me go *now*."

He stood his ground. "You put your name to a contract and we might get Nicky back, but you'll lose Terry for sure. We already know what we need to find him. Trust me... we can do this without any more agency help. We *have* to."

"We?"

"You're not going without me. This may be the last time we ever work together, and I want it to count."

"It'll count," I promised. "It'll count in spades."

Terry

I laid on the bed in nothing but a bathrobe, curled into a ball. It felt like there was a giant knot in my belly, pulling tighter with each breath. From the time Chip left with Doug I hadn't been able to do more than shower and pull the robe back on. When Kris offered to take care of Nicky's room I jumped at the chance, knowing I wouldn't be able to face his things just yet. In only four hours, since the moment I found his bed empty, the world had come crashing down on me and I was suffocating.

Chip was too calm from the outset. I wondered why—

and not without some anger—he wasn't raving like a lunatic and ready to explode. It was what I expected and what I wanted: an outraged, frenzied father desperate for his son. Instead, he stood there and watched with cold calculation total strangers tear apart our son's room. Life was collapsing around us and he was promising to take care of it. It was a certain promise; he would bring my baby home.

He hadn't said a word to the men who set about destroying Nick's room. He watched them like a hawk, but hadn't asked for names, hadn't thanked them. He never questioned what they were doing.

When Chip did come home I felt like that knot was about to pull and suddenly snap. I heard the front door open, and his hushed voice speaking to Kris, but there was no happy gurgling or even tired crying that told me Nicky was with him.

I pulled myself off of the bed and headed for the other room, and when I saw Chip standing there, my heart broke all over again.

Chip

Terry stood in the bedroom doorway, her eyes filling with tears, and my gut lurched. She expected me to be there with her son in my arms, and nothing I could say was going to change that. Now I had to tell her that someone she once loved was trying to destroy her.

How to do that without sending her over the edge?

"We know who took him."

She flew into my arms, burying her face against my chest. There was a flicker of an instant where she didn't want to know anymore than I wanted to have to tell her, but when I pulled her down to the couch, my arms still around her, she had to ask.

My mouth and lips went dry. "We can find him, Terry, but we need some information from you."

Astonished, she pulled away. "Me? Why?"

"Because you're the only one who knows him," I said cautiously. "We need to know everything we can about Matt Rhuele."

"This isn't possible," she blurted out, eyes wide with doubt. "He wouldn't do this. He couldn't. Chip, he was hurt when he realized I hadn't waited for him to come back, but he's not insane. You can't be serious!"

"You told me once when he was fixated on something he didn't let go."

"No!" she yelled. "Goddammit, you try again and this time come up with the right person!"

"Terry, stop," Doug was saying, reaching out for her before she could lunge at me. "He's telling you the truth. His thumbprint was on the rattle. DMV records coughed up the name Alvin Matthew Rhuele. It's not a mistake."

She stared at me angrily, jaw set. When I didn't look away, she let herself fall against me, head on my shoulder. "What," she said after a long time and without lifting her head, "do you need to know?"

"For starters, I need the most recent picture you have of him. And anything you can tell us about his family and friends. Anything, Terry."

"Okay." She sat up, brushing tears from her face. "Just ask me something and I'll try to answer."

I pulled away, sliding off the couch to sit on the hearth. I needed some distance so that I could think clearly.

"Where was he born?"

"San Francisco."

"Parents?"

"I think his mother is still in town. His father is dead."

"Brothers or sisters?"

She shook her head. "Only child."

"Friends? Any particular place he liked to hang out, maybe?"

She tried hard to think. "We had a lot of the same friends, but I didn't keep in touch with most of them and I don't know that he would, either. We all used to hang out at Scandia to play video games and miniature golf, but I think everyone outgrew that. He might not have, I don't know."

"What about hobbies?"

"Why? What good is that?"

"Hobbies," I repeated sternly.

She glared at me, understanding that I wasn't sitting there as the concerned husband and father, and she didn't like it at all. "I don't know… he liked music and sang some. He played around with motorcycles all the time, trying to take them apart and put them back together." She stopped to think. "He liked poker. Football. Baseball."

I looked to Doug for help, but all he did was shrug. "What about his mother's name?" I asked.

She thought for a moment. "Anne, I think."

"Anne Rhuele. It's a start." I turned to Doug. "We just have to decide what we tell people as we go along. We can't tell anyone the truth."

Terry's eyes shot open wide. "Wait a minute. What do you mean, tell people? You're not doing this, Chip."

"I am," I said firmly.

"The police…"

"Know nothing about this," I said. "We never reported it to them and we're not going to. I want Nick back *now*, Terry, and I know you do, too. Doug and I can find him long before the police could."

"I don't want to risk anything happening to you, too," she said in a small voice.

"I know what I'm doing, Terry. I'll find Matt, and I'll bring our son home. Today. I promised you that."

"We really can do this," Doug told her.

"What if he's hurt Nicky?"

"Then I'll kill him."

I dragged an old footlocker out of the back of the bedroom closet, pushing it across the floor. I'd never understood why I felt pressed to keep all the accumulated junk; when I put the lock on it I was certain I'd never need any of it again.

"You don't need a cover," I told Doug, "but I do. This guy knows what I look like and I need to be as far removed from that as I can. I don't want him to spot me first and run before I have a chance to catch him."

I dug into the locker pulled out an old leather motorcycle jacket, handing it to Doug. "Long time since I saw you in this," he said absently.

"You can wear it if you want." I dug down to the bottom of the locker and pulled out a pair of jeans so faded they were almost white, and a denim jacket that hadn't had sleeves on it since I was seventeen. "This one is mine."

"Tell you what," Doug grunted, trying the jacket on for size, "we sure won't win ourselves any fashion awards."

"That's okay," I muttered, "I already know I'm pretty." I dug into the front pocket for the knife I knew would be there. I held it up, and with the blink of an eye the blade popped open. "If this fuckup has harmed a single hair on my son's head…"

"Are you *sure* you want to do this?" Doug asked.

"Do you want to tell Terry we changed our minds, there's something better to do than patch her heart back together?"

"I know. It was just your chance to bow out and let someone from the agency do it."

"Not a chance... but I will borrow money from the agency."

He looked at me, puzzled.

"You gotta pay for information," I told him. "Nothing is free."

Terry

"I wonder what they're doing."

I sat on the floor with my back to the sofa, trying to hold myself together and not curl up in a little ball on floor. Kris handed me a cup of hot tea and sat across from me, propped up on pillows against the hearth. "I imagine," she said, sipping carefully, "that they're driving the streets around Matt's apartment or his mother's house, probably scaring the hell out of anyone watching them go by. Just don't worry about them... they can handle this."

"I went past worry before they left. I hit terrified about fifteen minutes ago."

"They'll find him."

I set the cup on an end table. "I just can't believe Matt would do this. He used to be crazy in a fun kind of way, but not this..."

"That was a long time ago," Kris said. "People change. Just look at your own husband—he's turned around a hundred and eighty degrees in just the last couple of years. You would have hated him six months before you met him."

I looked up at her. "I had the nasty feeling before he left that I was seeing some of that and I didn't like it. He almost looked happy."

"No, not happy," she said thoughtfully. "Chip's always been able to just step outside himself and into what ever façade he was creating, at least when it came to working."

"But he looked so..." I fumbled for the right word.

"Tough? He is tough."

"Not tough. Scary. He looked like all those guys that make you want to duck into a really crowded store to avoid. If I ran into him on the street looking like that, I'd be terrified. I sure wouldn't trust him."

She nodded, knowing exactly what I meant. "He didn't look like a businessman, did he? Even his friends and employees wouldn't recognize him without a second or third look. That's the whole idea."

Chip didn't shave, and while Doug went out to make last minute arrangements, Kris cut his hair brutally short. With his hair that short and a bandanna wrapped around his head, the sleeveless jacket and tight jeans, even I barely recognized him. The look in his eyes was completely different.

"What bothers me is that he seemed to enjoy it," I said. "All the planning and the disguising... he seemed completely comfortable with it."

"He is. It was his entire life for six years. Hell, the Charybdis was only a cover in the beginning, Terry. The agency built it for him. He got a crash course in small business management and had to step into that like it was just another assignment."

"Chip barely talks about that part of his life. I want to know more about what he did. I want an idea of what to expect."

Kris stared at me for a long time, and then nodded. "All right, but I doubt you're going to like it."

"I don't have to like it. I just have to know.

~

"*I'm making this official and I want no loose ends. Until this is fully resolved you'll suspend your regular activities and follow them.*"

"*Objective?*"

"*When they recover the boy I want his abductor to become a nonissue. No loose ends.*"

"*Why? Chip is likely to take care of this on his own. All of it.*"

"*No. Your job is to make sure the only thing he walks away with is his son. We don't want him tied to this any further than he needs to be. If he needs an alibi we'll create one for him. He's a potentially valuable asset to this agency and I want him viewing us favorably.*"

"*He's suppose to be free of all this.*"

"*As long as you hold up your end of it, he will be. But I won't risk him having a reason to refuse us the use of his considerable talents should you fail.*"

"*I won't.*"

"*Use whatever means you feel necessary. We'll have a team follow for cleanup when you give the word.*"

Chip

Matt Rhuele's apartment was occupied by a young couple and their two grown Rottweilers, both of which were promised to be trained to attack should we choose to step any further toward the door.

We chose not to.

We climbed back into Doug's convertible and drove slowly towards Anne Rhuele's address. I stared off to the side as he drove, and everywhere I looked there were families with small children, smiles punctuated by laughter and little hands reaching up to be held. We drove by the park and marching in a neat little row were five or six ducklings that I swore looked exactly like Quackers.

And everywhere we went I saw blonde baby boys that made me turn for a second look.

Anne Rhuele's house was half a block from the park, less than a mile from the apartment Terry had moved into and where she made space for me not even a year later. It was painted robin's egg blue and was bordered by brightly colored petunias that had grown like weeds, spilling from their beds and covering half the yard. As Doug knocked on the door I kept a wary eye out for bees.

"Mrs. Rhuele?" I said when the door began to creak open. "My name is Jeremy... I'm looking for Matt."

"Matt?" She opened the door all the way, eyeing me suspiciously. "Are you friends of his?"

I shook my head. Anne Rhuele was not what I expected. She didn't look any older than forty, maybe forty five, and was a slight, pretty woman with a dash of mischief in her eyes. Somehow I had expected her to be older and less than plain. "No ma'am," I replied carefully. "Just acquaintances. We were hoping we could find him here."

"What do you want with him?" she asked, her gaze shifting to Doug, who had wisely left the leather jacket in the car.

"We owe him some money," Doug told her.

"Yes," I agreed. "Matt did some work on my bike a long time ago and I didn't have the cash to pay him then. We went by his apartment but there's someone else living there now. Your name was in the phone book... I was hoping we'd get lucky and he'd be here."

"Matt fixed your bike?" She smiled softly and invited us inside. "You know, he probably doesn't expect you to pay him. He's like that, he'll do odd jobs but he doesn't want anything for it."

I nodded, wondering if she had any idea what her son was capable of. "Yes, ma'am, but I won't feel right until he gets exactly what he's due."

"I wish I could help you. Matt moved to San Francisco several months ago and I rarely hear from him. The last time he called he was going to move into a new apartment but he never called back to tell me the address."

"When did he move?" Doug asked casually, looking at the pictures lining her walls.

"Oh, it must have been seven or eight months ago. He found a job down there, said it was less painful than staying here."

I fidgeted restlessly. Eight months ago—he had probably been planning this from the moment Nick's birth announcement hit the newspaper. "Do you know where he works?" I asked. "It would be worth the drive down there to surprise him."

"Of course," she replied cheerfully. "He's a mechanic at Jolson's garage. It's somewhere downtown." She reached out for my hands, turning them over in her own, looking at them. "You're not a mechanic, are you? Your hands aren't stained the way my son's are."

"No ma'am. I don't fix things, I break them."

Doug snorted. "That's an understatement."

"Mrs. Rhuele," I said, forcing a smile, "could you get us the address of the garage? It would be a big help."

We both smiled politely as she left the room. How a woman that nice could raise a son so sadistic was beyond me.

"Check this out," Doug said, voice hushed. He pointed to the wall of pictures he was looking at, and my eyes settled on the one he wanted me to see. It was Terry, looking hardly any different, with her arms comfortable around Matt's waist. Senior prom, I thought. She loved him and he was less than three weeks away from breaking her heart.

"Do you know her?" his mother asked as she came back into the room.

I almost blurted out, hell yes, that's my wife, but bit it back. "No," I lied. "Just admiring her."

She went over and gazed at the picture. "She should be my daughter in law by now, but my son—God only knows what he was thinking. He still hasn't forgiven himself for letting her get away, especially after she went and married some boy she barely knew. She was such a nice girl."

Yeah lady, I thought bitterly, she still is and your son is trying to destroy her. "I suppose I'd be kicking myself too if I let a girl like that slip through my fingers. She looks special."

Doug tapped my shoulder. "Come on. We'd better go if you want to get down to San Francisco before the garage closes."

I turned to Anne. "Thank you, Mrs. Rhuele," I said, wishing her life wasn't going to be ripped apart when this was all over. "You've been a huge help, and I think Matt will be very surprised to see me again."

Kris

"I told you about Chip helping me out before, when I was almost raped." We still sat on the floor, lights dim. I felt like I was telling ghost stories to a group of girl scouts around a campfire, and the only thing missing was the smell of charred hot dogs and gooey marshmallows. "Not too long after that we had an assignment in Germany and Doug's cover was blown. He was caught before he could make his pickup… We were technically supposed to just leave him behind and let another team try to get him later, but Chip wouldn't leave without him.

"Terry, you wouldn't believe the balls he had... Doug was under guard and Chip walked up like he was some tourist asking for directions—in the middle of a secured building—and managed to get to the room where Doug was being held. He kicked out the window, they jumped out..."

I hesitated, and she was hanging on every word.

"Terry, they jumped out of this window and ran, had a storm of guards flying after them with guns aimed, and Chip tossed a grenade right into the middle of everything. Doug says it went off and blood was flying everywhere. It was damn near raining teeth, and Chip never looked back.

Chip

"Excuse me," Doug said, pushing open the grungy door to the garage office. "I'm looking for Matt Rhuele."

The man sitting behind the desk looked up, annoyed at the interruption. "Who?"

I walked in behind Doug. "Matt Rhuele," I repeated for him. "He works, here, doesn't he?"

Tony—according to his name tag—got up from his desk and pushed his way past us. He looked out into the work bay and then shook his head. "We got a guy here named Rhuele but the guys call him Cougar. But he's not here today."

My gut started to twist. "Where is he?"

Tony shrugged. "Called in sick. Who the hell knows? Flu's going around but I'd bet my left nut he's sleeping off a bender."

I wanted to pound my fist through the wall. "We need to find him. It's important."

"Yeah, I'll bet it is." He pulled the front door open to

answer a service bell.

Doug followed him out. "Yeah, it is. I owe him some money."

Tony started pumping the gas, keeping one eye on Doug. "For what?"

"Rebuilt engine for my bike."

"Uh huh." Tony was chuckling to himself as he counted out change for his customer. "He rebuilt your frigging engine and didn't collect."

"I didn't have the cash," Doug went on. "He told me I could bring it to him here."

"Yeah right. What the fuck do you want from me?"

"Just tell us where we can find him," I spoke up.

"For all I know he owes you not the other way around. You could be looking to collect. I'm not flipping the guy over just because you say so."

Doug threw his arms up as if he were disgusted. "Shit. Can I at least use the can?"

Tony nodded in the general direction of the garage. "Knock yourself out."

"Look," I grumbled, "if we wanted anything from him we sure wouldn't be standing here talking to you. Just give me his phone number... I'll call him and tell him to meet me here, you can keep an eye on us."

"Not a chance."

"Fine, *you* call him and tell him he has people waiting here."

I was about to pull out my wallet in hopes that a bribe might work when Doug came jogging out of the service station. "Just leave him a note," he told me. "He can find us if he wants his money."

"Can you do that much?" I glared at Tony and then

scribbled a phony name and number onto a scrap of paper he thrust at me. "If he doesn't call me by tomorrow, the job was free."

"I'll tack it to his timecard," he grumbled, walking away.

"And what the hell was that?" I asked Doug when we were back in the car. "Leave a goddamned note?"

"Doesn't matter," he said as he gunned the engine. "I got a look at his time card while I was supposed to be in the can. We don't need anything from this whiz. I got Matt's address."

The address Doug scrounged off the timecard turned out to be an old apartment building. Until that point, when we rounded a corner with expectations of the heavens opening and sunbeams pouring out over our destination, I kept telling myself it was all too easy, too frigging easy.

Doug pulled over to the side of the road and parked, staring at the ugly brick building on the other side of the street. I hated to think of my son here, in the grime and filth of a neighborhood long abandoned by families looking for their own slice of America in the heart of the city. "Son of a bitch," he muttered, pulling himself out from behind the wheel to sit on the top of the bench seat, staring out over the windshield. "There was no goddamned apartment number on that card."

"But we've narrowed it down," I mumbled.

"So what's next, Einstein? Go knock on every damned door in the building and hope we find him before a neighbor tips him off?"

"Presuming his mother hasn't already."

"We better hope she was solid about not having his number."

"She thinks her kid is a goddamned little angel. No reason for her to tip him off, not unless she pulled one over on us both, and I'm not that gullible."

He looked away from the building. "But are you that desperate?"

"I've been desperate before. Never sloppy." I squinted against the bright light, scrutinizing every window facing us from the apartment building, hoping to find one that had been covered with foil or cardboard, some sign that whoever was inside didn't want anyone looking in.

"We can't just sit here, Chip. We're way too obvious."

"Won't have to." I nodded towards the glass doors of the building. "Check out the number coming our way." I hopped up on the top of the seat next to Doug, whistling loudly.

"Jesus, Chip! What the hell—she's a hooker!"

"And not a half bad looking one, either. Get out." I swung my legs over the car door, landing on the sidewalk, and then leaned against the car. She walked over to us with an exaggerated slowness, obviously checking us both out.

"Two at a time, boys?"

"Something like that," I said, grinning. I met her gaze, hoping the long lingering look would work well enough to keep her from flipping me off and walking away.

"So," she said, glancing at Doug, "what'll it be and where?"

I looked around. There was a coffee shop within sight of the building. "For starters," I said, thumbing towards the shop, "food. We're starving. We can work the details out there."

"It's your money." She turned and headed in with me just a stride behind her. Doug moaned, heaved a good oh-what-the-fuck sigh, and followed.

We sat on either side of her at the table, a circular booth that was just dim enough to provide a little privacy and gave us a clear view of the building, but too dirty to even think about actually ordering food. Doug shifted nervously, eyes darting between the window and the hooker.

"So what's your name?" I asked, sliding my arm onto the seat behind her.

"You can call me Candy," she said, a blink away from rolling her eyes. "All boys like candy, don't they?"

"Sure," I replied, slow and deliberate. "I used to eat candy all the time."

Doug coughed and looked away.

"What about you?" she asked him.

"I'm a diabetic."

He glared at me over her head with a look that asked why I didn't just stick my tongue up her nose, it would be just as gross. I reached into my jacket pocket and fished out the picture of Matt that Terry had found stuck in a battered old paperback on the bookshelf. "Candy, do you know this guy?"

"Shit!" She tried to make a run for it, but found herself held down on both sides. "Fucking cops!"

"No," Doug said. "Not even close."

"Just take it easy." I relaxed my grip on her arm and flashed the picture again. "We just want to buy some time from you. We're not cops. All we need to know is if you know him, and where we can find him if you do."

She was trembling, nervous eyes darting between us. "Maybe."

"His name's Rhuele. You might know him as Alvin or Matt or Cougar."

"What do you want with him?"

"I just need to talk to the man," I told her. "It's nothing heavy."

The light bulb over Doug's head finally went off. "Candy, you're all right. The only thing we need from you is to know where he is. You know him, don't you? Otherwise you wouldn't be squirming right now."

"I know a lot of guys."

"Come on," I urged. "Just be straight with us and I'll make it worth your while." I took out my wallet, slowly pulling out one of the hundred dollar bills Doug borrowed from the agency. Her eyes were glued on it, wide open with horror when I tore it in half. "Take this."

She reached out and took the half I offered.

"You tell us what we need to know, and the other half is yours. Simple as that."

Candy watched as the other half of the bill disappeared into my pocket. She didn't have to think long. "All right, I know him. He lives across the hall from me, moved in just a couple weeks ago."

Hope suddenly surged through me. "Is he alone?"

Puzzled, she shrugged. "Well, yeah. Why?"

"It's important," Doug told her. He saw me swallow hard and knew I was close to pounding my head into the table. "Does he ever have anyone with him?"

"He had his little boy with him this morning, but that's it. He's just a baby."

I grabbed her face and kissed her cheek hard. "Candy, you're priceless." I gave her the other half of the hundred, and pulled out four more, tearing them in half. "If he's there, you get the other half of these. Which apartment?"

Sighing, she took the rest of the money. "Two B. Go through the door and up the landing, it'll be the second door on the right."

I slid out of the booth, leaning both hands into the table. "Wait here... if we find him, I'll be back with the rest of your cash."

She waved us off, doubting she would ever see the rest of that money, but she'd stay there and wait, just in case.

Terry

The mental picture I was developing was somewhat fuzzy, overlaid with the picture of Chip as I knew him and Chip as Kris described. The images meshed, but were just off center enough that I had a hard time seeing it all. "It's not that it's so hard to believe," I told Kris, "but it just doesn't feel real. I'm not even sure I can explain it."

"You don't have to. Even when you're living that life it feels surreal most of the time. Chip was just better at it than the rest of us. I really don't think he cared whether he lived or died... maybe that gave him the extra edge. I don't know... he was too young to hurt so much."

She stirred her tea slowly, watching it swirl in the cup. "You know," she continued, "he's had a damned hard life, but most of it has been his own doing."

"I thought his stepfather was more to blame. You should see the scars."

"I have seen them. Has he ever told you how they got there?"

I could see them in my mind, crisscrossing his chest, and the perfect white line that ran from nipple to nipple. "All he's ever said is that Grant is responsible. He couldn't even tell me what the fight was about."

"I don't think he's proud of it," she said. "Hell, he may not remember exactly. It's easier to swallow when you forget the particulars. Much less painful that way."

"I want to know why that son of a bitch mutilated my husband."

"I'd hardly call a few scars mutilation."

"Don't quibble over verbs. Adverbs. Nouns. Whatever… Just get on with it."

Kris pursed her lips thoughtfully, either debating whether or not to tell me or taking the time to dredge up the story from cobweb filled memories. She set the tea aside. "You know Chip and Grant never got along. Even when Chip was just a tiny thing they fought constantly. They both had these wide stubborn streaks and neither could give in… Anyway, when Chip was fourteen they had a real ripper of a fight and Chip ran away from home. Both Grant and Ron spent a week scouring half the state looking for him. They checked everywhere, friends, the hospitals, the police… even looked in the morgue."

"Where was he?"

"No one knew except Chip and he's never said. But his mother came home one afternoon and saw his stuff in the living room so she ran upstairs and bolted into his bedroom…" She broke off, raising her eyebrows uncertainly. "Are you sure you want to hear this?"

"Go on."

"Pat barged into his room and found him there with his sixteen year old girlfriend."

"Oh come on. He was only fourteen."

"I know," she nodded. "And I doubt that was the first time, either. In any case, he had the good sense to get the girl out of the house."

I gulped down the rest of my tea, now just lukewarm and with so much sugar it was like sludge going down. Fourteen. At that age I was barely aware of the boys around me and would have indulged my fantasies as just a chaste kiss on the cheek. "Where do the scars come in?"

"According to Ron, Pat suffered chest pains off and on for years, at least as long as he had known her and that was from her late teens. After Chip took off with his girlfriend she had a heart attack. She died before Grant could get her to the hospital."

"God..."

"Grant went nuts. The longer he waited for Chip to get home the more nuts he went, and when he did"—she made slashing motions with her hand—"he literally tore into Chip. He must have realized immediately what he'd done, because he had Chip at the ER within ten minutes."

"God, what they both must have gone through." I slowly shook my head, mentally running my fingers over those familiar ridges. "And they've hated each other all these years."

"Grant doesn't hate Chip."

"What?"

"He cares about Chip. Why do you think he didn't kick Chip out of his house after that? Even knowing he was someone else's son, he always made a home for him. The blame ended when he dropped the knife. Grant doesn't blame Chip, Chip blames Chip, and if he'd stop feeling so damned sorry for himself, he might realize that."

She reached for her tea again and added, "He's always used his bad relationship with Grant as an excuse for his recklessness. Sometimes I even believe him, but it's the only thing he wants to see."

"Chip is convinced Grant despises him," I said, head spinning. "It hurts him."

"Does a man who calls his worst enemy and pleads for a teenager's safety sound like a man who hates that kid? When

Chip left home Grant practically dropped to his knees and begged Ron to take him in, to the point he offered us a whole lot of cash to support him. We didn't take it, but Grant was terrified what would happen to Chip if he was on his own too early... Ron screwed it up in less than a month anyway."

Suddenly cold, I drew my knees up and wrapped my arms around them. It didn't help. "Look at him now. He stepped right back into the game without batting an eye."

"What does it matter," she asked, "as long as he finds your son?"

"What about when he comes home, Kris? What if he can't step away from it as easily as he steps into it?"

"Don't worry about it," she told me. "Just think about getting Nicky home."

Shadows care where they go. They do what they have to, but God, they care why.

He watched Chip and Doug run into the building across the street, whispering to himself, dear God, this is the only one that really matters.

Chip

I raced across the street, fueled by pure exhilaration. Doug nearly ripped the glass entryway door off its hinges and we both bounded up the three stairs of the landing; I started to reach for the doorknob but stopped just short of turning it. The man had just committed a felony, I reminded myself; there was no way that door would be unlocked. Even if it were, I couldn't run the risk of my son being in the arms of a suddenly startled and potentially armed psychopath.

"I'm pulling off to the side," I whispered. "I don't want him to see me through that peephole. You knock... say anything that will get him to open that door. Once it's open, we've got him."

Doug positioned himself in front of the door and I plastered myself to the wall to the left, knife twitching in my left hand. "Doug, this guy is huge, at least six-five and about two forty. He can squash you like a bug. When he starts to open the door, just get out of my way."

He nodded his agreement, acquiescing to my size and strength.

"Do it!" I whispered.

His fist pounded on the hollow wood, echoing in the empty hallway. He waited a moment and then knocked again, more insistent.

"Who is it?" A sleepy voice, irritated.

"Tony sent me from the garage," Doug answered, mind racing to stay one step ahead. "Wants me to see if you're all right, see if you need a doctor or something."

"Crap," the soft swear came. "Can't a guy take one lousy day off?"

I readied myself, hearing the fumbling of the lock and chain on the other side. Doug watched me from the corner of his eye, and when the door creaked open, he stepped aside. I spun in, catching Matt square in the center of his chest with the heel of my palm, sending him flying back.

"What the fuck?" he grunted, landing hard on the floor.

I reached him in one angry stride, grabbed the front of his shirt and lifted him off the floor. My fists seemed to move in slow motion, Matt's head bobbing with each blow. When I pinned him to the wall I saw Doug out of the corner of my eye opening doors, searching for Nicky.

"You tell me what the fuck you've done with my kid," I growled, hand closing around his neck, blood engorged veins popping out on his skin. "Tell me why you son of a bitch. Why the hell did you take my son?"

I loosened my grip, just a little, smashing his head against the wall once, hard.

Tears were streaming down his face, each breath an exercise in agony. "You have Terry," he sobbed, his voice coming out in barely understandable squeaks. "I'll never have her the way..." He was flailing at me weakly.

I slammed him back once more. "Not fucking good enough." I squeezed harder, looking at him through red clouded eyes.

"I just"—he tried vainly to suck in a deep breath—"wanted a small part of her."

Digging my fingers hard into his neck, I lifted him off the ground and slammed my knee into his groin, refusing to let him crumple to the floor. The knee jerked up again, and again. I flipped the knife open with my free hand, holding it inches away from the terrified eyes staring back at me. "You want to feel the pain you caused her? I can carve it in you."

"God... no," he barely whispered. "No."

"Your momma thinks you're a good boy, did you know that?" I snarled, wanting more than anything to run the blade across his face. I wanted blood to pay for Terry's pain. My pain. "Maybe I should dump your body on her doorstep. So she gets the message."

"Please... no."

"Shut up!" I lifted him forward, only to slam him back again. "You're paying for this, you little prick."

I had the knife under his chin, all it would have taken was a flick of the wrist to draw it across his throat, or up through his jaw.

It was the soft, satisfied baby belch that lifted the cloud

of rage, and the sound of Doug's voice telling me, "Chip, no. Not in front of Nick."

Rage drained from me like water from a broken bucket and I let go of Matt slowly. I closed the knife and shoved it into my pocket, surprised that Matt stayed on his feet, his back glued to the wall in terror.

Doug brought Nick from the back room and gently, reluctantly, handed him to me. He smelled like fresh fruit and baby powder, eyes blurry from being woken, one thumb jammed into his mouth.

"What now?" Doug asked, gesturing to Matt.

I could barely take my eyes off my son. "Leave him," I whispered. "Just leave him."

"I'll take care of him."

We both turned with a start toward the door. Ron stood there with fire dancing in his eyes and a small crossbow dangling casually from his hand. This was the hobby, the toy made from scratch that he was sure would work. Every detail his own.

"Take your boy and go," he ordered, his eyes fixed on the man cowering ten feet away. He never looked at me, though his eyes flicked for a bare second to Nicky.

Doug took my arm and propelled me through the door. As we ran down the landing we could hear Matt's frenzied pleading, the terror that swallowed every word. The sound, when it came, was not unlike the sick, wet thud of a watermelon being tossed off the balcony to the pavement below. It made me shudder, not because it was over, but because of the look in Ron's eyes.

"Don't forget about Candy," Doug reminded me once we were outside.

I drew a deep breath and nodded. She was still there,

waiting impatiently, staring into a small mirror as she fixed her makeup. I placed the remaining halves of the cash on the table, sliding onto the seat next to her.

"Thanks"—she stopped, looking straight at Nick. "What the hell are you doing with Cougar's baby?"

Doug jumped into the booth beside her, pinning her in once more. "He's not Cougar's son."

She looked at Nicky, and then up at me. Nick was resting with his head on my shoulder, fingers absently toying with the collar on my jacket. "He's yours, isn't he? That's what this was about."

"Yes," I said. "And we need for you to forget we were ever here, forget the whole thing. Forget about Cougar."

She was smiling at Nicky. "I can do that."

"In fact," I added, "it'd probably be best for you to not go near your apartment tonight. I'll pay for you to stay somewhere else."

"Hon," she said simply, "I work nights, unless you really haven't figured that out."

We left her and climbed into the car, Doug behind the wheel and me in the passenger seat, holding my son as close as I could. "This wasn't so bad," I murmured. "Only cost five hundred bucks."

Doug wasn't laughing when he turned to look at me. "Five hundred bucks? Hell, man, you'd have sold your soul if you had to."

I nodded grimly. "I know. My father sold his instead."

Doug

Nicky gurgled happily in spite of the fact that I had poked and probed nearly every inch of his body. He was quite content to sit naked on the exam table, slapping at anything that came within reach of his stubby little arms. We had been halfway home when Chip asked me to detour, to open the office and check Nick out before taking him to his mother.

"Just in case," he practically whispered.

"Perfectly happy, healthy nine month old boy," I pronounced, gently pulling the stethoscope out of Nicky's hands. "No bruises or scratches, no puncture marks, cuts, or evidence of invasion." I reached into the drawers under the table for a diaper. "You can dress him, just do it before he cuts loose on my table."

"Gladly." Chip eased Nick onto his back, lifting his legs to slide the diaper under him. "Well, little man, your mommy is going to be happy to see you."

"That's a slight understatement." I leaned over Nicky. "Your daddy doesn't have to stop at the twenty four hour Quickie Mart on the way home for a cup protector. Now mommy won't try to kick his balls up through his nose."

He took a playful swipe at my nose. "Oh shit."

"Yeah, Nicky," Chip laughed, "all the shit you want." He lifted his son off the table and was headed for the door when I stopped him, holding out my hands for Nick.

"As soon as you walk into that apartment, there's not another soul who will get to touch this boy for a week. I get to carry him to the car at least."

"Getting soft on us, doc?"

I laughed and kissed Nick on the forehead. "I've been real good about not sticking myself between you two since we found him. I want to hold my godson for five minutes."

"I owe you," Chip said seriously, locking the door behind us. "I mean it, Doug, I owe you my son's life. I couldn't have gone alone."

"Call it pay back for saving my ass so many times." I

handed Nick back to him at the car. "How much are we telling Terry?"

He didn't have to think. "Right up to the moment you found Nick in the bedroom. Nothing else happened. We'll figure out a way to keep the rest from her."

"Kris will want to know."

He settled Nick on his lap in the car. "Tell her. She has to know that they'd send someone to clean up this mess. I shouldn't have been so surprised... I *knew* they'd do this."

I started the engine and pulled out of the parking lot. "You knew," I said. "You just didn't count on it being Ron."

Chip

I wasn't sure what to expect when we came home, but I certainly didn't expect to throw the door open and find them both sprawled out on the living room floor, fast asleep. Somewhere in my mind was the image of Terry pacing the floor, wearing a path in the carpet, with Kris by her side, pleading for her to relax.

"So much for the hero's welcome," Doug chuckled.

"No kidding. They either had a hell of a lot of confidence in us, or none at all and terrified themselves into exhaustion."

Doug gazed down at Kris. She was curled in a tight little ball, clutching a pillow to her chest. "A little of both, maybe?"

I sat on the floor next to Terry with Nick in my lap. She was sound asleep but her face was still lined with worry, not resting even as tired as she was. I glanced at the clock over the mantel; it was after midnight. She'd been living on adrenaline since 7 a.m., a good 17 hours of terror.

Nicky leaned forward, reaching for her face. "Mommy honky."

I slid him off my lap and let him explore. He kneeled beside her head, fingers pulling at her lip. "Mommy honky," he repeated.

Doug laughed. "Where the hell did he learn that?"

Terry stirred, stretching her arms above her head. Nick crawled off toward Doug, pulling himself up using Doug's legs for balance. "Honky."

Suddenly, like a slap in the face, Terry's eyes shot open. "Honey, I'm home," I whispered, holding out my arms to catch her when she sprang up off the floor. "He was fine," I whispered against her hair. "Not a thing wrong with him."

She was crying again, wild heaving sobs that drew Kris awake and away from her pillow.

"It's okay, Terry, he's okay." I let her cling and cry for a moment, then pulled away. "Come on, I know you want to hold him."

Doug lifted him up just enough to set him on his hands and knees, patting him on the butt to get him to start crawling. He slapped his way across the floor and crawled into Terry's lap, ignoring her tight hug, still muttering "Mommy honky."

"Oh, God," she cried, "Nicky, just give Mommy a minute and she'll feed you, okay?"

Kris rolled to her knees and then got up. "You stay right there and hold onto that little man," she ordered. "Doug and I will invade your kitchen and find food for everyone."

Terry answered with a barely perceptible nod, one hand reaching for mine. She wanted her whole family close, and we sat there together on the floor, mixing tears with Nicky's exploring fingers and demands for food.

"I had no idea what he meant," I apologized. "I just thought he realized you were really white."

~

He stood in the phone booth, listening to the ring on the other end of the line, watching out the door as the last black car pulled away from the curb and disappeared into the night. Standing there he began to wonder just how much blood he truly had on his hands. Somewhere along the line he had lost count, and worse, he was beginning to not care. This one meant something, though, this was something he could connect with.

The ringing stopped and there was a pause.

"Maverick two," he said emotionlessly. "Objective complete." He hung up the phone and stood there, staring out at the street, wishing now more than ever that he could walk away and never look back.

They'd find him, though, and he had no desire to be the one stuck to a wall with an arrow through his head.

Doug

We stood in the kitchen for quite a while, staring into their pantry, trying to figure out what a nine month old baby eats in the middle of the night. Kris found boxes of cereal mix and jars of mushed up fruit, none of which we were convinced was the right thing to feed a kid who may not have eaten all day.

"Pancakes," she finally declared, and I knew better than to argue. He had four teeth; I would have made him a sandwich.

"You didn't miss much," I told her, reaching into the cupboard for plates. "Once we were pointed in the general direction, it only took a hooker to find him."

"Do I want to know?" she asked with a laugh.

"Her name was Candy," I said, trying not to laugh, too, "and she was sweet."

She was stirring the batter, using her elbow to point me to the right drawers for silverware. "So now you can honestly say you've paid a prostitute for services rendered. What happened after that?"

I set the forks on the table. "Christ, you should have seen Chip. He lit into this guy like a maniac and beat the snot out of him. I honestly think he intended to kill him. When I brought Nick out of the back room Chip had a knife at his throat and I'm pretty sure he was going to use it."

"That doesn't surprise me." She set the bowl aside. "How many people were there behind you waiting to finish it for him?"

"Just one."

She waited.

"Kris, it was Ron. Chip let this guy go and was ready to walk out of there with Nick and let him live... Ron walked through the door and ordered us out. So we left." I lifted my shoulders in a half shrug. I didn't have to say anything else.

She nodded as if she expected as much. "So it's really over, then. They don't have to worry about him coming back after Terry again?"

"Not in this lifetime."

"You're a good friend, Douglas Stone," she said quietly. She held out her arms and I stepped into them, sighing when she pulled me close. "I had a lot of time to think when you were gone. I honestly wasn't worried that you wouldn't come back without Nicky, or even coming back hurt, but the thought crossed my mind once or twice. It scared me."

"But Nicky's fine..."

"That's not it." She held on a little tighter, her breath warm on my shoulder. "You know, you have been so patient with me and put up with a lot of unreasonable demands... I have no right to keep sticking you in that position. It's always what I want and when I want it. I feel like a damned spoiled child, always getting my own way. We can't keep going on like this."

This is not something I want to hear, I thought dismally, dread starting to wash over me. "I told you I wouldn't put any pressure on you."

"And that's not fair to you." She lifted her head to look at me, her hand pressed to the stubble on my cheek. "In the long run, it's not fair to me, either."

"What, then?"

"You love Nick so much... you fawn over him like he was your own sometimes. I can't take away your chance to have that for yourself. I love you too much to hurt you like that."

"What are you saying?"

Her hand dropped from my face to my chest. "I'm going to have this baby, Doug. I just don't want to have it alone."

My hopes shot high again. "You won't. I'll be there, I swear."

"For how long? This is serious, Doug. We have to decide if we really want this much responsibility in our lives."

"You know how much I want. There's never been any question that I want it all."

"I need to hear it just one more time," she said.

"Kris," I breathed, holding her face between my hands, wondering if I hadn't fallen asleep out there on the floor with Nicky drooling all over me, hearing this just in a dream. "I love you. I want to spend the rest of my life with you. I want the whole bit, the house with a yard, a big ugly dog romping with our kids..."

"I hate dogs."

"Okay, then, a big ugly cat."

"I'm already thirty six, Doug."

"It's not too late. We can have it all if we really want it. There's not a thing standing in our way."

She waited, looking into my eyes.

"Marry me," I finally said.

She leaned forward, pressing her lips against mine. "Okay," she said, lips still touching. "Yes."

Kris

I'd never seen Doug pray, so I shared Chip's look of surprise when he asked if we would mind offering up some thanks before eating. Nick was digging his fingers into his food, his face already sticky from syrup, but there was no one at that table who would have asked him to please not go that route.

We all bowed our heads and listened to Doug's soft voice thank God for all the blessings in our lives, and the wisdom to be able to see the signs dangled in front of us. He prayed passionately, and when he was done there was a blanket of silence over the table.

Nick grabbed fists full of pancake and syrup, then leaned toward Chip. "Daddy kiss!" he demanded.

Chip smiled and leaned over to his son, who grabbed his face with both hands and planted a kiss on Chip's lips, leaving two perfect hand sized sticky prints on his days' growth of beard. "Daddy loves you, Nicky," he whispered to his son.

I glanced at Doug. He watched Chip nuzzle his son and allowed himself to see what he would have, sticky fingers and all.

~

Terry

"It's been a long day," Chip whispered, holding me close. We stood in the darkened bedroom; Chip and Doug had moved the crib next to our bed to appease any lingering fears I might have. We watched Nicky drift off, freshly bathed, his thumb stubbornly and firmly rooted in his mouth. "You should get some sleep, too, Terry."

"Not yet."

"Come on," he urged, trying to push me towards the bed. "You're exhausted. Just crawl into bed and I'll be there as soon as I shave."

I tightened my arms around his waist. His body was hot to the touch, and when I laid my face against his chest I could feel tiny beads of sweat pop up. "In a minute. Just let me hold you for a little bit."

His chest heaved with an exasperated sigh. "All right, I'll shave when I get up later. But get in bed... I can still hold you there."

I ruffled the stubble on his cheeks, still wet from the wash rag he'd used to wipe off the syrup, and climbed into bed, molding myself as close to him as I could. My hand automatically went back to his chest, tracing the scars, and for the moment all I could think about was how scared he must have been to come home to so much anguish and fear. The pain that provoked the attack was overwhelming; Chip had just come home at the wrong time. I doubted that his stepfather had ever intended to hurt him; he had been blinded by grief.

"I want to meet Grant," I said after a while.

Chip stiffened and jerked away. "What?"

"I mean it, Chip. It's time we buried old bones. You've both probably changed enough that you can make room for each other in your lives. Give him a chance to be someone for you for once. He's a lonely man... he doesn't even have his son."

"And whose fault is that? He sent Dave away, Terry. He didn't want to be bothered with his own flesh and blood, and Dave paid for it. The kid drugged himself into a stupor and took a header off a pier. Now you want me to crawl back there and offer Grant some kind of friendship?"

"I didn't say that."

"Then what do you want?"

"I want you to be as compassionate with him as you've learned to be with the rest of us. Maybe he's not the ogre you remember him to be."

"Just what makes you think that?"

I reached for his hand, winding my fingers through his. "Because you're not the ogre you used to be."

He closed his eyes and took a deep breath, exhaling in an exasperated half sigh. He had no argument.

"Just make the gesture, that's all I want."

His eyes opened, but he didn't say anything.

"Chip... your mother must have had a reason for loving him. Maybe you can find it."

"My mother," he pointed out abruptly, "was sleeping with two men at the same time for years, and they both knew about it. It wasn't your most conventional relationship."

"But there must have been something that made her stay with him," I argued. "Even after she had you, she stayed with him. Don't you want to know why?"

He relaxed and pulled me back into his arms. "I suppose." He lifted his head off the pillow to look at Nicky, who hadn't moved an inch. "We could have lost so much... That rattle you found was the only thing that gave us a clear line to him. I don't even want to think of what we would have been up against without it."

"You'd have found a way," I said, "though I'd hope you would have dressed a little better."

He laughed softly. "You loved it and you know it."

"All but the hair." I reached up and rubbed the top of his head. "I'll be glad when it grows out about an inch."

"I was thinking about just shaving my head."

"God, no," I laughed.

"Was just a thought." He lowered his face to mine and kissed me, long and very sweet. "Go to sleep already. It'll be daylight soon."

"You need sleep, too, mister, but I don't see you closing your eyes."

"I will," he promised, though I knew he would lay there and watch us both sleep until the sun was up and Doug or Kris was back to keep me company.

I fell asleep in his arms, feeling safe, thinking that there could never again be anything that could go wrong in our lives that would feel so horrible.

Chip

The house was pretty much like I remembered it: ostentatious, with perfectly lined and trimmed hedges, a lawn so green it looked as if it had been dyed, and brick that never seemed to age or get dirty. I stood on the long porch and looked out over the lawn; I could vaguely remember playing there with my brother, trying to teach him to catch a football, giving him a black eye when his hands slipped and the ball smashed into his face. The neighbors were always horrified to see us out there playing rough in the grass, complaining to our mother that we were making too much noise and leaving marks on the lawn; it looked bad for the neighborhood.

My mother didn't care.

On Dave's seventh birthday he asked for a pony; he didn't want to own the damn thing, he just wanted to ride a pony. Grant practically flipped the neighbors off and rented one, letting the owner lead Dave around the front yard for an hour, creating huge hoof shaped divots that sent the Chapman's next door into a near frenzy. This was an affluent neighborhood, after all. That sort of thing belonged in the middle class.

They were none too thrilled when I turned sixteen and bought a battered old Mustang, parking it on the street in front of the house. It desecrated the value of their precious and pretentious imports, but Grant never once suggested I move it or get rid of it. He seemed to enjoy any opportunity to irritate the wealthy snobs of the street.

The house was kept perfect, otherwise. You could balance anything on the tops of those bushes. Inside was so clean you could perform surgery on the kitchen floor. One tablespoon of spilled milk resulted in the entire floor being mopped; track two leaves in on a shoe and out came the vacuum cleaner. The only neutral zone was our bedrooms; if we wanted those to look like World War Three had just erupted, that was up to us. The floor of Dave's room was nearly always scattered with bits and pieces of whatever toy he had taken apart in hopes of discovering how it worked. Sometimes Grant would sit on the floor with him, trying to help him piece something back together, but he never complained about the broken things that were lost to Dave's curiosity.

Grant loved his son, and I could not understand why he'd sent him away.

I rang the doorbell, hoping no one would answer; at least then I'd be able to honestly tell Terry that I had tried. I had turned and was about to step off the porch when the slow creaking of the door hinges stopped me.

"Jeremy?"

"I was beginning to think you weren't home," I said, offering him my hand. "I would have called first... I wasn't sure you would see me."

"Ah, never." He beckoned me inside, leading me past the wide stairway to the family room. The first thing I noticed was the painting hanging over the fireplace.

"Do you remember it?" he asked. "I found it in the attic two years ago. I'd almost forgotten how beautiful your mother was."

I stood there, hands stuffed into my pockets, and stared at the woman holding her little boy. "So had I," I said.

Grant eased himself into the overstuffed chair that sat directly opposite the fireplace. "We never thought you'd sit still long enough to have the initial artwork done for that painting. There was always something else you had to be doing, even then."

"I never dreamed you'd hang that again," I told him, looking away from the image of my mother with her arms wrapped around me at an age not much older than Nicky. "After she died I thought I'd seen the last of it."

"Anger shouldn't last forever," he said, barely loud enough for me to hear. He looked sad, and as Terry suspected he would, very lonely.

I sat in the old leather chair next to Grant. For a man his age he looked too old. He was only what, I wondered? Maybe fifty five? He looked at least sixty, hair gray and skin sagging.

Everything was still in its place. All the little things that my mother had collected, the knick knacks and trinkets that

Grant had proclaimed to be a waste of time sat carefully on shelves, dutifully dusted. The only thing different was the portrait, which had been put away days after she died. Grant hadn't been able to bear the sight of her holding her son.

"How's the baby?" he asked suddenly.

"He's one of the reasons I'm here."

"He's all right isn't he?" He struggled to sit more upright, his voice tinged with panic. "What's wrong?"

That urgency surprised me. "He's fine. We just wanted you to see him, that's all. I was hoping you would come to dinner tonight, spend some time getting to know my wife and my son."

A tentative smile crossed his face. "Really now."

"I wouldn't be here otherwise," I said, wondering where all his fire was, the cruel barbs that tended to haunted me now and then. The old man sitting there was nothing close to the monster in my dreams. "Look, like it or not, you and I have a past. It's time we reconciled it and tried to get along. My little boy needs a grandfather and I won't cheat him out of that."

"You have a father," he said flatly.

"That's not the point. I want Nick to know you both. You're a key part of my past and I won't hide that from him." I looked up at the portrait again. "Maybe you can be the kind of grandfather to Nicky that you were as a father to Dave when he was little."

"I would like to see him," he said. "I don't want to cause problems for you, though. I know I put you through pain, Jeremy. I don't expect to be forgiven for it."

That was not what I expected from him. "Like you said… anger shouldn't last forever."

"No," he quietly agreed, his eyes following mine to the

painting. I wondered how much of his time was spent sitting there staring at it. "I wish your mother could see you now. She would be so proud of you."

"I wonder." She would have hated the choices I had made in my life, despised some of the things I had done.

"She was always proud of you, son. Thought you were strong and sure of yourself. I don't think there was a time when you didn't know what it is you wanted, and every time you went after it. She admired that in you. I think I did, too, though it scared me."

"I'm sorry."

"Sorry?" Grant looked over at me. "It was my problem, not yours. Perhaps if I'd been more patient…"

"I wasn't an easy kid to raise," I admitted.

"You had a temper," he agreed, "and you were stubborn and too smart for your own good. But you were never a problem."

The question that had bubbled in the back of my brain for years suddenly popped out. "Why did you let me stay here, Grant? You could have sent me to live with Ron the day she died."

"God, Jeremy, you don't cast out the people you love, even when it hurts."

That revelation was a kick in the head. I was out of the chair and standing in front of him. "You hate me."

He was shaking his head. "I know that's what you think," he said. "You were never ready to hear any different. You were just too angry."

I went over to the window, staring out at the tree that had frightened me most nights as a child. What was I supposed to think, or what was I supposed to feel? The fighting had always been intense and kept me constantly on edge. If there was love there, why had I never seen it?

"I don't expect you to feel any different than you always have," he said as if reading my mind. "The only thing left in this world that I want is for you to be happy. I don't expect anything from you."

I turned back, leaning on the wall by the window. "I am happy," I said. "I have more than I deserve. The last couple of years have been damned good to me. But you still haven't said if you'll come tonight. Terry is counting on it."

"I would never disappoint a beautiful woman," he said. "Of course I'll be there. It'll do me good to get out of this house for something besides work for a while. It's too damned quiet here."

"I'm surprised you never moved."

"I wanted to," he said, pulling himself out of the chair. "Several times. There's just something about this house I couldn't give up."

"All things considered, I'd think you'd want to get rid of all the reminders."

He was beside me, looking out the window. "Do you see the gouges in that tree?" he asked, pointing to the ugly gray slashes in the bark. "You did that when you were about ten years old. You took an ax out of the garage and wanted to cut the tree down, and would have if it hadn't been so hard. But if you look up," he tilted his head and tried to see a point past the ceiling, "you can see what's left of the tree house you tried to build just two years later."

Another cause for the neighborhood to get its collective shorts in a bunch.

"There are hundreds of little things like that around this house, Jeremy. Those are the reminders that I hang on to."

I left half an hour later not knowing what to think about

my stepfather.

He had tried to kill me. How could he think he ever loved me?

I stretched out on the bench, one shoulder pressed up against the cold metal lockers. Beads of sweat dripped from every pore in my body and every muscle was screaming at me. "Tell me why," I groaned, wiping sweat from my face with my shirt, "do I punish myself like this? There has to be a reason I torture myself."

"Because," Doug said as he pulled off his shoes, "you want to keep Terry lusting after your body."

"Terry would lust after a two by four if it had all the right working parts." I groaned, forcing myself to sit upright. "I should have just gone to bed when Kris showed up this morning. I think I slept for fifteen minutes."

"Terry get any sleep?"

I nodded. "As long as she could hear Nicky breathing right next to her, she was fine. I stayed up just in case she woke up and freaked out."

"How's she doing today? Clinging to Nick?"

"A little. I think she'll be okay, though."

"Give it a few days," he suggested, reaching into his locker for a towel. "It may not have fully sunk in yet. Don't be surprised if it does and she falls apart for a day or two."

"Nothing she does surprises me anymore. I've given up trying to figure out how her mind works."

"Is this something kinky I want to hear about?"

I detailed my meeting with Grant, and told him about Terry's sudden desire that we reconcile.

"Don't want to?" he asked when I finished.

"I don't know what to think." I peeled off my shoes and

tossed them into the locker on top of my street clothes. "I agreed to it even though I wasn't hot on the idea. She's asking a lot and she knows it."

"Then why do it?"

"Because you don't say no to a woman who's been stuck on an emotional roller coaster. I would have given her anything she asked." I reached for my own towel. "You should see the house, Doug. Grant has practically turned it into a shrine for my mother. Maybe I missed something when she was alive... he obviously loved her, I just don't remember seeing it."

"Children's eyes are different," he pointed out, heading for the steam room.

Walking in there was like stepping into a boiling hot cloud. I could barely make out the tile bench on the other side, and the smell of eucalyptus was thick. We both sat and leaned against the hot, wet wall.

"She wants to marry me," Doug said out of the blue.

"Come again?"

He was drawing the towel across his face. "Kris... she said she would marry me."

"Well it's about frigging time! When?"

"We didn't talk about it... but I don't want to give her enough time to change her mind. And I'd like to at least take her on a decent honeymoon before she gets too big to enjoy it."

"Then you'd better do it like yesterday," I laughed. "Pregnant women get really mean when they get big. It's even worse when they're in labor."

"I remember. I think if Terry could have gotten her hands on you she would have grabbed your nuts and pulled them down to your knees."

"There are some days I think she still wants to. Can you believe she's already talking about having another one?"

"Even after yesterday?"

"Especially after yesterday. Christ, I'm willing to bet I wind up with enough kids to field a baseball team. Nicky being gone definitely reinforced the idea of motherhood on her."

"Funny," Doug said, crawling off the bench and heading for the door, "it was Nicky being gone that made Kris realize she really does want to have the baby and get married. I wasn't going to say it before, but this whole mess turned out to be a blessing in disguise."

I nodded, but all I could think of was Matt Rhuele's pleading voice, begging for mercy, and the silence that followed. There was no blessing for him, I thought miserably. And his mother—if anyone's life was ripped open, it was hers. Where was the blessing for Anne Rhuele?

Kris

The sun was bright, and Ron shut his eyes against it, face turned toward the sky, ripples from the pond reflecting on his face. He stood near the water's edge, waiting, ignoring the ducks that were climbing over rocks to gather around his feet.

"I wanted you to hear it from me before you heard it from anyone else," I said, wishing he would sit on the bench with me.

He sighed and opened his eyes, looking down at the water. He tossed a handful of popcorn into the pond, watching as the ducks scrambled and splashed in after it. "All right, I'm listening," he said, eyes glued to the commotion in front of him.

I leaned forward, trying to see his face. "I'm marrying Doug," I said. "We haven't set a date yet, but it'll be soon."

He threw more popcorn into the water. His expression didn't change, but he swallowed hard, and I could hear it. "Somehow I'm not surprised. I think I should be, but I'm not."

"I just wanted to be the one to tell you."

He barely nodded, hand digging into the popcorn bag abruptly, flinging the kernels as far as he could. "Do you really love him?"

"Of course I do." I sighed, trying hard to not sound condescending. "Doug and I have been friends for a long time, Ron. It just grew from there."

"Doug's a good man." He refused to look at me. "Why are you telling me this, Kris? It's not like we stayed friends."

"I didn't want you to be hurt if you heard it from someone else. Or embarrassed. I know how I'd feel if the situation were reversed."

"Oh?" He forced himself to turn. "Hearing that I had a social life would bother you? Well, I don't. There's no one in my life, not even remotely, and I don't plan on ever getting burned again. It's something you'll never have to deal with."

That flash of temper, though I'd expected it at some point, took me by surprise. "Ron, I'm sorry."

"Don't be." He closed his eyes again for a brief moment, took a deep breath, and then opened them again. "You're entitled to a life. I honestly hope that you and Doug make it work. You deserve a chance at that."

"There's something else," I said, hoping he could maintain control. He didn't move, just stood rooted to his spot with ducks pecking at his shoes, staring at me. "I'm pregnant."

His gaze didn't waver, but he bit back several comments,

his jaw moving as he gritted his teeth together. "Good to know," he finally managed. "Congratulations."

"Look, I…"

He was shaking his head. "Kris, I won't lie and tell you how wonderful all of this is. It hurts like hell but I'll get over it. It *is* good to know what's going on in your life and how major it is. More than you can understand, I *needed* to know… Go and enjoy it, work hard at it to make it work, but don't waste any time worrying about how I'll feel. I'm not part of the game anymore and I'm not entitled to the details."

I felt the hot sting of tears in my eyes. How could I explain it to him? His feelings did matter. There was still that very fragile thread that linked us together. "I didn't want to hurt you."

"Just get on with your life," he said, "and be happy. Whatever I feel will be all right." He sighed hard and tried to force a smile. "You have to take what you can get, and it seems to me that a life with Doug and a couple of kids sounds pretty good. Just don't leave here thinking I hate you for it… I'm glad you're finally getting what you need."

He started to turn and walk away, turning the bag upside down and letting the popcorn float into the water. "I did love you, Ron," I said. "Right up to the very end, I loved you."

He crumpled the bag and shoved it into a trash can, his head barely turning toward me. "I know."

I watched him walk to the street, hands jammed into his pockets, head hung low. He sat in his car with his head on the steering wheel for a moment, then started it up and drove out of my life.

Chip

I stripped to my underwear and stretched out on top of the bed, ignoring the warning that screamed from the back of my mind that Terry would likely want to strangle me for messing up the bed. Bone tired, I would argue, overrides crisp, uncrumpled bedspreads.

I checked the clock by the bed. I could sleep for at least two hours and still have time to get ready for dinner. She would have to bite back any anger if I gave myself enough time to get things straightened up. I was capable of making a bed, even when I didn't see any point to it.

Nicky was asleep in the crib next to our bed, for once not fighting even the suggestion of an afternoon nap, and Terry was puttering around in the kitchen, cleaning everything in sight and polishing anything that was already clean but not sparkling. She'd survived the morning with the help of Kris's company, and by the time I came home her guard was relaxed enough that she didn't jump at every single sound; Nicky was not duct taped to her side but was playing with new blocks on the living room floor. I expected another night with him in our bedroom, but Terry had already mentioned moving the crib back to Nick's room before Grant arrived.

He was sleeping soundly, his thumb hanging halfway out of his mouth. I wasn't sure I was ready to move him out, not just yet.

I buried my head into the pillow and willed myself to drift off, counting on the music of his breathing and the sweet smell of baby powder to keep the nightmares at bay. My life was finally good; Terry was happy, Nicky was safe, and I felt about as relaxed and peaceful as my son looked. Salvation was right within my reach in the form of a blonde, nearly twenty one year old witch and her cherubic offspring.

So why, I wondered as the last shred of conscious thought slipped away, did I agree to dine with the devil?

Terry

I sat back, balancing Nick in my lap. He was wide awake, sucking eagerly on the juice bottle Chip offered him, his eyes glued to the stranger sitting on the sofa. I had to admit I'd been nervous about the evening, not knowing what to expect. For all the images I had about Chip's stepfather, he was just the opposite: easy going, open and friendly. I barely remembered him from our one brief encounter in the back of the chapel, and now he totally shattered my mental image of him. He was not the crotchety old man of my imagination. In fact, he was lively and almost gregarious, someone I could easily like if I could get past Chip's memories.

And Chip, for all his heel dragging and loud balking at the idea of Grant Davis shedding skin cells in his living room, was enjoying himself more than I would have thought possible. The conversation between the two was smooth and effortless; Chip obviously appreciated the man's mind and trusted his business sense. I was completely lost when the banter turned to the restaurant and Grant's advice that, despite the fact he dissected the entire operation, Chip soaked in graciously. He listened with respect and was courteous enough to ask for the names and numbers of Grant's financial advisors; I couldn't tell if he was being polite and humoring us both, or if he was genuinely interested.

"He had a head for business when he was little," Grant told me. "Every time I turned around he was coughing up ideas. After his brother had a pony for an afternoon, he wanted to buy a horse and charge the neighborhood kids three dollars each to ride it. And he wanted an interest free loan to get him started."

Chip grinned, stirring his drink with his finger. "It could have worked if the neighbors weren't so uptight. I only needed to sell a couple thousand rides to break even."

"So instead you opened a lemonade stand, and almost got me arrested."

"The lemonade was spiked," Chip explained. "But it was definitely popular."

"Your brother didn't start his scheming until his teens. He wrote from school telling me he *needed* a car, and he'd found a beautiful MG. It was cherry red and the engine was chromed. He swore he had to have it in order to take a job off campus."

"And you couldn't say no," Chip said.

"I chose not to. I knew he was lying, and he very easily could have learned the bus schedule to get into town, but I felt badly about him being there in the first place."

"Then why was he there in the first place?" Chip asked. I held my breath and prayed he could control his temper.

Grant ignored the hint of bitterness in Chip's voice. "It wasn't my choice, Jeremy. David wasn't happy in the public schools and he was drowning in boredom. It just didn't stretch him enough… his intelligence transcended remarkable."

"Dave didn't want to go," Chip argued. "He was scared to death."

"Wouldn't you be terrified if you were fourteen and leaving everything you knew behind? He wanted to go, he *begged* to go… but he was a child, of course he was scared."

Nick began to squirm so I set him on the floor and watched as he crawled over to the sofa and pulled himself up, his small fingers shyly touching Grant's leg. It was friendly contact at last, his curiosity outweighing his suspicions about the man who was stealing Daddy's attention.

"Hey little guy." Grant held his hands out and Nick stepped into them, more than happy to be pulled onto another lap. "Your daddy tells me you had quite an adventure yesterday."

"Fortunately he's no worse for the wear," Chip said.

"You were so lucky. No one should lose a child."

Nicky was gurgling, waving his chubby arms in front of Grant's face. When Nick reached up for his glasses, Grant traced his thumb over the mark under Nick's arm. "What's this?"

"Birthmark. It reminds me of the one Dave had."

"It's exactly like the one David had," Grant murmured. "I'd almost forgotten."

"Better on his arm than on his face…"

Grant nodded slowly. He planted a quick kiss on Nicky's head and then handed him over to Chip. "I really should be going," he said. "It's been a long day for you and I don't want to wear out my welcome."

Chip scrambled to his feet, handing Nick to me with one hand and Grant his jacket with the other. He looked confused but didn't say anything.

"Grant," I said, getting up to see him off, "it really was nice to have you here. Please don't let it be the only time." I crept up on my toes and kissed his cheek.

"Thank you." He offered his hand to Chip. "Be sure to call some of those people. They're the best in the business."

"Yeah, sure."

Grant slipped out the door and hurried down the hallway. Chip closed it, his eyebrows knotted in confusion. "What the hell was that?" he muttered.

"Maybe he really thought it was time for him to go."

Chip locked the door, checking it to be sure it stayed locked, and went over to the bar to pour himself another drink. "Or maybe," he said, ice cubes clinking against the glass, "he was just tired of the charade."

~

I shivered against the cold, and reached out to wrap myself around Chip's warm body. It took a moment before I realized that what I had in my arms was only his pillow, and fought to swim through the sleepy haze and open my eyes. Still groggy, I sat up, trying to adjust to the darkness. His side of the bed was empty and cold, and he wasn't in the bedroom. I swung my legs over the edge of the bed, reaching on the floor for my robe. The lights were off in the living room, and Nick's room was dark.

I tiptoed from the room, walking carefully in case he was asleep on the sofa. It was as empty and cold as his side of the bed. I ducked into the kitchen, and then into Nicky's room. All quiet.

As I turned from Nick's doorway I spotted him sitting out on the balcony, his feet propped up on the railing and chair tipped back precariously. I watched him for a minute, seeming to stare up at the night sky, wondering if he was even awake.

Out in his underwear no less, I noted as I stepped out onto the cold wood. Probably giving one of the neighbors a thrill.

"Are you all right?" I asked, pulling my robe tighter.

He didn't move, didn't turn to look at me as I lowered myself into the chair next to him. "I'm okay," he replied, voice gruff.

My eyes followed his hand to the bottle on the little round table between us; it was three quarters empty. "So, did we run out of water and you had to settle for vodka?"

"Very funny."

"How much have you had?"

He held up the bottle. "That much."

When his hand left the bottle I snatched it up and set it on the balcony floor out of his reach. "It's enough then. Chip, what's wrong?"

"Nothing," he grumbled. "I'm fine."

So damned stubborn. "No, you're not. You're sitting out here nearly naked, drinking enough to pollute an army. That's not fine."

He eased the chair back down, shifting it around so he could lean his elbows on the table. Like a storm out of nowhere, he started. "That bastard came in here, telling me what to do and how to do it—how to run my fucking restaurant, which I do damn well without his help. He lies about my brother... I know goddamn well Dave didn't want to be sent off to some piss ass boarding school—and then when he picks up *my* son and sees that he isn't perfect, just one fucking little red defect, he tears out of here like a bat out of hell. There's not a damn thing wrong with me, Terry, but that son of a bitch has a lot to answer for."

I stared at him, startled by the outburst.

"Nothing's changed," he went on, either not seeing or ignoring the anger flaring in my eyes. "He still wants to throw that same fucking knife any time he can."

"Stop it!" I hissed. "First off, you can cut it with the language, buster. Just because you're drunk doesn't mean you can start swearing at me."

"I'm sorry..."

I cut him off with a warning glance. "And second, what are you even talking about? Grant never once told you how to run your business. It was advice, pure and simple, and you *asked* him for it."

"Ter"—

"Third... you don't really know about your brother. You

weren't there, you'd left home by then. Maybe he really did want to go, but was still scared out of his mind by the idea of leaving home. And I doubt Grant thought Nicky is imperfect. You're just looking for trouble, Chip, and if I know you, you're going to find it!" I shot up out of the chair, sending it into the vodka bottle. "I'm going back to bed, and when you can manage to tear yourself away from your delusions, maybe then you can join me."

I pulled my robe off and tossed it onto the bedroom floor, then nearly body slammed myself into bed. Yelling at him was a first; it had just spilled out, boiling over the angrier I became. When I heard him in the bathroom ten minutes later, I rolled away from his side of the bed, afraid of how he would react.

The bed heaved with his weight and I waited for the fight to begin. It surprised me when he slipped his arms around me, pulling me tight against him, his lips barely brushing my ear.

"I'm sorry," he murmured. The kiss fell clumsily against my neck. "I love you, you know that."

I rolled back over. He looked like a little boy begging to be forgiven for stealing cookies before dinner. "I know you do," I whispered. "I just wish you had more of an open mind. Grant didn't try to hurt you tonight. You've got to stop thinking about him the way you did when you were little."

"I'll try," he promised. "Am I forgiven?"

I pushed him onto his back and slid on top of him. "You're forgiven. You smell like booze, but you're forgiven." I trailed kisses down his neck and chest, my fingers leaving a trail of goose bumps on his skin.

"Lord, woman, what you do to me."

I laughed softly, moving until my face was just above

his. "Evidently not enough. You're too drunk, and some parts of you are not cooperating."

He groaned, running a light finger over one of my breasts. "God, I'm sorry. I want to…"

"It's okay." I melted my lips against his, feeling very sorry for myself. "I'll get over it."

"Will you now?" He rolled quickly, pinning me beneath him. "You've never struck me as a woman willing to give up so easy."

"It's a lost cause. You can't."

"Ah, but you can."

"And how's that?" He raised his eyebrows, smiling. I could feel his lips and tongue moving slowly down my body, lingering and teasing until he heard me inhale sharply.

"Jesus, Chip," I moaned. "Just don't bite."

Chip

Ron sat with his feet on my desk, his fingers in front of his face forming a perfect upside down V that touched the tip of his nose. His deliberate attempt to look indifferent was offset by his eyes. They were clouded with worry, and he looked confused.

"I'm retiring soon," he said, relief touching each word. "Just one more assignment and I'm through."

I glanced up, feigning interest. "Full pension?"

"Not that it matters." He sat up, carefully setting his feet on the floor. "Look, I know you were surprised to see me the other day."

"A bit."

"It was necessary."

Necessary.

The pencil flew out of my hand, bouncing off the desk

and onto the floor. "You had a goddamned crossbow in your hand, Ron. I don't even want to know what you did with it, but I'm pretty sure Matt Rhuele isn't taking apart someone's engine today. Don't bullshit me about necessities. If I'd wanted the son of a bitch dead, I'd have killed him myself."

Ron leaned forward, his elbows on his knees. "I was sent to do it for you. You don't have a taste for blood anymore, Chip. I doubt you could have done it."

"I didn't *need* to! Nicky was safe, dammit. No one needed to die over this. And fuck—his *mother*... Who got the honor of telling her that her son is dead?"

"I didn't ask for the details, son, I just did what I was told."

Thinking about his mother was something I was avoiding; as relieved as I was to have my son home safe, I was sure she was more devastated by losing hers. The woman must have gone from full of life to the living dead in less than twenty four hours, and she had to guess that the two men she pointed in her son's direction were mostly responsible.

"Let's just drop the subject," I said. "I'm glad you're getting out of it. You never should have signed back on under these terms."

"I had nothing left to lose," he said. "I saw Kris yesterday."

"Oh?" I leaned back in the chair, fighting back a smile; Ron didn't need to know I was happy for Doug and Kris, not yet, anyway. "What'd she have to say?"

He snorted. "She's really going to do it isn't she?"

"It's what she's always wanted. Marriage, a baby, the whole bit."

"Don't remind me."

"Hey, she's happy. Don't begrudge her that."

"Me?" He seemed genuinely surprised. "It has nothing to do with me. I honestly hope they make it through the long haul. Just because she doesn't want me anymore doesn't mean I want her to be miserable. I'm not blind... those last couple years with me, she was miserable. I was happily married and she wasn't."

"Let her go."

"What the hell? I gave her the divorce she wanted, didn't I? I let go a long time ago."

Not that I believed him. "You still love her."

"I still care." He shifted uncomfortably. "All right, yes, I do still love her. I still hurt when I think about the way she left me. But it's my own damn fault and I'll deal with it."

"I'd say you'll get over it, but I doubt you will. This is a repeat performance, isn't it?"

"How would you feel if Terry walked out on you, especially to be with someone you considered a friend? You'd be picking off scabs, too."

The image of her stomping out the door couldn't even make it past a dubious consideration. "Terry's not going anywhere, Ron."

"Don't be so sure. Everything may be wonderful now, but you have no way of knowing what's going through her mind."

"The woman tends to amaze me sometimes, but I have the gut feeling that that I'd know it if she were tempted. And then I'd fight for her like hell."

"You would, wouldn't you?" He'd seen the end result of my temper up close more than once and knew what I might do. "Just keep her barefoot and pregnant, Chip. She'll be too tired to look around."

"She can look all she wants," I said, suddenly and inexplicably angry at the stupidities he must have committed in his marriage. "As for pregnant… that's up to her. My wife is a not-too-devout but still believing Catholic, Ron. How many kids we wind up with isn't my choice."

"Leaving it up to God? I thought you were smarter than that."

"Who better to leave it up to? If Terry wants a dozen kids and thinks it's some blessing from God, she can have a dozen kids. Or if all she wants is one or two, I'll be happy with that as well."

"You deserve a say…" he stopped when he heard soft knocking at the door.

"It's open," I called out. When the door swung open I shot a quick glance at Ron, praying he had sense enough to avoid a confrontation. In that moment I felt intensely uncomfortable, loyalties torn.

"The prodigal doctor," Ron grunted, turning away from the door. His feet found their way back to the top of my desk.

Doug glanced back and forth between us. "I just dropped by to see if you wanted to catch a ride to the gym."

I jumped to my feet, reaching for my keys. "As a matter of fact," I said, grateful for an easy out, "I lost track of time. Better to burn up your gas than mine."

"I get the message," Ron said, getting up. "I know my way out. Give me a call sometime when you have more than five minutes." He brushed past Doug, making sure he looked anywhere but at the doctor.

"Chip, I'm sorry," Doug said, watching Ron walk through the restaurant. "Believe me, I had no idea he was in here."

I closed and locked the office door. "Not a problem," I told him. "He walked in here a while ago like he's been here all along. In and out of my life like the wind."

"Like a shadow?"

"Like a goddamn shadow."

"I want your opinion on something." I could practically feel the sizzle as my skin touched the tile bench.

Doug tossed me a towel, sitting carefully as he leaned back. It was useless to try to look through the thick steam, so he closed his eyes and leaned his head back. "I'll give it a shot," he said. "What's on your mind?"

"Am I a hardass?"

"You really need me to answer that?" he laughed.

"Come on," I moaned, wiping the sweat off my face. "I'm serious. Terry doesn't think I'm terribly open minded."

Doug took a deep breath, towel pressed to his face to ward off the heat. "Depends on what the subject is. Sometimes you're fairly open minded, and then sometimes you're a real pain in the ass."

I sat up slowly to make sure I wouldn't get dizzy. "We had Grant over for dinner last night."

"Is he still alive?"

I ignored him. "By the time he left I was so pissed off it wasn't funny and it damn near caused a huge fight with Terry. She thinks I have a major case of tunnel vision where he's concerned."

"She's probably right."

I tried to stare at him through the haze. "Great. Who's side are you on, anyway?"

"You asked for my opinion, you didn't ask me to agree with you." He opened his eyes, leaning forward to rest his elbows on his knees. "I don't know the man, Chip. All I know is what you've told me and what Kris has said."

"Which is?"

"Not much. She doesn't seem to know a whole lot about him."

Bullshit, I thought, burying my face in the towel. Kris knew as much about my life as I did, possibly more. She'd always been able to read me like a book, and had the benefit of five years of Ron's pillow talk to fill in any blank spaces.

"Have you decided when you're getting married?" I asked, deliberately changing the subject.

"I'd do it today if I thought she would. All we've agreed on is soon."

"So what's wrong with today? Shag your ass out of here, go home, grab your woman, and head to Tahoe or Reno and get married already."

He peered at me over his towel. "She'd never go for that, Chip. I'm pretty sure she wants you and Terry there."

"So?" I stood up, gesturing for him to follow me out of the steam room. "We'll go get Terry and then grab Kris, and go get you hitched. Hell, it'll be fun. Nick might even sit still for it."

The smile that crept onto his face was uncertain. "What if she says no?"

"What if we don't give her a choice? Come on, Doug. Strike now while you can. You know she has this commitment thing... make the decision for her."

"Fine, but what if we get to the part where she's supposed to say I Do and says Hell No because she's pissed off?"

"Trust me," I said. "She'll love it. Just remember on your honeymoon that the lady is pregnant, doctor. Recall your own words of wisdom... avoid any and all labor inducing activities. And watch out for those air bubbles. You don't want the lady to blow up."

"God, you're an ass."

"Yeah, but I'm an ass who gets to be best man."

"Don't be so sure," he threatened. "There's always Nicky."

Chip

"So... do you feel any different?"

Kris was staring out the window of the hotel lobby, watching a group of kids splashing in the pool just a few yards away.

I slipped my arms around her to give her a hug. "Mrs. Douglas Stone. Definitely has a nice ring to it." I let her go, standing close beside her. "Your husband is arranging your honeymoon even as we speak."

"And your wife?"

"Helping him, I guess. Who knows? Sometimes I think she honestly believes that men aren't capable of making any kind of decision without a woman's help."

"And just whose idea was this, Chip? I didn't even figure out what was going on until we were halfway here."

"Doug just wanted you to have a wedding to remember."

"This reeks of you," she said, touching my cheek. "Just pushing us in the right direction? You were afraid I'd back out on him if I had enough time to think about it."

"Don't blame this on me. Doug said he wanted to marry you today. I just came along for the ride. I love that kidney busting drive up the mountain."

"You two are something, you know that?"

"We try," I beamed. "Hey, don't I get to kiss the bride?"

"Of course." She expected a quick brush on her cheek and wasn't prepared for the way I melted my lips to hers, for the passion that hid just behind the kiss, or for the way I lingered there. This kiss was a tease, almost an invitation for something more.

"You know," I said when I finally pulled away, "I really do love you. And I hope this all works for you and Doug as well as it has for Terry and me."

Kris wrapped her arms around me and hugged hard. "Thank you," she whispered in my ear. When she let go, there were tears brimming in her eyes. "I was so afraid that when I left your father I'd never see you again. I can't tell you how much you mean to me."

"You don't have to. You pulled me through more hell than anyone should ever go through, and you probably know me better than anyone else does. You should have known that no matter what, I'd never walk away from you." I brushed a tear off her cheek. "I have a feeling you and Doug will do great."

"Just don't ever kiss me like that again... This time it has to work, Chip. God, I love him."

"Just remember that. This time next year when you're up to your neck in wet diapers and baby spit, and you've been up all night with a kid cutting teeth and you don't think you can take much more, remember how you feel right now." I leaned over and kissed her again on the lips, but with much less fervor. "Look... Doug is itching to whisk you away and I seriously doubt his plans include standing around talking to me anymore. Be happy, Kris," I said, walking away. "Just let yourself be happy."

September 1977

Chip

The smell of sweat and steam and eucalyptus was by now so familiar to me that I didn't give it a second thought—which is probably why I found the look of absolute distaste on Grant's face amusing. He bounded through the front door of the gym enthusiastically and then stopped dead in his tracks when the acrid odor of a dozen people working out hit him. I wasn't entirely sure what he had expected, other than a room filled with single women in leotards stretching on the aerobics floor, but the proof that they were there to sweat had not been on his agenda.

He wanted to get out more and to meet, as he put it, all the foxy young things he could. I assured him that two hours in a co-ed health club was infinitely better than sitting at the end of the Charybdis's bar; in the gym he had the safety of a workout to hide behind. If whatever feminine prospect he worked up the nerve to speak with didn't meet his expectations, he could always turn his attention back to the weights.

The fact that he was as willing as he was to form a relationship—any kind of relationship—took me back a few steps.

It was a bit like walking on eggshells, waiting for the first crack. I was careful with what I said to him, and he measured each conversation, taking everything I told him at face value.

Six months was not enough time to mend the gap that had taken twenty four years to form. Grant was eager to try, and I agreed, reluctantly, to set aside my own personal prejudices. Terry had Nicky calling him Poppy; I wasn't left with much of a choice.

Either mend the fence or let the cattle through.

The time we spent together, which increased weekly and became less of a burden as time went by, had at least forced me to come to terms with the hard edge that had frightened me as a child. Showing affection was an alien concept to Grant, something he hadn't learned as a child. His attempts with Nicky were awkward and forced at first, made easier over time by Terry's insistence to always greet him with a hug and a kiss on the cheek. She never, I realized one afternoon when he tried to get out the front door quickly, let him leave without at least a hug.

The edge was beginning to soften, and I began to wonder how much of it had been just my imagination.

He loved my mother, of that I had no doubt. He lit up when he talked about her; all the memories he shared were warm and funny, and if Terry had never heard about any of the infighting and head butting, the image she would walk away from him with would be that of a typically happy family. I was finally beginning to realize he had chosen to stay in his marriage because he did love her, and that gave him the hope he needed to hang on.

If he'd been more able to show that love, it might have made all the difference in the world.

When it came right down to it, I was making the effort

to repair the gap between Grant and myself because of my mother's memory. Terry was right, there had to be something she clung to, a reason why she refused to leave him in spite of Ron. In spite of my existence. There was David, too; it was only beginning to dawn on me that he was not found under a rock in the back yard. He was proof my mother hadn't shut Grant out of her life, no matter how much I wanted to believe that she had.

I noticed, too, over the six months we took tentative steps towards each other, Grant stopped looking so old. He didn't live locked away behind the walls of his perpetual shrine to Pat Davis; he wanted out, he wanted to prowl the gym for women, and I figured there was just as much of a chance for him there as anyone else—more if he could flash his bank book. Plant word with the right woman and it would be all over the club within an hour. Take a look at the old guy with Chip, he's a keeper. He's rich.

Grant looked a little pale, though, still uncomfortable with the assault on his senses.

"Lift." Doug was spotting the weights, urging Grant to press them forward. The bar wobbled, lifted an inch or two, and stopped.

I sat on a stationary bike to Grant's right, pedaling with about half the intensity I should have. "Take a plate off," I told Doug, "before you kill him."

Sweat had begun to break out on Grant's face, tiny beads that popped out on his upper lip. "This is too much like work," he grunted.

Doug chuckled, taking the bar from him and setting it into the cradle. "Would you have come if we'd warned you?"

"I came," Grant said as he gripped the bar again, lowering it to his chest, "expecting a bevy of gorgeous women. All

I see are old broads with fat asses."

"Christ, Grant!" I stopped pedaling and wiped the sweat from my face with the tail of my shirt. "Come back on Friday night. No one comes here to work out then. It's nothing but picking out your bed partner for the weekend."

Doug was holding onto the weight bar, helping Grant lift it. "How would an old married man like yourself know that?"

"I wasn't born married, Doug."

"And I'm not married now," Grant puffed. "So tell me, where can I go in this town to meet a nice woman?"

"Doug's a newlywed, Grant," I said. "He doesn't look at women anymore."

"Bullshit," Doug countered. "I look, I just don't touch."

I started pedaling again, slowly. "How is the blushing bride? I haven't seen her in a couple weeks."

"God, she's huge."

Grant looked up at Doug, his eyebrows knotted. "Excuse me?"

"She's eight months pregnant," I explained.

Doug nodded. "I thought Terry got big there at the end, with Nick... she'd pale in comparison to Kris."

"Hell, Kris is just getting fat."

"All right, smart ass." Doug sat on the empty bench next to Grant, slipping his hands into weight gloves. "What about you? I thought Terry was all hot to have another kid, but I sure haven't given her a pregnancy test lately. Shooting blanks these days?"

"You got me," I shrugged. "Just haven't gotten lucky I suppose."

"Haven't gotten lucky, or haven't gotten it up?"

"*Excuse* me?" Grant sat up and rubbed his shoulders,

grimacing. There was the look I remembered, he was angry but not sure why.

I felt like a kid caught with his hand in the cookie jar. "Sorry. He tends to bring out the crudeness in me."

"You were born crude."

Grant turned to Doug. "You think he's bad now? This boy was like spit on a hot skillet. I never knew what was going to pop out at me. He learned to swear before he learned to walk."

"Oh, shit," I chuckled.

"Nicky's first words," Doug explained. "Still his favorite."

Grant laid back and wrapped his fingers around the weight bar and pushed, determined to try again. "Just like his father," he grunted.

I was looking at the digital readout on the bike, watching the RPM numbers steadily increase with effort; otherwise I might have seen the terror and anguish that wrenched Grant's face. What I heard first, instead, was the horrible choking sound and then Doug's demanding voice. I was off the bike and lifting the weight off Grant's chest in less than a second. What I noticed most of all, imprinted in my mind even as I raced to call the ambulance Doug commanded, was the bright strawberry red stain under my stepfather's right arm.

~

The antiseptic smell of the hospital was as foreign to me as the eucalyptus had been to Grant. I was uncomfortable, waiting there in sweat soaked clothes, trying to not breath in the sting of alcohol and betadine, and I couldn't unwrap my mind from around the picture of that red mark. It was a fluke, it had to be.

"He's in CCU," Doug told me. "To be honest, I don't think he'll survive the night. This was a major heart attack, Chip, and not his first one. If he codes again..."

I was pacing the waiting room, my own heart hammering wildly. "I've got to see him."

"I'm not sure that's the best idea right now. You're so pumped up you might panic him."

I stopped pacing. "Does he know?"

"That he might die? No one has gone in there and said in so many words, 'Mr. Davis, this is it,' but deep down? I'm sure he has a gut feeling."

"What caused it? Why now?"

"Any number of things... but if you're thinking of blaming yourself, don't. He wasn't working out very hard and he didn't seem to be under any significant stress. He has a history of cardiac disease and he's led a very sedentary life. I'm willing to bet his diet sucked, too. He's younger than I'd expect with his history, but it does happen."

"You've got to let me see him." I had been able to hold myself together long enough to call Terry, but the composure was beginning to give way to palpable fear. "Please."

Doug barely nodded, reluctantly giving his permission.

Grant's room in the cardiac care unit wasn't the dark, depressing tomb I'd expected; the wall facing the nurses station was glass, and although the room was filled with machines that beeped and hummed, it was relatively bright. Grant was stretched out on the bed, tubes and wires connected to his body, plastic tubing under his nose that delivered a steady stream of oxygen. His eyes were closed and the skin sagged from his face in a way that, would have made me think he had already died, if not for the slow rise and fall of his chest.

I reached for a chair by the door and pulled it to the side

of the bed, leaning my arms against the cold rails, wondering if I should wake him or leave him alone. Was he in there, just resting, or was his mind already gone, waiting somewhere out there in the ether for his body to give up?

"Jeremy?" The name sounded like a sigh rushing from deep inside.

I reached over the rail and set my hand on his arm.

"The letter," Grant whispered. "What"—he took a deep breath—"was in the letter?"

"What letter?"

His breathing was labored and uneasy, he struggled to draw in enough to speak. "Your mother," he managed. "Your wedding."

The image came to me instantly. Grant's hand thrust out at me, the faded white envelope. What had I done with it? It had never been opened; I'd never given it a second thought. I'd taken it and then what? Got in the car and drove off.

"Get some sleep. I'll tell you after you've had some rest."

I left the room, my head spinning and pain pounding between my temples. I remembered getting the letter. Why hadn't I read it, and what had I done with it?

"You okay?"

I leaned against the closed door, barely seeing Doug standing there. "Where's Terry? Is she here yet?"

He pointed toward the waiting room and I stomped past him, practically shoving him out of the way. Terry was sitting in the middle of a long line of plastic molded chairs, creases of worry drawn on her forehead and fear dancing in her eyes. When she saw me walking towards her she jumped up and tried to hug me, surprised when I pushed her back.

"I need you to think," I said, grabbing her arms. "You need to think hard."

"About what?"

"The day we got married Grant gave me a letter. He handed it to me just as we were leaving the chapel. Do you remember?"

She stepped back as I let her arms go. "Vaguely."

"What did I do with it?"

She sat back in the chair, biting her bottom lip, searching the recesses of her own memory. "All right... You took the envelope, and we got into the car. I can see it in your hand, you started to stick it in the inside pocket of your tux. No, you thought you'd lose it if you left it there, you might turn it in when you returned the tux." Her eyes closed, following my hand in her memory. "The glove compartment!" she blurted out. "You stuck it in there so that you could find it later."

"Shit." I threw myself into the chair next to her. "What are the odds it's still there?"

"What are the odds you've ever cleaned anything out of that car, Chip? There are still text books from high school behind the front seat. I'll go look." She stood up, looking down at me sadly. "He's dying, isn't he?"

"Probably."

How in the hell, I wondered, could I have just tossed it aside and not bothered to look in the envelope to see what it was. It could have been anything—a note from my brother, or an apology from Grant for all the years of inflamed confrontations. It could have been cash. It could have been something from my long dead mother. At the time I hadn't cared enough to think past the idea that I was driving off into a new life, and by God, there would be sex that night.

Terry was back in ten minutes, just enough time for me to start beating myself up mentally, and almost enough time for me to lose the fight. In her hand was a terribly wrinkled and rain stained white envelope, and she handed it to me without a word.

I took it, staring at the smudged lettering on the front. It was familiar handwriting, something I had seen on birthday cards and notes to school. My hands were shaking, but I tore one end of the envelope off and pulled out the fading piece of paper. I was vaguely aware of Terry lowering herself into the chair next to me, her warm hand on my neck, reassuring.

In my mind I could hear the musical lilt of my mother's tongue, feel her hand tousling my hair before she set into the kitchen to begin cooking dinner.

My dearest Jeremy,

Congratulations! You've survived your childhood, which is a sight more than I expect most days. Five years old and already I wonder from day to day how you will manage to make it to the next. It's your own doing, mind you, such a free spirit in such a small package.

Today you have a brother, and today you have a wife. Perhaps one day you'll learn to view the former as the blessing God intends him to be, and not the ruination of your existence.

I pray with all my heart that this letter never finds way to your hands; I want so much to be there the day you offer your heart to the woman who will love you for the rest of your life. The choice is not always an easy one. The comic turns of life sometimes offer us more choices than we can make, and surely by now you understand that I was never good at making those choices.

God grant me mercy, Jeremy, but I will lie to you through your life and tell you of a man who is your father, but truthfully, I do not know. The only certainties my heart can bear are that you have two men who love you as if you were their own, and their love for you is what binds them to me.

Surely now you know, love is such a precious thing to not be taken as lightly as I have done. Love this woman that God has brought to you, and never settle for the lesser choice. I do love your father, whichever he may be. For all my mistakes, I do.

All my love…

Terry

I watched as Chip crumpled the paper into a tight ball and hurled it savagely across the room. I wasn't sure what I was reading on his face, if it was anger or confusion, or a mixture of both. He sat so still, his eyes forward, glaring a hole into the wall in front of him.

"What is it?"

He took a few deep breaths and then vaulted from his seat, practically flying over to the small window ten feet away. "She used me," he growled. "I was just a pawn in her pathetic little game."

I went over to him, though I felt helpless and not sure what to say. "What was in the letter, Chip?"

"All these years, all these stinking, lousy years. I've spent my entire life certain that no matter how horrible I thought things were, at least I knew who I was. *I knew who I was!* She just fucking took that way from me, Terry… That lying *bitch* used me to keep Ron and Grant from walking out on her. She was nothing but a goddamned slut, and"—

I grabbed him by his chin. "Stop it. That woman was your mother and you damn well better not forget that."

"My mother," he fumed, "slept with two men on such a regular basis that she didn't know which one fathered her child. She married Grant but couldn't be bothered to play by the rules. So just what the hell do you call it, Terry?"

"Does it matter? You're here, no matter who your father is. How she lived her life was her choice, not yours. Let it go."

He stared at me, face hard and angry. "You remember the first time we had Grant to dinner? The night I was so fucking pissed off because I assumed he thought Nicky was imperfect because of his birthmark?"

I remembered too well.

"Dave had one, too, in just about the same place. When Grant dropped the weight bar today I jumped up to help Doug—Terry, Grant has an identical mark under his right arm, just like Nicky and just like Dave. He didn't leave because he was disappointed in anything. He left because the truth had just ripped right through him and he didn't know what to do."

Stunned silence was the only thing I could offer for several minutes. I understood Chip's anger, then, his feeling of utter betrayal.

He pounded the wall with his open hand. "Grant is my father."

I backed away from him, trying to absorb. "Chip, your scars…"

"Terrific, that's a nice thought. He almost tore his own son to shreds and didn't even know it. We never had a fucking chance."

"Sit down, Chip," I said. His world was falling apart piece by piece, and I didn't want to bring it tumbling down, but I had to tell him. "What do you remember about it? What made him do it?"

He sat down hard, crossing one leg over the other. His

foot was bouncing impatiently. "I've told you before, I don't remember. And it doesn't matter."

"I think it does. The night your mother died, think about it... What happened?"

"She had a heart attack, Terry. She'd had health problems her entire life." The foot was moving faster.

"What were you doing that night?"

He sighed hard. "Dammit, I don't know. What's the point?"

"The point is," I said, setting my hand on his chest, "that this happened the same night your mother died. She found you in your room with a girlfriend, remember? You left the house, and she had the heart attack while you were gone. It was when you came back late that night that Grant did this to you, wasn't it?"

He stared at me uncertainly, the memory flooding back to him at once; his eyes changed from doubt to pain as he recalled his mother's expression, and the hand that held the knife. "Grant was crying," he remembered. "He was in the kitchen and I came in... Oh my God, he thought I had killed her. Grant thought I'd killed her!"

I held him down, hand still pressing into his chest. His heart was thumping wildly, breath coming in ragged gasps. "Only for that moment, Chip. He came to his senses as soon as it was over. It was just grief... he didn't hate you. He's never hated you. He was just out of his mind with grief."

"But he already had the knife out when I got there. I walked in and his back was to the door, but he already had the knife in his hand. He jumped and turned around... Son of a bitch." He took in one deep, hard breath, and finally relaxed. "Goddamn, Terry, I don't think he intended to hurt me, I think he was going to kill himself."

"Then if you hadn't walked in… Chip, you probably saved the man's life."

"What do I do now? I can't go in there and read that letter to him."

If I had been looking for it, I would have seen the darkness that crept into his eyes, that odd mixture of terror and disbelief. I missed it, though, leaning towards him to kiss his cheek, and said, "You do what you have to do."

Chip

When I finally stood to go to Grant's room, my legs felt like rubber and my feet pounded hard on the dull tile, the shock of each step pulsating upward. I lingered by the door; Doug was inside scribbling on a clipboard, nodding at whatever tidbit Grant was telling him.

Do Not Resuscitate.

I went in and Doug patted me on the shoulder as he left. For a second I thought about asking him to stay, the coward in me not wanting to face someone else's mortality up close and personal.

"Look, don't say anything," I told him as I pulled the chair back to the side of the bed. "I have to tell you… These last few months have meant a lot to me, I need you to know that. You were right when you said that anger shouldn't last forever. I am sorry, so sorry, for all the hell I put you through. All I ever did was see things the way I wanted to see them and not the way that they really are. I am sorry."

His hand reached out for mine; I stood and leaned over the rail to make it easier for him. "You know, don't you?"

"You're my father," I said. "I know."

"The letter…"

"What?" I tried to sound surprised, as if it didn't matter,

but couldn't quite pull it off. "It wasn't much of anything, just that drippy stuff Mom liked. She did tell me, though, how much she loved you. She wanted me to know that, that she really did love you."

"Thank you." He closed his eyes and sighed. "God, I love you."

He drifted off, his hand going slack in mine. I sat by his bed as he slept, and was there hours later when the soft beep of the machine on the other side of the bed quickened, and then gave way to a high pitched, single toned squeal.

I stared at his still body for a long time, wondering what I should be feeling. I knew I felt a loss, and I felt betrayed, and that the chance to find whatever piece of myself that was missing was lost with the exhale of Grant's last breath.

Doug

Kris shifted restlessly. She couldn't sleep and knew I was lying there wide awake; she rolled slowly and pressed her belly up against me. I could feel the baby move, a slow, luxurious somersault punctuated by tiny knees and elbows. I turned onto my side, lying stomach to stomach with her, waiting for every movement; every time I felt the baby twist or turn I couldn't help but be overwhelmed.

More and more I found myself talking to God, grateful for every sleepless night and cranky morning Kris threw at me.

"Is Chip sure?" she asked, breaking the silence.

"Positive." Terry had shown me the letter and asked about the birthmark; why Chip didn't have one I couldn't say. He accepted it as fact that Grant was his father after all, and sat in the Cardiac Care Unit long after the body was cold, just staring into space. Nurses worked around him to unhook the

EKG machine and to pull out IV lines, floating around him with careful respect, not once suggesting that he wait outside, or that it was time to leave and let them take the body to the morgue.

He never cried; he simply stared at the turmoil of his past.

I tried to fit my arms around Kris, but couldn't quite reach. She rolled on to her other side and I snuggled against her back, resting my hand on top of her stomach.

"This will kill Ron," she whispered.

I pressed a kiss into her neck. "He never has to know."

Chip

I stood on the balcony, drinking straight from the bottle, swallowing liberal gulps that burned through my throat and into my gut. The air was chilly, but I didn't care. The only thing I cared about was numbing that vacuous feeling that was beginning to consume me. I couldn't focus on anything else, only the void that had formed and ballooned already to a size I was afraid I couldn't handle.

So I drank. It was easier to anesthetize everything than having to face it.

I could hear the soft footsteps behind me, and without looking I could see the disappointment that was staring back at me. She said she understood, but I doubted it.

How much time does it take to rebuild when everything has been torn down to the very foundation? What was supposed to fill in the gaps and cracks that were growing with every blink and every breath?

Why the hell did it matter?

The soft warmth of her hands felt strangely disconcerting on my skin. I wouldn't push her away, or ask her not to hold me. Part of my mind was whispering that she was hurting just as much, only this time I couldn't comfort her. Standing out there in the cool night air, it was all I could do to hold myself together.

And how to respond when she would certainly pry the bottle away from my fingers? I knew I'd let her. It was easier that way. Just like I knew I would follow her back into the apartment and, if she wanted, make love to her.

Just like I had before, so many times.

Performing was easy. Do the same mind numbing things day in and day out, and life can be tolerable. You go to work, come home and kiss your wife, play with the baby—meshing it all together without thinking of what might have been should have been easy.

I certainly didn't want to think about what might be if I didn't snap back fast. I'd lived in the dark places before, and hated myself when I was there.

It was beginning to obsess every waking thought; one ominous day out of my life was sending me into a downward spiral that I felt helpless to control. Grant had known and not said a word, not wanting to tip the cart over. If not for that small splotch of red I could have gone on blissfully ignorant and buried him without a second thought.

How many people might still be alive? I'd left Grant's house to be with my real father. It had been easy to run away and become part of the game, skilled cat and mouse quests that were often bloodier than I'd like to admit. It was excitement, adventure.

It wasn't real, not while I was in the middle of it. The guns were toys and the lives expendable.

Would I have stayed if I had realized that his efforts to discipline were made out of love and not hostility?

I handed the bottle to my wife without a word.

I had the family I wanted; all I needed to do was reach out, and there it was. Blood didn't matter. The ties were already there; I had what I'd made for myself. It should have been enough.

I reached for Terry and held her tight, the warmth of her wet tears trickling down my chest. She knew nothing she could say would help. It was a puzzle I had to finish, a piece I had to put into place myself. I didn't know if her tears were from grief or uncertainty, or even from fear that I would self-destruct right before her eyes.

I was too stupid to ask.

The one thing I did know, that ripped through me when I finally let them take Grant's body away, was how I felt.

I felt cheated.

~

We buried Grant four days after he died; it was a sad commentary on the man's life; for all the years he had lived in the community and the business his money generated, the only ones who bothered to show up were four people who either didn't know him, or didn't particularly give a damn about him for the greater part of his life. Terry cried, but otherwise there were no sad goodbyes, or anyone who sat at his graveside and spoke of the memories they would always have and how much they would miss him.

His funeral consisted of a well dug hole in the ground, a priest who offered the requisite send off, and handfuls of dirt tossed in after the coffin was lowered.

My only concession to being remotely sentimental was in making sure that he was buried next to my mother, her cracked and faded headstone replaced by heavy engraved granite that they could share for the next hundred years.

I had the opportunity to say something after the priest was finished, but couldn't think of a damn thing that would make a difference. *Sorry you're dead old man, but you're going to a better place.* I doubted he was going anywhere he'd enjoy or that it would be any better than the self imposed solitude of his life on earth.

Dave was buried somewhere nearby, but I didn't take the time to go look for his grave or make sure there were fresh flowers, or even that the site was cared for at all. Dan Martin was somewhere in the cemetery, but I hadn't bothered with his grave since his funeral, either. Brenda was far to the other side. Looking around was just a morbid reminder that I knew too many of the names on the headstones, and that I'd be there sooner than I'd like.

Kris was there over Doug's objections; she never knew Grant and didn't need to be there, especially suffering through baby bloat to the degree she was, but she insisted—what else would a friend do? Daddy dies so your friends rally around. I had selfish hopes that her water would break halfway through the homily, giving us a reason to end the funeral before it became a full blown farce.

Just stick the man in the ground and get it over with, he's dead and he probably doesn't give a damn about this anyway...

He was dead, he was buried, and I assumed that was the end of it.

A week later I found myself sitting in a too-comfortable chair in the middle of a dimly lit law office, surrounded on all sides by bookcases jammed with thick leather bound books that ran from floor to ceiling. The lawyer looked about fifteen years old, and I could only assume that this task was given to the new kid, something easy that he couldn't screw up.

"The basic gist of his will," the kid said, "is that the entire estate is yours."

"I don't want it."

He ignored me. "You get both houses…"

"I don't want them."

"…you get his real estate holdings…"

"I don't want them."

"…stocks, bonds, treasury notes…"

"Don't want them."

"…two cars…"

"Don't want them."

"…and roughly fifty million dollars."

"Excuse me?"

"You want that, I take it?"

"No, but I'm curious where he got that kind of money. I knew he was well off, but not that well off."

Junior simply shrugged. "Now you're that well off… I know, you don't want it. But you might, a year or two from now when reality sets in, or when you have several kids and are struggling to support them."

"I don't struggle," I said. I was sitting there in faded jeans and running shoes so worn the soles were starting to separate, so I could understand why he would assume I was a paycheck away from moving into a cardboard box; it was a point of pride to point out that I was fully capable of providing for my family.

"Regardless—it's still yours."

For sixteen years Grant had put clothes on my back, food on the table, and a roof over my head, but I swore, no more. I never intended to take another dime from him. The fact of his death didn't change that.

"He probably intended everything to go to my brother...
the will does state his possessions go to his son, right?"

He looked down, flipped through a few papers and said,
"Well, no. He specifically intended for a sizable trust fund to
go to David Mark Davis, but everything else was earmarked
for Jeremy Dwight Davis. He removed your brother's trust
fund quite a while back."

"At what point was I added to his will?"

More paper flipping. "You were made the prime benefi-
ciary about ten years ago."

Right after my mother died.

"It's time to face it, Mr. Davis—you're now a very
wealthy man. You may as well accept it, it was his wish, after
all."

Throughout the last years of his life Grant probably had
lots of wishes, but he didn't get those, either. He didn't have
a life beyond the Shrine To Patricia, his youngest son didn't
grow to adulthood, he never got to meet that bevy of beautiful young women hanging around the gym, he never once
heard me call him Dad. Or even hear me say I didn't think it
was the worst concept in the world.

I could sell it all and be done with it, wipe the last traces
of my mother's indecision from my life. Dispose of the cars,
the house, stocks and bonds, and blow off the money could
as easily as I could sneeze.

Or I could set it all aside for Nicky, and any brothers or
sisters he might have.

Or I could accept it graciously.

Or I could implode, and then nothing would matter.

~

Doug

"You're an idiot," I told Chip. "What the hell do you mean, you don't *want* Grant's estate? You're set for life!"

"Why would I want it?"

"Hell, I don't know. Compensation for years of shit? Because you're his heir? Because he wanted you to have everything? Why do you need a reason?"

He was standing behind the restaurant bar, digging under the counter for glasses and ice cubes. "Because," he said, dropping ice into a glass, "until about six months ago, the man was just some incident of my life. There was only a relationship because my wife insisted on it. Nothing in that entitles me to his money."

"You're an idiot," I repeated.

"So I'm a fucking moron. Ask me if I care."

"Have you told Terry any of this?"

"No." He filled both glasses with orange juice and vodka. "I don't know that I will."

"Christ…"

He lifted an eyebrow, his so-frigging-what look, and drained the screwdriver, pouring another before the ice had stopped spinning. "Look, there's no reason she should know, not if I dump the whole estate."

"She's your wife, Chip."

"Very astute." Another drink down the hatch. "Why would it matter?"

"Because she might have an opinion, for starters."

"She might." He poured vodka into the glass, pushing the juice aside. "But when it all comes down to it, he left his crap in my lap and I'm the one who has to deal with it. She'd agree if I said I didn't want anything to do with it."

"Yeah, if it were a tin shack out by the lake and a hundred

dollars in pizza coupons, maybe."

He frowned when Ted came in. "I'll take it under advisement," he said. Before Ted could open his mouth he added, "Take the bottle and you're fired."

"How many has he had?" Ted asked me.

"Two huge screwdrivers and a full glass of vodka."

Ted snatched the bottle off the counter. "So fire me. But you're done drinking here tonight."

"I mean it," Chip said, "I'll fire you."

"Fine, you do that. Doc, you gonna make sure he gets home in one piece?"

"You staying here till closing, Doug?" Chip asked. "Cause I've got a shit load of paperwork I still need to do before I go home."

"Do it tomorrow," Ted said.

"I thought I fired you."

"Yeah, well you can do that again tomorrow when you're sober. Just go home and have dinner with your wife and leave the rest of the stock alone."

"You can be a real prick sometimes, Ted."

"Come on, Chip," I said. If he fought leaving I'd be in for a truckload of trouble; sober he was a handful, drunk he was impossible. He shrugged it off, slugged back the rest of his drink, and stepped out from behind the bar, reminding Ted at least twice more that he was fired before I could get him out the door.

He didn't say a word on the ride home, and slammed the car door as hard as he could when he got out. Message received, Chip is pissed.

I should have stayed long enough to make sure he found his way through the door, but I didn't. He was halfway across the parking lot and headed in the right direction, so I took off. It wasn't until I was driving Terry around at midnight looking for him that I realized that was a boner of a mistake.

Chip

The pond at night has an almost magical quality to it. Street lights reflect off the water, and if you listen closely you can hear one or two ducks engaged in muted conversation. It was too dark to look for Quackers, but I was curious to see if he was still around. Surely by now some fed up female had pecked him to death.

I parked myself at the end of a teeter totter, and once in a while I'd push off with my feet, going just high enough that my toes left the ground, and then let it bang into the sand. If I went fast enough I felt that split second of floating; if I did it slow enough the hinges squealed and popped. It was a nice ten minute diversion, and when I got bored with it, I tipped the board so that I could lay on it, staring out over the water and up into the sky.

Someone up there had one wicked sense of humor. *Let's give Jeremy a rug of happy existence for a while, and when he's almost relaxed, yank it right out from under his feet. It'll be so much fun!*

Who was the brainiac who decided to name me Jeremy, anyway?

Chip wasn't any better. It was like an annoying little noise. Chip, chip, chip, chip, chip... Whose old block was I the chip off, anyway? Chip, Chipper, Chipster—Chip Dip when David was four and thought that was hysterical. Now Doug, he got a good name. Douglas. It sounded strong. Even his middle name was better. Vincent. That made Dwight sound backwards. Not So Bright Dwight. Jeremy Schmeremy, Not So Bright Dwight.

The brilliant parents that they were, they went with originality and named their second son David Davis. I wanted to call him Mark, but no. Dave was the only mutilation of his name allowed. Grant was a pain in the ass about names. "If I had wanted to call you Chip, I wouldn't have named you Jeremy. And if I wanted to call your brother Dave, I would have named him Dave."

Well, blow it out your ass. I had no idea who began calling me Chip, but it stuck.

I could have vented about the family name—what respectable Irish family takes an English name—but I had enough sensitivity to understand that much. Just barely. Grant and his parents hit Ellis Island and were reminded a dozen times while waiting in line, this is America, the Irish Need Not Apply—change your names while you can and don't speak until you can get rid of the brogue.

I probably had grandparents out there somewhere, or at the very least uncles and aunts and cousins, but no one had ever bothered to clue me in on who it was I might be looking for. Who were we before we were the Davis clan?

I was a Gallery before I was a Davis. At least I thought I was.

Someone should speak with Ron about that name. Change your name, bud. You look more like an Art, not a Ron. Or we can call you Shoot, middle initial N. Or any other Gallery that springs your way.

I should have grabbed the bottle of vodka before leaving the Charybdis. My family was more amusing through a haze of alcohol.

I turned my head at the sound of a heavy sigh; Terry was standing by the end of the teeter totter, bundled up in one of my old gray sweatshirts, the sleeves hanging off her hands;

well, I could only guess that much since she was standing there with her arms folded, but the shirt came down almost to her knees so it was a safe assumption.

"Were you planning on coming home tonight?" She wasn't sure yet whether she should be ticked off or worried, and was looking at me like, come on, give me a clue.

I looked back out at the water. "Eventually."

"Doug and I have been driving around looking for you for over an hour, Chip. Why didn't you let me know you'd be here?"

"Where's Nicky?"

"Kris is with him." She gestured for me to sit up, and I did. She straddled the board in front of me, her backside biting into the metal handles. "Now why are you out here and not at home?"

"Kris shouldn't be with Nicky," I said. "She should be at home in bed."

"So should you. Now answer me."

"I was looking for Quackers. I would've come home in a little bit."

"You're drunk."

"Not anymore."

"You're not going to tell me why you're out here in the middle of the night and why you couldn't let me know where you were?"

"I don't really know why I'm here," I said truthfully.

Sleeve covered hands went to my knees, rubbing me through the layers of fleece and denim. "Chip, are you okay?"

"I'm okay."

"Are you ready to go home?"

I peered over to the street, squinting through the darkness. "Doug over there?"

"He's waiting for us."

"Can we walk?"

"I don't think he'll mind."

I stood and helped her up. "Good. Cause I should probably tell you what happened today. Doug thinks you might have an opinion."

Terry

Chip sat at the kitchen table and stared into a glass of ice water while I reheated his dinner. He had talked all the way home, but as soon as we hit the door he clammed up; he grunted at Doug and barely acknowledged Kris, and would have made a beeline for the balcony if I hadn't steered him into the kitchen.

"You're too tired to decide anything," I told him, setting a plate on the table. "I don't understand the problem, though."

"There's no problem. I just don't want anything of his."

I sat down across from him. "It's an inheritance, Chip. If it had come from some long lost uncle you wouldn't think twice."

"But it didn't come from anyone else. I don't even understand why he left everything to me."

"Because," I said, "he wanted you to have it."

"I don't deserve it, Ter."

"Obviously he thought different." I pointed to his plate; he hadn't even picked up his fork. "Please, just eat. You don't have to decide your whole life tonight."

"Our life."

He was looking anywhere but at me, absently pushing food around on his plate. He looked so tired that getting the fork up to his mouth seemed like a monumental effort; his eyes had dark circles under them, and he leaned heavily on his elbows.

"You need to tell me what you think," he said.

I hadn't had much time to digest the facts much less think about what I wanted. "All I know is that Grant wanted…"

"I don't give a flying fuck *what* Grant wanted, Terry!"

"Chip…"

The fork dropped to the table, bouncing off his plate. "I asked what *you* think, not what my step"—he broke off and leaned back in the chair. "Fine, we can talk about it tomorrow, or the next day, or never. I just don't care."

I got up and left the room without another word. He was still in the kitchen when I went to bed, but I knew that when I got up in the morning the plate would still be on the table, the fork right where he had left it, and his dinner untouched.

Chip

Ending the day with a temper tantrum wasn't exactly what I had in mind. Terry stormed off to bed without so much as a good night kiss, and I wound up on the balcony in my underwear, thinking that I had to be one of the world's biggest fuck ups. I couldn't expect her to understand; the Grant she knew was not the man I grew up with.

The Grant she knew was funny, and even though he was uptight about it, loved her hugs and wanted more than anything to be Nick's Poppy. Grant The Stepfather was—what? I wondered suddenly.

What exactly had he done to me? We fought constantly and he grounded me every other week for some minor infraction that seemed insignificant in the grand scheme of things. If Dave spilled milk on the floor, that was too bad, it could be cleaned up. If I spilled… what did happen?

I wanted to say he knocked the snot out of me. I could clearly remember Dave's punishments—or lack thereof—but mine were a blur. Stay out past curfew, get grounded. Pee on the azaleas, get grounded. Pour gasoline on the neighbor's yard and burn your initials in their grass, and get grounded— for a few hours, anyway, long enough to make it look good.

Time spent in my room, I could remember clearly.

Terry was right, I was too tired to think straight. Sleep was coming in half hour snatches at best, and I spent more nights out on the balcony than I did in bed. I'd hold her until she fell asleep, then creep out of the room and sit outside until just before dawn. Yelling at her was the last thing I intended, but she couldn't understand. I couldn't take anything of Grants.

I hated the man.

She was asleep when I finally slipped into bed around three, and automatically rolled over to snuggle up to me. I had learned to sleep on my back, because no matter where I was in bed, most of the night she was there, too, tangling arms and legs around mine, her face mashed up against my shoulder or her head on my chest.

One of us should be comfortable, in any case. One of us should sleep.

When I was thirteen Grant walked into my bedroom—I was probably grounded for some minor offense; I remember being splayed out on the bed looking at some magazine— and dropped a box into the nightstand drawer. It was the closest thing we'd ever had to a sex talk; he closed the drawer, said "Don't get yourself caught, son," and walked out. It was a box of tightly foil-wrapped condoms, a baker's dozen, one for every year of my short life.

The supply never ran out, always replaced without request, and undoubtedly kept from my mother. I wondered why he'd done it in the first place, whether he recognized the restless stirrings in the already too tall teenager grouching life away in his house, or because he simply remembered his own adolescence. To me it was permission granted and opportunity not to be ignored.

My sex life began in the bushes that separated our back yard from the Chapman's next door; 15 year old Kim Chapman was more than willing to match her experience to my virginity. I don't know what she expected from me, but once the initial supply of condoms was exhausted I had moved on to someone else. And someone after that. Before the end of eighth grade I'd lost count.

By the time I turned 14 and started high school, I was fairly adept at getting what I wanted from the girls I was interested in, and I didn't think twice about moving on without an explanation. If there were any hearts broken along the way, I don't know, because I never cared enough to ask.

I was careful enough to not get caught; the few times I heard "you don't need that" I didn't listen.

So what was it about Terry that made me forget the Number One Rule of Seduction? The absence of protection didn't cross my mind until the weekend was over and we were sitting there in her bedroom, the urge to make her mine stabbing through my head as hard as it was burning through my heart.

She wouldn't have liked the teenager who abused just enough charm to convince impressionable girls that sex right then and there would be the single most important moment of their lives. She would have despised the arrogance; if she had met me before my sensibilities were bruised by guilt, she would have brushed me off and I'd have never seen her again.

Toward the end of my sophomore year, before I was

caught with my jeans around my ankles in the teacher's lounge and "strongly urged" to find education elsewhere, I took Linda Holtman to her junior prom. Linda wasn't a member of any of the popular cliques, but she was funny, and in an odd sort of way she was pretty. I asked her on a whim, figuring the investment of a little cash, plus a few hours stuffed into a tux, would have some sort of payoff at the end of the night. This was the prom, after all; all but 2 or 3 of the heterosexual males in that room expected sex in return for their efforts.

When I told her I'd reserved a room for when the dance was over, she stepped back and let me know in no uncertain terms *that* was not on her agenda for the night.

I told her that was fine, then left her in the middle of the dance floor and found a senior whose expectations were more in line with my own. I'd spent the money, rented the tux, reserved the room, and one way or the other I fully intended to be rewarded for my efforts. If Linda was hurt, I didn't care.

No, Terry definitely would not have had anything to do with the teenage version of me.

Weeks after Grant died she was still asking me on a daily basis if I was all right, trying to put her arms around me and make the pain go away, trying to get me to tell her what was bothering me—without coming right out and asking why I was being such an ass 90% of the time. She'd cook for me and I wouldn't eat. She'd put her arms around me and I'd stiffen up. She'd offer me backrubs to help me sleep, baths to relax me, and sex just for the hell of it.

Except for the sex—and only because I swore to myself I would never tell her no, not ever—I turned it all down. I walked away, left her angry and hurt, without any better explanation than the garbage I spilled out to women all my life.

I was leaving my wife standing in the middle of the dance floor, but this time I cared.

I just couldn't stop myself.

Terry

Steven Mark Stone came screaming into the world less than a month after Chip's 25th birthday, and the few times that he held his godson were the few times that Chip didn't act like he was looking at life through a wet, dark fog. A tiny toothless yawn almost pulled a smile out of him and seemed to fill him with a sense of longing, but when he handed the baby boy back to his mother, the fog redeveloped, and he was back where he began.

He raised an approving eyebrow when Nicky announced he was a big boy and no longer wanted to wear diapers; he wondered out loud if Nicky wasn't too young to potty train, but he went out and bought his son a step stool to stand on in the bathroom. Still, it didn't seem to have the same impact on him all the other milestones had. He acknowledged it, but just barely. Buy the boy a step stool and then forget about it.

Nicky was speaking in coherent sentences, and it seemed to bypass Chip that his son wasn't even a year and a half old.

He came home from the gym and peeled off his shoes and socks and shirt, then stretched out on the couch, the TV buzzing on the other side of the room. He watched it with eyes glazed over, either bored or just not giving a damn; I could hear a laugh track, but I never heard Chip laugh, or even grunt at something stupid. One show faded into another, commercials popping out loudly, and he didn't move.

Nicky was on the floor by the sofa with a dozen toy cars and trucks, driving them through the carpet while making motor sounds with his lips. Every few minutes he would rub his face into the carpet, wiping away the drool that dripped from his chin. Chip ignored the noise until Nick stood up with a truck in hand and walked over to him, slapping the wheels into Chip's chest.

"Pay twucks, Daddy."

I looked up from my book; he brushed Nick's hand aside and grunted, "not now, Nicky."

Nicky stood there, running the truck across Chip's chest and stomach, pushing it across the dips and valleys of his father's abdominal muscles, spit flying from his lips as he continued to make the sounds he was sure sounded exactly like a roaring engine.

"Don't, Nicky."

Nick stopped for half a second to wipe the drool off of his chin on Chip's arm, and then continued driving the truck across Chip's chest.

"Dammit, Nicky, I said no." He sat up and lifted Nicky, carrying him to the other side of the room where he sat him back down in the middle of all his cars. "Leave Daddy alone. I don't want to play right now."

Nicky dug around in the pile of cars and picked out his favorite blue truck and held it up to Chip. "You have dis one."

"Later." He went into the bedroom, and Nicky watched him until he was out of sight. I waited for the tears to start, but he simply put the truck down and started playing with another one.

Five minutes later Chip came out of the bedroom wearing a black sweatshirt, his shoes in hand. He sat on the sofa to put them on and Nick looked up, asking, "You eat cookies wif me?"

"Daddy's not hungry."

"You want milk?"

"I just said no, Nicky," Chip snapped.

I set my book aside and was ready to pick Nicky up to rescue his young ego from his father's bad mood; Chip stood up and reached for his keys and mumbled, "I'm going to the restaurant to get some work done."

He walked out the door without another word, slamming it behind him.

"Nicky," I picked him up, "do you still want a cookie?"

"Uh huh."

"Okay. Do you want milk, too?"

"Uh huh."

I carried him into the kitchen and set him in his booster seat. "Nicky, Daddy wasn't mad at you," I told him, pouring the milk into a plastic cup. "Daddy was just tired, and he had to go to work."

I handed him the cup and set a cookie on the table in front of him.

"Daddy loves you, you know."

He looked at the cookie and then at me. "I hab daddy's cookie?"

I hoped to wear Nick out with a long walk to the park; we fed the ducks and he squealed—partly out of fear and partly out of sheer joy—when they ate out of his hand. A dozen of them surrounded us, waddling right up to him, and a dozen more out on the water looked up with interest, but didn't bother to investigate what the little boy was offering. When all the duck food was gone we played in the giant sandbox, digging holes and building tiny castles that he flattened with his feet. He watched older kids play on the swing set and slides with some envy, but never asked if he could go onto the playground with them; when a breeze kicked up and blew over the water he announced it was time to go home because he was cold and the ducks had to take naps.

For dinner we had a picnic in the living room, munching on squares of cheese and bologna, while Big Bird paraded on the TV and Nick half paid attention to other kids talking to hairy hand puppets about the alphabet. He picked at a banana, digging out chunks that he mashed between his fingers before putting in his mouth.

He helped me clean up by carrying the banana peel to the kitchen, throwing it on top of the stove instead of into the trash can.

"Banana peels don't go there, Nicky."

"Dey do now."

I handed him the peel. "Put it where it belongs."

He rolled his little eyes and shoved it into the trash can.

I gave him a bath and then suffered through his nightly 'I don't want a diaper' whine, finally settling him into bed. We cuddled up against the pillows with a book and I read to him; when he still wasn't sleepy we pulled out a book and tried to come up with names for everything in the pictures.

"That's a kitty," I said when he pointed to a picture of a cat playing with a ball of yarn. "What sound does a kitty make?"

"Meow."

"Is a kitty like a puppy?"

He flipped to the next page, looking for a dog. "Puppies say 'woof,'" he said. "Dey babies."

"That's right. Kitties and puppies are babies."

"Dey not same."

"No. Kitties are baby cats and puppies are baby dogs."

"I not a baby."

"You're a big boy," I assured him. I pointed to another picture. "What's this?"

"Boat."

"That's right! Where does a boat go?"

He looked puzzled. "In da potty?"

After Nicky was asleep I stretched out on the sofa with a book and read for a while; when the words started swimming before my eyes I dimmed the light, leaving it just bright enough that Chip would be able to find his way through the apartment when he got home, and went to bed.

I woke up at 8 the next morning. His side of the bed was cold and hadn't been slept in, and the living room light was still on. He wasn't sitting out on the balcony, and his keys weren't on the stand by the door.

I picked up the phone and called his office, but there was no answer. I tried calling the bar, knowing that it was still too early for anyone to be there. The kitchen supervisor wouldn't be there for another two hours; three if they'd done the lunch prep before closing.

Nicky stumbled out of his room, clutching a teddy bear in one hand and rubbing tears from his eyes with the other.

"What's wrong, Nicky?"

"I wet."

"Aw, sweetheart, that's okay. We'll get you all cleaned up and dressed."

"I not a baby!"

I picked him up and hugged him. "I know. Nicky's a big boy, but even big boys have accidents."

"Do daddies?" he asked as I peeled off his diaper.

"Well no. Daddies are men. Men don't have accidents at night."

"I be a daddy?"

"When you're all grown up you can be," I said.

"I grow up?"

"You sure will." I pulled his pants up. "But don't grow up too fast, Mommy wants you to be a little boy for a while."

He frowned. "I a big boy."

Sigh.

After breakfast we drove past the park; I had dim hopes Chip would be there asleep on a bench or on a teeter totter, then headed for the restaurant. His car was parked in its usual space, but the doors were locked.

I strapped Nick back into his car seat and drove on, looking for a pay phone. I found one two blocks down at a convenience store, then sat there with the engine running, digging through my purse for change.

"You got pennies?" Nick asked.

"I don't think so, but Mommy is looking for dimes."

"Daddy gots dimes."

"I know, sweetheart," I laughed. "But Daddy isn't here and I need dimes now."

"Dimes der." He pointed at the glove compartment. "Daddy dimes der."

I opened it up, and sure enough, there were rolls of quarters and dimes. "How did you know that, Nicky?"

"I see'd Daddy."

"When he put the dimes in there?"

"Uh huh."

"Well you're a smart boy. I'm glad you remembered."

"Daddy buy candy."

"With the dimes?"

"Uh huh."

"It's too early for candy," I said, prying two dimes from the roll. "After lunch you remind me, and we'll go to the seven-eleven and you can buy a candy bar."

"Daddy go?"

"I don't know. Can Mommy take you?"

"Uh huh."

He went into the phone booth with me, watching closely as the dimes disappeared into the coin slot. I dialed Ted's number and prayed I wasn't waking him up after a long night working the bar.

He answered sleepily, accepted my apology, and then said that Chip had never come into work. He'd expected him most of the day, but had never seen him.

"What now?" I mumbled, hanging up the phone.

"Dimes," he said, slapping at the phone.

"Do you want to call someone?"

"No."

"You just want dimes."

"Uh huh."

I got more change from the car and fed it into the coin slot, then dialed Doug and Kris's number.

"I go Unca Doug?" Nicky asked as I was saying goodbye.

"You were eavesdropping," I teased. "Yes, we're going to go over to Uncle Doug and Aunt Kris's. Do you want to see their new baby?"

"No."

He settled into his car seat and held his arms out of the way while I buckled him in.

"Do you remember the baby's name?"

"Uh huh."

"What is it?"

"Stee-ben."

"Do you like Steven?"

"No."

"Why not?"

"Stinks."

"He just smells like a baby," I said.

"Stinks like poop."

The baby was asleep when we got there; Nick took a quick look at him and then, unimpressed, asked Kris if he could watch the TV. He settled on the floor and watched a rerun of Sesame Street, too caught up in trying to keep up with The Count and trying to figure out which One Of These Things was Not Like The Other to listen to the adults talking behind him.

"He only said he was going to work?" Doug asked.

"He said he was going to the restaurant to get some work done," I replied. "That was around three in the afternoon. Ted says he never showed up."

"But his car is there."

I nodded.

"Is he still in a bad mood?" Kris asked.

"Same grump he's been since Grant died. I hoped I'd find him at the park again… At what point do I call the police?"

"You don't," Kris said. "Chip's been a chronic runaway since he was nine years old. It seems like every time he gets hit with something he doesn't understand or something that pisses him off, he runs away. People quit looking for him when he turned eighteen… it's just his pattern. He always comes back, but no one knows where it is he slinks off to."

"Kris, I think he'd tell me before he just took off."

"If he was thinking clearly he would. If Chip's licking his wounds he's not thinking at all."

"His car is at the Charybdis," I said. "He can't have gone far."

"Terry…" Doug sighed, looked at Nick and then back at me. "I know where he is. I'll go after him."

"I'm going with you!"

"No. It'd be better if you didn't."

"Doug…"

"Really," he said. "Just let me go get him. You guys go do something today, have some fun. I'll have him back by tonight."

I sighed hard. "You expect me to just act like nothing is wrong?"

"Nothing happened to him, Terry. He just went off to be by himself. I'll go get him and take him back to your place."

"How can you be sure you know where he's at?" Kris asked.

"I just do."

"And you're not sharing?"

"No."

"So how is it for years the rest of us never had a clue, and you do?"

He looked at me. "You know where he went," he said. "If you stop and think, you know exactly where he runs to."

Doug

It took three hours to make a two hour drive. I wound up behind a motor home going 2 miles an hour in a no passing zone, and stayed there until we came up on a passing lane ten miles down the road; the old geezer driving it pulled into the far lane and let me speed by. I stuck my hand out the window and waved my thanks, then hoped he didn't mistake it for flipping him off.

Half a tank of gas and one hell of a backache later I pulled into the driveway. The house was dark and there wasn't a car anywhere near it. I tried the front door, but it was locked, and didn't bother ringing the doorbell because I knew he wouldn't answer.

I went around to the back of the house intending to try the back door. Chip was standing on the beach at the edge of the water, waves lapping around his ankles, soaking his shoes and the bottom of his jeans. His hands were stuffed into his pockets, and he was staring out at the ocean.

I leaned against the rail and watched him. He didn't move, not a twitch or turn of his head. I stayed on the porch for at least half an hour, waiting for him to turn and come up to the house.

He wasn't going to budge.

The wood steps creaked as my feet hit them, but he still didn't turn around. I knew he could hear me coming, and I was sure he knew it was me who was there. I stood next to him, straining to see what he was staring at so hard.

He stood there for another five minutes, then took a deep breath and said, "I was just looking for a way to plug up the whirlpool before Terry and Nicky get sucked under."

"It's time to go home," I said.

He didn't say another word. We climbed into the car and headed for home; he stared out the window and I knew better than to say anything, because he wouldn't be listening.

Instead of letting him out and trusting he would actually go into the apartment building and upstairs, I parked the car and went in with him. He took the steps slowly, opened the door quietly, and headed for the balcony once he was inside.

Terry was in the kitchen feeding Nicky. He smiled at me, but was too busy trying to rip his dinner into tiny pieces to say anything.

"He's out on the balcony," I told her. "He didn't say a

damn thing on the ride home, so I don't know exactly what's going through his head."

She looked at Nicky, and then at the kitchen door.

"Go ahead. I'll stay here and keep an eye on him."

"If he finishes the carrots," she said, pointing to a bag on the counter, "he can have a cookie."

"Two," Nick grunted.

"Thank you, Doug," she said, and then to Nicky, "One."

Terry

Chip was sitting on the balcony, his elbows on his knees and head in his hands. When I slid the door open he lifted his head, but didn't look at me; he stared off at some imaginary spot on the horizon and said, almost in a whisper, "I wasn't running away, I swear."

Chip

She wanted to know how I got to the beach.

I had no clue.

Terry

The only difference I could see between Chip and Nicky at the table was that after pushing his food around and pulling it into pieces, Nicky would eat. Chip slouched in his chair and pushed food around, taking an occasional small bite, until Nick was done and off playing in his bedroom. He'd drop his pretense then, and simply stare at the table, absently turning his fork over between his fingers.

"I can fix you something else," I offered.

"I'm not really hungry."

"I promise, it doesn't taste as bad as it looks."

"There's nothing wrong with your cooking, Terry."

I took the plates off the table and set them in the sink. "Are you going back to work tonight?"

"I should. You want help with the dishes?"

"No, there's not much to do."

"I'm coming home tonight," he said.

"I know."

He got up and pushed the kitchen door open; as it swung back in I heard a loud crack followed by Chip shouting, "Goddammit Nicky, pick your crap up off the floor!"

Nicky was standing in front of Chip when I came out of the kitchen, his eyes wide and flooded with tears.

"I swear to God, I'll throw it away if you don't take care of it." He was holding Nick's blue truck, scowling as he looked down.

"Daddy no."

"I mean it, Nicky. It's probably broken. If you don't take care of your stuff I'll toss it out."

Nicky dropped to his knees and started wailing.

I took the truck from Chip. The plastic was cracked down the middle, the metal holding the wheels together bent. "Chip, this is his favorite truck."

"Well, now it's his broken truck. He'll learn."

"Chip… he's just a baby."

He closed his eyes and sighed, then nodded. He reached down for Nicky, picked him up and said softly, "Nicky, I'm sorry. I didn't mean to step on it. I'll buy you a new one, I promise."

"Dat one," Nicky cried.

"Okay, I'll fix that one."

I shook my head; it couldn't be fixed. "Daddy has to buy a new one, Nicky. This one is broken and you could get an owie if you play with it."

Nicky cried even harder.

"I'll get you a better one," Chip promised.

"Bue one?"

"A blue one. A big blue one."

Nicky sniffed and wiped his nose across Chip's shoulder. "Daddy gots dimes?"

"Daddy has enough dimes to buy Nicky a new truck."

"Daddy buy candy?"

"If you want, I'll buy you a candy bar, too."

"Uh huh."

He put Nick down and watched him walk into his bedroom. "Don't ever let me yell at him like that again."

"We'll both yell once in a while, Chip."

"Not like that. That was just so fucking stupid..." He picked up his keys. "I'm not going to work after all. If Ted calls, tell him I'm out trying to spend my guilt away."

"Daddy sad," Nicky said, piling blocks and toy cars on top of his teddy bear. "Mommy kiss Daddy."

"I'll give Daddy a kiss when he comes home," I promised. "Are you sad about your truck?"

"No."

"That's good. I know Daddy felt bad when he broke it."

He kept piling toys on top of the bear and I was about to ask him why when the phone rang.

"You need to call Doug and get him to come over and watch Nicky," Chip said before I could get a word out.

"Why?"

"Because I need you to come bail me out of jail."

"You *punched* someone over a fender bender?"

"It was more than that," Chip said. "The son of a bitch

ran a red light and plowed into my car. I'll be damned lucky if it's not totaled."

"But you hit him, Chip!"

"Well, maybe now he'll think twice before running a red."

"Chip!"

"I did get Nicky's truck, though. We'll need to stop on the way home for the candy bar, unless I'm in trouble for promising him one. I know, I let him have too much crap."

We were on the front steps of the police station and I grabbed his arm to stop him. "Do you even hear yourself? You hit someone so hard he had to be taken to the ER. Over a car accident."

"Yes, I know. I was there."

"And that doesn't bother you?"

"No." He walked down the steps and onto the sidewalk. "Should it?"

October 1977

Terry

Chip's mood hovered like a dark storm cloud, the threat of torrential rain accompanied by thunder and lightning was always there; his temper was explosive and almost always irrational, and for whatever reason he was unwilling or unable to explain the wound he felt festering deep inside. In the time that had passed since Grant's death he was away more than he was home, and when he did come home he was either drunk or so surly he was unreachable. Each day was a new brick in the wall he built between himself and the world; every day it was that much more difficult to get past it.

I kept telling myself it was temporary, just a knee jerk reaction to grief he didn't understand; give him a few days, even a week or two, and he'd work through it.

A month after the funeral he was worse than ever.

Watching at him standing by the dresser, his hair wet and standing on end, pointing in every direction, I thought I could see what it was—he looked heartbroken. I wanted to get up and throw my arms around him, to pull him out of the shadows where he was hiding, but the last few weeks taught me that something so simple could backfire. He didn't want any of it.

I sat up in bed, drawing my knees up. He was stepping into his jeans, and just watching him caused a familiar ache to shoot through me. Even when it was the farthest thing from his mind, it was easy for him to make me want him.

"Nicky's still asleep," he said, not looking at me. "You might as well get some rest while you can."

"Or I could make you breakfast."

He reached into the drawer and pulled out a faded green t-shirt. "Save yourself the trouble. I'm not hungry and I need to get going."

"You can't go to work dressed like that. Besides, it's still early. Wouldn't you rather come back to bed for a while?"

"Not really." He turned his back to me and stared into the mirror, slowly pulling a comb through his hair. "But I will if you really want me to."

"No... it was just a suggestion."

He flicked water off his comb and shoved it into his back pocket. "I'm going to the gym before I go to the restaurant. I'll be home late tonight."

"Are you at least coming home for dinner?"

"I just said I'd be late, Terry." He reached down and grabbed his shoes. "I own a fucking restaurant. I'm sure if I look hard enough I can find food there."

"A simple no would have sufficed, Chip."

"Well... then no."

"I also need the checkbook." He was leaning on the edge of the dresser, staring at me crossly. The thought popped into my head that just a few weeks before he not only would have come back to bed at the first hint, he would have bounded across the room and jumped onto the bed, throwing his clothes in every direction. "I need to take Nicky shopping."

"Sure. Just what the hell is it Nicky has the urge to buy?"

I jumped out of the bed and was over to him in three angry steps. "I just asked you for the checkbook, is that such a problem? Your son has outgrown nearly everything he owns, or do you expect him to start walking around naked?"

"Stop it."

He tried to twist away but I put my hand on his chest and held him there. "Chip, tell me what's wrong."

"The only thing that's wrong," he said, pushing my hand away, "is that I'm going to be late. Doug is probably already at the gym." He started out the bedroom, with me a step behind. "Terry, I'm fine."

"No, you're not fine. If you were fine you wouldn't have broken your son's heart last night. He wanted to play, and you practically shoved him out of the room. You hurt his feelings, and that's not like you."

He dropped onto the couch to pull his shoes on. "I was tired and he was whining, Terry. You've got to do something about that. It's getting damned irritating."

"Chip, listen you yourself."

"Dammit, Terry!" he exploded. "Get off my back and stop nagging."

"This isn't nagging."

He was up and at the door, digging in the drawer of the stand for his keys. "Look, ignore me. No matter what I say it's going to come out wrong. I'll try to make it home for dinner but I can't promise anything. Payday is tomorrow and I haven't even started on it."

"Ted can handle it," I ventured, going over to him. "He has to be there late anyway."

"It's not his job, it's mine."

I slipped my arms around him. "So come home for a little while. I'll fix you dinner and give you a back rub."

"No promises."

He stiffened, wanting to escape out the door. Even at that point, I knew I could get him to put the keys back in the drawer and come back to bed, but it would be reluctantly and I wasn't willing to face that again. "Do I at least get a kiss?"

"Yeah, sure."

He bent his head to kiss me, just a quick peck on the lips, and was out the door before I could say goodbye.

Chip

It was the house, I decided. I didn't want the house. Living there would bring back too much of everything; no matter where I turned there would be a memory jumping out and taunting me. I just wanted to put it all behind me; Terry, I think, wanted me to be more forgiving, but I didn't think I had it in me to forgive being so used. How many times had my mother come close to telling me the truth? She must have realized that Ron wasn't going anywhere; he didn't give up his loves so easy. He fostered them against the world. He hurt easy, but he never would have left.

And it was funny how everyone commented on my eyes, my father's eyes. Kris has always told me I had my father's eyes. It wasn't something I saw when I looked in the mirror. The eyes that stared back definitely weren't Grant's, and now they weren't Ron's either.

I checked my watch. Terry would be angry, all right. There was no way she would believe I had worked on the payroll until well past midnight. The restaurant had closed an hour earlier and Ted would be shutting the bar down.

I had no idea why going home was so hard. I didn't

think it had anything to do with my wife or my son, but I was uncomfortable and it was just easier to stay away. If I waited until she was asleep I could slip into the apartment and sit on the balcony or watch TV and avoid the inevitable stress of trying not to fight.

"Want another one?" Ted asked, his tone suggesting he did not want to serve me. The two drinks I'd already had were more than enough.

"Sure. One for the road."

He held out his hand. "Your car keys first."

I cocked an eyebrow, trying to hide the scowl I felt coming on. I could argue until I was blue in the face, threaten to fire him—again—but it would be useless. "How in the hell do you think I'll get home tonight?" I asked, dropping the keys in his hand. "Flap my fucking arms and fly?"

"I'll call you a cab."

"Oh, that'll look great… the boss is plastered, so let's pack him into a taxi and send him on his merry way."

"If I were you I wouldn't be worrying how I looked to my employees. You're drunk and don't belong on the road. I sure as hell don't want to be the one to tell that young wife of yours when you plow your car into a brick wall that I let you out the door like this."

"She's going to wring my neck when I get home, anyway."

"As much time as you've spent warming the bar stools lately I can't say as how I'd blame her. I know my wife wouldn't put up with being ignored so much."

"I don't ignore my wife."

"Oh really?" He set the drink in front of me. "What would you call it? You're here long before we open every day and you're here after midnight almost every night. The few times

I've seen your wife in here lately you've said something stupid, or mean, and she leaves in tears. People notice. You're not doing a damn thing to enhance your reputation around here."

"So?"

"So patch up your marriage and stop using the bar to get away from it. This is the last night I serve you more than one drink—and if it's stronger than beer, you can kiss it off. If you're going to act like my sixteen year old son, then I'll start treating you like him."

I stared at him, disbelieving.

"You can fire me for real if you want, Chip. I can always get another job but you'll never get anyone as good to replace me." He took back the drink he was now sure would go untouched. "If you don't get your shit together she's going to leave you. Quit drinking so much."

"All right," I conceded. "Just give me back my keys and call a cab for me."

He tossed me my keys.

"I'm not an alcoholic, Ted. I don't drink that much."

"Not yet," he said, pushing a cup of coffee towards me, "but if you don't cut it out, you will be."

Terry

I was sitting up in bed, a small lamp on the night stand on and a book in my lap, when I heard Chip's keys fumbling in the lock. I listened for the sound of the balcony door to open, or the hiss of the TV as it came on, but he crept into the room, shoes in hand. He looked ragged and worn, and still looked sad.

"Ted called me," I said. "He thought I might be worried about you."

He tore off his shirt and tossed it aside. "Christ, you've got him spying on me?"

"Well, he was right. I was worried."

"What the hell for? You knew where I was." He stripped off the jeans and his underwear and fell into bed, smelling of Irish Whiskey and coffee.

I turned the light off and laid back. Chip rolled onto his side, away from me. "Knowing where you are doesn't mean I know if you're planning on coming home," I murmured.

"I'm here, aren't I?"

"Are you?" I tried to put my arms around him, ignoring how much he stiffened at first touch. He didn't push me away, though, and with a little persistence he relaxed.

"What is it you want, Terry?" he grumbled. "If you want sex, just say so."

"I don't want sex," I said, kissing his bare shoulder. "I want you to make love with me."

He rolled onto his back and sighed hard. "If it's what you want, all you have to do is say so. I'm willing to give you a tumble."

"No. Not the way you are now."

"Just what the hell is that supposed to mean? You keep saying one thing and then another... what am I supposed to think? If you're horny, do something about it. Use me. Just let me know one way or the other."

"This has nothing to do with sex," I whispered, rolling away from him. He had no idea, did he? He'd locked himself in his own little world and wasn't letting anyone in.

"I'll bite," he growled. "What is it?"

I wasn't sure I wanted to start anything, especially in bed, but if I let him get up he'd be out on the balcony—probably naked—and drinking again. It was difficult enough to talk to him when he was angry, it would be impossible if he got drunk. "I can't live with you like this," I finally said. "I feel like I'm living in a mine field. I never know when you're going to explode or what might set you off."

"You don't want to live with me anymore?" He sounded like a little boy, suddenly afraid.

"Chip, please. Quit trying to hear me and just start listening. You're twisting everything I say. I just wish you could calm down and talk to me."

"Do which? Listen or talk? I can't do both. It might be something inherently female, but the rest of us mere mortals can only do one or the other."

I bit my lip and prayed I could keep from crying. I couldn't tell if he was being deliberately obtuse, or if he was totally unaware of how he was talking me. "Let's just talk about it in the morning."

"Fine. Now do you want my body, which you can certainly have, or can I go to sleep?"

This can't be happening, I thought wildly. I'd been warned about his temper but had never been able to believe it. This was a man I could see using his hands to pound someone into a wall, someone who could go for the jugular and not wince. What if—and the thought nearly killed me—this is the way he really is? Perhaps he'd just had a couple of good years, and was starting to slide back into the old Chip Davis, the one I heard so much about but never thought really existed.

I lost the fight with the tears, but there was no way I would let him hear me cry.

Chip

This boy was like spit on a hot skillet. I never knew what was going to pop out at me.

I woke with a start, disoriented, the dream still fresh in my head. Those were the words I heard over and over again. Was that how I was? Unpredictable? I'd given Grant hell from day one, but I never thought of myself as capricious.

I stared down at Terry. She was curled on her side with her back to me, clutching a pillow. Even asleep she had that wild, bewildered look. Was that also how she saw me? Unreasonable and erratic?

I can't live with you like this anymore. I feel like I'm living in a mine field.

How many times had I reduced her to tears with the things I said? Ted warned I was losing her and it was beginning to dawn on me that I wasn't touching her fragile ego; she hadn't said or done anything she hadn't before. I had, and it was getting too easy to lash out at her. She was terrified, and only wanted to talk it out with me.

What could I say, though? Recognizing that you're a prick doesn't make it any easier to suddenly stop being one.

I cuddled up to her, carefully slipping my arms between her and the pillow. Maybe if she woke up she would think I'd done it in my sleep, and realize that no matter what I was saying and how idiotic I was behaving, I still needed her.

"I love you," I whispered in her ear, half hoping she was awake enough to hear me and half terrified that she'd roll over and tell me to go to hell. She snuggled back a touch, her foot sliding between my calves.

It occurred to me later that I could have woken her up with a long kiss, and done what she'd wanted before; I could have made love to her and meant it, I could have spent the rest of the night telling her how much I loved her and needed her, but the idiot that I am, I just placed a kiss on her neck and let myself drift off, falling back into the nightmares that had pricked at me for weeks.

    She was caught in the whirlpool and was fighting to keep
from being sucked under, and I wasn't doing anything to stop
it.

November 1977

Kris

I wasn't prepared for a mansion. When Terry invited me along to check out the house, I expected just that: a garden variety single family home with an average yard and a couple of trees thrown in for good measure. My notions were more along the lines of the small three bedroom house Doug had talked me into before the baby was born. Never in my wildest fantasies did I think that the house Chip inherited was big enough for a baseball team. Eight bedrooms, a den, a three car garage, and Grant had lived there alone for at least four years.

I followed Terry from room to room, making mental notes. The idea was to find a way to remodel and redecorate without tearing the house down to its foundation. Chip wanted it as far removed from its original state as possible.

Most of the bedrooms looked as if they had never been used. They were sparsely furnished and everything was coated with a fine layer of dust. Dave's room—I was certain it was his—still had all the trappings of a boy just on the verge of adolescence; walls covered by black light posters and pictures of rock stars, calendars of girls and sketches of cars, and at the end of his bed was a toy box still filled with tiny green army men and plastic tanks and trucks.

Chip's room was far less revealing. Almost everything he'd owned was gone. The walls were bare, the bed stripped down to a single sheet, the closet empty. Left standing in the corner was a dust covered twelve string guitar, the fret board streaked with wear, two broken strings hanging limp.

I was struck by the warmth when we entered the living room. The dark wood paneling gave it a rustic charm, the fireplace surrounded on both sides by chunks of jutting rock. I was drawn to the portrait hanging over the mantel, not missing the fact that Terry was also.

"So that's her," she muttered, sitting in front of the fireplace. "You know, Chip doesn't have any pictures of her."

"Is she what you expected?"

Terry studied the painting, her eyes shifting from the little boy to the woman and back again. Those eyes, devilish and mischievous, were definitely Chip's. "Kris, I don't know what to expect anymore," she said, her breath pushing the words out in a burst of pent up emotion. She was close to tears and not doing the greatest job of fighting them back.

"What is it? Is it redoing the house? Too big?"

"Chip won't even come here. He wants the whole thing finished first."

"Lots of painful memories, Terry. It's not easy for him."

"Easy for him?" she spat. "Kris, it's been well over two months since Grant died and he's just now getting around to taking care of all the odds and ends of the estate. He doesn't want to live here, ever, but he wants it redecorated. It doesn't make sense."

"He probably hasn't really made up his mind."

"Not about this, not about anything." She rested her head on her hands, running her fingers through her hair. "He doesn't know what he wants."

"This has nothing to do with Grant's estate or the house, does it?"

She blinked, tears spilling onto her cheeks. "He's withdrawn so far into himself its like living with a stranger."

"Sounds familiar."

"You don't understand. Kris, he won't talk to me, he barely looks at me... he won't touch me."

"Are you serious?" I was forming a mental picture of Chip in boxer shorts and an a-shirt, planted in front of the TV with a beer in one hand, waving at Nicky to get out of the way.

She shook her head, wiping the tears away with the back of her hand. "Dead serious."

"You mean he hasn't..."

"Oh, he has." The pained look would not go away. "If I make the first move and practically insist, he will, but he might as well not even be there. I got so tired of feeling like I was begging for affection—he's never come right out and said no, but..."

"You'd rather not at all," I finished for her.

"I just don't understand. Chip didn't even like Grant all that much. I can't believe he's grieving this deeply."

"Maybe it's not Grant, per se. Maybe he just feels like he lost something."

She was looking back up at the picture, riveted to the stunningly beautiful woman holding her impish son.

"She never stopped haunting Ron," I told her. "I don't think there's a day gone by that he hasn't mourned her. And Grant must have sat in this house day after day in the same spot you're in right now, staring at this picture."

"Chip loved her."

"And Chip feels betrayed. One by one they all did, with the possible exception of Dave, but he was too young to get caught up in all the crap."

"Chip has that look," she said. "His eyes are just like hers. He uses that look to get what he really wants. He can melt me to nothing with it and he knows it. I miss it."

"You feel betrayed, too."

"I want my husband back. He's right there but I miss him so much. All I want is for things to be the way they were before he read that damned letter." She was crying hard, her head buried against her folded arms in her lap.

I watched her cry; I remembered that pain too well. Even from the grave that woman wouldn't let go. If she couldn't have her men, no one could, and Chip was the only one really left. Grant and David were both gone, and Ron might as well have been. Doug had heard he was fading fast, dragging out his final assignment to the point of certain failure. There was only Chip.

I got up and stretched onto my toes to reach the wood frame of the portrait. With a little push it was off the wall and sliding into my hands. "It'll be in the attic," I said, offering her no choice. "Maybe someday Chip will be ready to see it again. Maybe someday you will, too."

I didn't think so. Five years of wrestling with Pat Davis's ghost taught me that much. I often wondered what her secret was, how she managed to keep such a tight, manipulative hold on the men in her life.

I found an old blanket and carefully wrapped it around the painting before stowing it in the attic. I was fairly sure it would stay there, but I left it within easy reach of the door, just in case.

Terry was sitting in the same chair when I returned, holding a photo album in her lap. It was filled with small black and white pictures, and a few faded color images. "Look at this," she said, waving me over.

I leaned over and looked; there were pages of family pictures, the four of them standing in front of the camera, smiling. "I wonder who took them."

"What do you notice?"

I looked closer. They appeared to be a perfectly normal, all American family, having their picture taken at parks and on the beach. Nothing out of the ordinary. "Chip was tall, even when he was a kid," I guessed.

"No. Look at the way they're paired off. In every single picture. David is standing in front of Pat, and Grant is next to Chip."

"With his arm around Chip in nearly every one of them," I noted.

"Chip doesn't look uncomfortable, and Grant looks happy. It's like he's glued to Chip."

"He loved Chip," I reminded her.

"But why doesn't Chip see that?"

"Chip saw," I said, taking the album from her and setting it on the hearth, "what he was taught to see."

She stood up and dug her keys from her purse, dangling them from her fingers nervously. "It's getting late. Nicky's probably already in bed and…"

"I know." I slipped into my jacket, wishing there was something I could do to make her feel better. "Doug's probably got his hands full, too. He's still not comfortable playing Daddy when there's no one there to rescue him."

"Is Steven still sleeping most of the time?"

"Mostly." I stepped out into the cool night air and waited

for Terry to lock the door. "Doug is calling him Spider, can you believe that?"

She managed a small smile. "Your son looked like a tiny spider monkey for the first week of his life, Kris."

"Don't encourage him!"

She unlocked the car and slid behind the wheel. "Trust me," she said, clicking her seat belt into place, "there are worse things in life you can be called besides Spider."

Chip

I lay in bed, listening to the tumble of Terry's keys in the front door lock. I'd left the bedroom door wide open, and except for dim light coming from the kitchen, the apartment was dark.

I didn't have to look to know what she was doing.

First to Nicky's room. It was a ritual, every night before turning in. Sometimes I'd hear her up in the middle of the night, her soft footsteps padding the short distance across the living room floor to his bedroom. Once she was satisfied everything was all right, she'd come back to bed, taking great care to climb in gently so she wouldn't wake me.

Most nights I was wide awake, staring into the darkness.

The sound of her footsteps was farther away. I soon heard the swish of water draining in the kitchen sink; she was cleaning up the mess I'd left from dinner, Nicky's leftover bits and pieces of hot dog, and my own mostly untouched plate.

Appetite was something that eluded me. I ate when I remembered, or when Terry coerced food into me. She began to use Nicky as a weapon in the war on food, pointing out what a bad example I was setting; after all, if Daddy didn't have to eat, why should Nicky?

The kid is a chowhound, I always thought when she started in on that, but I ate anyway, for no other reason than I was determined to not fight in front of him.

Some nights I even kept my dinner down.

I waited for a light to come on, or for her silhouette to creep through the bedroom door. I finally heard the groan of the sofa springs and the ear splitting silence that followed; I could almost see the throw pillow she held to her face, trying not to cry out loud.

More than anything I wanted to crawl out of bed and go to her, to just sit and hold her until there was nothing left to cry about. I stayed right where I was, my arms crossed behind my head, staring into the dark.

Nothing was working the way I wanted it to. The control I fought so hard to hold was just beyond where I could reach, and I couldn't remember when I'd last had a firm grasp on it. I could still do everything I was supposed to, mostly mechanical perfunctory movements that didn't hide a thing. Terry stopped touching me, stopped trying to hold or arouse me. She'd known from a night early on, when I'd done everything right, touched her in every way she liked; I sent her spiraling and quivering to the point of digging into my skin and damn near drawing blood. When she finally relaxed there was no denying that I just wasn't into it; I withdrew from her still hard and lay there not caring. She hadn't tried since then.

You have shit for brains, I told myself. How hard could it be to try and really mean it?

The muffled swish of nose spray came from the living room; I knew what it was because she used it so often after she cried. She could never breath afterwards.

Just tell her you love her, dammit. It may be your only chance.

I tensed up so hard I was trembling, muscle spasms that shot through my chest and arms. When I felt the bed heave I put my arms out and caught her before she could lay all the way back, pulling her to me tightly, shaking so hard I thought I could feel the bed move.

"Don't leave me."

Her arms tightened around me, and I could feel the warm trickle of more tears dribble across my skin.

It was the closest thing to an answer I got.

She set breakfast on the table, away from Nicky's eager fingers, a mound of soft, grossly yellow scrambled eggs. I stared at them, my stomach doing a slow agonizing turn. I couldn't eat, especially not something that looked as if it had already been chewed for me.

Terry handed Nick a plastic fork and scraped eggs onto his plate, watching me from the corner of her eye. "I called Doug this morning," she said, pouring juice into a cup and putting a plastic lid on it. "You need to see a doctor, Chip."

I started to protest but bit my tongue instead; you don't argue in front of the kid, he'll grow up weird and get a complex.

Maybe that was my problem, I thought, pushing the eggs around on my plate, avoiding Terry's gaze. Too much family conflict.

Hell.

What family?

I watched as the needle pushed through my skin, the blood that gurgled into the glass tube. The nurse took three ampules and then slapped a piece of gauze on the mark where the needle had been. Merciless bitch, I grumbled to myself.

"You really do look like hell," Doug said when she left. He was sitting on a small stool next to the exam table, clipboard in hand and stethoscope dangling from his neck. "How much weight do you think you've lost?"

I shrugged it off. "Five, maybe six pounds."

"Bullshit. You're down to one sixty five. You've lost at least twenty. Are you even eating? Or sleeping? You weren't exactly a heavyweight before, you know."

"I eat," I replied carefully. "Sleeping is a whole other matter. I doze off for a while and then realize I'm awake again. But I am eating."

"Like what?"

"Whatever Terry tells me to."

He didn't laugh. "I have to ask and don't explode because of it—are you taking anything I should know about?"

I hated taking aspirin for a headache, much less entertain the idea of anything stronger. I drank once in a while but Terry effectively put a stop to that by pouring every ounce of alcohol we owned down the kitchen sink. She went on faith alone that I would get the message. "Nothing, Doug, I swear."

He glanced down at his clipboard, then stood up. "Okay then, let's finish the physical to be on the safe side."

"All right. I'll turn my head and cough for you but you can forget about jamming your damned rubber gloved finger up my ass."

He tossed the clipboard aside and slipped the glove on. "Well my whole day will be shot now that I can't cop a feel on your prostate. I'll just have to be content with groping your balls."

Any other time I would have laughed.

"Look," he said, "I honestly don't think there's anything physically wrong with you."

"So I should see a shrink instead?"

"Maybe, maybe not. It could be that whatever is eating you up is something you have to work out for yourself."

I suddenly thought about Terry and how I was affecting her. An unexpected sting of tears hit my eyes and I blinked them back, not wanting even Doug to see me cry. "Doug, I don't have that kind of time."

His ungloved hand was on my shoulder. "Buddy, you have to figure it out or you'll flip out of your tree. Set a specific time for yourself and if you don't come out if it, then I'll set you up with a therapist."

I slid off the table, grimacing when I felt Doug's hand press into my groin. I turned my head and coughed when I was supposed to, and when Doug was done, peeling the glove off and throwing it away, I realized what it was. It was that familiar soul biting pressure, bearing down on my chest.

I was grateful for the time I had to slip back into my clothes. Of course there was nothing physically wrong with me. I was just turning into a frigging space cadet.

There was a small mirror above the sink, and I looked into it. True, there were dark circles under my eyes, but what was expected of a man who only slept in snatches for ten weeks? And I thought the lost weight looked good.

Terry hated it. Lately Terry hated everything.

I shook the thought away, feeling ashamed for even thinking it. She wasn't to blame for my temper or bad mood.

The man in the mirror scowled as he stared back. *Face it, it's all your own fault. You're a moody, self centered son of a bitch and you're breaking your wife's heart.*

I blinked hard. It was all bullshit.

~

I stretched out on the sofa in my office, telephone perched on my chest. If it rang I'd be up off the couch and across the room in a shot, probably trying to shove my heart back down through my throat.

I knew Terry was waiting at home for me to call. She would be sitting on the floor with Nicky, playing with cars or watching cartoons, the telephone an arm's length away.

I wasn't surprised when she only let it ring once. "I'm fine," I said.

After a moment's considered silence she asked, "Is that your opinion or Doug's?"

"Doug feels there's nothing physically wrong with me. Is that good enough?"

"It'll do."

"Dammit, Terry, what more do you want?" I was sitting up now, fingers gripping the phone so hard I was afraid the plastic would crack. "Do you want me to see a psychiatrist? Is that the next step?"

"Calm down, Chip. I just want to know what Doug thinks."

"I'm fine, Terry. Just ask him yourself." I was on the verge of shouting, speaking through clenched teeth. "I'm not a fucking loony bird, for Christ's sake."

"I just might do that."

"Do what?"

"Talk to Doug."

"Fine, Terry. Talk to the whole frigging world. Stick your head out the window and shout out that your husband is a certified A-one space cadet. I don't care!"

I slammed the phone down, hearing it ping, and instantly realized I had gone way over the line. When I called I wanted to reassure her, not spew out so much garbage that she'd be terrified of me coming home.

Smooth move. You really are an idiot.

Doug

"I need your help."

I looked up from a pile of charts, not at all surprised to see Terry standing in the doorway. I'd half expected her all day, certain that either Chip wouldn't call her or she wouldn't be satisfied with what he'd say.

I put down my pen and invited her into the office, pointing to the chair in front of my desk. "You talked to Chip?

"A while ago."

"There's nothing really wrong with him, Terry. Physically he's still in decent shape, though I'd be happier if he didn't look so damned tired."

"Doug, he gets worse every day."

"Moody, withdrawn, quick tempered? Like a two year old on the verge of a temper tantrum all day?"

"Exactly."

I got up from the desk and went over to her. I pulled another chair up to hers, reaching for her hands. "Chip gets like this," I explained. "Something throws him for a loop and if he doesn't understand it, he panics. The last time this happened it went on for about a year."

"A year of this?"

"It was bad enough I pulled him from duty. He couldn't think straight most of the time, and the tiniest things would set him off. It was terrifying to see him work through it, but eventually he did. With a little help I bet he could do it again."

She gripped at my hands with her fingers. "I had an idea, but it would mean saddling you and Kris with Nicky for a few days."

"Anything that will help."

"I need to get him away from here, just the two of us. He's mentioned wanting to borrow my dad's camper and go fishing or just camping for a while. I think now is the right time."

"Couldn't hurt."

"Oh, it could hurt, all right. It might be the biggest mistake of my life, but I have to take the chance. I can't take a year of this abuse." She looked away from me. "He hasn't hit me, but at this point I don't discount the possibility."

"He wouldn't, Terry." I sighed sadly when she looked back at me. "I know him. Chip would leave you before he started hitting you. If he's yelling all the time and treating you like crap, it's because you're the only one he can trust with his pain. Just don't let him scare you away. He *will* get through this."

"That's why I need to get him out of here, Doug. I know Ted will take care of the Charybdis, but it won't be so easy to get him to go with me."

"Don't give him a choice."

She pulled her hands way. "Sure. Like I can strong arm him into anything."

"Why not? We did it to Kris and that worked out great. We just showed up, shoved her into the car, and took off."

"Chip won't fall for that."

"He will," I promised. "Meet us at the gym this afternoon. Have Kris drive you over, and you can take off from there. Just don't give him a choice."

She looked uncertain.

"It'll work," I insisted. "And Nicky will have a blast with us." I pulled her to her feet, one hand under her chin. Her eyes were sparkling, wide open with trust. "Okay?"

"Okay." When I moved away to hang up my lab coat she said, "there's one more thing I'm not ready to tell him, and I doubt he's ready to hear it."

"What's that?" I grabbed my jacket and shrugged into it.

"I need you to confirm it for me first."

"Terry…"

She took a deep breath and let it out slowly. "I'm pregnant."

Chip fidgeted on the empty bench next to mine, watching the weight bar go up and down. He made it clear that the gym was not where he wanted to be; he didn't have the energy to grit through an entire workout, and said that the Nautilus machines scattered throughout the club looked less like exercise equipment than they did modern torture devices. He wanted to be huddled at the far end of the Charybdis's bar, a stiff drink in front of him and two or three already belted down.

The club was crowded and noisy, music blaring from the aerobics class at the far end of the room. Women were wandering between pieces of equipment, half of them seriously working out, half there to socialize and gossip; any other time it wouldn't have bothered me. Hell, any other time I might try to listen in and learn something.

Chip looked over me and watched women streaming off the aerobics floor. "This is terrific," he groaned. "Look who's here."

I lifted the bar back to the cradle and followed Chip's gaze. I couldn't believe our incredibly bad luck. "Son of a bitch. Blow Job Julie." She was something of an enigma in the club, being one of the women who used the facilities for both intense workouts and as a place to pick up men. When she was there she inevitably spent two or three hours sweating on the aerobics floor and on the weight machines, and another hour or two on the prowl. Her nickname—or so I was told—was well earned. I didn't want to find out, and Chip was in no position to even be tempted.

How could I explain this one to Terry?

"Don't encourage her, Chip. Just quit looking and maybe she'll go drape herself over someone else."

"Not a chance. She's targeted one of us and Julie Meyers doesn't give up easy."

I sat up. "Are you fucking nuts, Chip? The last thing I need is that horny twit breathing down my neck, and it wouldn't do you any good either."

"I can still play the game, Doug. A little harmless flirting never hurt anyone."

"You trust yourself to stop at that?"

He scooted over on the bench, making room for the tall brunette walking towards him. "We'll see, won't we?"

"Dammit…" I bit off the rest of what I wanted to say when she slid onto the bench next to him.

"You're looking pretty good these days," she told Chip. "I haven't seen you in a long time."

He tried smiling at her. It was forced but she was so intent on winning him over that she didn't seem to see it. "I've been around, Julie. Maybe you've just been too busy to notice."

"I always notice you, Chip. It's hard not to."

Watching them was an exercise in agony. It would kill Terry to see the way Chip was looking at the woman; it was the same look he had when he was younger, a raw animal hunger that would settle on him like a fog just before he'd disappear with whichever female he planned on spending the night.

It was too close for comfort.

"You two need a workout partner?" she asked. Her hand was on Chip's knee, slowly inching up his thigh. "I really do need help with my pecs."

"Your pectorals," Chip said, his eyes dropping to her bust, "look just fine."

She's going to grope him right here and he's going to let her.

"Chip…" I had to be sweating bullets.

"You could always help me work on my thighs," she said to Chip. I had ceased to exist to her. "My thighs always need work."

"Chip, your wife just walked through the front door," I hissed.

Julie's hand shot from his lap. "Wife? Since when do you have a wife?"

"Since about two years ago. It really has been a long time, hasn't it?"

"You prick! Just what the hell did you think you were doing?"

"Sorry, Julie," he said, "but the truth is, I wouldn't have done a thing. But thanks for the handshake."

"I'm not kidding," I said, watching Julie stomp off. "Terry really is here."

He turned on the bench and looked over at the front door. "Christ, do you realize how close I just came to having my nuts ripped off and shoved down my throat?"

"What, Terry's home vasectomy kit?"

"No shit. Alcohol and a rusty meat cleaver."

I was still groaning when Terry slid onto the bench next

to Chip, in the same spot Julie had been. I scooted over to make room for Kris, still looking at Chip; there was almost a smile there.

"We missed something," Kris said.

Chip shook his head. "It was nothing. Just having a laugh at the expense of an old friend."

"The one with her hand on your crotch?" Terry was glaring at him, eyes full of fire and anger, and worse for Chip, hurt. "Why don't you let us in on the joke?"

"Terry, it was nothing," I said. "The lady has a real problem and was trying to use Chip to solve it."

"She's the gym freak, Terry," Chip said. "She was offering free samples and was a little pissed off when we turned her down."

Terry's gaze was disbelieving.

"Babe, it was nothing."

She kept staring at him.

"Shit, Terry, what do you want? Should I just stay home so you can keep an eye on me? Well forget it. I'm a big boy and you're not my mother, so just fucking lay off." He was up and gone so fast it caught us all by surprise. She started to go after him, but I reached out and grabbed her wrist.

"Let him go. He'll be back in a few minutes, and if he's not I'll go after him."

Besides, I thought, you don't want to go out there and find him where I think he'll be.

Chip

I stormed out into the parking lot. I wasn't sure what I was doing, but inside I was boiling over, damning Terry for looking at me with even the most remote suspicion. If she figured I would do it, well then what the hell, why not do it?

Julie was sitting on the floor of her van, the side door slid open, her feet hanging out. She looked dejected and embarrassed.

My fault.

I walked over to the van, hoping I looked sympathetic. "Julie, I'm sorry," I said. "That was a cruel thing to do, but the last thing I expected was for my wife to suddenly show up."

"Funny, I hadn't heard you'd gotten married, Chip. Word gets around here pretty fast."

"I keep it pretty much to myself," I lied. I leaned against her van, my back to the door of the gym. "Look, I really am sorry. If she hadn't shown up—who knows?"

"Where is she now?"

I shrugged. "Working out with Doug and his wife, I suppose."

"So what do you want?" she sighed.

"To make it up to you."

She scooted back into the van. "Then come on in."

I looked around the parking lot, and when I was sure I wouldn't be seen, I followed her in. In one smooth movement she stripped off the leotard, stretching out on the thick floor carpet. I watched her, struck by the changes her body had undergone in the last few years. She was still in superb shape—proof that the gym was more than a social club to her—but the flaws of time were evident. Her make up was obviously thick; she was trying to hide age lines and the sagging of her skin. When I was eighteen I had guessed that she was in her mid thirties. She was by now, what? Forty? She looked older.

I pulled off my shirt and stretched out next to her. Her hands, cold as ice, reached for me before my back hit the floor. She slowly rubbed my chest, and trailed her lips across my stomach. It was when those cold fingers slipped beneath the waistband of my shorts and touched me with an aching familiarity that my brain began screaming.

"Making me work for it?" she breathed. "I can handle it, Chip, trust me."

I grabbed her hands and pulled away. I sat up slowly, unable to ignore the bewilderment on her face. That was something I was getting too good at. Charm a woman one minute and piss the hell out of her the next. "I can't, Julie, I'm sorry. I really am."

"What the fuck? I'm not good enough anymore?"

"That's not it at all. You're just not my wife. I can't do this to her."

She sat up, knees drawn protectively to her chest. "Then why are you here? To prove a point?"

"I swear to God, I don't know." I was staring down at my wedding ring, spinning it around on my finger. "We hit a rough patch... but I shouldn't have even thought of this."

She dug into a gym bag and pulled out a shirt and shorts, "You know," she grunted, trying to wiggle into the shorts, "most guys would have done it and felt guilty later. In my experience, that is."

"Yeah, well, we're idiots."

"You have any kids?"

"One... little boy, almost a year and a half old."

She slipped her arms into the shirt. "Then get your bony ass out of here. I don't do married men." She tugged the shirt down and laughed. "Well, I *do* married men, but not the ones I'm pretty sure have something they really want to go home to. So get out. And don't come back."

"Don't ever give it up, Julie," I said once I was outside

the van. "Someday you'll find the right one."

I slid the door shut and leaned against it. How in the hell was I ever going to get out of this one? Terry put up with a lot of crap, but this she wouldn't easily forgive.

"You are one first class moron, you pathetic son of a bitch."

I jumped, not expecting Doug to be there. The look on his face was pure disgust. "Save your sermon," I said, stepping away from the van when Julie started the engine. "I didn't do anything. I couldn't."

"How in the hell could you do this to Terry? She's sitting in there going half out of her mind worrying about you. You sure as shit didn't need to jump down her throat—and then to come out here with Julie? How fucking stupid are you?"

I sat down hard on the curb. "Pretty fucking stupid," I admitted. "But I'm not lying. Nothing happened."

"Yeah? Well if you expect your wife to believe that then you'd better do something about the trail of lipstick that runs straight into your shorts."

I groaned and used my shirt to wipe off the bright red lipstick. If I wanted to be careless and knock the wind right out of the marriage sails, that was the way to do it. "I swear, I never let it get that far. It's not that easy to make it with another woman when all you can see is your wife's face."

"You *don't* have my sympathy."

"I don't want your sympathy. What the hell am I going to tell Terry? This will kill her."

"Don't be an ass. You're going back in there and apologizing for acting like the royal fuckup that you are, but you're not making the mistake of telling her you came out here to get laid by the reigning blow queen. She doesn't deserve that."

I got up and shoved the stained t-shirt into the trash can by the front door and followed Doug inside. When I crossed the exercise floor I felt like I was moving in slow motion, my head muddled with Novocain. She was still in the same spot, eyes wet and red, watching me walk towards her.

"Terry, I…"

"Just drop it," she said. "I didn't come here to start another fight. You have about five minutes to get your stuff, and you're leaving with me."

Period. End of Discussion. I looked at Doug but he just shrugged and wasn't going to help me at all.

I went into the locker room and scrambled to change clothes.

This was my last chance, and I knew it.

"I'm sorry about what happened back there," I said. "You have every right to be pissed off."

She barely glanced at me, keeping her eyes instead on the road ahead. "I told you to forget it, Chip. You said it was nothing, then it was nothing."

I turned in my seat, leaning against the car door. All I could see was the dark outline of her face against the bright lights coming in through the window. "You want me to be totally honest with you?"

"I'm not sure."

"Ter... I don't know exactly what would have happened if you hadn't shown up. I can't honestly say it would have been easy to walk away."

"If you're trying to hurt me, you're doing a damn good job of it," she murmured.

"I probably would have. Walked away, I mean."

"You'll never know now, so just please drop it. I don't

want to hear about your relationship with her."

"There is no relationship."

"Has there ever been?"

A whole can of worms, I thought miserably.

You want to hear about the torrid sex we used to have in the back of her van? I was eighteen and it was terrific. She did things you're still too shy to try and taught me stuff that sends you over the edge. Is that what you want to hear?

"I thought you didn't want to hear about it."

She gripped the steering wheel hard; I could hear her fingers twist on the vinyl cover. "I suppose that says it all, doesn't it?"

"Julie was just a blip on my radar when I was a kid, never anything more than that."

"Fine."

"Terry…"

"Chip, you have a past. I get that."

The woman is falling apart inside and every word out of your mouth is just picking away at the pieces that haven't cracked yet.

"You still haven't told me where we're going," I said.

"Camping."

"Really?" The one and only time I had camped was on a spur of the moment trip with Ron and Dan when I was seventeen. None of us had a clue what we were doing; we spent half the night trying to figure out how to set up the tent and light a fire. Dan fished and caught a single two inch long blue gill, and he had to bring it back to the camp in a water filled baggy to show us before taking it back to release it. It was a three day disaster, and I loved it.

"We're going to my parents first, to get their camper," she said. "My dad can tell us where to go from there."

"Oh, great. Your mother hates me, Terry."

"That's my fault. I never should have told her we went away together before we got married. She didn't approve."

"Going up there without her grandson isn't going to help, either. She'll probably try to gouge my eyes out."

"Do me a favor, Chip."

"Anything."

"For the next five days, forget that we're parents. I want time for just us."

"Fair enough."

I settled back into the seat, watching the freeway rush towards us in the glare of the headlights. *Boy, you better be able to put out, or you'll crush her into nothing.*

The camper turned out to be a beat up old Chevy pickup truck with a fiberglass shell thrown on the back. It would do for a few days in the woods, but the kidney busting ride to Sterling Lake told me that was its limit. It was no wonder the truck stayed up on blocks in the side yard most of the time. Once a year in it was probably all Terry's parents could stand.

Her father, Paul, was a good natured man that I had taken to the first time we met, just days before our wedding. He either didn't know about or didn't mind his little girl's prenuptial activities; he treated me with the same friendly gusto he did everyone else, and made sure that I understood he immediately considered me to be a part of his family.

Her mother, on the other hand, was another matter. Sheila hated me from day one and I sensed the hostility from the moment we laid eyes on one another. Her reaction to me hadn't done anything to endear her to me, either. To learn that it stemmed from her disappointment that Terry had spent a weekend with me without the benefit of already being married didn't help any. I was thankful Terry turned out more like her father. I didn't think I could stand sleeping next to a cold fish night after night.

I realized while I was driving that was exactly what Terry was putting up with. I was doing a good job of playing the reluctant bride, 'doing my duty' when I thought I had to and nothing else. Most of the time I was surprised I was even able, though lately it wasn't an issue.

Even though the thick fog that was wrapped around me most of the time I knew she was being extraordinarily patient. She was taking all the abuse and rarely fought back. Her heart was breaking bit by bit but she was still there.

I pulled the truck to a slow, easy stop off the road near a campsite by the lake. Terry was dozing, her jacket rolled up and propped under her head for a pillow. Even in her sleep her eyebrows were furrowed together with worry. Zits, too, I noticed. She was breaking out.

With the truck finally still, I took the time to stretch my legs and stare out at the water. Trees had faded into autumn colors; the backdrop of the lake was dotted with the changing colors of the season and the bright green of pine.

Terry stirred and I slid across the rough vinyl bench seat, slipping my arm around her shoulders. It was a gesture so natural that it took a moment for me to understand the look of surprise when she finally woke up.

"Check it out," I said softly.

She struggled to sit up, shaking the heavy cloud of sleep away. "Wow… how long have I been asleep?"

"Not long enough to start drooling."

I wanted to lean over and kiss her, but she opened the door and hopped out. She was smiling, though, stretching her arms above her head and inhaling deeply. I sat in the truck, afraid to move, afraid to say or do anything that might wipe that smile away.

Later, I pulled the old lawn chairs out of the back of the camper and set them up, gently easing my weight into one of them, afraid it would cave in; it creaked and moaned, but held up. I stared out at the water and the ripples that shined in the moonlight. It reminded me of the duck pond but on a bigger scale, and much more quiet.

"You look sad." Terry pulled the other chair next to mine, close enough that she could reach out and touch my hand. I curled my fingers around hers, squeezing them lightly.

"I'm all right," I said, the chair complaining noisily when I tried to lean back. "I was just letting my mind wander."

"Then you're not angry with me for dragging you out here?"

"Are you kidding?" The notion surprised me. "Ter, this was a terrific idea. I wish it had been mine."

"It's just…" She sighed hard. "Don't take this the wrong way… but most of the time you're so moody and hard to talk to that I wasn't sure about this. It could've easily back fired."

"What'd you tell your dad? I saw you two huddled together in the kitchen before we left. I assume he wanted an explanation."

"I told him that I needed to get you away from every-thing before our marriage disintegrated. He understood."

Disintegrated.

She's probably one step away from leaving.

"I've been hell to live with, haven't I?" I asked, not need-ing an answer. "Babe, I'm sorry, I really am. This is just get-ting the best of me and I can't seem to stop… The last thing I want is to hurt you."

"But what is it?"

That plea was raw concern and fear rolled into one basic question. What is it? There was no way for me to describe all my demons. I didn't know how to tell her what it was like to be uncomfortable in my own skin, that detached, disjointed feeling. And the pressure—it was always there, pounding away at my chest.

She was waiting for a reply, and I shook my head, swallowing hard. "I don't know."

I got out of the chair and stood in front of her, my hands jammed down into my pockets. She watched me, waiting, while I struggled with tears that had unexpectedly filled my eyes. That happened more and more; I was fighting back the stinging sensation, determined to not cry.

"I'd make it all go away for you if I could," I finally said. "I don't like being like this, especially when it tears you apart. God, I hate it when I yell at you. You know that, don't you? I don't want… If I stay away from home too often, or I drink too much, it's because I don't know what else to do. If I'm not home then I'm not there to hurt you and I'm not there to disappoint Nicky. Jesus Christ, what am I doing to him? I don't want my son to think about me the way I think about Grant, and I don't want either one of you to be afraid of me…"

She stood, very carefully setting her hands on my chest. "I wish I could do something for you, Chip. Doug thinks you need to work this out for yourself, and that's what I want you to do while we're here. I don't care what it takes… if you have to scream it out and use me to listen, or you have to just cry until you're done crying, that's okay."

I lifted her hands off my chest and pulled her close to me. "Right now I don't want to scream or cry. And there is something you can do," I said, bending my head to kiss her. I felt as scared as she must have the first time we made love, and when I began to kiss her I was thinking, woman, this is for you.

I pulled her into the camper and made love with her, amazed to find out I was wrong.

It was for me.

"This is it. You've dragged this out so long they're all long past suspicious. One way or the other it should have been over with months ago.

"It's either now or never…if you don't finish it now someone else will come along and do it for you. The truth is, it's your job. So do it. Just do it. Do it."

He pulled the trigger. In that instant, it was all over.

He was finished.

Chip

The evening air had just a slight nip of cold in it, and a breeze was floating across the lake. I was resting under a tree—I have no idea what kind, only that it was dropping sap-sticky leaves on me and not needles—my back against the trunk, bark digging sharply into my skin. The fishing pole I'd borrowed from my father in law was on the ground next to me. I could feel my skin prickle with the sudden chill, but resisted the urge to go back to the camper for a shirt.

I closed my eyes, listening to her soft footsteps shuffling through the mast of grass and leaves. In my mind I could see her walking through the trees, the delicate, ever-slight sway of her hips.

"You awake?"

"Just barely." I opened my eyes. She had already guarded

against the chill setting in, wearing one of my bulky sweatshirts. Judging from the way it fit, I mused, that was all she had on. An old sweatshirt and skin tight jeans. She meant business.

"Do you mind a little company?"

I reached out, pulling her onto my lap. "I can always use your company."

"I thought I was supposed to find the world's greatest fisherman out here. What happened?"

"What happened," I said, lifting the pole off the ground, turning it over in my hand, "is that in order to catch a fish you have to mutilate those poor little worms, and I didn't have the heart to do that."

"So basically, you're too squeamish to bait your own hook."

"Basically, yup, that's it."

She put her arms around me, burying her head against my shoulder. "Then what have you been doing out here for the last couple of hours?"

"Abusing a brain cell or two."

"You're not supposed to be thinking about anything but us right now, mister," she said. "The whole idea is for you to stop fixating on your problems."

"I know. And I do feel a little better, I swear. It's just not that easy. I can sit here and fish, or go hiking, or even go freeze my nuts off in that water, but I have to take my brain along and it doesn't want to shut up."

"So what is it you're thinking about so hard?"

"You name it, I think about it. There's not one thing that hasn't crossed my mind in the last three months. I'm overloaded, Terry. My brain won't quit, even when I want it to, and it's killing me."

She lifted her head. "I think brooding is what you're doing. You've set yourself up for a constant game of 'what if.'"

"Enlighten me, Oh Blonde One."

"Ever since Grant died, or better yet, since you read your mother's letter, you keep asking yourself what if. What if you had known right from the start who your father was? What if your mother hadn't died? What if you had come home alone that night instead of sneaking your girlfriend into your room? What if Grant hadn't hurt you? What if you'd looked for Dave yourself instead of letting the agency do it? Is that what you've been doing all along? Wondering what might have been?"

"Mostly," I admitted. "I wonder what the possibilities are. You know, I don't think that even under the most normal circumstances Grant and I would have been close, but I'll never know. And my mother—Jesus, that woman—why did she use me like that? Just to keep her lover from taking off? That wasn't fair to Ron. He missed out on a normal married life. It goes on and on and on... that one stupid lie of hers changed everyone's lives."

She searched my face as I spoke, waiting for that hint of fear, and, I think, for the tears she was seeing so often. There was no trace of them now; this was just a laundry list of some of the things I knew had gone wrong. "Maybe it wasn't a lie," she said. "For all you know at first she honestly thought Ron was your father and didn't want to keep him out of your life. She was stuck between a rock and a hard place... she loved two men and couldn't bear to live without either one of them."

"But to sleep with both of them? So often that she didn't have a clue who my father was?"

"Chip," she sighed. "Be honest. How many times did

you sleep with a girl one night and someone else the next? It happened, didn't it?"

"My sex life is not the issue here!" I snapped, instantly regretting it. I had promised myself, no more tantrums. "All right, a few times. But sheesh, my mother?"

"Your mother was human, too, but she put herself into a position she couldn't get out of. Why do you think she wrote you that letter in the first place? I'm willing to bet there were hundreds of times she wanted to explain everything. That doesn't mean things would have been any different—or that you would have listened."

I closed my eyes again and leaned my head on the tree. "What about everything I've done, Terry? There's a good chance that if I had known Grant was my father, I never would have left home. I never would have pushed myself into that job, and a lot—I mean a lot—of people would still be alive. The blood on my hands won't come off, and all of it was probably avoidable."

"All right. Do you really want to play this game?"

I blinked my eyes open, waiting.

"Suppose you had stayed home with Grant, lived a typical teenager's life, nice and safe? You saved Kris from being raped. And you saved Doug from God knows what. What about the comfort Ron gets just from thinking you're his son? How many people are alive now that might not be because you risked your own life to save them? Okay, fine, you took a dangerous job but you were good at it and it meant the difference between living and dying for people we care about. Am I right?"

She was beginning to tremble, but wouldn't let me pull her any closer.

"What about it, Chip? You could have been buddy-buddy

with your father, but where would you be now? Going off to live with Ron got you here, didn't it? If it wasn't for Ron and Kris, you and I wouldn't be together. We never would have had the chance to fall in love. And Nicky—God, what about him? You can play what if all you want, but when it comes right down to it, I'll be damned if I'll sit here and dwell on things that would have kept us apart!"

"You're angry?" It was more of a supposition than a question. She finally melted against me.

"I'm not angry. I just want you to realize that things happened you had no control over, and it turned out for the best, didn't it?"

"I suppose, but I can't help the way I feel. You know I love you, I wouldn't change that for anything. I just can't help feeling cheated."

"I think you're depressed, Chip. Seriously. I thought at first it was Grant dying... but that's not it. You don't just have a bad case of the blues, you're seriously depressed."

"Do you want me to see a shrink?" I asked, hoping she'd say no.

She thought about it longer than I liked, but in the end said, "I'm hoping a few days out here with me will make you feel like a new man."

"Just as long as *you* don't feel like a new man... but if you think I should when we get back, I will."

She slid off my lap, crouching beside me. "Chip, I want you to be able to look at me the way you used to. I miss seeing that."

My fingers automatically reached out to touch her cheek. "It's still lurking around in here somewhere. I swear, you haven't seen the last of that look."

"And what are the chances of keeping you off the balcony

in the middle of the night?"

"Slim." I smiled weakly, tracing one finger along her jaw. "I need that space, Terry. I can't explain it, I just need it."

"Then can we compromise?"

"Name it."

"Not in your underwear anymore. Finding you out there like that makes me nervous for some reason."

"All right. I promise, before I step out onto the balcony, I'll take off my underwear."

"Chip…" she tried to be exasperated, tried hard, but was also trying not to smile.

"Terry." I stood up, reaching for her. "I'll promise you just about anything. I know what a shit I've been lately and I don't like it at all. Maybe you should scream back, shake me up a little. I'm not good at shielding the people I love."

"You tried."

"So I'll try harder."

"I'm not asking for a miracle."

"You are a miracle," I whispered, wrapping my arms around her. "If things were the other way around and you were being a perfect little bitch, I probably would have already walked out."

"Not a chance. I don't care how miserable I get, I would never let you get away. I'm too selfish for that and you know it."

"Bullshit. I can think of a lot of ways to describe you but selfish wouldn't make the list. You're a terrific wife and wonderful mother, and as a lover, trust me, you have no equal. But you're never selfish."

"I want to hear more about the lover part," she snickered, darting away from me. "Just how many women am I being compared to?"

"About three or four hundred," I said, hoping she'd think

it was a gross exaggeration. I followed her around the tree, letting her stay an arms' length away. "Does it matter? You're the one I come home to."

She was laughing. "No, but you let strange women in very tight, very sexy clothing grope you in public. I'm curious about her. Does she live up to the nickname?"

"I have no idea," I lied miserably.

"I think you do." She stopped running from me. I was standing there with my hands planted on my hips, not really sure where this was going. "I'm just curious, Chip. After all, I don't have anyone to compare your performance with."

"Does that bother you?"

She shook her head and came back to me. "No, it doesn't bother me," she said. "I wasn't serious."

"But I am." My hands went to her shoulders. "Look, I'm only going to bring this up once. If the curiosity got the better of you—about someone else, I mean—I would understand."

"What's this?" She stopped smiling. "Are you giving me permission to go out and have an affair?"

"No, that's not what I said. I just meant that if you let yourself stray just once, I could understand."

"You might understand, I really think you would, but you sure as hell would be hurt. Don't bullshit me, Chip. I don't need to measure you up against anyone else and I don't want you doing the same."

"I just meant…"

"I know what you meant. If I get restless or anything like that, I'll tell you. I won't go looking somewhere else."

"Look but don't touch? That's Doug's motto."

"And it's a damn good one. You know when I saw that woman's hand practically stuffed into your shorts I was hurt.

I won't deny that. But even if you don't know what you would have done, I do."

"Do you?"

"You'd have been terrified of getting caught."

"I did get caught," I pointed out. "I really am sorry, Terry. It'll never happen again."

"If you get the itch for a blow job in the gym parking lot or anywhere else for that matter, you come to me first. You raise a big enough fuss and I won't turn you down."

"Do I hear a lack of trust here now?"

"I trust you. And I don't want your permission to test drive any of the boys on the block. If you're not the best there is, then I don't want to know."

I bent over to kiss her, lips stopping just shy of hers. "I am the best," I whispered. One hand dropped from her shoulder and slowly crawled up underneath the too-big sweatshirt. "I may not have been the best lately, but I want to make it up to you now."

She shivered when my fingers brushed lightly on her breast. "If I don't feel it's adequate?"

"We just won't leave here until I get it perfect."

She drew in one long breath, fusing her lips against mine. "You'll have to try awfully hard," she said breathlessly a minute later, "to make it all the way to perfect."

For the first time in months, I felt confident.

Doug

"Are you all right?"

Kris stood at the kitchen sink, her hands plunged into hot, soapy water. I'd left her alone for a while, thinking that she needed to be by herself long enough to cry, but I didn't want to leave her there too long.

"Where are the kids?" she asked, ignoring the question.

I pulled a chair out from under the table and spun it around, sitting with my chin resting on the back. "Spider's asleep already. Nicky's sitting on the bed pretending to read out of catalog. At least I think he's pretending. That kid sharp is enough he might actually know how."

"Great." She pointed to the stack of dishes on the counter. "Would you mind drying those for me?"

I pushed off the chair and reached for the dish towel hanging on the oven door. She was purposely not looking at me. "It won't do any good to keep it bottled up, Kris."

"I'm fine." She plunged her hands, already fiery red, back into the water. "It just took me by surprise, that's all."

"You're not convincing me." I tossed the towel aside and tried to hold her, but she stiffened up, not wanting to give into it. "Kris, you loved the man once. Maybe a small part of you still does."

"I told you, I'm fine."

I reached into the water and pulled her hands out, forcing her to turn around. She went with it, hugging me tightly, the heat from the water on her hands soaking through my shirt.

"I don't love him at all," she insisted, letting the tears spill over. "It was just a surprise, that's all."

"Don't lie to yourself. You two were really good together once."

She pulled back, her tear-streaked face full of anger. "Why did he do it, Doug? What the hell made him even think of it?"

"I don't know."

"You know what this will do, don't you? This is going to kill Chip. Terry's out there trying to glue him back into one piece, and this will shatter him. He can't take it, he can't take something else going wrong."

I pulled her back into my embrace. "You just worry about pulling yourself together. I'll handle Chip when the time comes. It'll be all right."

I wasn't so sure, though, holding my wife while she cried, that anything would ever be all right for my young friend again.

Chip

The blanket was a reluctant concession to Terry's—and I felt misplaced—modesty. Laying on the thick down sleeping bag by the side of the lake at three in the morning, I doubted we'd be accidentally stumbled over by anyone. But I conceded, not only to the chill, but to the simple fact that she would be up and back in the camper before I'd be able to get to words out. Sex in the wild was one thing, but exposing all was another.

And damn it, the blanket itched.

"So tell me about your first love," she said, staring up at the clear night sky.

I abandoned my quest for more kisses. She had rolled onto her back and had that dreamy, satisfied look in her eyes. Renewed lust would have to wait. "I married my first love."

"Out of all your former conquests, there's not one you fell in love with?"

"Nope." I attempted another attack with my lips on her bare shoulder. "I was never in love before you. I'll admit to two case of pretty decent lust, though."

"Stop that. You're distracting me." She pushed me away playfully. "I'm pressing for details, Mr. Davis. What sort of woman besides me has a chance?"

"None at this stage of the game." I sighed dejectedly and rolled away, resting my head on arms crossed behind my head. "Did you ever think that I might not want to talk about any of the women that may or may not have been in my life? Maybe I'd rather hear about your first love."

"Philip Mathers, second grade. He kissed me during recess. I gave him a black eye. Other than that, I'm a total innocent."

"Bull. I doubt you were a total innocent even before I got my grubby hands on you."

"You had proof."

"Proof of what?" I tried to peel the blanket away from her. "Proof of your virginity? Sure, so what? I can think of lots of mind bending tricks that don't require going all the way. For all I know you spent the three years before I met you living in the back seat of some young stud's Dodge testing out the shocks. You could have done everything else in the book twice, and then some."

"I was completely virgin territory from the neck down. If I fogged up anyone's windows it wasn't because I put out much."

"Not even for whats-his-name?"

"Whats-his-name"—she poked at my ribs—"never tried. He knew how I felt. And I've already told you all the things I never tried. I don't want to talk about me, I want to talk about you and your four hundred women and two cases of lust."

"I suppose if I refuse I'm sleeping alone tonight?"

"You suppose right."

"Okay then." I turned on my side to face her, elbow digging into the soft covering on her father's sleeping bag. "Two major lusts. One I did something about, the other I refuse to talk about. Those are the ground rules. If you don't agree, then I'm not talking."

"Agreed."

"You won't like it," I warned. "It might confirm what your mother thinks about me. I'm just a young lech at heart."

"Speak, Irish." She poked at my ribs again.

"My junior year," I said, opting to look over her shoulder into the darkness rather than right at her. "I was conned into working in the teacher's lounge for the English department instead of taking study hall. Ms. Baxter had all this crap she wanted done and talked me into it. I was one stupid puppy, too... I spent about six weeks filling out these attendance cards and then filing them. I must have done over three thousand of them, all nice and neat and in alphabetical order. It was boring as hell but it beat being locked up in the library. Anyway, at some point it dawned on me that Miss Redmond used the lounge every time I was there, never more than a few feet away. I let my hormones push me into a few kinky fantasies... I never had the guts to say anything."

"But you did, eventually?"

"Sort of. I was just about done with all those damn cards and was putting the file away when I overheard her talking to another teacher. I tried to be cool and pretend I wasn't listening... I sent the whole damn card file flying when I heard her tell Mrs. Harryman that I was a walking erection."

"Oh my God," she snickered. "What did you do?"

"After I was done swearing up a storm because I knew I'd have to re-file all those stupid cards... I waited until Mrs. Harryman was gone and plopped myself down into the chair next to her and asked why the hell she'd said that. She just smiled nicely and gave me her address and told me if it was a lie, I'd have to prove it. She made it pretty clear she hoped it was the truth."

She sat up, pulling the blanket with her. "Chip, you had an affair with the head of the English department in high school? God, I remember her, too. She's a bitch!"

"Maybe in the classroom," I said. "Or maybe I turned her into one. She wasn't one with me, and in those days I didn't turn down that kind of invitation. I gave her what she wanted for a while."

"And then?"

"And then she wanted more than I was willing to even think about. I was only sixteen, Terry... She was talking like she couldn't wait until my senior year was over so that we wouldn't have to sneak around anymore. Hell, that was the best part. I was good at sneaking around, but she was getting careless."

"Is that why you quit school? Pressure from her?"

How much did she really want to know, I wondered. "Not exactly. Are you sure you want the gory details?"

"I do."

"I quit school," I said, not sure she really did, "because I was asked to leave. Let's just say we got caught and the end result wasn't pretty."

"Oh my God." She was laughing, though. "I'm sorry, but I keep picturing the ice queen who tried to get us to take Chaucer seriously. I never would have thought this woman was doing the man I'd marry. Why didn't she get fired?"

"She was suspended for a year, I think. And by the time you had her for English, I wasn't 'doing' her. By then I was using someone else."

"All four hundred of them."

"Ahhhh, yeah."

"How many, really, Chip?"

"Too many. I'm not proud of it, Ter. Can we just say I'd

never be able to make a list and get it right?"

"Was it really that many? In the hundreds?"

I didn't know what to tell her. She'd either think I was a freak, or bragging.

"Wow," she said after a while. "I'm surprised your winky hasn't fallen off."

"My what? Is that what you're telling Nicky it is? His little winky?"

"Well… yes."

"If it makes you feel any better," I said, "I've made love with you more than I've had sex with all names on my would-be list combined. And you're a lot more fun."

"So I get to be the one who breaks it," she snickered.

"You're welcome to try."

"But you won't tell me about this second major lust of yours, the one you did nothing about."

"Some private things are meant to stay that way. I'm sorry."

"Don't be." She pulled the blanket away a bit, offering me the chance to sit up and share it with her. I smiled and pulled myself into it, slipping my arms around her. "Besides," she said, "I don't think I need for you to tell me to know."

"Really now."

She rested her head on my shoulder. "It's still there, too. I can see it sometimes when you look at her… A touch that lasts a fraction longer than it should, a hug that's a little too intense for friends. I'm not complaining, Irish, not at all. Not as long as you lust after me more."

"Are you willing to put a name with the woman you think it is?"

"Why wouldn't I be?"

"Jealousy, if you're right."

She pulled back and looked at me seriously. "Now why on earth would I ever be jealous of Kris? Just because you have the occasional fantasy doesn't mean I feel threatened. You wanted her years ago and were too chicken to do anything about it."

"You're too smart for your own good, woman."

"True." She kissed me lightly. "And I wouldn't be at all surprised if somewhere down the line you worked up the nerve to do something about it."

"Not likely."

"About as likely as me taking you up on your offer to screw some poor unsuspecting guy just to compare models? I didn't say you'd go to bed with her, I just said you'd do something about it. Like maybe admit to her you think she's incredibly sexy and has tortured you for years."

"Not likely," I repeated. "Besides, I'm sure Doug tells her those things all the time."

"I doubt it. He's too typically male. Typical males never say the right thing when they should."

"Oh?" I began a renewed attack on her, teasing her neck with my lips. "I'm a blundering idiot, in other words? Never remember to tell you what it is you do to me? Never know when I should mention how incredible you are, or how much I love you?"

"You may be the exception... but I can't believe you went to bed with a bitch like Miss Redmond."

"Went to bed with you, didn't I?"

The pain in my ribs, I was sure, would go away in about three or four days.

"You're mean, woman."

"But you love me anyway."

"That I do," I said.

She kissed me, deep and slow. "Can I tell you something?"

"After that kiss? Anything."

"You loved Grant, too." Her finger went over my lips, stopping me before I could erupt. "Just listen to me, okay?"

I nodded.

"Every time I go over to the house, I wind up sitting in the living room looking through all these old pictures of your family. It doesn't matter where you were, in every single family photo you're right there by Grant, he has his arm around you, and you don't look bothered by it at all. I kept thinking it was just a habit you got into when you were little..."

"But?"

"But I kept looking, and in the pictures without Grant, you didn't look the same. You looked uncomfortable, like you needed to get away from something. I found a few with just you and Dave where you almost looked happy. But for the most part, you and Grant are practically joined at the hip in all of them, and instead of looking like you're irritated, you look like you feel safe."

"Where are you going with this?"

"I'm getting there. Just answer something—don't stop to think about the answer, just say the first thing that comes into your head, okay?"

"Okay."

"When you think about all the crap in your life, who are the most angry with?"

"My mother." I felt like someone had just punched me in the chest and knocked the wind out of me. "My mother," I repeated slowly.

"When you read that letter, you said you felt betrayed, right?"

"I still do."

"And manipulated?"

I nodded again.

"Didn't you feel manipulated before she died, Chip? All those years of being the glue that held everything together for her? Didn't you feel that pressure, even when you were Nicky's age?"

I had to think about it. "A while back," I said, "I figured that Grant had never really abused me, not until the night she died. I just didn't understand why I always *felt* abused."

"Blaming him was easier, Chip. You didn't know he was your father, and since she was dead..."

"You think all this crap I kept stored up was because of her, not Grant?"

"It doesn't matter what I think. What matters"—she kissed my chest—"is what you feel in here."

I had no idea what to say. We dropped the blanket and were holding on to each other; I could feel my heart pounding hard, I knew she felt it too.

"It's okay. There's nothing wrong with you having loved Grant, and there's nothing wrong with you being angry at her. She made some really big mistakes."

"But they were just mistakes," I murmured. "I didn't hate her, Terry, I don't think I ever hated her."

"Of course you didn't. But she let you think Grant was the root of all your restlessness... she never let you know it was just because you were a restless kind of kid. Somewhere deep inside you knew that, that's why her letter hurt so much. It took away the one reason you had for protecting yourself against all that old pain. But you loved her, in spite of it."

"I just never liked her."

"That's okay. There's no law that says you have to like your relatives."

"I like you," I said. "And I think it's safe to go home."

Doug

I slid onto the barstool, my arms crossed in front of me on the bar. Getting Chip to come with me had been amazingly easy; Nicky had just fallen asleep when they pulled into the driveway, and Kris, using her best mother's tone, convinced Terry to let him finish his nap before they took him home. Under her warning that he'd be subject to endless comparison of the boys' milestone moments if he stayed, Chip agreed it was a good time to occupy a couple of vacant chairs at the restaurant.

"Who's driving?" Ted asked, setting cocktail napkins in front of us.

I barely glanced at him. "I am. Better just bring me a Coke."

"Seven and Seven, and make it a really big one," Chip told him. "One of us should enjoy this anyway. The drinks are free, Doug, we can always call one of our wives to come get us."

I wanted to be able to think clearly—and control Chip if I had to—and one drink would be enough to put me away. On the other hand, I wanted Chip as numb as possible.

"So what kind of torture did you perform on my son to knock him out like that?" he asked when the drinks came. "He hates naps. Terry usually has to staple him to the bed, and then the little shit won't go to sleep."

I sipped at the Coke. "Three hours at the playground this morning might have had something to do with it. I promised your wife he would have a good time with us. I couldn't disappoint her."

"Neither could I."

How do I tell him? "How was it? You look a hell of a lot better now than you did a few days ago."

"Terry should play doctor more often." He grinned, and popped a pretzel into his mouth. "At least she seems better at it than some people I know."

"I doubt I'm equipped to treat you the way she does." I set my glass on the napkin, watching beads of water drip from the rim and soak into the paper. "Did you catch hell for Julie?"

"Not exactly. I spent some time apologizing for it, but she didn't want details." He took a long sip of his drink; Ted was generous, it had to be at least a triple, and for that I was grateful. "Terry didn't seem to think I'd have let it go any further than it did. Just a grope on the weight bench."

"Would you have?"

He looked doubtful. "The mood I was in? Seriously? I can kid myself all I want, but the truth is, is she hadn't shown up when she did, even you couldn't have stopped me. I probably would have killed myself later, but I know damn well where this boy would have headed."

"You still went out to her van."

"And all I could see was the look on Terry's face. The woman haunts me, Doug. I couldn't get it up."

I watched him drain the last of his drink and order another. Ted started to balk, but when I nodded, he took the empty glass and poured another. "You didn't tell Terry that, did you?"

"I might be dumb as a rock but I'm not completely stupid. I've hurt her enough as it is. Fortunately, she has more faith in me than I do."

"But you're feeling better? No more gloom and doom?"

He sighed, shrugging. "Not as much of it, I hope. I have to admit, I didn't leave there feeling as spectacular as I want her to think... but dammit, she was thinking about leaving me. I'm not about to let that happen. I didn't let myself yell at her the entire time we were out there. Hell, we did more talking in those few days than I think we've done since Nicky was born. There might be a little cloud still following me around, but I think I'll survive it."

Don't be so sure...

"Even if it didn't do me that much, it did a world of good for Terry and right now that's all that matters."

"Nick had a good time," I said.

He caught the edge in my voice, the shadow of doubt that was lingering there. "You better tell me what's bugging you," he said, pushing his drink aside. "Something's not right."

Not now, you're not ready.

"Nicky's okay, isn't he? Did he get hurt? Sick?"

"Your son is just fine," I replied, voice thick. I wondered if he was drunk enough, if there was enough alcohol pulsing through his veins to deaden the blow. "He ran around at top speed the whole time you were gone. Kris thinks you feed the kid amphetamines."

"Cut the crap, Doug. I'm getting the feeling you didn't drag me here to talk about our kids or what kind of gymnastics Terry had me doing out by the lake. You want me drunk on purpose, and I want to know why."

"Maybe in your office."

Chip tried to relax, easing back onto the stool he'd been halfway off. "Here is just fine. What is it? What happened?"

I stared into my soda for a long time, wishing I had the stomach for something stronger. It would have been easier if Chip had come home still angry at the whole world. Terry had done her job too well; he seemed mostly happy now.

I took a deep breath and said, "It's Ron."

"Oh, Jesus." His uncertainty fanned into full blown fear. He swallowed the rest of his drink in one gulp; without asking he knew to expect the worst. He'd been waiting for bad news from the day Ron had signed his new contract. "Who got him?"

I had to force myself to look at him. For everything that Chip had been through, he was still incredibly young. I was looking at someone barely twenty five years old, a man coping with more pain than should have been given to anyone over an entire lifetime. Now one of the last links to his past, as fragile as it had become, was being ripped away.

"No one. Ron got himself."

"What?" He flinched, grabbing onto the edge of the bar. "What the hell did he do?"

I tried not to pull up the image of my wife's ex-husband sitting there, his service gun wedged angrily into his mouth. The touch of irony, as I saw it, Ron's final gesture to the agency and the world, was to finish his career in the way he saw it, locked in a toilet stall not fifty feet from Alex Barstow's plush blood red office.

"He ate his gun, Chip."

"Oh, Jesus," he swore again, looking like he was about to throw up everything he'd had to drink. "When?"

"Three nights ago. He..."

"Son of a fucking bitch. I'm screwing my brains out and the closest thing I have to a father is desperate enough to blow his..."

"Stop it." I grabbed onto his arm firmly, desperately wanting to say the right thing. "Don't ever confuse the two. The fact that Ron chose to end his life when he did and how he did has nothing to do with what you do with Terry. If you start putting the two together, you'll take it out on her in the long run."

"I always do, don't I?"

"You don't have to, not this time. Remember, this is going to knock her off her feet, too."

His eyes glazed over, and he stared ahead into nothing, then blinked; it was like a wave of calm had washed over him. "Why did he do it?"

"I don't know. He didn't leave a note or anything."

"And you're sure it was suicide? Could we be looking at a repeat of Dan?"

"No. It was pretty clear cut. It was one hell of a mess, but I'm positive it was suicide."

"I want to know why." He slid off the stool, steadying himself against the bar. Two drinks too many on an empty stomach.

"Where are you going?"

"You're driving me to headquarters," he said flatly, "and you're going to get me in to see Alex Barstow."

Terry

There was a long silence, punctuated only by smothered sniffles. I sat on the sofa in Doug and Kris's living room, awe stricken, while Kris struggled to keep her tears under control. I wasn't sure if it was shock or indifference, but the news didn't have much of an impact. Chip warned me, after all: Ron has a year, maybe two if he plays his cards right. He was right; two years was about all Ron could handle.

I couldn't imagine how miserable he must have felt. Chip was evasive about the job Ron had taken, but that in itself made me certain that it was beyond the realm of dangerous.

There had been no mercy in Chip's voice when he gave Ron a life expectancy of two years. He was disgusted enough that I didn't press the matter.

All that mattered now was that Chip had gotten away from it all, he was no longer a part of it. But how would he react? He was expecting it, wasn't he? He had already prepared himself for the inevitable.

I was sorry for Ron, sorry for Kris, but more than anything, I was terrified for Chip.

Chip

Just standing there, I knew that I was more drunk than I was sober, and in all fairness I should keep my mouth shut. The circumstances weren't fair, though, and I damn well wanted answers. Doug stood just behind me with one hand trying to hold me up while I fought from swaying back and forth in front of the Secretary General.

Alex Barstow sat behind his massive desk, his face a mask of patience as he endured my tirade. Or perhaps he was bored and wasn't even listening; I went on for a long time, spitting out half formed thoughts and accusations.

"I'll tell you once more," he said carefully. "The reason for his unfortunate passing has not yet been determined."

"Oh, poop. Your morons probably don't give a rat's ass why Ron decided to redecorate the can with his brain. Who's even looking? And where?"

"Take it easy," Doug said, steadying me.

Barstow leaned back, ignoring any sarcasm I threw at him. "Our 'morons' are very interested in his suicide. It coincides with his inability to complete an assignment. I am very curious—and very disturbed."

"Barstow, I knew you were disturbed the first time I laid

eyes on you." I stumbled forward, placing my hands flat on the top of his desk. "But you're not stupid, are you? Amazing how easy it was for me to get out of my contract. The whole team just vaporized. Kris was let go, Dan is dead... for what? You kept Douggie here because you paid for all that medical crap stuffed between his ears. What about the rest of us? How expendable were we?"

"Exactly what is your point?"

"My point is that you found a way to conveniently get rid of us all one way or the other. You let me go with some chicken shit of an excuse of a suspension and let me keep the restaurant, you used my supposed mistake into forcing Dan to retire the team, and refused to take Kris back. There was never a fucking soviet plane to steal, was there? You just timed it to be sure I wouldn't be here. And you knew Kris's marriage was on the rocks, didn't you? You knew Ron would be a damned good maverick, and you went after him when he was down."

Doug was at my side, urging me to back off.

"We all know who killed Dan Martin, don't we, Alex?"

"Chip..." Doug was pulling at my arm.

"He knew too much and was getting a little soft and couldn't be trusted anymore. Might have talked, am I right? But Kris and I, we could keep our mouths shut. We both stayed close to the doctor here, so you knew we'd never so much as squeak."

Barstow held up a hand to stop Doug from pulling me away. I stood up, weaved horribly, and dropped into the chair.

"Am I on someone's list?" I asked.

The silence was nerve wracking, but I was willing to wait as long as I had to for an answer. "All right," he finally said, motioning for Doug to sit. "You're somewhat perceptive,

Mr. Davis. Yes—the dissolution of your team was manufactured. We needed Ron and secured his confidence in the only manner he would allow. His wife was let go because Dan Martin knew she was leaving him and he felt she was ready to quit on her own. Dr. Stone agreed to remain as a medical consultant."

"And Dan?" I prompted.

"His death was a mistake," he said, voice touched with a tinge of sadness. "It was my fault. No, he didn't kill himself. I allowed disinformation to leave this office, and it was interpreted by others that he was not leaving on his own accord. In this business that makes a tremendous difference. He was never intended to be anyone's target. So yes, it is completely my fault.

"I've never felt it necessary to be concerned with either you or Mrs. Stone, because as much as you think you know, what you know is relatively unimportant... You are not, nor will you be, on anyone's list. I gave my word a long time ago that you and your family would be kept safe. I keep my word."

I stared at him blankly.

"Don't misunderstand me," Barstow went on, "you had definite potential and we had plans for you. There was simply no way of securing your father without letting you go first. It was his only demand. He agreed to become our primary maverick on the condition that you be dismissed, without prejudice or penalty."

I felt the blood drain from my head and thought for a moment I might pass out. "Why all the help, then? When I needed to find my brother, and then my son..."

"Because there is always the spark of hope that at some point you will want to return on your own. Mr. Davis—Chip—I wish I could tell you why he killed himself. The simple truth is that we just don't know."

"I want to help," I said. "Trust me with the records of his last few assignments. Let me figure it out."

Barstow looked to Doug, who nodded.

"Go home and sober up. I'll make sure you have access to anything you need."

I got up and started for the door, stopping before I opened it. "Your spark of hope?" I said to Barstow.

"Yes?"

I shook my head. "My wife would kill me."

Terry

Kris handed me a glass of wine and then sipped nervously at hers. The crying had finally stopped and she was able to talk, sniffling as she spoke. Her eyes were puffy and red and her hair was flying in all directions from the abuse it had taken, all the times in the past hour she had run her hands through it.

"You have to understand, I love Doug with all my heart, but when I told Ron I was pregnant and getting married again, I felt like I was crushing him into dust. When he killed himself I lost any chance to tell him how sorry I am."

"I think he knows."

"But *I'll* never know, that's the whole point. I can never tell him that even though I'm happy with Doug, and even though I couldn't live with him anymore, I still loved him just a little bit. Dammit, even Doug knows it! I just never completely stopped loving him."

Doug

I pulled the car into the driveway, not moving from behind the wheel after I shut the engine off. Chip had his head leaning against the window, his eyes fixed on something in front of him.

"You miss it, don't you?" I asked. "If it wasn't for Terry, you'd go back."

He blinked hard. "In a flash."

Terry

I closed the door to Nicky's bedroom and walked across the carpet to where Chip was sprawled out on the floor. He had his back against the chair, watching me come towards him. His eyes, though tired and bloodshot, still had that hungry look from the night before. I'd noticed it just before dawn broke, when I woke to find him sitting on the hard camper bed, watching me. It had confused him when I started to cry, but that was the look I'd been missing.

He had unloaded and opened up so much, only to come home and find another hole punctured in his life.

"Is he asleep or did you just give up?" He was fighting to keep his own eyes open, though I wasn't sure if that was effects from the drinking he'd done or stress from the news.

"Wide awake." I dropped onto the couch, kicking off my shoes. "I think he'll stay in bed, though."

"Little shit didn't even miss us. I expected at least a 'hi, Daddy.' Instead I get 'you gots dimes?' He damned near patted me down looking for money."

"He has his priorities." I felt a wave of weariness sweep over me that made my bones ache. I looked at Chip, and seeing the lines of fatigue cut into his face, pulled myself up and suggested it was time to follow Nicky's lead and go to bed.

When the lights were out I laid there listening to him breath. I knew he'd have a hard time falling asleep. "Are you sure you want to do this, Chip?" I whispered. "Wouldn't it be a whole lot easier to leave it up to someone else?"

"No one else gives a shit. The few who might care are too busy to spare the time."

"You expected it, though. Maybe the job just got to be too much for him."

Chip sighed and rolled onto his side. "He was ready to retire, Terry. He told me a few months ago that he had just one case left, and then he'd be finished. I thought he was looking forward to it."

"Maybe. A lot of men don't like letting go. Retiring just reminds them that they're getting up there. Ron might not have been able to face not having his job to go to."

"Ter, I'm going to tell you something, but it goes no further than this bed. Not to Kris, not to anyone, not ever. You have to swear to it."

I wasn't sure I wanted to know, but whispered, "You have my word."

"I'm not sure how much I've told you before... Ron had a horrible job, Terry. It was a living nightmare. Have you ever heard me mention the term 'maverick renegade'?"

"No."

"It's an operative classification. A maverick is someone who works alone, with little or no agency support. A renegade is someone who basically is supposed to put themselves into the fire first—someone who's willing to be damn near reckless and not worry about the consequences.

"It gets more intricate when you break things down into classes. A maverick class one hunts people down and brings them back, usually to serve out federal warrants. The military calls them 'chasers' but this is on a slightly bigger scale—like a bounty hunter for the worst of the worst. A class two is more ruthless in what they do... they not only hunt people down, but get rid of anything in the way and usually the target as well."

"Ron?"

"Class two."

"What does it mean, Chip? What did Ron do?"

"Ron was an assassin."

I stared into the darkness, where I knew Chip's face was. This was impossible, not Ron.

"You have to trust me when I say he went into it for reasons he thought where important."

"Then this is the truth? It's not some sick joke?"

"No. It's why I've got to find out why he decided to end it all. A while back he was talking about being free of it, he had one last case to get through. It just doesn't make sense."

To hell with it, I thought wildly, pushing him onto his back so that I could lay with my head on his shoulder. "So what can you do? He didn't leave a note."

"He left a shop card," he said. "I can use it to find out what he's been up to for the past year or so. Maybe a mistake came back to haunt him. I just want to see what the computer spits out. I've got to be able to pin a reason on it."

"As long as I'm under some kind of oath, then I have a few questions. Like how you got involved in the first place. I've never understood that, you were so young."

"I *was* young… and they were stupid." His arms went around me. "I went to live with Ron and Kris… she was great about it, in spite of the fact they'd only been married a little while. She never made me feel like I was intruding in anything. Anyway, I was getting pretty hard to handle and Ron was trying to reign me in a bit. I just kind of stumbled onto it. He didn't trust me enough to leave me home alone, so they dragged me off on what was supposed to be some kind of family vacation... I wasn't stupid. They kept disappearing for these huge chunks of time, and Kris was pretty inept sometimes. I chased after her like a lonely puppy and she led me right into it. When I proved to be helpful, Dan saw the possibilities. He put me together with Doug and we took off like a couple of rockets when we weren't screwing around. I did enough things right that he was able to go to the agency and get me a place on his team. They never asked how old I was, not then."

"What about Doug? How did he get into it?"

"Legacy. His father was a field agent and they recruited him right off his residency. That's his story, anyway. I strongly suspect it was set up before he went to medical school."

"What a waste of a good doctor."

"No kidding. But we needed him. All that crap he has spinning around in his head helped out more than once."

"Have you ever been hurt?"

"Not really. Bumps and bruises. I never needed Doug for that."

"Kris says you were damned good at it."

"I suppose. But it's over, Terry, I'm not going back to it. If you're worried that doing this for Ron will get me sucked back into it, don't. It would have to be something major for me to even consider it again."

I didn't ask what something major might be. I just relaxed and let myself be happy with the idea that he was there, and he wasn't going to spend his night shivering on the balcony in his underwear.

Chip

The logs for all the work Ron had done over the course of two years were stored on several floppy disks; I had his shop card, which was not much more than heavy computer paper covered with a series of code numbers, and use of a computer terminal in the basement. It took one of the programmers an hour to show me how to load the right disks and how to switch back and forth between them without losing any data or screen display. I had to give him credit for his patience; he could have whipped the information through in fifteen minutes, but he would have no clue what he was looking for.

I sat in front of the terminal for a long time, staring at the card in my hands. It was the key to Ron's life, or to the end of it. The minute I typed in the first code I was responsible for the information that would pop up, and I wasn't sure I wanted that. What was just a jumble of numbers would quickly become the names of real people with personal lives. Connected to every one of those names there had to be family left behind, people who wondered what had happened, and why.

I had a hard enough time dealing with the knowledge that I'd left families suffering as the result of my work; to deliberately search for someone and end their life was almost impossible to comprehend.

It was too high a price to pay for my freedom.

They would have reassigned you, Ron, I thought, fingering the worn edges of the card. *There has to be a reason, I don't believe you gave in to the pressure and I don't believe you were depressed over retiring. You wouldn't have left without saying goodbye, not without a reason.*

There were four sets of numbers on the card; Ron had probably gone through a dozen or more over two years, and was probably more successful than I'd like to think.

I'd called him a murderer, and I'd meant it.

He should have told me why.

I typed in the first long number and waited, the cursor blinking on the screen as the disk spun noisily. Was it hard for him, I wondered, sitting there waiting for this same information, or had he learned not to care?

I doubted it, and by the time the screen changed, I was sure of it. You can't not care.

```
WALKER, DAVID
CODE: MAYOR
DECEASED
CONTINUE?
```

Code Mayor? A team leader? Why the hell was Ron chasing a team leader?

I poked at the Y and waited impatiently.

```
LEADER SW REGION
FEDERAL WARRANT SERVED
LKL: DALLAS TEXAS
SWM : NKF
CHARGE: HOMICIDE, SUBORDINATE MEMBER (2)
CHARGE: TREASON
CHARGE: DESERTION
CONTINUE?
```

Yes.

```
MAYOR TARGET MR2
OBJECTIVE COMPLETE
END
```

Single white male, no known family. Killed off two of his own team members. Wanted for treason and desertion. Awfully convenient, but this isn't it.

I placed a small X next to the code and went to the next. It was easier to type, less threatening; what I was reading felt impersonal, if I ignored the fact that I was so closely tied to the man who was responsible for ending this person's life.

```
KRANTZ, MARK
CODE: RENEGADE 1
DECEASED
CONTINUE?
```

Yes.

```
ASSOC. OPERATIVE
FEDERAL WARRANT ISSUED
LKL: WASHINGTON DC
MWM 2DC
CHARGE: ATTEMPT ASSAS. COMMANDER IN CHIEF
CHARGE: TREASON
CONTINUE?
```

Yes.

```
RENEGADE 1 TARGET MR2
OBJECTIVE COMPLETE
END
```

Touché, Ron. This moron had two kids and probably didn't think twice about them. Going after the President? I wonder what his wife thinks of him now...

I was disappointed; there was nothing there that would throw Ron off track. In a morbid way I understood the point of getting rid of these two—Ron was tracking treasonous operatives and field agents, getting rid of the people who knew enough to leave a trail of national destruction behind them, people who could no longer be trusted.

There was never a moment when I didn't trust every person on my team with my life; when Kris found herself at the controls of a plane she'd never seen before but needed to fly in order to get us all out safely, I didn't think twice. She would do it. She had to do it. She had blind trust from every member of that team.

I couldn't imagine being with people who would turn on me, let alone the entire country.

I marked off the code and typed in the next one.

```
FALATI, MARCIA
CODE: MAYOR
DECEASED
CONTINUE?
```

Yes.

```
TEAM LEADER NO. CA REGION
CONVICTED IN ABSTENTIA
LKL: TRAVIS AFB, CA
MWF SPOUSE USAF E-5
CHARGE: CRIMES VS. USA
CHARGE: D/A
CONTINUE?
```

Yes.

```
MAYOR TARGET MR2
OBJECTIVE COMPLETE
END
```

Another team leader gone off the deep end, and for what? Crimes against the U.S? She left behind a husband.
Holy shit, she was a double agent...

I remembered her, too, passed her more than once in the halls. She struck me as cold, either too good for the rest of us, or more likely, too enamored with her own position to be bothered with the peons who did the dirty work.

Her husband was an air force sergeant; if he was still alive someone had been awake enough to realize he had no clue what his wife did for a living. He probably thought he'd gotten lucky, a cushy job at the same base, never facing the chance of being transferred out yet having every opportunity to promote. He could have served his 20 years at the same place and retired as a master sergeant, never the wiser.

If he was still alive, he was now probably shining some captain's boots in the Azores.

She was pretty enough, too, at least enough to turn a few heads before realizing she was untouchable. Maybe not to Ron, though. Ron was just high enough up the ladder, had enough rank and seniority to make him worth her time. Lovers? He was tight lipped about any personal life, other than mooning over Kris. Could the man have died from a broken heart?

I went on to the next one, making a mental note to keep Marcia Falati in mind. She would be worth researching.

STEVENS CHRIS
CODE: N/A
RELEASED
CONTINUE?

Released? You never got to this one, Ron?
Yes.

INACTIVE FILE
ASSOC. OPERATIVE EASTERN REGION

```
LKL: MIAMI, FL
SWM:NKF
CONVICTED IN ABSENTIA
CHARGE: SODOMY OF A MINOR
CHARGE: RAPE OF A MINOR
CHARGE: HOMICIDE TEAM MAYOR
CHARGE: HOMICIDE TEAM MEMBER (3)
CHARGE: DESERTION
CHARGE: TREASON
CONTINUE?
```

Yes. Hell yes.

```
FUGITIVE TARGET MR2
AWAITING OBJECTIVE
END
```

What kind of bastard is this? Ron, why the hell didn't you finish this? If this was the last case, this should have been the easiest one to justify. Getting him would atone for all the others. Why the hell did you stop?

I picked up the card and stared at it, willing some sort of revelation to come. That last number practically glowed; it was Ron's last assignment and the one he would have no qualms about. This was one any of us would have done. It was worse, as far as I was concerned, than Marcia, accused and convicted of betraying her country. What could have possible stopped him?

Ron…Why?

"Any luck today?"

I turned the water on, hot and hard, and stuck my face into the spray. My head was pounding, throbbing pain that pulsated with precision at my temples. "I don't know," I said.

"I might have something."

Doug stood in the doorway of the gym's shower room, holding a towel around his waist. He was still covered with a oily layer of sweat, his hair matted to his head, wet and wild. "Well, I'm heading into the steam room if you want to mull it over. Sometimes two heads really are better than one."

I turned the shower off, shaking water from my hair. My muscles screamed at me, every movement an exercise in pain. I could quit; Terry wouldn't mind an extra inch or two around my waist and it wasn't as if I was prowling for women anymore. I didn't need my body as bait. If it wasn't for the eight hundred dollars I coughed up every year just to walk through the front door, I'd be tempted. Vanity just wasn't worth it.

"All right, doc," I groaned, stretching out on the wet tile, "put your brain into gear. Mine's not working anymore."

"Whatcha got?"

Not much, I thought dismally. "The shop card from Ron's personal effects only had four entries on it. The first two I doubt mean anything in the long run."

"The last two?"

"You remember Marcia Falati? She used to work out of headquarters. Tall red head, married to a security cop on base."

"The iceberg that sunk the Titanic. What about her?"

"Any chance she had something going with Ron?"

Doug was quiet for a moment, but couldn't stop the slip of laughter. The lady, and he used the term loosely, was nobody's idea of a good time. Even her own team members hated her. "Come on, Ron couldn't have been that desperate."

"Why the hell not? Look, she was the last case he finished. Somewhere between her and his last assignment—which he dragged out for months—he killed himself. The only thing I can think of is that maybe he did have something going with her and that he cared about her. The next case was a real bastard, Doug. No one would feel the least bit guilty about taking that one on."

"But Falati? The woman was nothing but frost."

"Maybe." I wiped the sweat out of my eyes, considering. "How many times have we gone after women no one else would?"

"Shit, I don't know. Why?"

"Face it, it's crude, but I can remember more than a couple times when I purposely went after women who weren't even halfway onto the good looking side of the playground just because I thought they'd put out easier. You've done it, too. Women that didn't otherwise get attention."

"Well, yeah… That doesn't mean I'm proud of it."

"Maybe Ron saw through something in her. Marcia might not have been aloof, she might have been terrified. She was damn young to have her own team and it was a hell of a lot of pressure. So much pressure that she sold out. Just because she ignored the rest of us doesn't mean she didn't warm up to Ron."

"What about her husband?"

"A cover. I'm sure she was doing him, too, but he was a cover. I checked him out… he's squeaky clean. It's a sure bet he had no idea what his wife was up to. The team that cleaned up after Ron put it on record that they were certain he had no idea what she did for a living. He was devastated… he still thinks she was just some junior exec at a research company."

"Still…" Doug was shaking his head, drops of sweat and steam dripping from the tips of his hair. "It doesn't feel right. I don't think Ron had a social life. I never heard a thing about him with Marcia or anyone else, and that crap gets around."

"Doesn't mean it didn't happen," I argued. "Ron probably got as horny as the next guy."

"You're grasping at straws. My gut tells me Marcia had nothing to do with Ron."

"Straws are all I have to grasp at."

He was probably right. If there had been any emotional involvement he never would have finished the assignment, he would have passed it on to someone else.

Or taken her and run like hell.

"Are you sure you want to do this? You may be too close to it to be objective."

"God, you sound like Terry. I'll do it myself, Doug. I doubt anyone else would."

"At least get someone to help you."

"Hell, no one in that agency is going to lift a finger for this. The general climate is pretty cool… I think they were all wary of him. I can't expect any help."

"I'll help you," he said. "I liked Ron once, and I probably still would if I hadn't ended up liking Kris more. He was a decent guy and deserves to have a clear name. I don't particularly like hearing people call him a coward."

"They're really calling him that?"

"Only those who don't have the balls to step into his shoes. Chip, I'll help you for no other reason than I love my wife and this is killing her, too."

"Then you'd better call her and tell her you're going to be late," I said, getting up. "We're going back to HQ."

Terry

I was curled up on the couch when Chip slipped through the door at one in the morning. The living room was dim, just one small lamp on behind me, giving me enough light to read by. When I heard him close the door I tossed the book aside and sat up.

"Angel, I'm sorry," he started, hoping to smooth it over before it started.

"It's okay," I said. "I talked to Kris earlier and she warned me I might not even see you tonight, but you could have called."

He pulled off his sports coat, looking guilty. "I know, I just got so busy…"

"Chip, I *was* worried. If Kris hadn't called me, I'd be frantic by now. I don't mind if you're going to be out late, but I need to know."

"Yes, mommy."

"I'm not mad," I said. He was hiding a smile behind that sheepish look; I was probably the first person to ever give him a curfew. "Are you hungry? I saved you some dinner."

He nodded, pulling off his tie. "I could eat a horse. I might have had lunch. I don't remember."

I fought the wave of nausea that poked at me when I got up to go into the kitchen. I felt as tired as he looked, and as soon as he'd eaten I wanted to drop into bed like a rock and not move for the rest of the night.

"It's kinda nice out tonight," he said, rummaging through the refrigerator for something besides juice or diet soda. "Want to sit out on the balcony with me?"

"That depends." I tossed his plate into the toaster oven. "Will you have clothes on?"

"Fully dressed, I promised."

He was quiet while he ate, and even though I knew he needed my company, I just wanted to climb into my warm bed.

"It was a colossal waste of time," he said after a while, so quietly I wasn't sure he'd spoken at first. "I may just be spinning my wheels. Maybe Ron did just fall off his rocker."

I didn't believe it, and I knew he didn't either. "Don't expect the answers to fall into your lap."

"It should be so easy…" He put his feet up on the railing and tipped his chair back. "I'm missing something. I might not even be on the right track."

"Can I help?"

"I'm afraid not."

I stood to stretch and stepped over to the wood railing. An acerbic, bitter taste filled my mouth, and with it came another wave of nausea. I gripped at the rail, steadying myself, wishing he would finish and go to bed.

"You look terrific," he said, nearly whispering. "You could make a guy want you, you know."

The fatigue exploded. "Is that all you think about? I'm not your goddamned sex slave, Chip. I'm good for a hell of a lot more than keeping your house clean and your bed warm!"

The expression on his face was nearly laughable. He pulled his feet off the rail and set the chair upright, staring at me, astonished. He slowly got up and took the short step to me, all the while never taking his eyes off my face. "Where did that come from?"

"God, Chip, I'm sorry," I said, falling against him. "I don't know why I said that. I'm tired and haven't felt well all day."

"Are you sick? Do you feel bad enough you need to see a doctor?"

I resisted the urge to tell him I already had. "I'm fine, Chip. I just need to go to bed."

"So go. I'll be there in a few minutes."

The irony of unreasonable temper was not lost on him. From the bedroom I heard him go back into the kitchen and turn water on, rinsing his plate off, and the sound of cupboard doors open and close as he put away dishes I'd washed earlier.

I would have thanked him for it, but by the time he came to bed I was sound asleep.

Chip

It was still dark when I dragged myself out of bed. I was bone tired, but it would be easier to plow through more files if I could work in the peace and quiet of a vacant office. I had only been able to sleep in snatches, and knew Terry slept fitfully. She had moaned so many times during the night, tossing and turning, that it was just easier to get up. I dressed in the dark, not wanting to ruin any chance she had for a little rest before Nicky was up.

Before I left I scribbled a note so that she wouldn't worry, carefully adding that I might be late again. Something had set her off and I didn't want a repeat. How could she possibly feel like a sex slave when it had been all she could do to get my attention for almost three months? I was a slob, I knew that, I took advantage of knowing I could drop my clothes anywhere in the house and she'd pick them up; I couldn't scrub a toilet to save my life and I habitually left dirty dishes in the sink, but I still couldn't see where she'd been coming from.

Granted, she could have been furious with me for wandering in at one in the morning, but even if she hadn't been forewarned, she would have dropped it after an honest apology. Her patience was saving my sanity.

I pushed aside the file I'd been looking at but not reading.

Something was eating at her. It had to be my fault. I thought she was content being a wife and mother, she never hinted that she wanted to go back to work or had other aspirations. Leaving her job had been her decision; I supported it, but I hadn't asked her to.

Maybe she needs to hear it from you, encourage her to stretch her wings a little…Go back to work, or back to school…

On the other hand, I realized, rubbing at my tired eyes, I wanted to pull my wings in a little. The Charybdis didn't need me. Ted could run it with his eyes closed and probably deserved more credit for its success than he'd been given. All I knew for certain was that I was bored with it. In fact, sitting there surrounded by files and scraps of computer paper with numbers and notes scribbled on them, staying at home with my wife and son was very attractive.

I pulled the file back where I could read it. Something in my gut kept screaming that Ron's decision to die lay somewhere between his last two cases, and I couldn't help wondering if there was something that wasn't on record that had eluded the grapevine.

"So," Doug said as he came in, "how goes it?"

"It goes absolutely no where. I'm drawing a complete blank."

He sat across from me and pushed a McDonald's bag across the table. "I figured I'd find you here already and presumed you skipped breakfast. Eat something so you don't get sick. You're way too skinny."

"Well you're awfully pretty, too." When the aroma of food hit me I realized how hungry I actually was. "Did you catch hell for being so late last night?"

"Kris was asleep by the time I got home, but I scored

some brownie points for being awake when Spider woke up for his bottle. She finally got to sleep through the night."

"I'm not sure if I'm in trouble or not," I said between bites. "Terry was fine at first, but later she jumped on me."

"She was worried."

"No... Kris warned her I'd be late. All I did—and I swear it was innocent—was tell her she looked terrific. Next thing I know she's jumping down my throat telling me she's not my goddamn sex slave."

"She was probably tired, Chip. Nicky must have been crawling all over her yesterday. Remember, he hadn't seen her in five days."

"Hell, you're probably right."

"Besides," he chuckled, "I hear from a reliable source you haven't been exactly burning up the sheets lately anyway."

"Shit." I crumpled up the bag and tossed it into a trash can across the room. "Just how much do they tell each other, anyway?"

"You and I are better than the soaps. I wouldn't be surprised if they tell each other all our kinky habits."

I flipped through the pages of the file, hoping something would jump out at me. "I don't doubt it. I suspect Terry pumps Kris for information more than anything. Stuff she isn't comfortable asking me."

"Major insight for a complete ass," he said. "Such as?"

Where was the comfort of the steam room when I needed it? "Terry was a virgin when I met her."

"And you took care of that for her."

I nodded. "Remember the weekend a couple years ago when Dan nearly bent himself in two because he couldn't find me?"

"The beginning of the end."

"If I had known before we took off, I doubt I would have laid a hand on her. It surprised the hell out of me."

"Pissed you off?"

"Hell no. I think I knew then that I wanted to spend the rest of my life with her. My radar was on the fritz on purpose…" I pushed the file aside, chalking it up as a lost cause. "I did something beyond stupid a few days ago."

"More stupid than usual?"

"She started cracking jokes about not having anything to measure me against, not knowing if I'm as good in bed as I allude to. She was trying to be funny, but the truth is, she's right. She has no clue."

"What the hell did you do this time?"

"I told her," I said slowly, drawing a deep breath, "that I would understand if just once she let her curiosity get the better of her. I basically told her she could sleep with someone else."

"Are you fucking loony? Why the hell would you set yourself up for something like that?"

"Because even though she was kidding around, it hit home. She *doesn't* know. I worry about her thinking that she made a mistake. I know that what I've got with her is so good I take it for granted, but she has no idea."

"You *are* fucking loony. Are you sure that wasn't your ego talking? Face it, Chip, you've been with a lot of women and I bet most of them told you how good you are. You just wish she knew what she's got."

"Maybe."

"What's it matter anyway as long as you're both happy? Hell, look at Kris and me. I know she's got a string of men behind her and sometimes I wonder how I stack up, but it's not eating away at me."

"I told you it was beyond stupid. It's just"—I stopped, realizing he was practically staring at me. Other than Terry, though, Doug was the one person who would understand. "She's my life, Doug. Nothing else matters. Not the crap with my mother, or with Grant, not even Ron. When she dragged me out to that lake it woke me up... she even told her dad she was getting me away because our marriage was disintegrating. I can't hurt her anymore. If I lost her I know I'd die. I'd just curl up and die."

I waited for the smart remark.

"I understand," he finally said. "I feel that way about Kris. Ron felt that way about your mom. I don't care what anyone says, I think it's us that gets nuts when we're in love. Women just seem to handle it better."

It hit me out of no where. I felt like the world slipped on its axis for half a second and tried to spin me out of my chair.

"Holy God in heaven. Doug, you're not going to believe it."

Terry

I rolled over and opened one eye. I somehow knew I'd be looking into those sweet blue eyes, baby fine hair tousled in all directions. It was what pulled me awake, the feeling he was there and waiting.

"Hi, Mommy."

I smiled at him. "Hi, Nicky."

"Gotta go potty, Mommy." He stomped off to the bathroom, standing at the door, waiting.

I forced myself to sit up and slowly crawled from the bed. When did he start talking so well? And where is my baby? The little boy climbing onto the step stool was just that, a little boy. I felt a little sad when I pulled off his diaper and realized it was bone dry. He'd made it through the night again, and there he was, standing on the stool Chip bought him, peeing up a storm.

While Nicky finished, I looked into the mirror and brushed my hair. From the moment my feet hit the floor I was fighting nausea, seemingly endless waves that pestered me all day. It was getting to the point where I wouldn't be able to hide it any longer. I'd come close to throwing up on Chip just hours before, and it wouldn't be much longer before I started to show.

"Done, Mommy." He climbed off the stool and waited there, half naked and not caring. "I want Daddy."

"Daddy has to work today, Nicky. I'll play with you if you want."

He frowned, shaking his head. "I want Daddy."

Oh, great, I thought miserably. "Sweetheart, Daddy's not home. He had to go to work. Now, are you hungry? Do you want me to make you some eggs?"

He pursed his lips together seriously, regarding me suspiciously. "Daddy makes toast."

"Okay then," I agreed, "I'll make you some toast."

"No!" He stomped away angrily, shouting, "You make eggs!"

I looked back into the mirror. This is one of the good mornings, I reminded myself. Are you sure you want to do this again?

"Mommy?" Nicky was back, he had one foot through a pair of training pants and socks clenched in his fist. "I love you."

Definitely.

Chip

"I am so amazingly, astronomically stupid," I swore as I ran down the corridor with Doug following me. We headed towards the computer lab, and I kept up my self abrasive litany the entire time. "I can't believe how fucking dumb I am."

"What? *What?*"

I ignored him and pulled Ron's shop card out of my pocket. The cursor on the screen was blinking, waiting. "Watch this," I said. "Don't think about it. If you were Ron and this popped up on your screen, what would you do?"

```
STEVENS, CHRIS
CODE: N/A
RELEASED
CONTINUE?
```

"I don't understand," Doug mumbled. "This has to be a mistake. Chip, goddammit, this has to be a royal mistake!"

"That's just it." I tapped my finger on the screen. "You're seeing the same thing Ron did. That's *Christopher* Stevens, Doug. It's not your wife. This"—I punched the Y on the keyboard—"is the rest."

"Shiiiiit."

"Don't you get it? Ron never got this far. He punched in the code and read Chris Stevens, and in his mind it was his Kris."

"My Kris."

"Fine, your Kris. Jesus, Doug, he saw the same thing you did. And he would die before he'd hurt her. It rattled him so much he didn't read any further... if he did he would have realized. Ron killed himself so he wouldn't have to be the one to kill Kris or be around to see someone else do it for him."

Doug was reaching for a chair, fumbling and trying not to go to his knees. He was starting to shake, barely able to talk. "Chip, she can't know…"

"She won't," I assured him. "No one will."

"Then what do we do?"

I put the shop card in my pocket—it could be burned—and erased the floppy disk. "We let it go, Doug. People will think what they want no matter what we say. I'm satisfied he was just reacting out of his own sense of honor. Let's just say the evidence was inconclusive. Barstow will go with that if I promise to not make anymore waves. Payback for letting Dan die, I don't know. But he'll let it go if I will."

He didn't hear me. "Chip, he really loved her. All this time she's thought he never let go of your mother enough to love anyone else, and all along he loved Kris."

"Maybe that's it. He didn't love my mother enough to give her the freedom to be just with Grant… but he did Kris, he loved her enough to let her have you, and enough to die before his world existed without her."

"I'm gonna get sick."

"Doug, she loves *you* like that, you know that, don't you?"

He said he did, but he was turning different shades of green and needed to get out of there. I pocketed the floppy disk, thinking I might be able to burn it, too, and suggested we head for the gym, where we could hide in the steam room, someplace he could let it out if he had to.

The steam was thick and the benches almost too hot; I stretched out on one and Doug sat on the upper bench, his face buried in his towel. He was quiet for a long time, but didn't move, sweat running off him in huge drops.

I knew Ron loved Kris, but I never would have guessed how much.

My mind was wandering; Doug finally dropped the towel and said out of nowhere, "I haven't had sex in three months."

"I'm sorry," I laughed. "But don't look at me. You're cute but I don't swing your way."

"We need to double date. You need to spend some more time with Terry, and I'm just dying to get some, period. Let's get a babysitter and surprise them with a night out. Make it as romantic as hell."

"Sure, and a double date is romantic."

"They'll like it."

He wanted to take her out, but he didn't want to be alone and in a position where he'd be tempted to tell her anything.

"That they will." I sat up, shaking off some of the sweat. "You know, for a couple of guys our age, I think we're too married for out own good."

He threw the door open and stepped out into the locker room. "Yeah? Well it beats the alternative."

Doug

"Thirty seven." Kris sighed and buried her face into her pillow. "I wasn't ever supposed to get this old."

I laughed and tried to snuggle up to her. "You're not old. Thirty years from now, you'll be old. Old ladies don't keep their husbands on the dance floor half the night, and old ladies don't come home and keep their husbands up until dawn doing unspeakable things."

"I have gray hairs," she moaned.

I pulled her hair away from her face. "Motherhood."

"Young husband," she countered. "I'm not looking forward to three years from now when I hit forty and you're still comfortably in your thirties."

"I'll be the age you are now. Probably even have more gray hair than you do."

"I should hope so. You do realize that when you turn forty I'm trading you in for two twenties?"

"Nah, you don't want to break in anyone new. You just about have me trained."

"I suppose."

"I'm resigning from the agency, Kris," I said suddenly, surprised to hear the words tumble from my own mouth.

She rolled over onto her side, hand on my arm. "Are you sure you want to do that?"

The tone of hope in her voice was undeniable. "I'm sure. I don't want to take the chance that they'll yank the rug right out from under my feet and assign me to a new team. All I want now is to set up my own practice and help you populate the world with little Stones."

"One more, maybe." she murmured. "You may have the stamina for a house full, but I don't think I do."

"That's okay. I don't care how many kids we have. We can always borrow Chip and Terry's when the parental urge strikes."

"Kids? Plural?"

"I'm not saying a word. Patient confidentiality and all that crap, you know."

She shoved me onto my back and straddled me. "Crap is a good word. Tell me what you know, Doug. If you were all that hot on ethics you wouldn't be their doctor in the first place. So tell me or I'll start plucking out chest hairs."

She had a hair between two fingers and was tugging.

"She's pregnant," I chuckled. "But Chip doesn't know it, yet, so you have to keep it to yourself. And forget about me sending them to someone else. I'm damn well going to be the one who delivers all the little Chip clones."

She laughed and bent over to kiss me. "I love you, mister," she said with her lips still on mine. "Don't you ever forget that."

Chip

I was propped up on one elbow, watching Terry sleep. The worry that had knotted her eyebrows was gone and she looked more peaceful than she had in months. I resisted the urge draw her out of sleep slowly with a deep kiss.

Hell, I was still a little overwhelmed by how passionate she'd been; I had it in my mind that we'd come home, dance a little more in the living room, or cuddle up on the couch and talk. I wasn't going to push her towards the bedroom.

She wasn't my sex slave, after all.

That was my plan until she kissed me and every consideration I'd had was gone. We left a trail of clothing all the way to the edge of the bed, too anxious to have each other to care.

You can't be a gentleman when the woman has no intention of being a lady.

"I can't believe you're still here," I whispered, pushing a lock of hair from her face. "You deserve a hell of a lot better than me."

"Probably," she groaned.

I kissed her softly. "I thought you were asleep. Did I wake you?"

"Probably." She propped the pillows behind her and sat up, leaning on them. "God, my head hurts."

"Hangover?"

"I didn't drink anything. You're the one who should be passed out cold. You drink too much, Chip."

"Guilty," I admitted. "But I didn't think that would turn you into a tea-totaler."

"I'm not. Just careful."

"And still half asleep."

She flashed a smile, bright and challenging. "So wake me up, mister. You're either still drunk or still horny, and either way I think I'm up for the rest of the night. So help me out."

"My pleasure." I started at her lips and slowly worked my way down, soaking in how silky smooth she felt. I slipped on the bed, sliding my body further down hers.

"Chip, don't!"

The urgency of her cry and the way her fingers grappled wildly at my hair froze me. "Why not? I thought you liked this."

"I do," she moaned. "Doug said not to."

"Come on, that was way back when you were pregnant and we've"—I stopped short, suddenly aware how stiff she was laying there. I slowly rubbed my hand over her belly, and placed a long, wet kiss there. "How far along are you?"

"Almost four months."

Four months seemed like an eternity.

"Chip?"

I moved until my face was just above hers. "Woman, you are the most incredible gift I could have ever gotten."

"Chip, the baby…"

"The baby is perfect," I said. "God, I'm feeling so many different things right now I don't know what to tell you."

"Just tell me how much you love me."

"Lady, I love you like no one could possibly understand." I kissed her again. "I'll move into the house if you want, Terry. I would guess that by now all the ghosts are gone."

"Are you sure?"

"As sure as I'll ever be. And I'm turning the Charybdis over to Ted."

"Why?"

"Because I'm bored with it and he's good at it. I don't want to sell it, but I think it's time to move on to something else."

"Then what will you do?"

"Doesn't matter. Anything. Maybe nothing at first. I'll hang around all day and drive you nuts. Play with Nicky. Go back to school. With what Grant left us we could both forget working for the rest of our lives if we wanted. But I want something we can build from scratch, something that's really ours and not something that got dumped on me. The restaurant isn't me, Ter... I'm not the monster I named it after anymore."

"What if you get restless?"

"Then you'll grab me by the nipples and shake me back to reality again. I've got to grow up, Terry. I want to do something new, but I want it to be for us, and for our kids. I want it to be forever."

"Forever's a pretty long time, Chip."

Hell, that might be long enough.

December 25, 1977

Chip

A cemetery on Christmas Day should be gloomy; winter should cast a pall over the morning sky, and there should be a thick haze pressing down into the day. Instead, it was bright and sunny, the bite of cold air stinging my cheeks and numbing my nose.

Terry waited with Nick while I searched for the right headstones; she sat on a bench with him on her lap, giving me the privacy I needed yet hadn't had to ask for. I stepped carefully between graves, trying to not violate someone's final resting place with the scuffed and dirty soles of my shoes. Fresh flowers dotted the landscape, splashes of color glaring brightly against the headstones.

I found Brenda's grave on the far side of the cemetery, devoid of anything that would whisper to the world there was someone buried there who mattered. No one laid flowers for her or treated her grave with the care and respect it deserved; her stone was a small metal plaque set into the ground. It bore her name and the years she lived, but nothing else. I stood and stared at it, trying to remember the girl she had been before I ripped her heart out. I needed to apologize, to tell her that I honestly had wanted to help her out of the life she was stuck in, but not the way it turned out.

You should have had it all, and I should have helped you find a way to get it, even if it wasn't with me.

The day was meant for reconciliation, and I had too many apologies to keep buried inside.

I found my brother's grave; I just needed to see his name, and wanted desperately for him to know that if I could do it all over again, I'd be a better brother. I would make time for him. I'd make the effort to be sure he wasn't drifting alone, and I'd find him myself.

Dan's grave was less than 100 feet away, the grass covering it dry and brittle, dirt building in the etchings of his name. *I'd be a better friend, Dan. If I had known the day you fired me what was looming ahead, I'd have told you that I did think of you as a friend. I'd have been better at it.*

The image of him hanging from that thick rope in his office was burned into my brain; he wanted a life and a family, and had he lived, I'd have been there to cheer him on. He needed to know that; I needed him to know that.

I stood in front of Ron's grave; there were fresh flowers tucked into a metal vase, the white marble headstone wiped clean, and a grave blanket woven with pine was tucked on the ground like a freshly laundered quilt. Someone else felt the same urge, someone else wanted to care for him, even when we hadn't gotten it right while he was alive.

I wondered if Doug had come with her, or if she spent her Christmas morning there alone, tending to this site with what love she had left to give him.

Doug would understand.

No matter what, you're a father to me and I'll always

love you like you were. It was too high a price to pay for my freedom, and I'm sorry you never knew that you were genuinely loved. We loved you, Ron, we both loved you. God knows we did, even if we never had the guts to say it enough.

Terry kept Nick on her lap as I walked back towards them; he strained to slide off and run to me, but I had one more stop to make.

I knelt in front of my parents' graves. It took me a long time to figure out what I wanted to tell my mother; I wanted her to know that I didn't have to understand her, but I did love her. No matter how screwed up her life was, and how hard it was for her to choose between them, I know she loved me deeply. She must have been one hell of a woman for two men to be that devoted to her.

Mostly, I was there because I had to tell Grant how sorry I was for being blind all those years, for not wanting to see the truth. Especially for not remembering how much he must have loved me when I was little and how safe I felt with him. How hard it must have been to let me go.

"I want that kind of grace in my life," I whispered, "and I wish I had loved you the way you loved me... but I'm getting there. I just need you to know that it's all right. It's okay that you're my father. I appreciate it all, everything you did and every sacrifice you made. I'll find a way to honor you."

Somehow, I will.

Charybdis was originally published in 2001; the sequel, *As Simple As That* was published in 2002, and the final book of the series, *Finding Father Rabbit*, will be available in August 2003.

About The Author

K.A. Thompson is a freelance writer and the editor of Martial Artists Wired. Currently living in Ohio, the author is married to a United States Air Force Nurse Anesthetist. They have an adult son.

www.ingramcontent.com/pod-product-compliance
Lightning Source LLC
Chambersburg PA
CBHW031417240626
47154CB00001B/82